Malum Discordiae

Ashlyn Drewek

Fox Hollow Books

Cover design by Teresa Conner at Wolf Sparrow Creations

For Anna –

You have inspired me more than you know. Tennebrose wouldn't be here without you.

спасибо

CONTENTS

Foreword

This book contains references to animal cruelty, alcohol/drug use, death of children, murder, suicide, and dubious sexual consent. Reader discretion is advised.

Preface + Glossary

The terms used throughout this book may look familiar to Christians but in this context they refer to the Winslow witch community. As happened so often throughout history, persecuted religious groups tended to hide their own beliefs within the larger, accepted religion around them. The most recognizable example in America is Voodoo — a combination of West African religious traditions blended with Catholicism, meaning African spirits were "renamed" for the Catholic saint they resembled. Hence why Marie Laveau, the famous "Voodoo Queen" of New Orleans was also a devout Catholic.

In my world, the Winslow witches used syncretism to hide *their* magic within the larger community by disguising it in terms from Puritan doctrine consistent with the time period in which they colonized America, particularly the mid-to-late seventeenth century.

Over time, the terms stuck, in part because that was the tradition established and also because it *continued* to serve them. Even as the rest of the community became more secularized and there was less of an emphasis on religion, the Winslow Congregation could continue to operate under the very noses of their non-magical neighbors without drawing attention to themselves. After all, as members of the founding families, who would question their dedication to tradition?

So in order to avoid confusion with the real meaning behind these terms, here are *my* definitions as they relate to the Winslow witches.

Book of Transactions — an ongoing book that documents everything discussed and voted on at Meetings. It also records witches' general information, such as their names, powers, the date of their conversion, births, marriages, and deaths.

Committee — the thirteen Selectmen, including the Deacon, who preside over the Congregation, acting as a governing council.

Congregation — the collective of the Winslow witches.* Once a witch is accepted into the Congregation, they cannot leave "until Removed by Consent of the Committee or Removed by Death."

*The term "coven" was not used in reference to a group of witches until Margaret Murray's *The Witch-Cult in Western Europe* was published in 1921. Historical sources themselves only refer to congregations and sabbats.

Conversion — the sacred rite all Winslow witches go through at the age of thirteen to either accept or reject their powers. If they reject their powers, they are no longer privy to the inner workings of the Congregation. If they accept their powers, their information is recorded in the Book of Transactions and they are bound to the Congregation (see above). The process of conversion is different for each witch, dependent upon their individual magic.

Covenant — an agreement set down by the Congregation, detailing the rules as they pertain to the use of magic against fellow witches and non-witches. Not to be confused with a regular "covenant," which is any other agreement or pact between witches and other magical beings.

Deacon — an elected position and the final authority of the Committee. Leads the Meetings and networks with other witches outside the community when needed. Presumably, this position goes to the most powerful witch.

Meeting — a planned gathering for the Congregation where important news is conveyed, traditions are taught, public grievances are aired, and socialization in general. These are not religious in nature, but have more of a political and social feel.

Meetinghouse — where the witches congregate for Meetings, trials, and certain group rituals. In the spirit of their Puritan ancestors, it is devoid of decorations or stained glass. It is also not considered a sacred space in any religious sense of the word.

Selectmen — one elder from each of the original thirteen bloodlines. How they are chosen is up to each family. The Selectmen form the Committee and govern the Congregation as well as most of the town of Winslow.

Tithing Man — serves as an independent authority, outside of the Committee. Their role is to watch over the Congregation and keep order amongst the members. They are tasked with handling minor disputes and reporting to the Committee if anyone is not adhering to the Covenant.

Latin Terms

Astra inclinant, sed non obligant — *The stars incline us, they do not bind us*

Exilium — *Banish; banished*

In nomine et virtute domini nostri Jesu Christi — *In the Name and by the power of Our Lord Jesus Christ*

In nomine Patris et fillii et Spiritus Sancti — *In the name of the Father, the Son, and the Holy Spirit*

Malum Discordiae — *Apple of discord*

Mors omnibus — *Death to all*

Ne te quaesiveris extra — *Do not seek outside yourself*

Pulvis et umbra sumus — *We are dust and shadow*

"Now, by the stock
and honor of my kin,
To strike him dead I
hold it not a sin"

Tybalt Capulet
Romeo & Juliet

Ego coniuro vos omnes superdictos spiritus demones
per piissimam et misericordissimam et intemeratam ac
incorruptam virginem Mariam matrem domini
nostri Ihesu Christi, que pro miseris peccatoribus mortem
sumens nos ad celestem patriam revocavit.
Item ego coniuro vos superdictos spiritus per omnes
sanctos et sanctas dei et per omnes apostolos martires
confessores virgines et viduas. Et per hec
preciosissima ac ineffabilia nomina omnium creatoris
quibus omnes ligantur et que tremunt omnia
celestia terrestria et infernalia. On. Ya. Ely.
Sother. Adonay. El. Sabaoth. Messyas.
Alazabuta. et Osion. Et ego coniuro vos et ex-
orcizo per virtutem et potenciam omnium principum re-
gum demonum maiorum vestrorum et per virtutem et pos-
sibilitatem ac potenciam vestram et per habitacu-
lum vestrum et per hec formam et per omnes figuras in
quo permanetis quatenus
vos insolubiliter ad me
potenciam alli-
gatam ad
me sine
dilacione
venire
debeatis
in ta-
li habitu
ut ma-
nifeste
non timeatis

The Founding Families of Winslow

Dane

Green

Hewitt

Northrup

Tenney

Ambrose

Colburn

Corbin

Oliver

Simms

Ainsworth

Treadwell

Winslow

vt die dnica in meridie & debes tenui ferire
ensem lucidissimum & aurem vivum et cum
dco ense in quodam remoto loco facere cir
culos quibus factis cum acie predicti ensis sup
terra debes .xvj. noia vt inferius apparebit &
illa figura quibus factis debes figere versus
orientem in interiori circulo dictum ensem
vt hec figuratio demonstrat

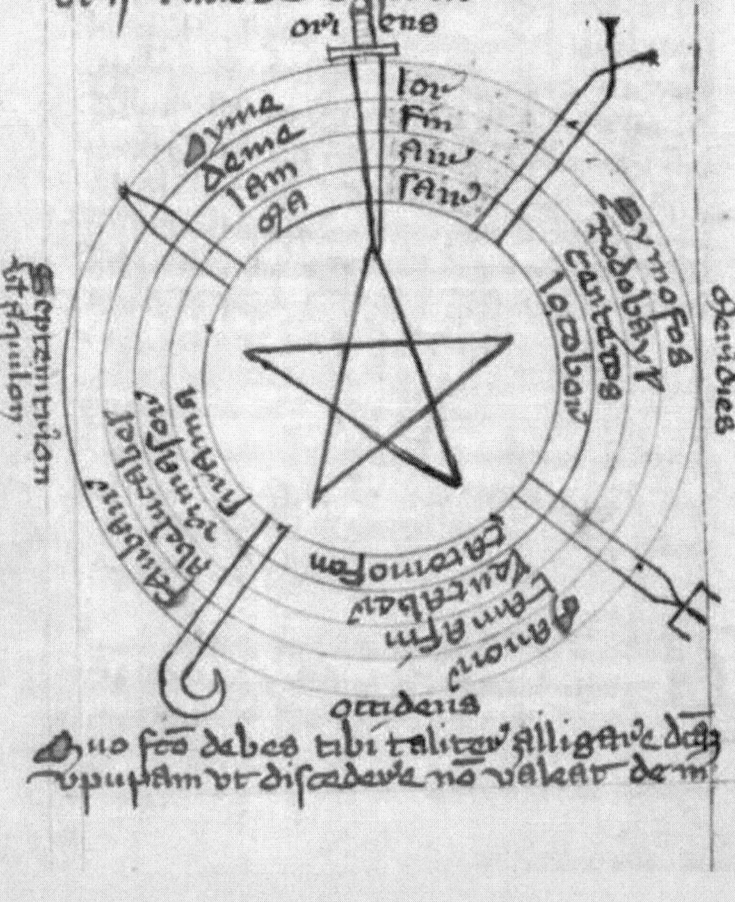

Quo facto debes tibi taliter alligare de
upupam vt discedere non valeat de m

The Ambrose & Corbin Family Tree

Signu[m] die martis q[ue] e[st] planeta diei martis

Sigillu[m] martis q[uod] d[ebet] fieri martio ascendente

Signu[m] martis q[ue] e[st] planeta martis diei

Sigillu[m] iouis q[uod] fieri deb[et] ioue ascendente

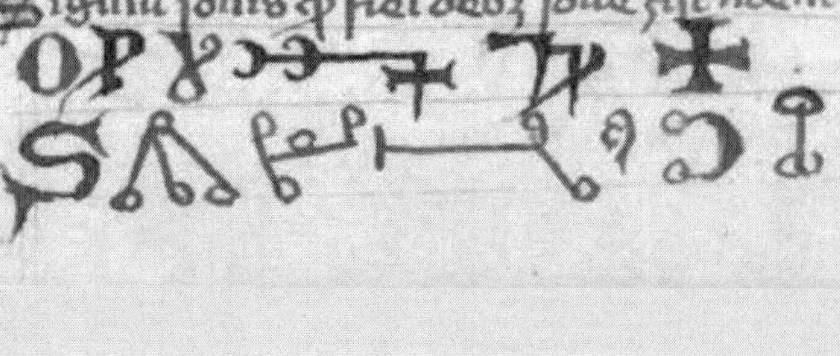

The Hewitt Family Tree

George Hewitt — Marian Tenney

- Graeme Hewitt
- Owen Hewitt (deceased)

Hic incipit speculum Floron. Si vis fieri
speculum de puro chalibe ad mensuram
palme unius in rotundo. habeat quoque in ma-
nubrium ad tenendum et sit illuminatum et lu-
cidum ut ensis. Sit quoque factum in nomine Floron
et in circuitu istius speculi ex alia parte non
lucida sint hec decem nomina cum hiis de-
cem caracteribus descripta et nomen Flo-
ron sit in medio scriptum. postquam fuit
factum in loco sacrato ungatur de puro bal-
samo ex parte lucida et subfumigetur taliter

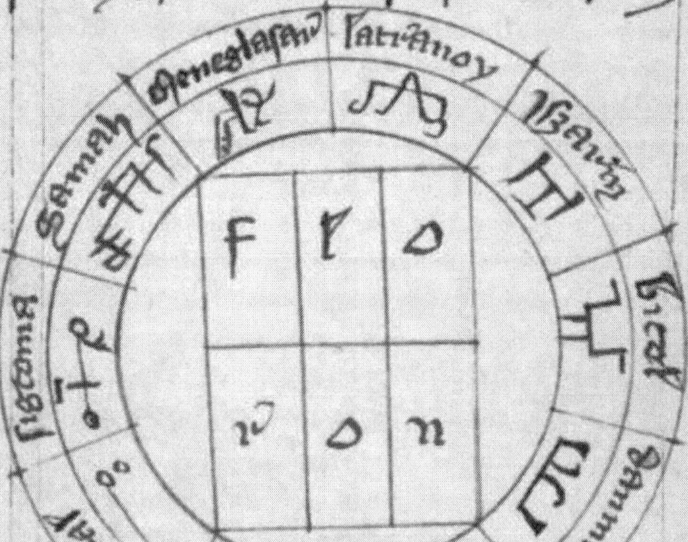

The Northrup Family Tree

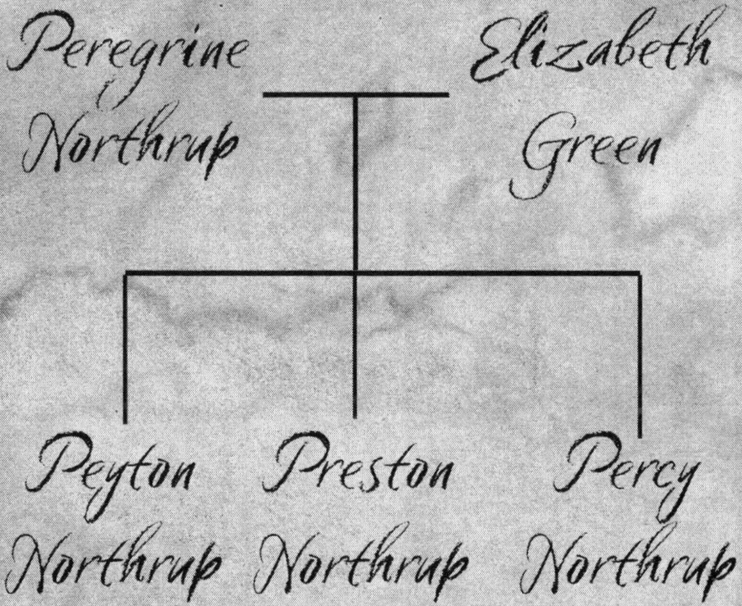

tia deitatis sum i vivi in hac vi dei virtute
te exorcizamus. bylet per honorem primus tui sancti-
et per illud sacramentum quod tu nocturna matri
tua fecisti vos ut in similitudine tua et non in
corporum similitudine ad serviendum et ad sa
dandum nobiscum in quacumque hora vel quod servimus
te in speculo isto pacifice ac humiliter et sine
ulla deformitate te mihi ostendas et sim
plus ut duo ut potestas deservivus tuus quod vo
tam de futuro quam de preterito aut de qua
cumque alia re dubitabili de qua scire voluero
michi dant vera responsa ut signa in dei vir
tute et opera. Istud vero speculum debet
formari ad modum clypei ut. Alio modo
volvens in cuius girum hec nomina depingan
tur. Deus sanctus. deus optimus. deus fortis. deus immorta
lis per futura secula. Et circa duo latera super
ordo sigilla Salo
monis depingan
tur. Inferius in
fima vero clypei
minus sigillum Salo
monis et in medio
speculi hoc nomen
Bylet depinga
tur ut in hac
patebit figura
hec visa ponitur

"What, drawn, and
talk of peace?
I hate the word.
As I hate hell,
all Montagues,
and thee."

Tybalt Capulet
Romeo & Juliet

Chapter One
Cassius

"Put the skull down and let's go already!"

Sending a quick glare at the impatient pain in the ass in the doorway, I hefted the yellowed human skull in my hands and poured the water out from inside the cranium. Shaking the last drops free, I set it inside its iron cage and returned the whole thing to its place on the shelf next to the others: horses, cats, birds. An assortment of skulls for whatever you might need.

In this case, I needed information from the seventeenth century. I was hoping by using a skull from that era I'd finally get my answer. Sadly, I didn't and I didn't have time to try again with my cousin huffing and sighing and shuffling his feet every five seconds. Not to mention the incessant dinging from his cell phone as a flurry of texts came through.

"I was in the middle of something," I sniffed at Lennox on my way by. "As if you couldn't tell."

"Uh-huh." He shook his head, rolling his dark eyes skyward and shoving his phone in his pocket. I don't know why he bothered. It chimed again within seconds. "You just got home! And instead of spending time with yours truly, you go straight for the skulls. Typical. Do I even want to know what you're looking for?"

"You know damn well what I'm looking for. The same thing *you* should have been looking for while I was gone."

"The folios," he said flatly. "Always the folios. You're like a dog with a bone."

It was my turn to roll my eyes as I headed up the curved, stone staircase. Pushing through the heavy door at the top, I tapped one finger against the worn wood, waiting for Lennox to saunter his ass out before I closed it again. I turned the heavy, black key in the lock and pocketed it, raising my brows at him. "Remind me again why you insisted on dragging me to this party? Arden is there and clearly anxious for your arrival, along with God knows whoever else has been blowing up your phone, so you don't exactly need me."

"Because, Cassius Corbin, you pain in my ass, it is tradition."

"For you, perhaps. I've been excused from Winslow traditions for the past few years. Remember?" I smirked at him and folded my arms across my chest.

"You are my cousin and I've missed you! Is it so wrong to want to spend time with you now that you're back?" He threw his arm around my shoulders and steered me down the hallway, as if I was going to magically escape. I mean, I could have. But since he had most of the same powers, it's not like I'd get very far.

Nevertheless, I gave him a disbelieving look.

"Ok, fine. It's Preston's annual back-to-school bash and I need a wingman."

"You have Arden," I pointed out on the way to the front door. "Other than Preston and you two idiots, I don't know anyone in this town anymore and I'd like to keep it that way. I'm not here to make friends. I'm here to find the—"

"Folios. Yes. I know." He made an exasperated growling sound. "We'll find the damn folios! But before we go on a magical treasure hunt, can you please try to have a little bit of fun? Just a speck. You're too young to be this… *not* fun."

"Fun? You want to talk about fun?" I raised my eyebrows at him. "Like that time you blew out all the windows at the meetinghouse? Or the time you set fire to the Deacon's car and blamed it on the Tenney brats?"

"Why would you even bring up the window thing?" He looked wounded, clutching his chest. "And the car *was* the Tenney brats. I maintain my innocence."

"Well, thanks to that little temper tantrum, I've been the pride and joy of the Corbin line ever since." I smiled brightly at him. "So, thanks, Cuz."

"Good thing I'm an *Ambrose* then," he tossed back, shoving me out the door and down the front steps.

The Northrup's massive house was set near the center of Winslow, in the colonial part of town. A striking three-story building, it dominated the block much like Peregrine Northrup dominated as Deacon of our secret little community.

Thankfully, his son, Preston, wasn't as much of an asshole as his father was. Or, at least, he wasn't the last time I saw him. But that was six years ago. Who knew how much had changed.

Arden was waiting for us in the front yard when we strolled up, thumbing through his phone. "About time. I was beginning to think you ditched me."

"Cash was going to," Lennox said, smacking my stomach with the back of his hand. "But *I'd* never do that to you."

"Blow me," I muttered, leading the way into the house.

The sooner we made our appearance, the sooner I could get the hell out of here. The air outside had already dropped by ten degrees and the scent of rain permeated the night. Claudia had let the supply of storm water run low while I was away and I'd much rather be home setting out glass bottles in the garden than schmoozing with the drunken imbeciles wandering around, chest-bumping each other and gossiping about people I didn't know, nor care, about.

Per Preston's rules, all keys and cell phones were immediately deposited into a large basket the moment we crossed the threshold. You could only get them back when you were leaving and after he established you were sober. There would be no DUIs or incriminating evidence of any kind stemming from the Northrup residence. It was his one nod to responsibility and it was non-negotiable.

"Any other members here?" Lennox asked Arden as we took up residency in an unoccupied corner of the living room, watching the collection of teenagers and twenty-somethings milling about.

"Not that I've seen," Arden replied offhandedly, sipping something out of a red plastic cup.

"Have you been looking?" Lennox challenged, plucking the cup out of Arden's hand and taking a sip. "Or are you only looking for Sophia?"

Arden rolled his eyes, reclaiming his cup. "Yes, and no. It's only been the three of us so far, aside from Preston and India. Grayson said he was coming after he gets off work. I haven't talked to anyone else, though."

"Good. We'll have strength in numbers in case anyone *else* shows up."

I didn't miss the way Lennox emphasized the word or the silent conversation that shot between the two of them. While I appreciated the fact they were trying to be considerate of my feelings, *not* saying the name of my family's arch-nemesis just made it awkward. It was already weird as hell being back in Winslow, I didn't need to be constantly reminded of the reason why I was gone in the first place. My own memories did that for me.

"I'm getting a drink. A *real* drink," I huffed, stalking away from both of them.

Meandering through the house, I made my way through the crowd to the kitchen. Rather than partake in whatever piss-colored beer was flowing into plastic cups, I helped myself to an actual glass from the cupboard and mixed a gin and tonic. The perk of growing up with Preston was knowing where his mother stashed the good liquor. Thankfully not everything had changed in six years.

"Doth my eyes deceive me? Can it be, at long last? Is that Cassius Corbin that stands before me?" a male voice said, right before a pair of hands landed on my shoulders and gave me a shake. "I didn't know you were home, man!"

"Preston," I murmured in acknowledgment, taking a fortifying sip of my drink. And let the interrogations begin...

"When did you get back?" Preston asked, circling around to the front and snagging a bottle of whiskey before I closed the cabinet.

"About a week ago."

"Cool, cool. How was England, or wherever your father shuffled you off to?"

"It was fine," I said with a fleeting smile, even if "fine" was the last word I'd use to describe my trans-Atlantic exile. Oh, I'm sorry. *Boarding school.* That sounded nicer.

"Well, I'm glad you're back, man. Try not to do anything freaky, though, ok? Dad comes home tomorrow and blood is really fucking hard to get out of the carpet."

"I told you, you have to get it while it's fresh. Otherwise, let it dry and then use a brush to break up the particles." I pantomimed scrubbing and gave him a warm smile, knowing it was completely at odds with the subject matter.

He laughed and shook his head. "Catch you later, Cash." Calling out to someone else, he darted off into the crowd.

Topping off my drink, I turned to go when I collided with another body. Clear liquid sloshed over my hand, the smell of juniper and citrus wafting between us.

"Oh, shit!" The guy grabbed my glass with one hand and steadied me with the other. "I'm sorry! I was trying to sneak by you. My bad."

"It's fine," I replied automatically, shaking as much liquid off my hand as I could before wiping the rest on my leg. "I should have looked where I was going."

The moment I lifted my gaze to his I was struck dumb. A pair of mismatched eyes stared back, a crystalline blue and a fern green, framed by long, dark lashes. Obviously I knew people could have two different colored eyes, but I had never witnessed it in person before. Simply put, they were the most striking thing I'd ever seen, set in one of the most attractive faces I'd ever seen — male *or* female.

"I'm Graeme," he said with a slow smile, letting go to offer his hand.

"Cash." I slipped mine into his, forcing myself to stop staring like a moron and offer him a polite smile. Electricity rippled through my palm as soon as it made contact with his skin. I retracted it quickly under the pretense of needing to wipe off more liquor. But what the fuck? *That* had never happened before. Whatever it was, I hoped to hell he didn't feel it.

"Just like the Man in Black." He gave me a once-over that made heat flare in my cheeks. The fact I was in a black sweater and black jeans probably didn't help dissuade the comparison.

"Something like that," I murmured, rocking back on my

heels. A second too late, I realized he probably didn't hear me over the loud bass of the music. I could hardly hear myself, let alone him.

"Cool necklace," he said, leaning in again.

I followed his gaze to the center of my chest. The necklace in question was a silver crow skull with a sigil carved into the rounded part of the head. The wickedly sharp beak had caught me on more than one occasion, but I refused to take it off. It was a gift from my mother on my tenth birthday and one of the few things I'd been allowed to take with me in the dead of night when Dad packed me off to the UK.

"Thanks," I said, tucking it away and hoping he didn't ask a follow-up question. Thankfully, he didn't.

"So, I take it you know Preston?"

I nodded. "You?"

"Yeah. He's dating my best friend, so we're acquainted." His attention darted past me for a minute when someone shouted his name. He laughed and pointed at them with a grin, clearly answering some silent gesture behind me. "Don't even think about it, bro!"

"Well, it was nice meeting you." Happy to have found an escape, I turned to go, but Graeme shifted closer. His hand landed on my bicep, his mouth by my ear.

"It's starting to get a little crowded, don't you think?" Graeme asked, his voice and his breath combined giving me goosebumps. "You want to go out back? I could really use some fresh air."

Before I even knew what was happening, I nodded and followed him through the kitchen and out to the sprawling brick patio.

Someone had started a bonfire in the elaborately constructed pit in the center, but it was abandoned now, with chairs and empty beer bottles scattered everywhere.

Graeme settled on the brick bench, his gaze following me

as I dropped into the vacant space next to him. "I don't think I've ever seen you at one of Preston's parties before."

"I try to avoid them," I said with a laugh that I hoped came off as more charming than nervous. Why was I so fucking nervous? It's not like parties were unheard of in England. I'd been to my fair share, made awkward small talk with people there just as I was doing now. Except, this felt different. Clearly it was a sign I needed more alcohol, so I gulped down some more gin, waiting for the warmth to spread throughout my body and calm my ass down.

My laugh must have passed as real since he laughed too. "Yeah, I don't blame you. They can get a little crazy sometimes. Not much else to do around here, I guess."

"Is this your kind of scene, then? Crazy house parties?"

He tossed a glance over his shoulder at the house in question. Inside, someone hollered, followed by glass shattering. Hopefully it wasn't one of Mrs. Northrup's antiques.

When he turned around again, his nose was wrinkled and he shook his head. "Nah. I'd much rather be out in the woods or something like this, right here."

Before I asked what he meant, he shifted forward slightly, extending his hands and warming them near the fire. The wind picked up, circling the flames and gusting the heat toward us. A few stray embers floated downward, snuffing themselves out before they reached the ground.

"The woods?" He didn't exactly strike me as the outdoorsy type. Maybe it was because he was too pretty. Then again, people probably didn't think I ventured outside, either, since I'd been saddled with the bookworm label.

"Yeah, like the North Woods. You ever been?"

I almost laughed. Except for the last six years, I'd spent more time in those woods than I had in my own house. "Yeah, I've been there. It's been a while, though."

"Everyone in town says they're haunted." He shot me a wry grin. "Ever see a ghost while you're out there?"

I couldn't help but laugh that time. *A* ghost? Try *dozens* of ghosts. But that wasn't exactly something I was going to share, especially with anyone outside my family. "You must be talking about Black Mary."

He laughed and shrugged. "Unless there's another ghost that's terrified Winslow for the past three hundred years?"

Thunder rumbled overhead, giving me a safe segue, away from the topic of my martyred and vilified ancestor. "Looks like we're in for a hell of a storm," I said, turning my attention to the roiling clouds.

Graeme followed my gaze upward, a smile spreading over his face. "Oh yeah. It's gonna be wicked."

Something in the way he said it sent a chill down my spine. Stealing a glance at him out of the corner of my eye, a second chill chased the first. He was looking right at me, a mischievous sparkle in his eyes.

"Do you like storms?" he asked.

"Yeah, I guess," I replied hesitantly, trying to figure out what his angle was. It wasn't the usual topic of conversation, at least for Americans. I'd had plenty of idle chit-chat about the weather overseas.

"I get the sense you're more of a snowstorm type of person, though. Not so much the thunder and lightning kind."

I tried to ignore the fact he'd correctly pegged my favorite season and adopted a more skeptical expression. "What makes you say that?"

"Something about you," he replied, unabashedly raking his gaze up and down. My body was definitely warmer now, and I was pretty sure it didn't have anything to do with the fire *or* the booze.

"So what kind of storm do *you* prefer?" I countered, trying to get a grip on myself.

He smiled slyly. Before he could answer, the logs in front of us hissed as the first raindrops fell.

"I guess I should really get going," I said, hopping off the bench and darting toward the house.

"In this?" he asked, following after me. Thunder clapped a second before the skies opened, unleashing a torrent of rain.

"It's just rain."

As if incensed by the challenge, a cold wind ripped across the yard, slamming me backward into Graeme. His steady hands caught me once again, practically searing my skin through my sweater.

"Seems like it's more than that," he replied with a devilish grin. Reaching around me, he kept one hand on my arm while he opened the patio door with the other.

Almost as soon as we stepped inside, the weather took a turn for the worse.

The wind screamed outside and rain beat the glass so hard I was afraid it was going to shatter at any moment. I'd no more than formed the thought when the lights went out, plunging the house into total darkness. A few girls shrieked. At first, I thought it was the storm scaring them, but then I heard more than one guy laugh and try to high-five their friends in the dark while the girls scolded them.

Too bad I didn't have Lennox's abilities. It would have been so easy for him to spark a little flame, use a little magic, but sadly that wasn't an option for more than one reason. One, I *didn't* have his abilities. And two, even if I did, I couldn't broadcast that information to these people. Since our thoughtful host confiscated everyone's cell phone upon arrival, I didn't even have *that* as a light source, which meant Graeme and I bumbled along in the dark.

"I know someplace we can go to wait it out," Graeme

murmured. His fingers encircled my arm and he gave a small tug in the direction he wanted me to walk.

"Where?"

He didn't answer. Instead, he let his hand slide down my forearm, intertwining our fingers.

Following him through the dark house, I skimmed my other hand along the wall, trying to reorient myself with the layout. I was fairly certain we were headed toward the Deacon's office. There was at least a fireplace in there if the power stayed off for too long.

Closing the door behind us, Graeme chuckled softly. "Told you it was going to be wicked."

"You were right. What should we do now?"

His breath caressed my face a moment before the warm, plush feeling of his lips pressed against mine. Freezing in place, I didn't quite know how to respond. I mean, the advance wasn't entirely unwelcome but damn. I didn't expect a hook up *here*, of all places.

My reaction, or non-reaction, didn't seem to faze him. He shifted closer, one hand gripping my waist. The other threaded through the hair at the back of my neck, adjusting the angle for a deeper kiss. My skin tingled everywhere he touched me, whether it was with his hands or his mouth.

As the shock of his advance wore off, I kissed him back. Sucking gently on his lower lip, I relished the moan in the back of his throat and the way he pulled me closer. He slipped his tongue into my mouth, swirling it around mine in the most sensuous way. It wasn't hard to imagine him savoring other parts of me, too. If things kept going the way they were, I'd probably get to find out sooner, rather than later.

Proving my point, his cock was right there, hard and straining against his jeans. Rubbing my equally hard dick against his was the only way to bring an iota of relief, but it still wasn't enough.

As if he could read my thoughts, he palmed my dick, gripping me through the denim and stroking my length. Lightning flashed outside, briefly illuminating his face and the fact he licked his perfect lips. The next thing I knew, his fingers unzipped my pants and pushed them down to the tops of my thighs. My cock sprang free, jutting between us in the dark. He found it quickly and resumed stroking it as he dropped to his knees.

Shit… Was this really happening? A flutter of nerves spiraled through my stomach but I wasn't about to stop him.

Just like the kiss, I felt his breath on my skin before his mouth made contact. The flat of his tongue licked me from base to tip, again and again. He flicked the ridge at the bottom and then sucked the crown into his mouth.

I sighed, running my fingers through his silky hair, still damp from the rain. My cock slid deeper and deeper until I was buried in his throat. He gagged a bit but stayed where he was, swallowing all of me.

"Oh, fuck," I gasped, hoping I didn't lose control right then and there. This really *was* happening. With a guy whose name I'd learned like twenty minutes ago. I tried not to overanalyze it but it was still hard to wrap my head around, even as he massaged the underside of my shaft with his tongue.

His hand slipped between my thighs and drifted upward, rubbing my balls while he backed off of my cock, gasping for a full breath. "Did you like that?"

"Yeah," I breathed, bracing myself against something in the dark. A table, a desk. Something sturdy with a hard, blunt edge that pressed into the backs of my thighs. "It felt amazing."

He hummed his acknowledgment around my dick and dove in again, sucking and licking and driving me crazy. Not being able to see what he was doing made it all the more intense. Every sensation was magnified in the dark, from the drag of his tongue to the gentle scrape of his teeth. The anticipation of what was coming next only added to the experience.

"God, yes. Just like that." Fuck... I wasn't going to be able to hold out for much longer.

He sucked and teased my crown with his tongue at the same time he stroked my shaft with increasing speed and pressure.

"You're going to make me come," I panted, the tingling in my balls growing with each second.

He popped off my cock with another gasp for air. "Do it, baby. I want to taste your cum." I'd barely registered the command before he latched onto my dick again, somehow sucking even harder.

"Oh my God... Fuck!" I thrust into his mouth, burying myself all the way. His fingers dug into my ass, pulling me in, holding me there while my orgasm unloaded down the back of his throat, pulse after pulse. The tingling hadn't stopped, even after he wrung every fucking drop out of me. What the hell was *that* about? Jesus... I made a mental note to look into it later when some of the blood flow returned to my brain.

Breathing hard, I eased my dick out of his mouth and stumbled back, hitting the hard surface again. "Oh, fuck... That was..."

"Incredible?" He chuckled and rose to his feet, licking and kissing my exposed skin on his way up, from the V of my groin, up my abs. Once he was vertical, he pulled my pants up over my hips before leaning in and kissing my neck, pressing his pelvis into mine.

"Your turn?" I asked, tipping my head back to give his mouth more room to maneuver.

"If you insist," he murmured before biting my shoulder,

his hands splaying beneath my sweater and running up my back. It felt like my whole fucking body was vibrating. If he noticed any shaking, he didn't say anything. Or hell, maybe he took it as a compliment.

The lights flickered and turned on again.

If it was possible, Graeme looked even sexier than he had before we came into this room. My hands had disheveled his dark hair and the intense kissing made his pillowy lips redder than before. That mischievous sparkle in his beautiful eyes was still there, practically glimmering every time the lightning flashed outside.

I slipped my fingers into his hair and pulled his face closer to mine. Our lips were a breath apart when the door opened.

Leaping away from each other like someone threw ice water on us, I hoped like hell it wasn't Peregrine Northrup storming in. There was no way to safely explain our presence in his office, a room that had been off-limits my entire life. And even though his powers didn't include telepathy, as far as I was aware, I was sure the guilt of what we'd done was written all over my face.

Thankfully, it was only my cousin, which was still bad but not Deacon-Northrup bad.

"There you are," Lennox said. Well, snarled. He might have been speaking to me, but his black gaze was pinned to Graeme. "We've been looking for you."

"Yeah, we were just… talking. Then the lights went out." I gave Lennox a fleeting smile, trying to figure out why he looked so extraordinarily pissed. I mean, *he* was the one who damn near dragged me out of the house and now he was pissed I was actually socializing?

"You ready to go?" Despite the inflection in his voice, it was *not* a question. We hadn't even been here that long, but something told me the party was definitely over.

I tossed a quick glance toward Graeme, hoping Lennox would take a hint. "Yeah. I'll be right there."

My asshole cousin didn't move. His black gaze turned on me, as piercing as if he'd actually stabbed me.

I winced, recognizing a command when I saw one. Or rather, *felt* by the invisible knife prodding my back — just a little telekinesis courtesy of his mother's side of the family.

Ducking my head, I hurried to join him before he produced a real knife and *really* made me regret coming out.

"Can I get your number?" Graeme asked, taking a step after me.

I turned to look at him, but Lennox grabbed my arm and yanked me out of the room.

"I can't believe you were just talking to him," Lennox growled, dragging me through the crowd like I was a child instead of a college-bound eighteen-year-old. "What the fuck is wrong with you?!"

"What is your problem?" In spite of myself, I stole another glance over my shoulder at Graeme. He had rejoined his friends, sipping a drink and watching me with those mismatched eyes, a small crease between his dark brows. "Who is he?"

"Oh my God!" Lennox stopped abruptly next to Arden and whipped around to face me. "That's Graeme *Hewitt*, you moron! George Hewitt's son!"

Every cell in my body turned to ice until I was frozen from the inside out. My breathing was so fast and shallow, I didn't know if the oxygen was even making it to its destination. Anger, nausea, hatred, humiliation, it all churned in the pit of my stomach like toxic waste.

He was a *Hewitt*?!

That meant he was a witch.

That meant he was…

Forcing myself to swallow, I avoided looking at either of

them and concentrated on trying to slow my breathing. Gin bubbled inside me, threatening to come out at any second.

"What about Graeme Hewitt?" Arden piped up, looking between Lennox and I expectantly. "Causing trouble again, I take it? Someone really needs to knock that asshole off his fucking pedestal. He's not Deacon *yet*, for Christ's sake."

"Cassius was just *talking* to him," Lennox answered, his teeth on edge.

Arden's eyes nearly popped out of his head. "But his dad..."

The voice was mine, but the words were hollow. "Murdered my mother."

Chapter Two

Graeme

As soon as I re-emerged from Peregrine's office, India's wide-eyed stare locked on me as I made my way toward her. I kept glancing at Cash, keeping an eye on him as he cut across the room, hoping maybe he'd ditch the prick and come back to me.

Cash looked back precisely one time. His spine went straight and he looked like he'd seen a ghost — which, in Preston's house, was entirely possible, given how old it was.

He and his friends left moments after in what was obviously a hurry. Lennox Ambrose, his tall, dark, and asshole of a friend, apparently, was the last to leave, giving me a lethal look before he disappeared.

"What the fuck?" India hissed. "What did he want with you?"

"Who?" I asked, sipping the drink she held out to me and hoping she wasn't talking about the guy I'd been eye-fucking across the room since the minute he walked in. From the edge of her tone, I assumed she meant Lennox, not the mysterious guy Lennox just snatched away from me like the selfish dick he was.

"Cassius Corbin! Who else?!" She stared at me like I'd lost my mind. At that point, maybe I had. Or maybe it was all of the alcohol. The very name she said sent a shudder down my spine even though I clung to the stupid hope she was wrong.

I knew Lennox.

I knew his prissy BFF Arden.

Aside from Winslow being a relatively small community, I'd had the misfortune of attending the same private academy with those two since sixth grade.

That meant she really was talking about Cash.

And Cash must have been... short for fucking Cassius. Cassius *Corbin*. The answer had been right in front of my fucking face with that goddamn necklace he was wearing. I thought it was him being edgy. No. It was him announcing his twisted-as-fuck lineage. Flaunting it, even!

I laughed into my cup like it was all a big fucking joke and promptly drained it, hoping the beer would keep me from throwing up where I stood. My stomach twisted in knots, but I wouldn't let on that India caught me unaware. I already felt like the biggest fucking idiot on the planet without her chiming in on the subject or agreeing one thousand percent.

Cassius fucking Corbin.

The son and heir to the family who'd hated mine since the beginning of time, the family I was taught to hate from the moment I drew breath.

More importantly, he was the son of the woman who killed my brother.

Cassius fucking Corbin.

The guy I thought was *so* hot from the minute he stepped through the door, with his dark hair and pale skin, looking like a dark academia snack. The one who smelled like expensive soap and evergreens. I'd pursued him until I had him. And I fucking *had* him!

Instead of killing him, what did I do? I blew him in the dark like a fucking moron.

I was about to blow again — goddamn vomit everywhere

— when Preston returned, handing India another red plastic cup. "What are we laughing about?"

"What an idiot Graeme is," India replied with a light laugh, tossing her copper hair over her shoulder and thankfully glossing over the whole incident. It was bad enough she knew, I didn't need Preston weighing in on it either. "He let this storm get out of hand just to win a bet. Now it's going to rain for the rest of the night, so no bonfire for us."

"If you're going to make the power go out, could you at least warn me first? I was in the bathroom. Makes things a little awkward," Preston said with a chuckle.

I forced myself to laugh with them, hoping it sounded natural and not like I wanted to curl up in a hole and die.

"Yeah, if you're going to be *Deacon*" — India practically growled the last word — "one day, then you better master your magic. You can't let your emotions win."

Preston nudged me with his elbow. "Take it from the son of a Deacon, you definitely want to establish a happy place in your head. All of the petty bullshit the Congregation brings to you? We can't have a blizzard in July because you get pissed off at someone. Dad blew the roof off the old Middlewich barn one day because he got so pissed. The Congregation wasn't happy."

"Yeah. You're right. I'll work on it." I forced another laugh and waved my cup at them. "I'm gonna get a refill." Or thirty.

For the rest of the night, I joked and acted like I wasn't guzzling beer to try and get the taste of Cassius out of my mouth.

The taste I eventually overcame, but the feeling? That would never go away. Sucking the dick of the enemy. I'd done a lot of shit I wasn't proud of over the nineteen years of my life, but I'd never stooped *that* low.

What the fuck was wrong with me?!

A week later, I was still fuming about the whole incident, but my period of self-flagellation was over. Now? I was thoroughly pissed at *him* for breaking protocol. Didn't he know the rules? They'd only been around for three fucking centuries! Corbins and Hewitts were to avoid each other like the plague. The only time we should be in the same vicinity as one another was at a Meeting, surrounded by the rest of the Congregation so no one did anything stupid. That's how it was supposed to work. They stay away from us; we stay away from them. And for the past six years, I hadn't seen a single fucking Corbin. Their asshole relatives, like the Ambroses, sure, but not the murdering Necromancers themselves.

So what the fuck was Cassius doing at a back-to-school party for Tennebrose University? He didn't fucking *go* here, did he? Shit...

I mean, it shouldn't have been surprising. All of the Winslow witches were given the opportunity to attend Tennebrose. It was one of the few places you could safely work on your craft and no one was the wiser. After all, university was supposed to prepare you for the rest of your life and our lives revolved around our ancestral magic whether we wanted them to or not.

But I never saw that blue-eyed asshole in all my years at King Street Academy with his prick of a cousin Lennox. I highly doubted someone as stuck up as a Corbin would attend Winslow High with the rest of the peasants. The rumors that he was disfigured clearly weren't true. So where the hell had he been hiding all these years? Had he really been locked up in his father's creepy castle in the woods this whole time?

I'd no more than remembered Cassius's smug smirk at the party when the Devil himself appeared in my actual line of sight.

Sitting on the ledge overlooking the sunken garden outside the university library, Cassius had a book in his lap but he wasn't reading. His attention was focused on the crow sitting next to him. The bird ruffled its feathers and sidestepped closer to Cassius, depositing something in his outstretched hand.

Smiling at whatever it was, he inclined his head and said something to the bird. From my vantage point, it looked like he actually *thanked* it. Like it could understand.

The crow cawed loudly and took off with a few flaps of its wings, disappearing into the sky overhead.

Cassius's smile vanished in the blink of an eye. As if he knew he was being watched, a cold mask slammed into place while he glanced around, methodically searching the faces of people walking by. The moment his eyes landed on me, a jab of white-hot pain ripped through my stomach.

By the time I stormed over to him, he was on his feet, his hands clenched at his sides.

"What the fuck do *you* want?" he spat, looking me over with nothing but contempt on his chiseled face. If it was possible, he might have been even hotter when he was angry. God, I fucking hated him.

"I could ask you the same thing, asshole." It was a pathetic comeback, but it was really all I had. While I dreaded the idea of seeing him again and had spent the week trying to come up with some sort of plan for when it happened, I wasn't actually planning on having a verbal sparring match first thing in the morning. I was barely awake as it was, except for my dick, who apparently decided to join the fray as soon as Cassius spoke. Traitor.

Luckily, Cassius didn't seem to notice. He was too busy glaring at me like an insect he was about to set on fire with a magnifying glass because crushing them under his shoe was just too quick. "In case it's escaped your attention, fuck wit, this is a library. People come here to learn."

"I meant Tennebrose, you dick," I spat back. Even though I was pretty sure I knew the answer, I wanted to hear it from him directly. "Shouldn't your kind be off terrorizing unsuspecting villagers or something?"

"*My* kind?" His blue eyes flashed, registering surprise and insult all at once. "What is *that* supposed to mean?"

"You know what it means, Necromancer." Anger boiled inside me at his offended tone. What right did a Corbin have to be fucking offended? Was he in that much denial about how fucked up his family was? No wonder they were all murderers.

"I'd watch your fucking mouth if I were you."

"Why? You didn't mind it last week." Oh my God… I couldn't believe I fucking brought that up! Well, it was too late now. Might as well roll with it and see if I could use it to my advantage. Pushing my shoulders back, I assessed him with a sneer. "I guess I didn't realize how twisted you people really were. Get a good laugh with your buddies over the whole thing? A Corbin fucking over a Hewitt. *Again*. Real original."

"*You're* the one who approached me. *Twice*, I might add." His lip curled as he took a step closer, his hands clenching at his sides. "If you know what's good for you, there won't be a third time."

I matched his step with one of my own, eyes narrowing. "Is that a threat?"

"It's a fucking promise." A fine, black mist swirled around

his hands. It wouldn't have been noticeable against his black coat to anyone walking by, but I knew whatever it was was *not* good. "You're lucky I don't kill you right here."

"Guess it's true what they say," I said, glaring at his hands pointedly before my gaze snapped up to his. "The apple doesn't fall far from the tree."

Rage twisted the sharp lines of his face. He lifted one hand, the black swirls intensifying as they wove through his fingers, churning into a ball.

Before he could cast whatever dark magic he was concocting, both of my hands flew up in defense. A rush of wind whipped around me, dispelling the mist like a puff of smoke.

Even after I lowered my hands, the winds didn't stop. They continued to stream past me with the force of a hurricane, pushing Cassius backward one step at a time. When he reached the edge of the ledge, I could almost see a gust twisting around his torso. I blinked, right as the wind threw him backward into the air.

"No!" I took a step after him, my hand outstretched, but it was too late. He'd fallen out of view with a yelp, followed by a sickening crunch.

"Shit, shit, shit." Raking my hands through my hair, my brain whirred a hundred miles a minute before I latched onto one thought — get the fuck out of there.

Glancing around, I snatched my backpack off the ground and slung it over my shoulder, walking away as calmly as I could so I didn't draw any attention to myself.

I didn't walk over to the ledge or look at what was happening down below. I didn't have to, because I'd heard it. His body hit the paved terrace at the bottom, at least twenty feet down in the sunken garden, with a heavy thud. I also heard a wet, crunchy sort of sound that could have only been his skull splitting open, like dropping a pumpkin from up high.

Swearing under my breath, I hoped for two things: one, that no one saw; and two, that Cassius Corbin was fucking dead.

Chapter Three
Cassius

My head was still pounding when I woke up the next morning and dragged my ass to my eight o'clock botany class. If it was any other class, I might have been tempted to blow it off. Unfortunately, it was a requirement. Not a university requirement related to my degree in any way, shape, or form. It was a *magical* requirement, which meant I'd better not piss off my elders on the first day.

Smoothing my hair down over the back of my skull for the hundredth time since waking up, I marched straight to the back of the science room and took a seat at one of the long, black tables. Hopefully, between the product and my paranoia, the giant scab leftover from yesterday would stay hidden and no one would ask what happened. Before I left the house, my sister assured me no one could see but handed me a small pot of salve for it anyway.

All I could say was thank God for crows. They sought out Lennox on my behalf and alerted him to my situation before anyone else found me. A normal person would have called 911 and *that* would have presented a whole host of problems the Congregation would *not* want to deal with.

Witches may have founded Winslow and built Tennebrose University and we may have spent centuries infiltrating the highest levels of local government, but none of that meant the average citizen was supposed to know of our existence *or* our abilities.

I didn't want to have to explain to a mortal how Graeme Hewitt threw me off a fucking ledge without even touching me, nor did I want to have to explain to a fellow witch the reason behind it. Although it was a given that our families hated each other and historically spent most of their time trying to exterminate the other, the Selectmen would still want to know *why*. For every murder, honor killing, or act of retribution, there was a detailed account logged in the Book of Transactions. All except for the original offense, of course, the one that started the feud. That explanation had been lost to history and all we had to go on were family stories of he-said/she-said.

Instead of turning me over to the elders for an investigation, Lennox worked his magic, repairing some of the internal damage in my head. As soon as I was conscious, he rushed me home to Claudia to mend the rest.

Each of us had our gifts, but in this instance I was especially lucky my sister was a bone witch. She fused my skull back together better than any of her fellow doctors could in half the time. When she was finished, she smeared a sticky, foul-smelling salve over the gash and proceeded to hen peck me for the rest of the night. Fluffed pillows, repeated tonics, and zero movement allowed according to the junior Doctor Corbin. I was grateful our father wasn't home, otherwise I would have had both of them treating me like an invalid.

"He could have killed you," Claudia seethed hours later, tucking a blanket around me rather roughly considering her rule against me moving. "You need to report him to the Committee."

"I'm fine," I sighed. "And I'm not reporting anyone."

Lennox had been perfectly fine avenging my honor the

old-fashioned way. He wanted to seek out Graeme and melt the skin off his bones, but Claudia insisted we rise above our stupid reputation and let the elders decide what punishment was appropriate.

She ignored me, punching a pillow into submission and building a nest around me in bed.

"Besides," I continued glumly. "You know the Deacon is best friends with his father. It won't do any good."

"The Deacon is only one man. The rest of the Selectmen still have a say. There are thirteen for a reason."

"And how many of them would side with Necromancers?"

"Enough."

"They didn't before…"

Her irritated glare softened into a wince. She turned away quickly, rearranging the stuff on my nightstand to make it easier to reach — books, water, phone, a huge chunk of obsidian. The usual. "This is different. It was unprovoked."

"It wasn't," I admitted through clenched teeth. Grabbing the comforter in my fist, I smoothed it out again, avoiding the exasperated look I could feel radiating from her general direction. "I was going to hit him first. He beat me to it."

It was her turn to sigh as she sank onto the edge of my bed, grasping my forearm gently. "Oh, Cash…"

"I know… Now that I know we're going to be on campus together, I'll do a better job of staying away from him. Promise."

"You better," she said sternly before leaning forward, pressing a kiss to my forehead. "I'm not losing any more family members."

I nodded mutely, watching her leave.

For the rest of the night, my thoughts were consumed with Graeme Hewitt. Conflicting thoughts at that — memories of his mouth on mine, along with the look on his face before he threw me off that fucking wall. It was pure anger, followed by pure horror right before I plummeted downward. I didn't know what his powers were, exactly, but I knew now I had to be mindful of his hands. Hands that lit my skin on fire, stroking and grabbing and touching just right—

A cold breeze whisked through the classroom, eliminating any inappropriate thoughts in a flash and slamming me right back into the present. I glanced at the row of windows on the far side of the room but they were all closed. The breeze came from another source, then.

Dread circled in the pit of my stomach as I turned toward the door, watching as my nemesis practically floated into the room.

Mr. Popular. Mr. Perfect.

Graeme waved and laughed with someone as he walked by their table. He slapped them on the shoulder and took another step down the aisle before stopping dead in his tracks, his mismatched eyes locked on mine.

Anger and power rippled through me, pricking my hands as it manifested in the telltale black mist. I hid them beneath the table, but let it grow anyway. My promise to Claudia was the only thing that kept my ass in the chair, even though my pride demanded yesterday's insult not go unchecked.

Like a heat-seeking missile, Graeme marched straight to my table. Planting both hands on the edge, he leaned down, lowering his voice. "You've got to be fucking kidding me."

"Aw, you didn't think I was that easy to kill, did you?" I gave him a faux pout. Just seeing him made my heart rate go up, which in turn renewed the painful thumping in my head.

"What the fuck are you doing here?"

"Wow." Staring at him for a beat, I waited to see if that was a serious question or not. I mean, first the library and now a classroom. People routinely knocked the American education system, but I didn't think a private academy would pass along someone *that* far behind their peers. "For being in an advanced botany class, you're not very bright."

"Fuck off," he snapped, his face inching closer. "You're not in any of my other classes so what are you doing in this one?"

"Well, your majesty, it's a requirement for us. Remember?" I flashed him a bitter smile.

He huffed and stomped away with a withering glare.

I expelled a short breath, waving the black mist away before it started curling out from beneath the table. With my luck, someone would think it was a fire and sound the alarm.

Graeme threw his backpack onto the table right across the aisle. When my head jerked in his direction, he met my bewildered expression with a brilliant smile, the kind that belonged on the cover of a magazine somewhere. I fucking hated him and the audacity of every breath he took.

"What are you doing?" I asked. There were scores of open seats, literally anywhere else. Why the fuck was he sitting right next to me?

His dazzling smile turned vicious. "What does it look like, genius?"

Beneath the table, I twisted my hand in a circle, gathering the mist back into a ball. Stealing a quick glance at the rest of the class, I launched the mist across the aisle, hitting him square in the chest.

He flew backward out of his chair, knocking it over in the process, and landed on his back with a grunt.

A series of gasps sounded in the front of the room. A few people ventured over to ask if he was ok and offered to help him up. He laughed off their questions and concern, blaming the freshly waxed floors and how he'd been perched on the edge of his chair.

I, on the other hand, retrieved a notebook and a pen from my messenger bag, pretending to be oblivious to what was happening five feet away from me.

Graeme got to his feet rather slowly, holding his chest with one hand and straightening his chair.

"Move, or I'll do it again," I said, not even bothering to look at him. Dragging one of our required texts closer, I flipped through it casually.

"Fuck you," he said under his breath. "I'm not sitting anywhere in this room if my back is facing you. Can't make it too easy for you to put a fucking knife in it."

"Oh, I wouldn't worry about that." It was my turn to give him a radiant smile just to watch his jaw tighten. "I'll let you see it coming."

"I'm sure you would, you sick prick."

I held his glare, maintaining my smile even though my face was killing me. The black mist spread through my fingers, twisting and churning into another little ball. Without warning, I whipped it in his direction.

This time, his hands flew up. A gust of wind clashed with the mist, scattering it.

"Nice trick," he growled next to me.

"Better than being a pompous windbag." The wind resumed with a flick of his wrist, sweeping my notebook and pen off the tabletop. Asshole.

Rolling my eyes, I stooped and retrieved them only to slam them back into place. "How mature. I'm positively trembling in fear over your awesome powers. Oh, please don't hurt me with witch wind!"

"Seemed to work pretty well for me yesterday, didn't it?" He smirked triumphantly.

"You smug son of—" I was halfway out of my chair when Dr. Ainsworth walked in, smiling brightly and greeting the first couple of students.

Grudgingly, I resumed my seat as the professor nodded his greetings to some students he wasn't acquainted with. His gaze swept the rest of the class in an orderly fashion. The second it landed on me, his smile vanished. I might have been offended, but his gaze flicked across the aisle to Graeme and back again, equally displeased having a Hewitt in class.

As one of the Winslow elders, he shouldn't be the least bit surprised to find two witches in his botany class. After all, *he* was the one who insisted botany be a requirement for graduation. Therefore, I'm sure his shock had everything to do with who we were, in particular, and that we were in such close proximity to one another. The fact each of us was still breathing was a bonus — it meant no paperwork for him as the Congregation's Tithing Man, a tedious position designed to keep Covenant members in line instead of burdening the Selectmen with trivial offenses when they had much more important matters to handle — like hiding our existence from the rest of the town.

Ainsworth regained his composure fairly quickly and set his bag on the desk. "And let's begin!"

With that, the first-day lecture was underway.

I tried to focus on what Ainsworth was saying, following along on the syllabus and brainstorming ideas for the central project driving our grade for the semester. Tried, and failed. Knowing Graeme was right next to me, even if it was five feet away, was unnerving. Every time my papers ruffled or I swore something brushed through my hair, I'd send a glare in Graeme's direction only to find him paying rapt attention to our professor.

As soon as we were dismissed, I snatched my bag off the table and bolted for the door. Thankfully, Ainsworth didn't try to stop me for some sort of conference with his royal majesty. *I* knew what the fucking rules were — clearly someone needed to inform Mr. Hewitt.

Being that botany was my only class for the day, it meant I could get the hell out of this building and away from Graeme Hewitt as fast as my legs would carry me.

Jogging down the front steps of Dane Hall, I hitched my bag on my shoulder and headed for the parking lot down the road.

I didn't make it very far before an all-too-familiar wind pushed against my back. Hard. Come to think of it, it was the same feeling I had that night at Preston's when the wind pushed me into him. Asshole!

Stopping abruptly, my molars ground together, but I refused to turn around. Rather than looking at Graeme and making my blood pressure spike for the umpteenth time, I searched the nearby trees instead. "You're either dumber than I previously thought or you *must* have a death wish."

"For a Necromancer, you sure are a fucking coward," Graeme said behind me. "You won't even turn around and talk to me like a man."

My spine straightened, tension rippling down the bones and spreading through the rest of my body. "What are you going to do? Blow me again?"

"Fuck you!"

I pivoted on my heel, facing him with a dark smile. "Don't be so sensitive. I was talking about your pathetic little puff of wind from earlier."

Rage flickered across his face with every breath, every muscle tightening. "I don't even know why I thought I could talk to you like a normal person."

"I'll tell you why. You couldn't kill me so now you're trying to make nice in the hope that I don't creep into your bedroom at night and do all sorts of dark, dastardly things to you." I pretended to have a revelation, considering my own words with a pensive expression. "On second thought, maybe you'd like it."

Seething through his teeth, his fingers curled at his sides. Wind swirled around my legs and swept upward, encasing me in my own miniature tornado. Guess I struck a nerve.

Any attempt to move was met with a gust, shoving me backward. I closed my eyes against the stinging wind and used the howling in my ears to my advantage, quieting my mind.

I searched out the family of crows roosting in the trees across the street. Once the connection was fixed in my mind's eye, my "sight" returned through their eyes. The birds buzzed in anticipation, watching the ruckus down below with the utmost curiosity.

Go.

Shrieking and cawing, the crows burst out of the trees. In a sweeping arc, they dove at Graeme. A dozen wings flapped, black beaks and claws gouging and scratching at whatever they could reach.

Graeme yelped and ducked, covering his head with his arms, swearing at me and my winged crusaders. His witch wind immediately stopped, releasing me from the miniature cyclone.

I could have let him go. I didn't. The crows continued to swarm him. Folding my arms over my chest, I cocked my head, watching the scene with my real gaze. Whenever a beak or a claw ripped into him and he hissed or cried out in pain, I felt a piece of my family's name restored.

A female scream sounded above the chaos.

My attention snapped to the doorway of Dane Hall. A pair of girls had emerged from the building, pointing and shrieking at Graeme's crow-covered body. I only recognized one — Sophia, the girl Arden was supposedly interested in. Sophia retreated back inside while the other girl stood frozen, her hands over her mouth and eyes wide.

With an annoyed growl, I dispersed the birds with my gratitude and rushed over to Graeme, pretending to be as concerned as she was.

"There are people watching, you idiot," I growled, seizing

a handful of his shirt and yanking him to his feet. Scratches crisscrossed his face, blood beading on his skin and soaking through small tears in his shirt.

He smacked my hand off and shoved me in the chest, his eyes flashing with barely-contained fury. “Get the fuck away from me!”

As soon as I regained my footing, I closed the distance again and shoved him back. “I don’t know how many times I have to tell you, Hewitt, but stay the fuck away from *me*.”

“Or what?” Graeme’s face hardened, his beautiful mouth twisting to a snarl. “You’ll sic your fucking birds on me again? Nice try but I’m not scared of a party trick.”

I snorted, giving him a once over. “Is everything out of your mouth a lie?”

“What the fuck are you talking about?”

“You *are* afraid.” I edged closer, so close I could feel the heat rolling off of him. “I can smell it on you.”

He held firm, but his eyes tightened at the corners. Just a flicker, enough to let me know I struck another nerve. He didn’t like when people saw beneath his pretty, popular image. And he definitely didn’t like being called out on it. Duly noted.

I reached up and swiped my thumb along the gash on his cheekbone, collecting the beads of blood. Before he realized what I was doing, before I even had time to think of the ramifications, I lifted it to my mouth and sucked the blood off the pad of my thumb.

His lips parted, his eyes widening. Surprisingly, he was speechless.

For that brief moment, I saw myself through his eyes — the memory of Preston’s party by the fire, what I looked like while he was on his knees in front of me, the anger in my face outside the university library. It was a jumble of emotions I was all too familiar with. But it was comforting, at least, to know I wasn't the only one struggling with our current predicament.

I licked my lips and lowered my hand, my gaze locked on his. "Just what I thought."

He swallowed but pushed his shoulders back. "What?"

Allowing myself a small smirk, I gave him a pointed once over and spun on my heel, striding away.

"What the fuck did you just do? Cassius!"

My smirk spread into a full-fledged smile. The only answer I gave him was laughter, like the villain he wanted me to be.

Chapter Four
Graeme

I had one measly day between my first class with Cassius and the next. One measly day to figure out how our next interaction was going to go down. One day to see if he'd cursed me somehow by licking my blood like a fucking psycho. And one day to come up with some sort of plan.

But first things first. I needed to fix my mangled face.

After his little freak show with the crows, I drove straight to India's house.

"You will never believe what just fucking happened," I said, storming inside as soon as she opened the door.

"Oh my God! What happened to your face?" She pushed the door shut and hurried after me into the kitchen.

"Cassius fucking Corbin." I grabbed an apple out of the large wooden bowl on the counter and proceeded to the kitchen table, depositing myself in a chair with zero grace. I didn't know what his middle name was, but from the moment I learned who he was, that was the only thing I could call him — Cassius fucking Corbin.

"But how?"

"Goddamn crows. He was controlling them somehow, I know it." I took a vicious bite out of the apple.

She tucked one leg beneath her and sat on the chair across from me, frowning. "You have to tell the Deacon."

"Absolutely not!"

"Why not? He attacked you with magic. That's against the Covenant."

"Because then that asshole is going to tell Peregrine I threw him off a ledge yesterday." Shaking my head, I turned my glare to the apple in my hand. "Actually, I'm kind of surprised he didn't already tell someone."

India groaned. "Graeme…"

"I know!" I sighed and set the apple on the table, no longer the least bit hungry. "I didn't exactly *mean* to, but he was doing this freaky shit with his hands and I just reacted."

She propped her elbow on the table and held her head in her hand, the curtain of her copper hair falling to the side. "What are you going to tell your parents about your face?"

"I was hoping you could help with that."

"Better wait for my mom. I wouldn't want to make you any uglier than you already are." She wrinkled her nose at me with an impish grin before adding, "But she won't be home until six."

I shrugged. "That's fine by me."

"Won't your dad freak if you're not home by dinner?"

"Not if he knows I'm here." I slid my phone out of my pocket and shot him a quick text before he sent a stupid search-and-rescue team after me.

A second later, I got the typical response: **Be home by curfew.** As if I'd dare press my luck.

"So what are you going to do about Cassius?" India asked.

"I have no fucking clue." Thinking about him made me furious all over again. It's like he knew just what to say to piss me off in zero-to-sixty. Was he telepathic? Or just an asshole? "Hey, what do you know about blood magic?"

"Enough to not mess around with it. Why?"

I gestured vaguely toward my face. "He licked it."

"He licked you?" Her blue eyes popped open.

"No. He touched the blood and licked it off his finger. Why would he do that?"

She straightened, folding her arms over her chest, brow furrowed. Her brain was probably in the midst of sorting through the hundreds of books she'd read, searching for the answer. "I mean, usually blood magic is reserved for power spells, like protection or curses. But that's using it as an ingredient. For him to ingest it, I'd think he's trying to gain control over your spirit. That's what they do, right? Spirit work?"

He was already in my fucking head. Taking over my spirit probably wouldn't be that hard at this point. "Can you do that from one tiny drop of blood?"

"I have no idea. I'm just telling you what the books say. Maybe it didn't mean anything and he did it to fuck with you."

"Yeah, maybe. If I start acting weird, then I guess you'll know why."

"You're already weird," she said with a laugh.

I feigned offense. "Shh! I have an image to protect."

"Not in this house, you don't. Here you're the guy who still jumps in puddles and nurses woodland critters back to health." She gave me a pointed look and rose from the table, crossing over to the fridge to grab a couple bottles of water. "You're never going to be cool to me, even if they do name you the next Deacon."

"Yeah, yeah."

By the time Thursday morning rolled around, I was still as clueless about Cassius as I was Tuesday afternoon. Even with India's help, I never came up with a solid plan of action. She suggested I keep as far away from him as possible. Knowing I'd be three feet away from him in Ainsworth's class made that kind of *im*possible, but I promised her anyway.

Except, I never made it to class.

A large crowd gathered outside Dane Hall, talking excitedly or crying. Two police officers were barely visible beyond the crowd, a strip of yellow tape flashing into view now again between the backpacks and bodies.

In the center of the circle, someone was sprawled on the ground. A girl, judging from the fanned-out brunette hair and chipped pink nail polish visible on one hand.

"Who is that?" I murmured to the person closest to me.

A guy I recognized from class the other day turned to answer. "I think her name was Melanie?" He deferred to the petite blonde next to him. "Mel, right?"

The blonde sniffed and nodded, wiping her cheeks. "Yeah. We had bio-chem together."

"What happened?" I asked.

The blonde broke down into full-on sobbing, burying her face into the guy's chest. He shrugged but over the top of her head he slashed a finger across his throat, like he was decapitating his own head.

My gaze snapped back to the center of the circle. Instead of focusing on the dead girl, it landed on a black figure on the other side of the crowd and the pair of blue eyes burning into my very soul.

Cassius Corbin.

The corner of his mouth turned down in the faintest hint of a sneer as his gaze dropped to the body. He remained unmoved by whatever he saw. Cold-hearted bastard.

The crowd shifted and I finally saw the dead girl's face. Her eyes were empty sockets, blood splattered everywhere. But even more disturbing was the fact her head was lying a full foot above her shoulders.

Melanie turned out to be the girl who saw our fight the other day. Well, one of them. She was the one who screamed, ultimately making Cassius call off his stupid birds. Now she was dead and I had more than a sneaking suspicion her motherfucking killer was standing just a few feet away from her corpse, reliving the thrill of the kill like the psycho he was.

"Get these people back," a man snapped as he barged onto the scene, shouldering through the onlookers like a line-backer. It was Thomas Treadwell, the chief of Winslow PD himself — and another witch.

At the sight of the chief, Cassius skulked away. There may as well have been a neon sign flashing over his head that read GUILTY with a giant fucking arrow pointed at him.

Never one to leave well enough alone, as my mother used to say, I went after him. His strides lengthened, like he knew I was behind him. Unfortunately for him, my legs were just as long and it wasn't hard to catch up.

"Going somewhere?" I said over his shoulder. "Off to find your next victim, maybe?"

He drew up short and spun quickly, nearly crashing into me. "You have *got* to be one of the dumbest people I've ever met. I can't believe you're actually trying to cause another scene when Treadwell is *right* there."

"If it gets his attention, then so be it. I'm not about to let a murdering witch stroll around campus like he owns the fucking place."

His jaw clenched a split second before he shoved me in the chest. "You'd know all about murder, wouldn't you?"

I stumbled back a step but regained my footing, squaring off again. "My father had every right to kill your mother for what she did. What excuse are *you* going to use for the Committee?"

For a split second, he looked genuinely confused. "What are you talking about?"

I tossed my head toward the dead girl. "Couldn't control yourself the other day, so you come back and take it out on her? Pretty childish, Corbin. Mortals never stand a chance."

He glanced toward the circle of people. It was filled with police now, pushing students away, giving the detectives room to work. When his gaze returned to mine, his eyes narrowed. "You are *not* going to pin your fuck-up on me. Go find another patsy. Now that your pretty face is miraculously healed, I'm sure you can find someone even dumber than you to take the blame. That's what you Hewitts do, after all. Blame other people for your misdeeds."

"*My* fuck-up?" I took a step closer, lowering my voice. "You think *I* killed her? Why the fuck would *I* kill her?"

"Well, *I* didn't fucking kill her."

"Then who did?" This ought to be good. I'm sure he had his alibi all planned out. I couldn't wait to see who he was going to frame for this.

A dark glint crept into his eyes. "One way to find out. If you're not too chickenshit, that is."

I drew myself up straighter, despite the fact I didn't want *any* part of what he was planning. "Tell me when and where, asshole."

"Morgue. Midnight." His gaze raked over me slowly before he turned and strode away.

I'd just walked in the front door and was in the process of hanging up my coat when Dad stormed around the corner.

"Where have you been?" he demanded, checking his watch. I don't know why, considering it was only ten o'clock in the *morning* and nowhere near close to breaking his ridiculous curfew, for God's sake.

"Uh, school?" I toed off the last shoe and turned to face him with raised brows. "Why?"

"Thomas said he saw you at campus over two hours ago. Where have you been? I know classes were canceled for the day. So where were you?"

"I went for a walk. Is that ok with you?" Fucking Treadwell. There were goddamn spies all over this town.

"How many times have I told you not to go into those woods by yourself?"

A weary sigh escaped me before I could stop it. "It's fine, Dad. I've never seen a ghost let alone been attacked by one."

"That doesn't mean she isn't watching you. And speaking of Black Mary, why in God's name were you with that Corbin boy? Was he with you in the woods? Did he hurt you? I swear to God, Graeme—"

"Oh my God! Stop!" If Dad wasn't on the verge of stroking out right in front of me, I would have tried to lie. But since Treadwell fucked me already by ratting me out, I figured the truth was easier. "We're in Ainsworth's class together, ok? It was nothing. No, he wasn't with me. I just wanted to clear my head."

His jaw clenched before he spoke. "I'm calling Samuel right now. This is completely unacceptable!" He actually turned to go before I caught his arm and pulled him to a stop.

"No, Dad! It's fine. It's just one class. Besides, this isn't high school. You can't call my teachers and get me special treatment anymore." As if it wasn't embarrassing enough back then... if he did it now, I'd be fucking mortified. I was supposed to be an adult, but even at nineteen I still had to toe the line and do everything my dad said. Why? A combination of fear, the concept of filial piety, and a big ass dose of guilt.

"It's not fine!" Dad continued, the vein in his forehead throbbing harder. "I don't want those people around you. Period. Lord knows what they're capable of. Just look at the mother, may she rot in whatever Hell she's in. You don't need to be subjected to their kind any more than absolutely necessary."

My God, graduation couldn't come fast enough. Maybe I could take summer classes to speed things along. Although it wouldn't do me that much good. I'd still be stuck in Winslow for the foreseeable future, like a prison sentence with no hope of parole. "I can handle it. Ok? I can handle *him*. Don't call anyone. Or email. Or send a strongly worded letter. I've got this."

"I don't like it, Graeme. Not one bit. I don't want you talking to that boy again. Do you hear me? Don't even look at him!"

"Why would I talk to him?" I threw my hands up, all but scraping the bottom of the patience barrel. "He's the son of a killer." Just like me — the parallel of which was not, lost on me.

Dad stared at me, his eyes narrowed, like he was trying to decide whether or not to believe me. I glared back, refusing to be the one to break first. He was looking out for me, I got that, but for fuck's sake already. When would I be allowed to live my life? Would there ever be a time I could escape the fucking cloud that hung over this family? Over me?

A tiny, crystal bell chimed, immediately ending the showdown. Dad looked away first, only because that bell meant my mother was summoning one of us. When no one responded fast enough, she called out pathetically for him.

"George! I need my pills."

"Coming, dear." He shook his head, puffing out a breath. "Do *not* tell your mother about any of this. I don't even want that family's name uttered in her presence. You know what kind of condition she's in." Far be it for me to tell him she'd been in that fucking condition for six years. Losing Owen broke her and she never bothered picking up the pieces; it didn't matter she still had a husband and another son who needed her.

"Fine. Whatever." I held my hands up in surrender and headed for the living room. It's not like I wanted to come home and gush to either of them about how dreamy Cassius was. Dark hair, blue eyes, pale skin. Cheekbones that could cut fucking glass. As much as I hated to admit it, and despite the fact he was a Corbin, he was still fucking hot. But neither of my parents needed to know my feelings on that — or the fact we'd already had two duels and it was only the second week of class.

Flopping on the couch, I held the remote in my hand but didn't bother turning on the TV. It wouldn't have mattered. I couldn't get Cassius out of my damn head even when I tried.

Chapter Five
Cassius

I wouldn't exactly say I was *sneaking* out of the house, but I definitely didn't want to draw attention to the fact I was leaving at such a late hour. I knew Dad had a day full of surgeries planned, so he'd gone to bed early, but who knew where Claudia was. Since she was still in her residency, there was no rhyme or reason to her schedule. And after the whole library thing, she would *not* be ok with me running off to meet up with the asshole who cracked open my skull.

Luckily for me, there was more than one way to get out of the house.

Climbing over the balcony railing, I perched on the edge before stepping out to the side. Once I got a foothold on the lip of the ornamental stone, I grabbed onto the lattice and made my way down easily enough.

Dropping to the ground, I dusted my hands off and adjusted the bag on my shoulder before setting off for the garage.

Making my way back to Winslow proper on autopilot, I drove to the hospital and parked. I had no idea what kind of car Graeme had, so I didn't bother waiting around. He'd have to find his own way in if he wasn't too chickenshit. Just because he may or may not have ventured into the North

Woods on his own didn't mean he was up for the task at hand.

Slipping in through the ER doors, I walked through the near-silent halls, ducking into a stairwell and heading down to the basement. Even though it wasn't spelled out for the public, I made my way to the morgue with ease. It helped that my family worked in and out of this hospital regularly. Plus, I had literally been here a few days ago, chatting with Dr. Dane about taking on an internship position in the morgue.

Letting myself in, I flicked on the lights and surveyed the sterile room. There was a single autopsy table, unoccupied, and the giant stainless steel cooler on the far side of the room. Lucky for me, it wasn't the kind with the individual drawers that made moving bodies doubly tedious. This one was like any other industrial walk-in cooler, except it was chock full of dead people instead of food.

Shrugging the bag off my shoulder, I propped the cooler door open with it and stepped inside.

There were half a dozen corpses to pick from. Since I didn't know her name, the tags were pretty much useless beyond indicating gender. I unzipped the first body bag, to no avail.

It took three more attempts before I found my murdered classmate.

Wheeling her out into the open, I unzipped the bag down to her abdomen and pushed the plastic away from her face.

"Huh." I considered the sight before me with raised brows. She really was decapitated. Here I thought it had just been a stupid rumor on campus. For once the gossips were right.

Lifting her head out of the bag, I held it between my hands, studying her face. Beyond the actual decapitation, the first thing I noticed was that her eyes were missing. The sunken, half-open eyelids were a clue, as was all of the dried blood running down her face.

Tilting the head, I studied the inside of her neck. The cut was clean, like it had been made in one blow. Unless someone was carrying around a portable guillotine, I doubted any mere mortal could have made a cut like that. Maybe a katana by an expert swordsman. *Maybe*. But who the hell fit that bill in a small town in rural Massachusetts?

"Admiring your handiwork?" a male voice asked, dripping in disdain.

My jaw clenched involuntarily. I knew it was Graeme without even having to turn around. His voice had haunted my dreams since the first night I laid eyes on him.

"Finally plucked up the courage, I see," I threw back, laying the girl's head in the bag where it belonged.

"Unlike you freaks, my family isn't into corpses. I actually had to Google where the hell I was going." He approached the gurney cautiously, as if the corpse in question was going to sit up and grab him at any minute.

I smirked and cocked my head. "No, of course not. You tree-hugging hippies can't stand the sight of blood. Especially your own."

He glared at me in return, but for once didn't have some dumb ass comeback.

Doing my best to ignore the irritation of his mere presence, I retrieved my bag and returned to my original place before rummaging through it.

"What are you doing?" he asked as I walked to his side of the table and plopped a couple of black candles on the floor behind him. He actually sounded nervous. How cute.

"Setting the mood for Round Two." I rolled my eyes and kept going. "It's a circle, dipshit. You know, those things that keep you safe during a spell?"

His hands clenched so hard I heard his knuckles crack. It

was either that or he chipped a tooth by grinding them. "I swear to God… if I had known who you were, I would have—"

"Would have what?" I stepped toe-to-toe with him, scouring his face for the rest of the threat. "Tell me."

His Adam's apple bobbed a split second before he leaned away from me. The fight hadn't left his eyes, but he wasn't going to pursue it, either. I didn't know whether to feel triumphant or disappointed.

"Let's get this shit over with," he growled.

"Either you're in this circle, or you're out. If you're in, then you're in until the end. There's no backing out once it starts." I held his gaze, hoping he realized how serious I was. Personally, I didn't give a shit what happened to him but I didn't need him trashing my circle and making things infinitely more difficult for me.

"I'm in," he said, his chin tipping up ever so slightly.

"You better be. Or *I'll* be the least of your worries if you break the circle." I set another candle down at the dead girl's feet. Grabbing a few more out of my bag, I completed the rough shape and lit the candle closest to me. Before I could touch the lighter to the next wick, it burst into flames with a crackle of electricity.

My gaze snapped up to Graeme and narrowed. Well, *that* was a new aspect to his powers. Guess I was lucky he didn't decide to use that one on campus the other day and fry my ass.

"Allow me." Graeme met my glare with a smug smile and continued lighting each candle with a flick of his fingers and the tiny blue sparks. Show off.

The memory of our first meeting hit me so hard that my hand virtually tingled all over again, putting two and two together. Goddamn it! That weird zap of electricity — that was *him*. He said he didn't know who I was, but maybe it had been some sort of a test to see if I was a witch or not. Maybe because I didn't react, he assumed I was only human.

I refused to acknowledge his rather impressive skill and focused on what I was here to do — which was getting answers. Whenever there was a murder in the witch community, the suspicion always fell on my family first. This time I'd beat them to the punch and offer up the real murderer before they had time to fabricate a case against any one of us.

As if he could read my mind, Graeme spouted off with another question. "If you can just ask a ghost and find out the answer so damn easily, then why didn't Treadwell come do this?"

"Because you need a Necromancer, moron."

"Why don't you do it *for* him, dickhead?"

"Yeah, right," I scoffed. "First of all, thanks to a smear campaign that's lasted a millennium, no one consults Necromancers anymore. And secondly, even if they did, who would believe us?"

"Then why should *I* believe you?"

"I don't give a shit if you do or not. Now shut up already so we can get out of here before we get caught." I'd had enough of his questions and his fucking attitude for one day. Closing my eyes, I laid one hand over the girl's forehead and the other above her heart, concentrating on clearing my mind of all the unnecessary bullshit — like the fact I could smell Graeme's cologne over the smell of death and chemicals.

The lights above us went out. A swath of darkness swept through the room, cocooning us in shadows.

"What the..." Graeme whispered, his shoes squeaking on the linoleum as he no doubt pivoted to look around. "What did you do?"

I wanted to tell him to shut up — *again* — but I doubled

down on my effort to concentrate, murmuring the spell to conjure her spirit.

Since she was only recently deceased, it didn't take long to summon the girl's soul back to our realm. Once I felt the rush of cold air pierce through my chest and latch on, I knew I had her.

Opening my eyes, I blinked to readjust them to the dimness and stared at the wavy, decapitated head hovering over the body. She looked even worse than her corpse. Black holes gaped at me where her eyes should have been, had they not been ripped out. Phantom blood dripped down both cheeks and her hair hung in a matted mess. It was just her head, as detached from her spirit body as it was from her corporal one.

"Holy fucking shit!" Graeme's eyes were as wide as saucers. It looked like his grip on the metal stretcher was the only thing keeping him upright at the moment. "Why does she look like that?!"

I couldn't help but smirk at the horrified look on his face. "Aw, what's the matter? Never seen a spirit before? Murder victims are always the best. *So* gruesome to look at. Sometimes you can even smell them, they're so real."

"Fuck off."

"What's going on?" her ghostly voice rasped. Her head bobbed back and forth, like she was looking for us despite not having any sight.

"We have some questions for you," I replied.

"Questions?"

"Who killed you?" In a normal conversation it wasn't very polite to jump into the heart of the matter, but when you were dealing with spirits, it was best to get it over and done with. The longer things dragged out, the more unreliable their memories became and the more wiggle room you gave demons to cross over without permission.

"I don't know," she answered, choking back a sob.

"You didn't see them?"

"My eyes! They took my eyes!"

"Melanie," Graeme said, his voice strangely soothing considering he was having his own freakout a minute ago. "Listen to me, ok? This is really important."

Her head swung in his general direction, adding to my irritation. He wasn't a fucking Necromancer. She was under *no* obligation to answer him or obey his commands, yet there she was, fixating on him.

"What *was* the last thing you saw?" I interjected.

"Crows!" Her head whipped toward me, her lower lip quivering. "I saw the crows attacking!"

I glanced at Graeme, not the least bit surprised to see his accusatory glare on me. If I didn't find something to exonerate myself soon, the dick across from me was going to go straight to Treadwell and tattle about our fight. Then all of this would have been for nothing.

"And the blood. So much blood..." Melanie gazed down at her body, like she could actually see it.

"Where did the blood come from?"

"Everywhere. It came from everywhere." Well, that wasn't surprising with a decapitation. "My heart hurts so much. Why is this happening?"

"Your heart?" I blinked, moving my hands to the hem of her sweater and lifting it upward.

Graeme's hands came down on mine roughly before I could pull it up all the way. "What the fuck do you think you're doing?"

"What the fuck do *you* think I'm doing?"

"Have some respect!"

"Necromancers have more respect for the dead than any of you fucking nature witches," I snarled, ripping my hands out of his. I yanked her sweater up the rest of the way, over the breasts he was so stupidly (and needlessly) protective of.

Carved above Melanie's heart was a sigil — a *demon's* sigil. It was crude and hastily done, featuring a combination of three horizontal lines, tiny circles, and two small Latin crosses atop a larger one, situated at the apex of a triangle.

"Oh, fuck," I murmured, tracing one of the lines, trying to see if I could pick up on anything the demon may have left behind — like a name, which would have been fantastic.

Graeme slapped my hand away from the corpse. "Don't touch her like that!"

"Jesus Christ, are you serious?! I'm not getting off on this, you sick fuck. I'm looking for trace elements of the fucking demon!"

His eyes widened. "Demon? What demon? What are you talking about?"

I stared at him for a beat. "Wow… I hope your good looks hold out because there's clearly not much going on upstairs."

"Fuck off! I told you my family doesn't do this shit!"

Rolling my eyes, I pulled Melanie's shirt back down and returned my focus to her before he could distract me anymore. "Do you remember what happened?"

She whimpered and shook her head.

"Did they speak to you? Say anything, anything at all?"

The head shook back and forth again.

"Did you see the person? A glimpse? Anything?" The tiny bit of hope I had prior to this was a second away from being snuffed out.

"Just the knife," she moaned. "It was a pretty knife. But it was cold when it cut me. Like ice."

Graeme made a face. "What was so pretty about it?"

She considered me for a moment, her head bobbing like an apple in water. "The crow. The way the black jewels glittered in its eyes as it swooped at me."

"Jewels?" I asked, though my mouth felt like cotton. Demons and crows. So much for exonerating my family.

"Black ones," she repeated dully. "For the eyes. Crow eyes."

A nauseating feeling settled in the pit of my stomach. The black, bloody holes in her skull bored into mine.

"Mors omnibus, Cassius Corbin," she hissed. *Death to all.*

The head bobbed closer, phantom blood dripping from the corner of her mouth. As the droplets fell, they morphed into black feathers. Crow feathers.

I dismissed the spirit with a sharp wave of my hand. The severed head, along with the ghostly feathers, evaporated like wisps of smoke. The shadows around us winked out of being, returning us to the garish fluorescent lights in the morgue.

"What the fuck?" Graeme demanded. "Why did you do that?"

With a snap of my fingers, the candles extinguished themselves. I snatched the candle closest to me and threw it into my bag. Black wax splashed all over the back of my hand, but the pain barely registered. I had to get home. Quickly.

"What are you doing now?" he asked, his dark brows furrowed. "What did all of that mean?"

"I have to go."

"Why? What are you not telling me?"

Stuffing the rest of the candles into the bag, I slammed the body back into the cooler and was halfway to the door when Graeme grabbed the strap over my shoulder and yanked me to a halt.

"I asked you a question, Corbin. She kept saying 'crow' and then she called you by name. As much as you like to think I'm an idiot, I'm not. So start talking."

"Let go of me." I tried to jerk the strap out of his hand, but he held on, stumbling forward a step and nearly crashing into me.

"I don't think so. You don't get to haul me in here for your little magic show and then bolt at the last second."

"I really don't have time for this, Graeme."

His eyes widened slightly, as did mine at the sound of his name. His actual name — not his last name or an insult. Whatever. I was fucking tired and had more important things on my mind, like a murderous demon on the loose and my family taking the fall for it — again.

The elevator in the hallway dinged. We both froze, Graeme's hand still clutching the leather strap on my shoulder. Shoes tapped across the floor, along with a squeaky wheel rolling down the linoleum. As soon as the automatic doors to the morgue started to open, I shoved Graeme toward the far end of the massive refrigerator.

"What the fu—"

"Shut up!" I hissed. "And don't move."

Once he was tucked away, I hurried back to the center of the room and resumed a perfectly casual stance. I hooked my thumb in the pocket of my jeans and glanced around like I was merely bored and my heart wasn't two seconds away from jumping out of my skin.

Instead, the guy bustling into the morgue was the one who jumped and grabbed his chest. "Oh, Jesus, man! You scared me!"

"Sorry, Dustin." I forced a smile to my face, thanking God for a small favor. Out of all of the orderlies in the hospital, it was the one infatuated with my sister. There was no way he'd give me grief about being in here without permission. "I was, um, looking for my pen. I think I left it here the other day after that interview."

Dustin smiled and waved me off, not even questioning the

fact it was so late to retrieve *anything*, let alone something as trivial as a pen. "Oh, I haven't seen it. If I do, I can text you... or give it to Claudia. You know. If she's around. If that's easier."

"Yeah, that'd be great. Thanks." I shifted the strap on my shoulder and started for the door, glancing over my shoulder now and again. Graeme was still pressed against the wall, as flat as humanly possible. Even from a distance I could see him mouth "What the fuck?!" at me while I tried to make my getaway.

Blissfully unaware, Dustin wheeled the empty gurney further into the room, headed straight for Graeme's hiding place.

My primary concern was saving my own skin, but letting Graeme get busted would land me in the same hot water. As much as I liked watching him squirm, I couldn't let him get caught.

"Hey, Dustin?" I blurted out before I even had a fully-formed plan in my brain. Scratching the back of my neck, I grasped for something — anything — to get Dustin's attention back on me. "Did you ever ask her out?"

Dustin stopped in his tracks and gave me a baffled look. "What?"

"Claudia? I mean, I know she can be a little, um, hard to read. But I think she likes you." Oh my God, my sister was going to fucking kill me. The only thing Claudia liked was surgery and magic. Hopefully she'd let the poor bastard down gently.

"Really?" A small smile crossed his face. Rather than continuing on with the gurney, he shoved it toward the corner and let it roll the rest of the way. "Did she say something? About me?"

Graeme caught the gurney right before it slammed into his pelvis, shooting another glare in my direction like *I* was the one who almost crushed his dick. Ungrateful asshole. I should have let him get caught.

"Mhmm. Yeah." I nodded, hoping my expression was even partially believable. "You helped her with that car accident victim?" Living in an area with twisty roads, hills, and plenty of deer, it seemed like a safe guess.

Dustin's smile brightened. "Oh yeah! That was brutal. The tree branch went right through the guy's stomach. I had to hold the branch for her while she cut it out."

"Yep. That's the one," I replied with a smile. "So, um, while I'm here. Do you know anything about the girl from campus?"

"Oh! Dude. So get this. Her head was" — he whistled and sliced his hand across his throat — "clean off. But that's not the worst part. Someone cut her eyes out, too!"

"Is that so?" I stuffed my hands in my pockets and followed him into the cooler when he beckoned. As soon as his back was turned, I waved spastically at Graeme to make a run for the door. "Pre- or post-mortem, do you know?"

"Pre. Sick, bro. Check out this blood." Dustin unzipped the bag with a grin. If he noticed any of the hardened black wax on the inside of the plastic, he didn't say anything.

I feigned interest in the gaping sockets, but I couldn't help glancing over my shoulder. Graeme was right outside the door, peering in at us with furrowed brows. Gritting my teeth, I tossed my head toward the door again since he clearly wasn't getting the hint.

Just as Dustin took a step back, I leaned in, pointing at the clean slice through her neck. "What can you tell me about that? Looks like a sword or something, right? Because an axe would have that chiseled edge?"

Dustin sighed and shrugged, gesturing helplessly. "Best guess is some kind of big, super sharp knife. The M.E. is coming tomorrow for the autopsy so hopefully they'll have a better idea. It's weird though, right? I've never seen anything like it."

"Yeah, it is. Well, I'll get out of your way. If you find my pen, just let me know. Or Claudia. It was our grandfather's. Can't believe I lost it." I gave him a fleeting smile and smacked my forehead with my palm.

"Sure thing. Take it easy, Cash."

I backed out of the cooler, hoping like hell Graeme finally left. When I spun at the last possible moment, the room was empty.

Exhaling a sigh of relief, I exited as quickly as I could, darting through the halls until I resurfaced outside the hospital.

Sadly, while Graeme had left the room, he hadn't left the property. The minute I had my car in sight, I also had *him* in sight, leaning against my hood with his arms crossed.

"Get off my car," I snapped, opening the passenger door and chucking my bag onto the seat, the candles and crystals clacking together.

"You seem to be in an awful hurry all of a sudden."

"It's late. I'm tired."

"You're the one who wanted to meet at midnight," he tossed back, stepping in front of me, blocking my way to my car door.

"Because it's the best time to cross over, you idiot." Even my insults were starting to sound weary. Aside from the fact spirit work *was* exhausting in and of itself, I had to get back to the house to settle a concern gnawing at me.

Graeme's lip curled as his mismatched eyes raked up and down my body. "You are so fucking full of yourself, aren't you?"

I scoffed and sidestepped him, slamming my shoulder into his. "Whatever you say." I truly didn't have the energy to fight him at the moment. My mind was focused on more important things — namely, how a girl who was just murdered was able to accurately describe my family's ritual knife and why that knife was used to gouge out her eyes and more than likely carve a demon's sigil into her flesh.

Graeme grabbed my sweater in both hands and slammed me into the side of my car, his nose millimeters from mine. "What game do you think you're playing, Corbin?"

"Wouldn't you like to know?" I tried to shove him off, but he hung on, dragging me closer in the process.

With his lips parted, he looked like he was seconds away from spouting off with something else — or kissing me. I didn't know what he was waiting for, but the seconds dragged by, our chests pressed together, engaged in a heated staring contest. Swallowing thickly, he pushed away from me with none of the earlier force.

"I'm going to figure it out," he said, taking a step backward, keeping his gaze on me like I might suddenly attack. Given our history, he wasn't entirely wrong. If I had the energy, I might have been tempted.

As soon as he rounded my car, he headed straight for his Jeep, throwing glares over his shoulder now and again.

We both climbed inside our respective vehicles at the same time, but he was the first to leave. I exhaled a breath and closed my eyes, my head thumping back against the headrest.

I actually wished him luck in his endeavor to figure this whole mess out, because I had no fucking clue. The mission to find my family's folios was officially on the back burner until I could get this new mess sorted out. I just hoped Graeme Hewitt stayed the hell out of my way.

Chapter Six

Graeme

I spent the night tossing and turning, all because of fucking Cassius and his mind games. It went without saying I'd never met anyone like him, which meant I had no idea how to respond to his relentless antagonism. Growing up in a community as close-knit as Winslow meant most of the people I interacted with were other witches or mortals who were, for the most part, blissfully unaware of our presence.

Of course, Lennox and Arden had been the bane of my school years until they graduated, but their torment was mostly kept to one-upping each other in class or competing for the same position on the swim team. They didn't seek me out in public and I steered clear of them if I spied them first.

Not Cassius.

I may have approached him, but he certainly didn't shy away from the confrontation. For every insult I lobbed at him, he dished it right back. It was pretty safe to say Lennox and Arden hated me, but they weren't so openly hostile. Not like him.

Except, he wasn't always like that. Before I knew who he really was, before he knew who *I* was, he had been reserved, almost shy, unsure of himself. And in the hospital parking lot, he looked... different. That seance or whatever the hell it was did something to him but damned if I knew what it was. If there was a flash of vulnerability, it was gone just as quick, locked behind his ice-cold Corbin persona.

The whole morgue thing was creepy as shit, but I chalked it up to my inexperience with dead people. Other than my brother's funeral, I hadn't been to many. The goal of Hewitt witches was to be in harmony with nature, to give life to the things around us, and protect the natural order. Death may have been a part of life, but not in the way the Necromancers used it.

An involuntary shudder ran down my spine. Every time I closed my eyes I saw that girl's floating head. The way her bloody eye sockets stared at me, like she could see right through me. I'd never be able to forget her face. Or Cassius's. What he looked like up close, under the moonlight. How it made his eyes look damn near silver. Just like they had when the lightning flashed, right before I—

Fuck, Graeme! Don't even go there. I'd given myself enough grief over the past few weeks, I didn't need to keep circling back to the biggest fuck-up of my life. In retrospect, it was probably the second biggest fuck-up, but I didn't want to think about either of them. Ever.

After virtually no sleep, it was a miracle I climbed out of bed in time for my meeting with Ainsworth. In lieu of actual classes this week, he'd arranged one-on-ones at his office to discuss our projects and see how we were doing in the wake of Melanie's murder. I, on the other hand, was hoping he could shed some light on the whole demon thing Cassius refused to talk about. It's not like I could ask my dad about any of it and I highly doubted India knew much in the way of demons, either. It wasn't a topic nature witches tended to delve into, but the Tithing Man would probably know.

A faint buzzing hummed through my chest as I jogged up the steps of Dane Hall. I stole a glance at the gray sky overhead, but it didn't feel atmospheric. I didn't know what the hell it felt like... The only thing I could liken it to was when you stuck a nine-volt battery on your tongue as a kid. It didn't hurt, but there was definitely a tingle.

The closer I got to Ainsworth's office, the buzzing increased to a thrumming. Right then and there, I knew, like a sixth sense, Cassius was nearby. This weird shit started the night of Preston's party and it only ever acted up when he was around, projecting his creepy, Necromancer energy into the world.

Halting in my tracks, I searched the hallway for any sign of him. A few students milled about, talking with one another or various faculty members. Nowhere in the crowd did I spy my rival, but the buzzing didn't dissipate. He had to be there. Lurking like the freak show he was.

Without locating him, I huffed and continued on to Ainsworth's door. Knocking once, I was surprised to see it was already cracked. When it swung open completely, the thrumming inside my ribs almost exploded.

Fucking Cassius.

He jerked back like I punched him, his pale eyes flying open. A split second later, his marble face rearranged itself to the most disgusted look possible while his attention turned to our traitorous professor. "Sir?"

"Ah, Graeme. Right on time. Please come sit." Dr. Ainsworth gestured to the two empty chairs across from him. Cassius's bag was already sitting next to one, which meant he wasn't leaving anytime soon, otherwise he would have grabbed it *before* opening the door. Did Ainsworth seriously double-book us? What an asshole!

"I'll stand," I said, brushing past Cassius on my way into the cramped office.

Cassius closed the door behind me. Or, slammed it. He

gave Ainsworth an irritated glance and resumed his seat, his lips forming the hardest line I'd ever seen.

"I'm sure you know why you're both here," Ainsworth said, lacing his fingers together on the top of his desk calendar.

Cassius sniffed and looked away, suddenly very interested in the plant in the corner of the room.

Rolling my eyes, I crossed my arms over my chest, looking in the opposite direction so I wasn't even glaring at the same damn plant. It was bad enough I had to breathe the same air as him.

"Right." Dr. Ainsworth sighed. Whatever hope he'd had of this being an easy or agreeable conversation went right out the window with his weary exhale. "I know this is a required class for both of you. All I want is for us to come up with some sort of agreement that assures me you two won't kill each other until after the semester is over. Can you do that?"

Tiny little prickles jabbed at my skin, but only on my left side. I stole a glance at Cassius. He looked away immediately, his head whipping forward again. Of course he wouldn't agree to that. Mr. High and Mighty Necromancer? Strike a bargain with a lowly nature witch? Ha!

Dr. Ainsworth wasn't deterred by our silence. "Let me be clear, then. If you use magic against each other again, you know I'll have to report it to the Deacon." He raised his brows, giving us each a long, pointed stare.

"But, I—"

"He's the one—"

Ainsworth raised his hand, silencing our dueling defenses. "I don't care. You both know the rules. Tennebrose is neutral territory. Using magic against one another, no matter your grievances, is forbidden. I saw your little performance the other day with the tornado," he said, staring at me.

I swallowed thickly, the heat rising in my cheeks.

Cassius snorted, a smirk lifting the corner of his mouth.

"And yours with the crows," Ainsworth added quickly, wiping the look off Cassius's face. "Do you have any idea what kind of problems that would create for the Congregation? It's bad enough we have this murder to deal with. You're lucky no one saw you two on top of it."

"Melanie saw," I spit out, feeling the need to defend myself before Cassius somehow turned this into my fault.

Ainsworth ripped his reading glasses off his face. "Are you sure?"

"Very," Cassius added glumly.

Leaning back in his chair, Dr. Ainsworth sighed and pinched the bridge of his nose. "Did anyone *else* see?"

I stole a glance at Cassius again. He looked up at almost the same time and caught my eye before looking away.

When he didn't get an answer, Ainsworth's eyes popped open and narrowed on each of us in turn. We shook our heads.

"No," I muttered.

"I don't think so," Cassius said.

"Good. I'm sure it's an unfortunate coincidence. Wrong time, wrong place, and all of that." Ainsworth drove the heels of his hands into his eyes and rubbed them vigorously before sliding his glasses back on. "Alright. Now. Tell me about your projects."

"Our projects?" I blinked at him. Was he serious? Not that they were secret, but how did he expect us to chat about school work after calling us out on our little duel? He was the Tithing Man — it was his job to keep us in line. I thought he'd have some sort of magical punishment in mind, or at least an ass chewing.

"Poison," Cassius said, brushing a non-existent speck of lint off his knee. Oh, of course he had a fucking answer prepared. He probably went home the first day and did all of the assignments for the rest of the semester. Kiss ass. “Reconstructing Acqua Tofana.”

I snorted. And of course he’d pick something morbid. Why wouldn’t he want to grow a hybrid plant or something? No… let’s recreate a poison from the seventeenth century!

Ainsworth smiled, apparently pleased with the little psycho’s project. “Wonderful! I can’t wait to follow your progress.”

“I’m also doing poison,” I said, keeping my gaze locked on Cassius. He straightened his spine in his chair and turned his head slightly, but his gaze remained fixed on something across the room.

“Wonderful! Tell me more.”

“Poisoned apples. Seeing if the myth is true, once and for all, if you can grow them from a seed.”

“You’re going to *grow* poisoned apples?” Dr. Ainsworth asked, his brows lifting.

A muscle in the side of Cassius’s jaw clenched.

“Yep.” I made sure the ‘p’ popped for effect. I wanted to see if Cassius’s whole head would actually explode, or just the vein throbbing in his temple, a ribbon of blue beneath his pale skin.

His reaction was even better than I could have hoped. Flying out of his chair, he closed the distance on me in a flash. With how fast he moved, a rush of air swept over me, enveloping me in a scent I was coming to recognize as him, some odd combination of leather and lavender. His blue eyes may as well have been blood red with how much anger surged through him, spewing out of his hands in that black mist he loved so much.

Before I could even summon the teeniest bit of my own magic, something wrapped around me from behind and yanked me backward, slamming me into the wall. Feet dangling in the air, the force continued to crush me, squeezing the air out of my lungs and trapping my hands at my sides.

I managed to look over at Cassius, surprised and relieved to see he was suffering the same fate on the opposite wall. Giant vines held each of us in their crushing grip, like a couple of mice to a python. Dr. Ainsworth stood in the middle, one hand held out in either direction. The more he squeezed his fingers, the more the vines squeezed us, until we both squeaked helplessly. To say he was disappointed would have been a massive understatement.

"What did I *just* say?!" His narrowed gaze latched onto Cassius until Cassius looked away, then it was my turn to get the death stare. "You can*not* use magic against one another! Not here. And certainly not in front of *me,* you morons! Why don't you just have it out in front of the Deacon while you're at it? Hell, why stop there? Fight to the death in front of the whole Congregation at the next Meeting! Bring shame on both of your families and throw away three hundred years' worth of magic! Go ahead!"

I ducked my head, trying to avoid the heat from Ainsworth's glare. My stomach twisted from more than the vines squeezing it. This wasn't me. I wasn't even interested in magic; I think Ainsworth had seen enough of me growing up to know that. But this was what happened any time I was within fifty feet of Cassius Corbin — another side of me came out I never knew existed. It was feral and unpredictable. More than anything, it was dangerous.

After a moment of letting us wallow in our mutual shame, the vines loosened enough so we could breathe, but not move.

Ainsworth cleared his throat and continued with a more optimistic tone. "Thanks to you two, I have the perfect solution to this little problem. This is now a *partnered* assignment—"

We both exploded at the same time.

"Are you kidding me?!"

"You can't be serious!"

Ainsworth kept talking over us. "—and you two *will be* partners. Effective immediately. Since you're both working on poison, come to some sort of agreement on what your topic will be and submit a proposal by the end of next week."

"Professor, I don't want to sound contrary, but I can't jeopardize my GPA over something as trivial as 'teamwork.' Neither my magic nor my chosen profession requires anyone else's assistance," Cassius said, as entreatingly as possible. God, he was such a snob! "And I'm not about to leave my fate in the hands of a Hewitt." The way he spewed my last name, with so much venom and blinding hatred, actually stung a little.

"I understand, Cassius," Dr. Ainsworth replied with a placating smile. "My answer remains the same."

It was my turn to try and object, though certainly not for his sake. "Professor, you know I—"

"Enough! I have made my decision and that is absolutely final. If neither of you like it, feel free to drop my class." He snapped his fingers and pointed, like he'd been struck with a thought. "Oh, that's right. This is the only time either of you will be able to take it since we rotate classes every three years. And before you get hopeful, I'll make damn sure I'm on sabbatical your final year." He directed his scowl at Cassius, probably since he was the freshman in the room. Ainsworth already knew he had me by the balls. "So if you have any hope of graduating before you're thirty, I suggest you learn to cooperate!"

Cassius swore under his breath.

I, on the other hand, exhaled a resigned sigh.

"If I let you down, what are you going to do?" Ainsworth asked, glancing between us.

"Nothing, sir," Cassius mumbled.

Ainsworth looked at me next.

"Nothing," I agreed with a huff.

The vines pulled us both off the wall and brought us to the center of the room, setting us on our feet directly in front of one another. They loosened again, allowing us to move one arm.

Ainsworth cleared his throat pointedly.

I rolled my eyes and stuck out my hand.

Cassius just glared at me, as cold and unmoving as stone. The vines around his torso tightened, creaking softly. He fought it as long as he could before a wince cracked his face and he shoved his hand into mine.

Electricity rippled across my palm as soon as it made contact with his.

Cassius's gaze snapped upward, the silent accusation floating across the narrow space.

Before he could say anything, I ripped my hand out of his.

The vines dropped from both of us, coiling around our feet like thick, green ropes. "Good luck on your project, boys," our professor said cheerily, waving us out of his office.

Although I took Ainsworth's wave and his well wishes as my cue to leave, I waited for the vines to retract into the plants from which they came before I dared to move an inch. Balling my traitorous hand into a fist, I bolted for the door at the first opportunity.

Cassius was quick to follow, chasing me down the hallway and into the stairwell. He nearly caught me on the landing but I leapt down the remaining stairs.

Before I could reach the door handle, the whole stairwell was plunged into a darkness so thick I couldn't even see my hand in front of my face.

"You've got to be kidding me." I spun in a circle, trying in vain to see where Cassius was lurking. I summoned a quick gust of wind, but it didn't do anything to dispel the looming blackness. So, apparently his shadows were a different sort of magic than his mist. Good to know. "Where are you, you asshole?"

"What the fuck was that all about up there?"

Even if I couldn't see him — or anything, for that matter — I could feel him, just like before. The buzzing in my chest ebbed and flowed every time I lunged at the spot I thought he was. Even though my hands kept coming up empty, the buzzing never went away.

"What are you talking about?" I snapped, swatting at nothing again.

"Ainsworth said no magic and you fucking shock me right in front of him?"

"I didn't shock you. It must have been static electricity," I snapped in my defense, hating with every fiber of my being that he felt my magic. It was one thing to make a little spark to light a candle, it was another to showcase a larger power. The less the Corbins knew about my abilities, the safer I was. "Stop trying to blame me for everything. You're the one breaking the Covenant right now with this little freak show!"

The shadows peeled back like a curtain and disappeared, revealing Cassius right in front of my face. "I knew Hewitts were liars, but I've only just realized how shitty you are at it."

"Deflecting once again, I see." I glared at him to drive home my deeper meaning. "I'm not the one hiding something, Corbin."

"I'm not hiding anything!"

"Then what was all that bullshit at the morgue?" Instead of answering, he tried to walk past me. I grabbed his sleeve and yanked him to a stop. "Case in point. I ask a question you don't like and you walk away."

"Touch me again and I'll send you to the Land of the Dead myself." He jerked his arm free, his blue eyes cold and hard, completely unlike the first time we'd ever met, when I stupidly wanted to get to know him. Or at least fuck him. Sometimes I couldn't even comprehend the two versions of him were the same person — Cash, the sexy, shy guy, and Cassius, the psycho Necromancer.

"I can't wait for the day when you're begging me to touch you." I let my gaze drop to his mouth, not even trying to be subtle anymore. Electricity rippled across more than my hands at the memory of his searing kiss and I licked my lips involuntarily. God, why did he have to be hot? And smart. And fucking infuriating.

Instead of falling for my innuendo or letting himself get sidetracked by any smidge of a pleasant memory, Cassius kept his chin lifted, shoulders square, like the Prince of Darkness he was. "I'll never beg you for anything."

"Whatever you say."

I thoroughly enjoyed the anger in his eyes as he processed my retort. Taking my leave once and for all, I strolled out of the stairwell, leaving him to stew.

Chapter Seven
Cassius

My hand was still tingling by the time I made it back to my house. Fucking Graeme. He could claim he didn't use magic against me all he wanted, I had the proof in every nerve he electrocuted. I couldn't believe he'd be so reckless with Ainsworth literally a foot away. Fucking hypocrite. Crying about *me* breaking the Covenant when he did it every single goddamn time he touched me!

I slammed through the side door of the house and all but threw my messenger bag and coat on the hall tree. Now that I was home, I shoved Graeme Hewitt to the back of my mind and focused on something far more important — what the dead girl told me.

After my return trip from the hospital, I scaled the decorative lattice and climbed over the railing again right as Claudia walked into my bedroom.

Closing the balcony door behind me, I met her in the center of the room, brows raised and heart racing a million miles a minute. "What's up? What are you doing awake?"

"Catching up on patient files. Heard you moving around," she replied. "Why are you up so late?"

"Couldn't sleep. Too much on my mind." Bit of an understatement, but it's not like I could explain any of that to her.

"Thinking about your classmate?"

"Yeah." It wasn't technically a lie.

She touched my cheek gently. I hoped she didn't realize how cold my skin was from being outside. "You don't have anything to worry about."

"How do you know?"

"Because I know Treadwell and I know he'll do everything he can to find the killer. He's a hard ass, but he cares more about justice than the Deacon does."

"Do you think it was a witch?" I asked. "Or… something else?"

A small crease formed between her dark brows. "Why would you think that?"

"She was decapitated with a sword. Plus, someone cut her eyes out and carved what looked like a sigil into her skin. Like, maybe, a demon sigil."

The crease deepened. "That doesn't necessarily mean it was a witch *or* a demon. And how do you know all of that, anyway? It wasn't in the paper."

"I… saw her. This morning. Before Treadwell got there." Fuck! Get it together, Cash!

Claudia shrugged, shaking her head and apparently buying my explanation. "I don't know. I've never heard of a demon leaving their own sigil behind. It doesn't make sense. And I can't believe a witch would mark a mortal's soul like that *or* give a demon any sort of power."

"Well someone did..." I shoved my hands in my pockets, trying to find a logical explanation.

"I mean, serial killers like trophies, right? So maybe they're just crazy. Or it's some idiot kid trying to stir up another cult crisis."

"Yeah, maybe." Her lack of concern was a bit of a relief, but I was still annoyed at myself. Maybe I was reading too much into it. Maybe that sigil was… random? Some stupid cult thing or a crazy person, like she said? No. I couldn't even *remotely* convince myself a witch wasn't one hundred percent behind this. I just needed more proof.

Claudia left shortly thereafter but I couldn't risk getting caught going down to the basement. Other than spellwork, there was absolutely no viable reason for me to be down there at one o'clock in the morning. Looking for answers had to wait until I knew I had the house to myself.

Thankfully, I only had to wait until that afternoon, after the meeting with Ainsworth.

"Dad? Claudia?" I called into the empty house. Neither of their cars were in the garage, but I wanted to double-check before I cut across the kitchen and pulled open the heavy wooden door that led downstairs.

Storming into the ritual space, I marched straight to the huge cabinet set against one wall and pulled out the center drawer. Before I even opened the carved box, I knew the knife was missing. I knew it because that dead girl's eerily accurate description kept playing over and over in my head.

Still, I *had* to be sure.

Opening the lid, I was met with an impression of the knife on the red velvet and a sinking feeling in the pit of my stomach.

It was gone.

"Shit!"

Slamming the box closed, I shoved it back in the drawer and stared at the cabinet. The list of suspects was both short and complicated — the only people who knew about *us* were other witches. But who among them knew about this room? I mean, every family had their designated ritual space but that didn't mean someone coming into our house would know where to look.

Who the fuck would be stupid enough to break into our house in the first place? And what did they get out of using our ritual knife to summon a demon with a nice, tasty human soul and then subsequently murder said girl?

Someone intent on framing us, that's who. And that's where it got complicated. As far as motive went, most of our miserable little community had motive for wanting us gone. There were only a handful of families who dared to ally themselves with us, so that ruled them out. The rest of the Congregation? They were all fair game, starting with the fucking Hewitts as Enemy Number One.

As much as I wanted to drive over to that asshole's house and take my knife back, I knew I had to play it smart. Telling Dad would throw another log on the proverbial fire (i.e. the feud) or get me shipped overseas again. Telling Claudia was pretty much the same thing as telling Dad, except she'd *definitely* take her allegation to the Selectmen and demand an investigation. *Then* my ass would be shipped overseas to finish college. Treadwell was busy with the murder, so telling him that one of the weapons used to kill that girl was conveniently missing from our basement was absolutely out of the question.

Slipping my phone out, I called the only person I could think of to help me sort out this shitty mess — Lennox.

"What's up?" he asked.

"I have a huge problem and I really need your help."

"Of course. Anything. What happened?"

"Someone stole the crow knife."

The other line went quiet until I heard footsteps and a door close. "Say that again?"

I took a deep breath and exhaled it before repeating it as clearly as I could. "Someone stole the crow knife. They used it to summon a demon and murder that girl on campus yesterday."

"What the fuck, Cash? Did you tell your dad?"

"No! I'm telling you!"

"Ok. Fuck. Let's think." I could picture him and the variety of faces he made while arguing with himself silently. "Ok. How do you even know that's what happened?"

"I..." I closed my eyes and groaned out the last bit. "Went to the morgue."

Lennox sighed. "Why? Why would you do that? You don't need the practice, Cash! You've been talking to spirits since you were three."

There was no way I could tell him about Graeme, so I made a noncommittal noise and cast about for another answer. "Curiosity? I don't know. I've never talked to a murder victim before."

"So did she say who killed her?"

"No. But she described the knife. And I saw the sigil with my own eyes."

"Which demon was it for?"

"I don't know."

"What do you mean you don't know? It's kind of important to know which one it was if you want to make sure it doesn't happen again."

"There's seventy-two sigils in one book alone! I don't have them all memorized!"

"Ugh. Can you draw it from memory or scry for it again or something so we can compare it to the ones we know of?"

"Yeah, I'll get right on it," I snapped. Before we got too far off track, I circled back around to the reason I called. "In the meantime, what am I supposed to do now? Someone already used the knife to kill one person, what happens if they send a demon after someone else? Or if they come back into the house for more shit?"

"Like what? The Book?"

"It wouldn't be the first time someone tried to steal it. Think about it. A knife that has the ability to kill any demon? The Book with our most powerful spells? They're only missing one piece. If they get it, they could destroy all of us." Just thinking about it made me ill. No one had tried to take the Book since I was a kid, when a group of then-teenage witches broke in on a dare and tried to retrieve it. Maybe someone got the itch again now that they were adults. Maybe the knife and the murder were meant as some sort of distraction so they could come back and finish the job.

"It would be stupid for any non-Necromancer to take it," Lennox said with a scoff. "The Book will kill them before they read off the first spell. Well, I mean, the demons will kill them. But you know what I mean. And besides, it's not as powerful without the missing folios. That's why we don't use it anymore, remember?"

"You and I know that, but the other witches don't. Either they don't know about the missing folios or..." A thought hit me like a tidal wave of nausea. "What if they do? What if *they* have them?"

"You think someone found the missing folios? After all this time?"

"Someone has to know where they are. And maybe that someone wants the rest of the Book."

"Ok. I have class until three. I'll swing by after that and we can scry for the knife, ok? Hopefully it's not as warded as the damn folios. But if you're right — which I hope you're not — then maybe finding the knife will take us to them and we can reclaim what's ours."

"Yeah. Sure. I'll be here."

"Don't tell anyone! Ok? We'll figure this out."

"Thanks, Lennox."

I waited impatiently for the appointed hour. Before he even got there, I set up everything on the altar. Laying out a crystal grid, I set a silver bowl in the center and topped it with one of the crow skulls.

Once everything was in place, I headed back upstairs.

Claudia came down the main staircase as I was going up. She wrapped her arms around me wordlessly.

"What's wrong? And when did you get home?" I asked.

She pushed me out at arm's length and tilted her head to the side, giving me that motherly look she'd perfected over my lifetime, well before Mom was even gone. "Just now. Treadwell called a Meeting."

I stiffened. "When?"

"Tonight."

"Did he say why?"

She shrugged. "I didn't hear. But I can only assume it's about the murder. I guess you were right about it being a witch."

"Great…" I slipped away from her and kept going up the stairs, pausing near the top. "Oh, Lennox is coming by later."

"Alright. I'm on my way back out, anyway. I forgot something at the hospital."

I nodded and headed up the rest of the stairs.

Treadwell called the Meeting, not the Deacon. That couldn't have been a good sign. That meant he knew it wasn't a regular murder. But how much did he know? Was the Meeting a chance for a community briefing or the start of the next trial? The last one, against George Hewitt, hadn't exactly gone in my family's favor. Why should this time be any different?

By the time Lennox showed up, I was thoroughly convinced someone in my family was going to jail. Not just regular jail, for regular people with steel bars and a little yard time. No, the jail for members of the Congregation was so much worse. Solitary, in the middle of the woods, underground. For however long they decided to leave you there. It could be centuries if they *really* wanted to punish you.

Lennox knocked on my open bedroom door and stuck his head in. "Hey. Didn't you hear me calling?"

I jumped and whirled toward him. "No. Sorry." Striding past him, I moved down the hallway to the stairs.

"Jesus. Slow down already."

"I can't. There's a Meeting tonight."

"Yeah, I heard."

"We have to find that knife."

"We will. Relax."

"I'll relax when I know we have it back." I yanked open the heavy basement door and hurried down the stone steps.

"Are you sure you checked everywhere?" Lennox asked when we hit the bottom.

"Yes! We only ever put it one spot and it's fucking gone!"

Lennox sidestepped me and approached the large cabinet. Sliding open the center drawer, he gestured to the ornate box inside. "Is that what you're talking about?"

"Yeah."

He nodded and lifted the lid, freezing in place.

"What? What is it?" I rushed to his side, gripping the edge of the cabinet. "What the fuck?!"

The crow knife was there. *Right there*. Right where it was supposed to be. The black-jeweled eyes glittered and the silver blade winked in the dim lighting, like it was pleased with itself for pulling some elaborate prank.

"I swear to God, it was gone." I looked at Lennox, eyes wide. "I put all this shit out because I thought we were going to have to—"

"I know, Cash." He patted my cheek lightly. "I believe you. But it's back now, so we can relax."

"But how?"

"I don't know. Frankly, I don't care. Maybe it was a demon fucking with you. Or maybe Claudia used it and forgot to put it back until just now. Who knows with objects like these. You know half of them have a will of their own.

Remember when Grandma's tarot cards got pissed off at her and they kept disappearing for weeks?"

"I'm putting it somewhere else in the meantime. We'll use a regular knife until this whole thing is over with. I can't chance it wandering off again."

He nodded. "That's probably a good idea."

I nodded too and grabbed the box, heading back up the stairs. Once we made it out of the basement, Lennox pushed the door shut.

"Don't forget to lock it," I said over my shoulder. Stopping abruptly, I turned and looked at the door again. In my haste to get to the basement, I didn't even realize that the door was already unlocked, the iron key a perpetual weight in my pocket.

"What's wrong?" he asked, his head tilting.

"I didn't have to unlock the door." Did that mean someone was in here, just now, putting the knife back? Were they *still* here?

"But we're the only ones here." Lennox looked around slowly. "Aren't we?"

"We're supposed to be." I glanced around the immediate area, looking for any oddities in the air, a shimmer, a ripple, anything to indicate a demon moving about.

After a few minutes of absolute stillness, I said, "I'll see you at the Meeting." I started to walk away when his voice stopped me again.

"Are you sure? If there's a demon in the house, I don't think you should be alone, Cash."

"There's enough wards in place. I'll be fine."

"Ok…"

Nodding, I ducked out the back door and set off for the gardens with the box.

Chapter Eight
Graeme

The smells of fall permeated campus. A midday rain on old stones, wet leaves, and damp woodsmoke all swirled together on the slight breeze. By the time I was done with the rest of my classes, the wrought-iron lampposts were on, illuminating the sidewalks with hazy yellow light.

It was this time of year, these smells, this indescribable atmosphere, that made me feel the most aligned with my powers. As chaotic as autumn weather was, it was like a salve to my soul. It made me feel alive. It was the only time I felt like myself since the rest of the time I had to present the perfect Hewitt image. I was, after all, the only living heir — the last chance for the line to carry on, a fact I was reminded of daily by my dear old dad.

On the way to the parking garage, my cell phone chirped.

I fished it out of my pocket, eyes widening at the text from India.

Meeting at 7

That couldn't have been good… It wasn't a regular Meeting day. If I was a betting man, I'd say it had everything to do with the dead girl on campus.

You coming?

I texted back quickly. ***Yeah see you there***

Just as I slipped my phone back into my pocket, the lamp at the end of the block went dark. Then the one next to it. Down the row of lights, each one blacked out, like someone snuffing a candle one by one.

Turning slowly, I surveyed the surrounding buildings. All of a sudden, I was completely alone.

The hairs on the back of my neck stood on end. That little voice inside told me to run, first as a suggestion and then as a scream. I only lingered for a minute before backing up slowly, my gaze sweeping back and forth as the strange darkness continued to press in on me from all sides.

I turned to run when something slammed into me from behind, sending me sprawling onto the sidewalk. "Fuck!" My palms were shredded from the concrete, but I was more concerned with getting back on my feet as quickly as possible.

As soon as I did, whatever it was hit me again.

I had enough time to brace for it and throw up a current of air, knocking most of the force away. Channeling as much wind as I could, I flung my hands to the sides, sending a sweeping gale in a circle around me.

The darkness didn't dissipate. Just like earlier in the stairwell. Motherfucker.

"Cassius?!" I turned in a circle, looking for any sign of the sneaky bastard.

Something sharp sliced across my bicep.

I hissed and jerked away from it, clamping a hand over the sting. Even if I couldn't see shit, I knew I was bleeding from the feeling alone.

"Meeting got you scared?" I shouted into the darkness. "Is that why you're here? Afraid I'll tell everyone about our little trip to the morgue? That Melanie basically named your fucking family!"

Another biting pain slashed across my back. I staggered forward with a yelp, dropping to one knee.

"Two can play this game." Closing my eyes, I pulled all of the water vapor in the air toward me as fast as I could. The closer it got, and the more I summoned, the thicker the fog around me became. It made breathing a bit tricky with the sudden surge of humidity, but hopefully it meant that asshole couldn't breathe either. The other hope was that he wouldn't be able to see me through my magic, since he was apparently unhindered by his own.

After a few minutes without any more attacks, I stood slowly, keeping the fog close. Hearing nothing, seeing nothing, I moved toward the parking garage.

As soon as I stepped off the sidewalk, yellow light flooded the top of my hazy cloud.

I dispelled it with a wave of my hand and looked around.

The street lamps were all shining. A handful of students were walking from building to building, chatting or texting.

It was as if nothing had happened. Nothing at all.

Looking down at my bloody palm, I swallowed thickly and hurried off to my Jeep.

India met me outside the meetinghouse. Her eyes widened as soon as I came into full view. "What do you think—oh my God! What happened to you?"

"Fucking Corbin just attacked me."

"What?!"

"Yeah. Can you help me clean this up? My dad will flip his shit if he sees me like this."

"I'm not my mother," she said, like I didn't already know that.

"I don't care about the fucking scar. Just stop the bleeding!"

"Ugh. Come on." She dragged me over to her car and pulled a first aid kit out of her trunk.

I shrugged out of my bloody jacket and peeled off the shirt underneath, assessing the giant slash across my arm. Fucker. Standing half-naked in front of the meetinghouse probably wasn't a good idea, but I didn't have time to go home and change and I sure as shit wasn't going to miss whatever this emergency session was all about.

"Oh my God. What did he do to you?" India touched my back gingerly, her warm fingers pressing along my rapidly cooling skin. When I tried to look over my shoulder, she shoved my face forward again. "Don't move. I don't want you making it worse."

"I don't know what it was. It felt like a knife. I never actually saw it. I didn't see anything."

A warm heat traced along my back, moving slowly from one side to the other, almost to the point of pain. "How could you not see him? He'd have to be super close to do this."

"He does this thing with shadows. It'd be cool if it wasn't so fucking creepy."

"The whole family is creepy. I wish they'd just leave already."

"You and me both."

"Speak of the devil." India's hands stilled on my back as Cassius rolled by in his fucking Lexus, his dark brows furrowed. He faked a confused expression so fucking well, I should put him up for an Academy Award.

He parked at the opposite end of the parking lot and climbed out. I could tell his gaze landed on mine as soon as an icy pain bored into my skull. Even though I was only shirtless, I suddenly felt completely naked in front of him with the way he was staring at me.

Then Lennox and Cassius's sister joined him and the spell was broken. The three of them walked into the building through the western door, looking like emissaries from Satan himself.

"Your shirt is ruined," India said, holding it out to me anyway. I hadn't even realized she was finished bandaging my arm.

"That's fine. Hey, can I sit with you? I don't want to have to explain the blood to my dad."

"Yeah, of course." She squeezed my hand and headed toward the eastern side of the building.

Every step I took reignited the stinging across my back. Even breathing felt like it reopened the wound. Still, I wouldn't let it deter me from this Meeting, or from having it out with Cassius when it was over.

Chapter Nine
Cassius

It had been years since I stepped foot in the meetinghouse. The last time was the emergency session called on the night of my mother's murder. The very next night my father packed me up and sent me across the Atlantic for boarding school because he didn't trust the assholes in this town. Guess he was right not to.

Nothing had changed inside the massive wooden structure for three hundred years, so I don't know why I thought anything would be different after a scant six. It was still an open, rectangular room with exposed wooden beams and errant cobwebs. A gallery sat on one end of the building, opposite a pulpit. There were very few windows; the only light came from the gas lamps that ringed the perimeter or hung from support beams throughout the space. The middle of the room was filled with box pews, like a giant maze.

Even after all these years, I still knew the way to my family's box. Maybe it was one of those things encoded in my DNA or the fucking trauma of my last memory in this place.

I opened the little swinging door and held it open for Claudia, exchanging a look with Lennox as he stepped into the Ambrose box.

Before I sat, I cast a wary glance around the room, scoping out the Hewitt box across the aisle. Surprisingly, the only one there was the murderer himself, George Hewitt. I knew I saw Graeme when I pulled in. He was hard to miss without a fucking shirt on. So where was he?

Scanning the rest of the boxes, I spied him in the Tenney's pew. The redhead at his side could have only been India Tenney. She saw me first, not even bothering to hide her scowl. Graeme was next, his mismatched eyes narrowing as soon as they spotted me.

I ground my molars and sat, purposely sitting with my back to that side of the aisle. It was bad enough being in the same building as him twice in one day, I didn't need to look at him if I didn't absolutely have to.

"Is Dad coming?" I asked Claudia, trying to ignore the whispering from across the way. It wasn't just the Hewitts and the Tenneys. Whoever wasn't aligned with my family were all surprised by my return and were doing a shitty job of keeping those thoughts to themselves. From the snippets I could hear, there were several reasons for my sudden departure six years ago.

Monsters. All of them.

He's not disfigured. Didn't they say he was disfigured?

I heard he burned his last school to the ground.

He doesn't look touched.

I still say he's the one who did it. Poor Lydia.

My head whipped around at that one, trying to pinpoint the source.

Claudia touched my cheek and turned my face back toward her. "He's coming. One of his surgeries ran late."

When Chief Treadwell walked in, all talking immediately ceased. He nodded his greetings as he made his way toward the front of the room, taking a seat below the pulpit.

Dr. Ainsworth came next. Ever the teacher, he scanned the room, looking like he was doing a headcount on his way to the front. Then again, he probably was. Anyone who failed to show got a personal visit from him to discuss the reason why. After he shook hands with Treadwell, he took a chair on the other side of the pulpit.

Dad slipped in the west door and marched straight to our box. He hadn't even changed out of his scrubs.

"Cassius," he said as soon as the door swung open.

I stood and stepped into his warm embrace.

He touched my cheek before turning to Claudia and hugging her as well. "Are you two ok?"

"Of course, Dad." Claudia gave him a reassuring smile.

"We all know emergency sessions are never good," Dad said, sitting next to Claudia, where they could both see the pulpit without having to crane their heads.

"Deacon's here," I muttered, watching Peregrine Northrup sweep through the southern door, smiling and nodding like the king he thought he was.

Peregrine didn't waste any time marching up the curved, wooden stairs to the pulpit. As soon as the giant clock in the tower overhead struck seven, he spread his hands and smiled. "Thank you all for coming on such short notice. Chief Treadwell has a few things he'd like to address with the Congregation. Chief?"

Treadwell nodded and stood, walking to the center of the aisle below the pulpit. "As I'm sure you've all heard, there was a murder on campus this week. While the victim doesn't have any relation to our community, I'm afraid her murderer does.

"For starters, the girl's eyes were taken prior to her death. Whether they were taken as part of a spell or to prevent her from seeing her attacker, either on earth or in the spirit world, we don't know.

"The odds a regular murderer would take the eyes are slim to none. Also, mortals would have a hard time decapitating their victim so quickly, and without being seen, which is why I believe the murderer is one of our own. Winslow PD is working day and night to solve this, so I urge anyone with information to come forward immediately so I can facilitate a resolution that is beneficial to all involved." He nodded at the conclusion of his little speech and returned to his seat.

I was surprised he didn't mention the demon's sigil or the fact a sword was used in the decapitation — a weapon more than one demon still preferred. Maybe he didn't want to tip his hand.

Dr. Ainsworth stood next and took Treadwell's empty spot on the floor. "I know I am not law enforcement in the traditional sense, but as the Tithing Man, I also urge anyone with information to come forward. No matter what the reason was, we can only help you if you come to us."

Maybe it was my imagination, but I swore Ainsworth's gaze landed directly on me as he spoke his last sentence.

Swallowing thickly, I looked away.

Claudia squeezed my hand. Without looking up at her, I squeezed it in return.

"So please, be careful," Peregrine said, gripping the edge of the pulpit. "Watch over one another."

Dismissed, we exited our pew and headed for the western door. So much for learning anything useful.

A cool wind swept over my face before I got too far. I glanced over my shoulder, teeth already clenching.

Graeme was leaning against the side of a box pew, his hands shoved in his pockets, staring at the dancing flame in the hurricane lamp across from him. He may have looked bored, but I knew that little breeze was his doing.

"I have to talk to Ainsworth real quick. I'll meet you at home," I murmured to Claudia.

As soon as she was gone, I spun on the ball of my foot and stalked over to the pew. Instead of facing Graeme directly, I leaned against the corner near him, staring at the southern door. The important Congregation members left through it, talking in hushed tones to one another.

"What the fuck do you want?" I snapped as soon as no one else was in earshot.

"Nice trick with the lights earlier. And the knife work. Same one you used on that dead chick?"

"I told you, I didn't fucking kill her."

"Just like you didn't try to kill me, right?"

"Oh my God. You're still crying about that? It was a couple of scratches from some birds. Get over it. You threw me off a fucking wall!"

He whipped around the corner, coming nose-to-nose with me. "I'm not talking about the crows. I'm talking about earlier *tonight*, outside of the parking garage."

"I don't know what you think you saw, but it wasn't me. I wasn't anywhere near campus tonight."

"Then I'm sure I'm imagining this," he snapped, turning his back to me and peeling his shirt off again like a lunatic. His bicep was bandaged, but there wasn't a bandaid big enough to cover the giant slash marks across his back. There were three horizontal lines, partially healed. Probably thanks to the Tenney girl. But blood had started to surface at the bottom corner of the deepest cut with all of his jerking around.

I dragged the tip of one finger along the gash, collecting what I could. Before I could lift it to my lips to see what the fuck he was talking about, he spun again and grabbed my wrist, eyes narrowed at his blood on my hand.

"Don't even think about pulling any of that Dracula shit."

"Scared of what else I might see?" I sent a pointed glance southward, returning my gaze to his with a dark smile.

He scoffed, but he didn't let go. "I'm not scared of you *or* your sick fucking fetish. On the contrary, I feel sad for you."

"How do you function with that little pea-brain in your

head? I'm surprised you can even make it through one day without getting hit by a fucking bus."

"Same as I'm surprised you can make it through a day without killing someone. Is that why you're back? On the lam from wherever it is you've been hiding out all these years?"

I rolled my eyes and yanked my wrist out of his grasp. "Were you dropped on your head as a child? Or is this genetics? You know, I blame the inbreeding."

"Oh, that's rich, coming from a fucking Necromancer. Your kind is on the verge of extinction. Let's hope it's soon. The world will be better off."

I tsked him. "Hate to break it to you, but the dark arts aren't going anywhere. So you and all of the other self-proclaimed 'good' witches need to learn your place."

"Elitist, much? Or just planning on world domination? I hear Hitler liked the occult. What are the odds he and Himmler were fucking Necromancers?"

I shoved him in the chest as hard as I could. "You self-righteous piece of shit!"

He stumbled but maintained his balance. "Is that the best you got? Let me guess. You used up all your energy earlier attacking me like a fucking pussy in the dark?"

Rage exploded inside of me, manifesting in a crackling ball of black mist twisting between my hands. It was the size of a beach ball when I threw it at him as hard as I fucking could.

The mist detonated like a bomb between us. A ball of fire erupted in the middle, sending tiny black shards flying out in every direction like an explosion of glass.

I threw my arm up over my face and spun away from the blast.

"Enough!" a female voice roared.

Lowering my arm cautiously, I watched India storm

forward, her hands still glowing from the fire. She stepped in front of Graeme and the flames reignited on her hands. "If you know what's good for you, you'll slither back to whatever hole you crawled out of."

I scoffed and shook my head. There was no point in arguing. Nothing I said or did would ever change their twisted perception of me or my family. I hadn't even been home a month and I was already sick of defending my honor.

"Fuck you. *Both* of you." I snapped my fingers, extinguishing every single flame in the building, including the ones glowing on India's hands. As the shadows descended, I made my exit before I could be accused of murdering anyone else.

Chapter Ten
Graeme

Of course Cassius and I didn't discuss our stupid project in the midst of slinging barbs at one another. I honestly didn't give a shit what he wanted to do — if he wanted to do anything at all. I was sticking with my experiment, mostly because it would finally give me the answers I wanted. Well, there was only one answer I was after — did Lydia Corbin murder my brother or not?

Everyone said she did. It was a given. She married a Corbin and Corbins and Hewitts had hated each other since the founding of the colony. According to family lore, a Corbin boy fell in love with a Hewitt girl and when she refused his hand, he murdered her. The Hewitts, then, murdered the Corbin boy. And we'd hated each other ever since. Winslow's very own witchy Hatfield and McCoy. Lydia and Owen were just the latest victims in a centuries-old feud.

I could never forget the night she brought my little brother's limp body to our front door. Dressed in a riding outfit, her long, dark hair swirling around her as she ran with him. She cradled his body against her chest as if he were her own, a fact I found odd, even then. She explained to my parents how she found him like that while out for a ride. He was in her orchard, facedown on the ground, already dead. According to her. The enemy.

One autumn afternoon, Owen was a spirited nine-year-old, running off to play with his friend Percy. Just a few hours later, he was dead. And I, the responsible thirteen-year-old who was supposed to be watching him, was entirely to blame because I *didn't* watch him. I'd overheard my parents talking about the "big celebration" coming up, that it was time for me to make my conversion and fully step into my powers. I'd fled to the North Woods in the hope I could outrun the Congregation's plans for me, their future Deacon. I came home just after dark, in time to witness Lydia's death.

My father didn't listen to Lydia's explanation. He didn't believe she simply found him like that. A Necromancer shows up with a dead body and you're supposed to believe they weren't involved, when their entire magic system is based around death? Lying wretch, he called her above my mother's ear-piercing sobbing. In the blink of an eye, Lydia was dead — collapsed on the front step next to my brother's body, blood trickling from her nose but otherwise unblemished. I still don't know how my father killed her, only that he did.

Word spread through the Congregation like wildfire and everyone assembled at the meetinghouse within the hour, including the children.

Percy Northrup was the only one brought to testify. He was the only one who *could* testify since he was the only witness left alive. And according to the Deacon's eight-year-old son, Owen ate a poisoned apple off of Lydia's tree and fell over dead.

Caius Corbin refuted every part of Percy's testimony and begged the Congregation to let him summon the spirits of both parties. The majority refused to be swayed, claiming he'd only use his abilities to swing the verdict his way. The

Ambroses were the only ones who vouched for him, but as Lydia's kin, their loyalty was beyond suspect. The rest of the dark families, those aligned with the Corbins, wisely kept their mouths shut.

The Deacon and the Selectmen met and decided — justice had already been served. The Hewitts lost a son. The Corbins a wife and mother. Neither family would suffer any more casualties at the hands of the Selectmen.

But something about that night never sat right with me. Maybe it was the way Lydia cried while talking to my mother. Maybe it was the fact everyone believed an eight-year-old. Or maybe I was just looking for someone else to blame instead of myself. Because if I'd been watching him, instead of running to the woods by myself, then he would have never gone over there. He would have never eaten that stupid apple. And he would have never fucking died.

And now, six years later, I was poking at Fate, daring it to bite me in the ass as some form of karmic justice.

Hopping over the old wooden fence, I adjusted my bag's strap on my shoulder and set off toward the Corbin's orchard.

Everyone in Winslow knew about the Corbin's apples. It's what their family was known for — well, what the regular folk knew them for anyway. They only saw the massive, castle-like house and elaborate gardens and were awed by a pillar of old New England wealth.

The Winslow witches? We saw the lair of demons.

Until Cassius. God, he confused the hell out of me.

He was beyond infuriating but he also made me feel things I shouldn't *want* to feel. I didn't know if I was coming or going when it came to him. Our first meeting was... well, an experience I'd never forget. Followed quickly by unbridled hatred and contempt. And now I had to see him in class for the rest of the damn semester or until one of us killed the other. Some days I wasn't sure which would come first.

Since the rows of trees weren't labeled, I wandered the orchard, collecting an apple here and there whenever one looked like it might be a different variety. Once my bag was full and my shoulder ached from the added weight, I started toward the fence again.

An odd thundering sound stopped me in my tracks. I glanced up at the clear, blue sky before something told me I should turn around.

Sliding a cautious glance over my shoulder, I whipped around fully when I saw a black horse charging at me. I scrambled out of the way, ducking between two trees as the horse slid to a halt, snorting and stomping its massive hooves.

"What the hell do you think you're doing?" an all-too-familiar voice snapped.

I stepped out from between the trees, finally realizing Cassius was mounted on top of the animal, in a fucking repeat of the events from six years ago. Dressed in a black shirt and tight, gray pants, he nearly blended in with the horse, like a villain in a movie. He was even wearing black leather gloves. If only he had a cape or a mustache to twirl.

"Working on *my* project," I shot back.

"You're trespassing."

"Meaning what? You're going to kill me now?"

His eyes narrowed on the bag. With a flick of his wrist, it was ripped from my shoulder and thrown several feet away, apples scattering everywhere. "Meaning you're leaving without them."

As if sensing his rider's anger, the horse stamped its hoof again and tossed its head, jangling the reins.

Was he serious? "You literally have an orchard full!"

"Yes, you're right. *I* do. The *Corbins* do. The Hewitts do *not.*" His heel shifted slightly in the stirrup. The horse surged forward, taking abnormally high steps as it pranced toward me, stomping the ground as it went.

I backed up quickly, holding my hands up in surrender. They said discretion was the better part of valor and I wasn't fucking dying just to get a passing grade in Ainsworth's class. "I'm going. Ok? You don't have to be such an asshole."

The horse kept coming anyway.

Cassius smirked. "You should be grateful I'm *just* an asshole. If I were anyone else in my family, you would be dead already."

"I don't know what's stopping you. Unless you need me alive for one of your sick fucking rituals."

"What are you talking about?"

"The fact you people eat human flesh and keep the bones like souvenirs? Ring any bells?" I probably shouldn't have said any of that, but it was out of my mouth before I could help it. The rest of the world had the Bogeyman to terrorize their children and keep them in line; witches in Winslow had the Corbin family. So it was all too easy for a lifetime's worth of conditioning to spew out of me for no good reason.

The horse reared, so close to my face I felt the fuzzy hair on its hooves brush my skin.

Stumbling backward, I landed hard on my ass and threw my hands up in anticipation of being crushed. The air tingled with electricity and a rush of wind swept past me. A bolt of lightning slammed into the ground between the horse and I, scorching the earth and flinging bits of mud and grass everywhere.

The horse reared again, letting out a surprised whinny as it pawed the air.

Sadly, it wasn't enough to throw his asshole rider off. Cassius clung to the long, curly mane until the horse's front hooves landed on the ground. He leaned forward, whispering softly to the animal. "Shhh. Lucius. You're alright. Easy, boy. It's ok... You're ok."

He stroked its neck in a surprisingly gentle manner for someone whose family got off on death and torture. As soon as it calmed down, his glare returned to me in full force. "Do *not* use magic against my horse!"

"Then keep your fucking horse away from me!" In truth, I hadn't *meant* to use it at all. It just sort of... happened. Just like on the ledge by the library when I sent him sailing. The goal was to knock him down, not throw him twenty feet in the air and drop him on concrete.

"Ainsworth might have forced our hand, but consider this your last warning, Stormbringer." He snarled the last word, as if it was supposed to be an insult. "If I ever catch you on my property again, I *will* kill you and keep your skull as a fucking souvenir." He pulled the horse's reins to the side and clicked his tongue. Casting one final withering look over his shoulder, he gave the horse a swift kick and galloped away.

Cold drops of rain plunked on my head, picking up in intensity the longer I sat there. I glared up at the sky, knowing full well it wasn't supposed to rain today.

Speaking of which...

Stormbringer?

Is that what they called weather witches? I mean, it was fitting, but also kind of... dramatic? Then again, it *was* coming from a Necromancer. They were nothing if not dramatic.

Glancing around, I exhaled and got to my feet. I snagged my bag off the ground and slung it over my shoulder again, trudging back to the car. Rain chased me the entire way. By the time I slid behind the wheel of my Jeep, I was soaked and shivering.

Tossing my bag in the passenger seat, I started the engine and pulled the seatbelt across myself. Something red caught my eye in my periphery and I glanced at the seat beside me again.

Peeking out underneath one of the pocket flaps on my backpack was a splash of dark red.

I pushed the material aside and grinned.

There was one, perfect apple sitting on the seat. One perfect apple that asshole's magic hadn't knocked loose.

Fuck you, Cassius. *And* the horse you rode in on.

Chapter Eleven
Cassius

Graeme's unexpected and unwanted arrival reminded me of two things. One, he was a fucking asshole. On top of that, he was an asshole with *weather* magic. Not just air elements, as I previously assumed. Weather magic could be a problem depending on how far he wanted to push his side of the feud. Although, he seemed surprised when I called him Stormbringer. Maybe he didn't know the extent of his own powers, in which case I stood a fighting chance if he ever decided to put them to full use.

And reminder two — I needed that asshole to get a passing grade in Ainsworth's class. As much as I wanted to do the project on my own, I knew Ainsworth would never let that fly.

Since my stupid project partner wanted to test his little theory about growing poisoned apples, I would oblige him. We'd recreate Acqua Tofana, or some version of it, and see if it could be delivered via apple. The historical documents said it took four doses to simulate a natural death. Maybe we could increase the lethality to one dose. Or one bite. Whatever. Time would tell.

To make sure we were still cooperating, Ainsworth held both of us back after class the following week. Literally held us back, with vines wrapped around my hands so tightly I couldn't do the most basic magic even if I wanted to. The fact Graeme was in a similar situation only made me feel slightly better.

"Perhaps I didn't make myself clear?" Ainsworth asked, taking his glasses off and polishing them on the hem of his shirt. "You were supposed to submit your proposal last week. Where is it?"

"It's my fault," Graeme blurted out. "I was supposed to email it. I guess I forgot."

I shot him a look of surprise, quickly wiping it away when Ainsworth turned toward me for confirmation. I merely offered a nod, hoping he didn't press for more.

"Alright. Email it to me before five tonight." The vines loosened briefly, only to tighten up again. "But before you leave, why don't you tell me what you're planning?" He zeroed in on Graeme again, since the dumb ass nominated himself as our spokesperson.

"We were, um, going to—"

I cleared my throat, smoothing out Graeme's blundering. "Reproduce Acqua Tofana, as I said, and see if those properties can be transferred to the pips before planting."

Out of the corner of my eye, I could see Graeme staring at me, but I refused to look at him or the dopey surprise on his face.

Ainsworth smiled. "Wonderful. See? That wasn't so hard, now was it?" The vines finally fell to the floor and retracted out of sight. "Enjoy the rest of your day, gentlemen!"

I grabbed my messenger bag from where I'd dropped it and hightailed it out of the classroom before our mad professor had any more questions or bright ideas.

"Wait up," Graeme called out behind me.

Pretending I didn't hear him, I kept going at exactly the same pace. Ok, it was a smidge quicker. Sadly, it didn't deter him. Graeme's fingers snagged my coat sleeve, jerking me to a halt. I knocked his hand away from my arm roughly. "Don't fucking touch me!"

"Well, if you would have stopped, I wouldn't have to touch you!" He looked like he was at his wit's end already. Good. Maybe I could push him over the edge.

"Oh, that's right. I forgot," I sneered, taking a step closer with every word until I was practically on top of him. "I'm supposed to show deference to you because you're a fucking Hewitt and Hewitts always get what they want. Isn't that right? So tell me, *Hewitt*, what the fuck do you want? What can this disgusting, flesh-eating Necromancer do for you?"

He bristled, the cords in his throat tightening, but he didn't make any sort of move to put space between us again. "Our project, you arrogant asshole. You actually thought about it?"

"Clearly more than you have." No fun. He genuinely wanted to talk. Given what a pain in the ass he was and the fact I had more important shit to do, like demon research, I didn't feel like sticking around to push his buttons anymore. I pivoted on the ball of my foot and continued on my way. Much to my annoyance, Graeme fell into step next to me, matching each of my strides.

"Look, I don't like this arrangement any more than you do," he said.

"I doubt that."

"But," he snapped, talking over me, "we need to deal with it. Try and find a way to work together."

"Don't worry about it. I'll put your name on the paper and call it a day."

Graeme scoffed. "I don't think so."

"Fine, I'll take all the credit then and you can do whatever the hell you want. You were planning to anyway."

His arm shot out in front of me a second before he

appeared in my field of vision. I crashed right into it, into him, and bounced back with a glare.

"You know what? Do whatever project *you* want. I don't fucking care." The corners of his eyes tightened, along with a muscle in his cheek. It was on the green side of his eyes and I swear the more pissed he got, the darker it turned. "Just tell me one thing and I'll fucking leave you alone forever."

I arched a brow at him, waiting.

"All of the bullshit aside. Forget the rumors, forget all the bad blood. Answer honestly. Does your family really grow poisoned apples?"

"Oh yeah." I smiled darkly, taking a step closer. He swallowed but held his ground when I leaned closer to his face, lowering my voice. "Just like we fuck goats and sacrifice babies under a full moon." Slamming my shoulder into his, I shoved past him with a growl.

"How did my brother really die?"

His question brought me to a screeching halt. My spine went rigid and my heart stuttered. He was the only one who had ever asked that question. In six years, he was the *only* one who actually left room for an alternative explanation. Or maybe I was more brain-damaged from that fall than I originally realized.

When he spoke again, his voice was right behind me and much softer than before. Even the air around him felt sad as he dropped the Hewitt act, letting me catch a glimpse of the boy from the party once again. "Please, Cassius. That's all I want to know."

As much as I hated him, hated his whole fucking family, I couldn't blame him. If it was Claudia who died, I'd want answers too and nothing would stop me from getting them.

Turning slowly, I stuffed my prior anger back into its box and faced him with a neutral expression. "I don't know. Honestly."

His shoulders slumped, his jeweled eyes dropping along with them. Some sort of emotion fluttered through the center of my chest. Sympathy? I wasn't sure. Before I could figure out what it was, my mouth carried on before my brain could stop it.

I inhaled a breath with a grimace, spitting out my next words as quickly as I could. "But I know how we can find out."

Chapter Twelve

Graeme

This was one of my worst decisions ever. Right behind giving my mortal enemy a blowjob.

Parking my Jeep next to the fence, I hopped out and stared at the vastness of the Corbin's apple orchard. My ass still hurt from the last time I was here and Cassius's stupid horse almost trampled me to death. Pretty sure my tailbone was bruised thanks to him. And now here I was again, climbing the fence for a second time.

I didn't have to wait long before a familiar thundering sounded, shaking the ground. Just like last time, Cassius appeared on a black horse in the distance, flying down the lane, headed straight toward me. This time he was wearing a pair of tight burgundy pants and a black, short-sleeve polo despite the chilly afternoon. He slowed the horse to a walk and stopped right in front of me, holding out a black-gloved hand wordlessly.

"What?" I glanced from his hand to the horse, just now realizing he didn't even have a saddle. "*I'm* not getting on that thing. Are you nuts?"

"You want to walk all the way back to the house?" Cassius retracted his hand and adjusted his grip on the reins. "Be my guest. I'll see you after nightfall. Hopefully no one else in my family catches you before then."

"I mean, couldn't you have brought two? Or something?"

"And *that* wouldn't have been the least bit suspicious. 'Oh, hey, Dad. Don't mind me while I, a single rider, take *two* horses out for a hack.'"

Point taken, dick. "How the hell am I supposed to get up there?"

He gestured to the fence with an incredibly bored expression and held his hand out again.

Rolling my eyes, I trudged back to the fence and climbed up onto the middle rung.

Cassius maneuvered the horse forward, walking up right alongside me. He held his hand steady, giving me a balancing point as I swung my leg over and more or less plopped onto the horse's back behind him.

"You're going to have to get closer than that unless you want to throw off the balance completely," Cassius said, glancing over his shoulder.

Biting my lip, I inched forward.

"Closer," he huffed.

Silently swearing at him behind his back, I slid a bit more until I was practically flush with him.

He reached behind him and grabbed my hand, plastering it to his waist. "Hold on," Cassius said right before he made a clicking sound and tapped the horse with his heels.

As soon as we lurched forward, I grabbed Cassius with the other hand as well, clinging to his shirt with zero regard for how it might have looked. Apparently that amused him enough to the point where he chuckled instead of snarling at me to stop wrinkling his shirt.

"Shut up," I snapped, trying to loosen my grip only to latch on again with the horse's next step. At this rate, I was going to be hanging on to him like a fucking koala by the time we got to where we were going.

"First time on a horse?"

“Other than a pony ride? Yeah. I prefer riding things that I can control.”

He snorted. “That’s gotta be rough for your dating life.”

I glared at the back of his head. “Oh my God, you’re so funny! Not.”

He shrugged. The muscles in his abdomen tightened, which gave me the impression he was still laughing, however silently. A part of me might have been miffed he was laughing at my expense, but another part was happy to see him in a good mood. It was a welcome change from our usual interactions.

As the horse lumbered on, the breeze shifted. The tree branches swayed overhead, bobbing with fruit. The scent of apples and something else, like sweet grass, were the first things I smelled, followed by the distinct smell of rain.

“We should hurry,” I said, glancing up at the gray sky.

“Why?”

The clouds answered for me, sprinkling the first cold drops of rain. One droplet slipped inside my shirt and rolled down my back, between my shoulder blades. An involuntary shiver raced down my spine after it.

“It was a joke,” Cassius said with a sigh. “You don’t have to throw a tantrum, for Christ’s sake.”

“It’s not me.”

“Can’t you stop it?”

“It’s easier to start a storm than it is to stop it.”

“Great.” He made the clicking noise again with his tongue. The horse picked up speed from a casual walk to something a little quicker.

I couldn’t help but notice Cassius’s ass, especially since my hands were holding onto his waist mere inches above it. The faster the horse walked, the more swing there was to his hips, like he was melded together with the horse. Maybe that's how he was able to ride without a saddle. Or it was his thighs, flexing with—

Thunder clapped above us, like the universe itself was reprimanding me for the dirty path my thoughts started wandering.

Jesus Christ, Graeme! Do not get a fucking hard-on right now! He would *never* let me live that one down.

Rain fell faster, blurring the landscape into a wash of grays and browns with pops of the bright red apples. Lightning flickered up in the clouds, followed almost immediately by a boom of thunder. Shit. The storm was closer than I originally thought.

Cassius must have known it too. He reached across himself and grabbed my hand, pulling it even further around his waist so I was forced to hug his back. Before I could ask what the fuck he was doing, he kicked the horse and we were off. I don't know if it was a gallop or what, but it felt like we were flying through the orchard.

I pressed my cheek to his shoulder blade and closed my eyes, praying to God I didn't fall off and *really* embarrass myself. Or break a limb. You know. Priorities.

Even going as fast as we were, it still took what seemed like forever before the horse left the orchard, dashed across an elaborate garden, and clopped to a halt inside a miniature brick castle that was, in fact, a stable.

Cassius swung his leg over the horse's neck and slid off, turning to me expectantly, with his hands up, like he was going to catch me.

"Fuck off," I grumbled, mimicking what he did and dropping to my feet without his help. The minute I landed, my legs bowed out. It took me a few steps to feel remotely normal again, although I was pretty sure I'd have to ice my groin in the morning. "You do this shit for fun?"

"When I'm not harvesting organs and snatching unsuspecting children from their beds." He gave me a pointed look and walked off with his horse, disappearing into one of the stalls. The horse's curly black tail swished, like it, too, was irritated with me.

Smart ass.

I crossed my arms over my chest and wandered around the stable. A few horses peeked their heads out of their stalls, huffing or chewing hay. Almost everywhere I looked, there were cats. On the rafters, on the soaring stacks of hay bales, even one who was brave enough to be sitting on the actual back of a horse.

"They keep the mice away," Cassius said, reappearing behind me as a fat calico rammed its head against my shin. "I'm not planning to take over the world with an army of cats."

"I didn't say anything."

"No, but I'm sure you were about to."

A small frown pulled the corners of my mouth. He took offense when I meant none and slung verbal daggers any chance he could. Sad to say, the rush of our sparring matches no longer held the same appeal. I couldn't help but wonder if we'd ever speak civilly to one another again.

"So now what?" I asked, shoving my hands in my front pockets.

"I'm going to go get cleaned up and then I'm going to get what we need for the spell."

"What's that?"

"My mother's ashes." He held my gaze for several seconds, though it seemed like a lifetime, like he was waiting for me to make some sort of disparaging comment. I didn't give him the satisfaction even though I had a thousand questions running through my head — none of them disparaging.

Instead, I walked over to a bench and made a show of sitting down, to wait patiently.

Squaring his shoulders, Cassius turned and walked in the opposite direction, his knee-high boots clicking across the cobblestones.

I bit my lips and leaned to the side, watching him move further away. Those burgundy pants were so goddamn tight you could bounce a quarter off his ass. Sadly, there was no conceivable way to tell him *not* to change, so I'd just have to enjoy every second of watching him walk away.

The calico jumped up onto the seat next to me and bonked its head into my elbow, meowing loudly.

I smiled and scratched the cat's head, happy to have the company while I waited.

Chapter Thirteen
Cassius

"What's in there?" Graeme asked, his voice full of awe as we passed the heavy, iron gates that sectioned off part of the garden. Rain pelted our umbrellas relentlessly to the point where my pants were soaked from the knees down. His jeans looked to be in a similar state. Thankfully, we were getting close.

"It's the poison garden," I replied, prepared for the onslaught of snide comments. "Feel free to taste, touch, and smell whatever you'd like in there."

He glared at me through the wall of sideways rain. "You were nice for, like, five minutes. Can you try going back to that for a change? It might make this whole thing easier for both of us."

"Oh, am I making you uncomfortable, your majesty? Please, allow me to change my ways to accommodate your sensitive disposition."

He exhaled a sharp breath, staring straight ahead. "Fine," he said after a minute. "Keep being an asshole. Just tell me where we're going."

"To the crypt." I also kept my gaze straight ahead, counting down the seconds until his witchy little mind blew.

"Did you say crypt?!" Ah. There it was. "Like the place

with dead bodies? That kind of crypt? You literally have a *crypt* in your backyard?!"

"What else should we do with our dead? Stuff them and hang them above the fireplace like a fucking trophy? Put them in a glass coffee table?" I rolled my eyes at the idea of Grandma chilling in the living room while the family had afternoon tea over her corpse. And just when I thought he might be over his dickish comments.

"I don't know," he sputtered, gesturing while he searched for the words. "How about bury them in a cemetery like normal people?"

"So your kind can dig them up and defile them? Thanks, but no thanks. We'll keep them here where we know they're safe."

Graeme stopped, looking horrified. "Oh my God! We wouldn't do that. We would *never* do that!"

I didn't bother waiting for him and kept walking. "Right… Just like you people wouldn't raze an entire village to the ground and force the Congregation to kowtow to your name for centuries. And surely you wouldn't drag a man out of bed in the middle of the night and hang him, either, without any provocation. Or murder a woman simply trying to return a dead child to his parents."

I forced myself to breathe calmly while I waited for another comeback, some justification for his family's laundry list of heinous attacks against my family, but it didn't come. When I stole a glance at him, he was beside me again. A frown marred his face, but it wasn't at me — he was staring at the ground.

A twinge of remorse shot through me until I reminded myself where, exactly, we were going. He could sulk as much as he wanted. His father was the reason my mother was dead. Even if it didn't hurt so much anymore, the pain would never go away entirely. Each new milestone in my life was another reminder that she wasn't there — and George Hewitt was the reason why.

We didn't speak again until we stopped in front of the Corbin mausoleum. It was a large, dark granite structure, its doors and windows constructed of wrought iron and stained glass. Even someone as stuck up as a Hewitt would have to admit the building was beautiful, despite its morbid purpose.

With a wave of my hand, the doors swung outward. As soon as I stepped inside, a section of the floor pulled away, revealing the stairs that led down into the crypt. I shook off my umbrella and propped it inside the door, candles sparking to life all on their own.

I was halfway down the stairs when Graeme's voice stopped me.

"Seriously?"

Pausing, I turned and looked up at him. "What?"

He shook his head and jogged down the stairs, passing me with an amused snort. "Only you people would have a secret tunnel into a creepy-ass crypt, buried in the backyard."

"It's not creepy," I countered, feeling more than a little insulted on behalf of all my ancestors. "It's my family."

The lines of his face softened. It almost looked like regret. Except, I knew better.

Whatever it was, I ignored it and carried on, leading the way past the dark hallways that shot off in every direction, each lined with dozens of niches to hold the varying branches of the Corbin line.

"You cremate everyone?" Graeme asked, looking around with wide eyes. If he was expecting piles of bones or human skins hung like tapestries, I'm sure he was disappointed. It may have been underground, but it was clean and fairly bright with all of the sconces lining the walls.

"Yes," I huffed.

"Why? I'm asking for real."

"Why the fuck do you care?"

He shrugged, stuffing his hands into his pockets. "Just wondering. Trying to make conversation. Seemed appropriate, given our surroundings."

I realized I *might* have been overreacting, so I gave myself a mental slap and exhaled another calming breath. When I answered his question, I made sure to drop the hostility from my tone. "What I said before *was* the real reason. You can't resurrect someone if there isn't a body. You might still be able to reach the spirit, but at least the physical form of the person can't be turned against you."

"Yeah, but who would do that?" The horror was back in his tone. When I spun abruptly, it was on his face, too, mixed with confusion.

"Oh my God. Do you know *anything* about Necromancy beyond the scary stories you good little witches tell each other at sleepovers?"

"I know all I need to know about Necromancy," he spat back.

Eyes narrowed, I took a step forward, praying he did something stupid. "This ought to be good. Lay it on me, genius."

"You people are the reason the witchcraft trials even started!" he said with a snarl. "If you weren't so obsessed with demonic magic, none of this would have happened and we wouldn't have to hide who we are! But no. Power-hungry Necromancers couldn't leave well enough alone!"

"I am so fucking sick of you looking down your nose at us! You're no better than the magistrates who signed the fucking death warrants! Better to kill what scares you, rather than try to understand it, right? You people hate what you fear and it's pathetic!"

"Pathetic? What's pathetic is the fact you're clinging to a

form of magic that should have been wiped out centuries ago! Then we wouldn't be in this mess!"

I shoved him in the chest as hard as I could. "You are such a self-centered, arrogant asshole! The sight of you makes me fucking sick."

"You'll be happy to know the feeling is mutual!"

"The sooner this is over, the better for everyone. You can go back to your bubble, pretending I'm the fucking villain instead of taking a long look in the mirror and realizing what a pathetic waste of magic you are."

All of a sudden his hands were on my chest, tangled in my shirt. He drove me back against the stone wall so hard the air went out of me. Before I could even think about escaping, his body pressed against mine, trapping me there between him and the stone. "Has anyone ever told *you* what a self-centered, arrogant asshole *you* are?"

"Get off of me." Regardless of the fact we were about to rip each other apart, being this close to him made my heartbeat stutter, just like it did the first time I saw him. Why did he have to be so goddamn attractive? He was like a snake in the garden — his beauty lured you in, then a fucking viper leapt out when you least expected it.

The command made him smirk and shove more weight against me. "Make me."

"You're such a child." Ironic, considering he was at least a year older than me. Gritting my teeth, power prickled as it surged through my hands.

He must have realized what I was doing because the next thing I knew he grabbed both of my wrists in one hand and slammed them above my head.

"No magic," he snapped, the heat from his gaze burning into mine.

"Pussy." I all but hissed the word, moving my face a fraction of an inch closer to his.

"Don't push me, Corbin."

"Am I supposed to be afraid of you?" I snorted out a derisive laugh. "You're a disgrace to weather witches throughout time. Stormbringer my ass."

Electricity darted down both of my arms, ripping through my nerve endings with each painful volt. "Stormy enough for you, asshole?"

I grimaced, grinding out a "Fuck you!" while trying to keep myself upright.

"Maybe that's what your problem is," Graeme growled, pushing his hips into me. His cock was already hard-as-steel, rubbing against mine and throwing fuel on the fire I was trying — and failing — to snuff out. "Maybe you're so hard up for it, that's why you're such a miserable prick."

"I'm not hard up for anything, you idiot. Least of all *you*." Except my own hard-on obliterated that defense. I couldn't even think straight when he was around. My head hated him for a thousand reasons, but there was a *want* in my blood I couldn't deny. It had been there since Preston's party — the first time he touched me, smiled at me. And, of course, kissed me.

"Then why is your dick so hard, baby?" he asked, reaching for my belt buckle.

I didn't stop him from yanking it open or from freeing the top button, nor did I have a good answer to his stupid question. The only answer I had was so fucking wrong, it both thrilled and infuriated me. Before I blurted it out like a moron, I clenched my molars together. Glaring over his shoulder, I simply willed him to be the better person instead of actually trying to stop him from whatever it was he was about to do.

A soft and husky laugh reverberated next to my ear, as if he could sense my internal distress and was enjoying every second of it. His tongue came next, tracing the shell of my ear while he pulled my zipper down.

Jesus Christ, Cassius…

As soon as the pressure on my wrists slackened, I came to my fucking senses. Ripping myself out of his one-handed grip, I shoved him away from me again. I couldn't just stand there and do *nothing*. I was a fucking Corbin and this had already gone too far. "Don't touch me."

"You want to top? That's fine," he said, undoing his belt and jeans as well.

"I don't want anything to do with you."

"That's not what your dick says."

"I think *you're* the one who's hard up since you won't take 'no' for a fucking answer."

"Yeah, you're right," Graeme said with a dark smile, swaggering forward and closing the distance. "Nothing gets me going like a smart-mouth prick who looks down on everyone and everything." He put his hands on either side of me, caging me against the wall. A moment later, his tongue skipped along my throat, making its way up to my jaw.

I turned to see what he was doing, right as his tongue crested my chin and went straight to my mouth, invading it the same way he'd invaded my thoughts from the first moment I laid eyes on him. Still, I resisted. I pushed against his chest and pulled back as much as I could with the stone behind me.

He caught my wrists and pinned them again, pressing his body against mine even harder. Angling his face, he resumed his attack on my mouth, slipping his tongue inside deeper. As much as I hated him, I couldn't help the strangled moan that worked its way out of my throat.

When we broke away for air, he pulled back a bit, looking at me with lust-drunk eyes. It was the same way he'd looked the night of Preston's party before either of us knew who the other was, before the line in the sand was drawn. Back when we were just two people, connected by luck or fate or hormones — not hatred. They say there's a fine line between love and hate. But what about *lust* and hate? Where did that fall on the spectrum?

"This changes nothing," I snarled, slipping my hands inside his waistband and pushing his pants and underwear down past his hips.

"I still fucking hate you," he agreed, leaning back to tear his shirt over his head and toss it aside, stepping out of his jeans while he was at it. As soon as he was naked, he yanked my shirt off and knelt in front of me, dragging my pants downward as he went.

"Once. To get it out of our system. And then back to figuring the other shit out."

"Once," he agreed, his breath washing over my dick before he kissed the head gently. His tongue flicked out over the slit, licking away the pre-cum. I sighed and leaned back, running my fingers through his dark hair as his head bobbed in front of me, sucking and swallowing my length in his infuriatingly perfect mouth.

My hips flicked now and again, shoving my cock that little bit deeper. Part of it was to remind him he wasn't completely in charge. The other part was fucking animal instinct. No surprise I was turned on by what he was doing with his mouth, but when I saw he was jacking himself off at the same time, I almost lost it. He glared up at me now and again but never once slowed down until he popped off the end and spat out a new command. "Turn around."

And I did. I have no idea why I did. I shouldn't have. I shouldn't be doing any of it. I should have told him to go to hell. I shouldn't have braced myself against the wall and arched my back in anticipation of what was coming next.

His hands ran down the small of my back and caressed

my ass cheeks, almost reverently. When his lips pressed against one, then the other, my breath caught. It left me entirely when he spread them apart and his tongue lashed out, trailing up and down my backside. From hole to balls, and back up, over and over, until he concentrated his efforts on the hole itself, licking and swirling and sucking like I'd never experienced before.

"Fuck me..." I closed my eyes and pressed my forehead against the smooth stone, fingers clawing against the hard surface. Why did it have to feel so good? Why did *he* have to make it feel so good?

He pulled away with a low chuckle, massaging my ass cheeks. "Is that good, baby?"

"Shut up," I snapped back, nearly sighing when he picked up where he left off.

This time, he pressed against my entrance with a finger, sinking it inside with zero warning. I exhaled sharply and pushed back, overriding my surprise and the initial burn by taking control.

He slid his finger in and out while his mouth dropped lower, licking my balls and the crown of my cock.

God, I hated him. I hated what he was doing. I hated that I felt like I was going to come undone at any second and his dick wasn't even inside me yet. I hated that the best sex of my fucking life was with Graeme fucking Hewitt.

Two fingers slipped inside, stroking me, while he kept teasing my cock with his mouth. When a third wedged its way inside, I nearly came unglued.

"Oh, fuck..." I squeezed my eyes shut as my balls tightened.

He stopped abruptly and got to his feet. "Oh, no you don't. You don't get to come until I say so."

I turned to glare at him, but he shoved me forward again, flattening my chest against the wall. "You're afraid of a horse and you think you can control me?"

"Watch and learn, baby." His lips brushed the back of my neck right before he bit me. His cock slipped between my cheeks, pressing against my hole while he continued to bite and suck my neck and shoulder.

"What are you waiting for?" I panted, flicking my hips backward, trying to get him to hurry before I came to my senses. "Don't tell me you're going to back out now."

"I'm not doing this for you," he shot back, pushing the head of his cock inside with a groan.

"Whatever you have to tell yourself." After a surprised gasp, I bit my lip, attempting to stifle my moan as he breached the ring of muscles. "About time. I was beginning to—"

He drove his cock deeper, stealing my breath and whatever the hell I was going to say next. "What was that?" he asked with another husky laugh, his fingers tightening against my hips so hard I was probably going to have bruises. "Were you saying something?"

"Fuck you," I snapped a moment before he thrust in again.

"No, baby. Fuck *you*."

Despite the extraordinary prep, or maybe because of it, he didn't waste his time being slow or gentle. Each thrust was hard and fast, his pelvis coming flush with my ass again and again, like a machine. I couldn't remember a time I'd been fucked so ruthlessly. Then again, I didn't make it a habit of falling into bed with my family's sworn enemy.

One of his hands slipped around my waist, gripping my cock. "Say my name, Cassius," he said right next to my ear, twisting and stroking me in time to his cock moving in and out.

"What?" I could barely think and he wanted me to talk?

"Say it," he growled, his teeth grazing the side of my neck. "I want you to acknowledge who's fucking you right now."

"No." In all honesty, I would have called him whatever he wanted as long as he didn't stop. But I had to at least try and hang on to a shred of dignity.

The hand that was still holding my hip came up and grabbed the back of my neck, shoving my face against the wall and pinning me in place while he fucked me harder. "Fucking say it, Cash. Whose cock is buried so deep in your ass you can't stand it?"

"Graeme," I blurted out, squeezing my eyes shut as my body hurtled toward release. "It's Graeme! Fuck me, it's Graeme!"

One more thrust, one more stroke, and I was done for. The warm pressure in my balls fucking exploded, unloading my cum all over the stone wall. If it weren't for the fact Graeme was holding me in place, I'm pretty sure I would have wound up in a puddle on the floor.

I almost didn't realize he had pulled out until he collapsed against my back, grunting through his own orgasm. His cum shot out on the floor between our feet. I suppose I should have been grateful for small favors — cleanup wouldn't be that much of a pain now and I'd be able to save some sort of face with the fact he didn't actually come *inside* me. Not that my pride mattered much at this point…

"Fuck me," Graeme panted, his warm breath caressing the back of my neck. "That was hot."

It was. Hot and fulfilling and fucking wrong. Graeme was everything I shouldn't want in one giant, peculiar-eyed package.

"If you're finished, I have work to do." I shrugged him off and pushed away from the wall roughly. Snatching my pants off the ground, I slipped into them again, keeping my back to him.

"That's it? Just gonna fuck and run? Again?"

I whipped around, advancing on him in long strides.

"Don't act like you're innocent in all of this. You're the one who came on to me at that party. And you're the one who pushed for this."

He held his ground, his eyes darkening. "You wanted it just as much as me. *Both* times. Don't even deny it."

"What I want is for you to stay the fuck away from me. If putting out is the only way to make that happen? So be it. As soon as we have our answers, all bets are off."

A flicker of emotion darted across his face. Like a wince. But it was gone too fast to say for certain. "Meaning what? You're going to kill me?"

"If I have to." I may have said the words, but I doubted how much I meant them anymore. Maybe it was some lingering emotion, given what we'd just done. It had to have been because there was no way I would ever *want* a Hewitt to live. If I could somehow annihilate the whole family in one go, I would. That would bring an end to the feud for sure.

Graeme took a step forward, his chin tipped up. "Then why wait? Why not get it over with now?"

I gave him a once-over and took a purposeful step back, away from the temptation presented by his still-naked body. Um, his vulnerability. The vulnerability *of* him being naked. That's what I meant. "You're not worth the effort."

"Fuck you, Cash." His voice wavered at the end and he swallowed hard, his Adam's apple betraying the movement.

"Unfortunately for you, it was a one-time thing. Remember?" With a smirk, I pivoted on my heel and stormed off.

Chapter Fourteen
Cassius

Venturing into the spirit world was never easy, but it was even more nerve-racking with an audience. Normally there was no way in hell I'd do something like this with Graeme around, but I didn't have much of a choice. He wasn't leaving until he had answers. So who better to ask than my mother?

After sneaking Graeme into the house from the side garden, I hurried him through the study and down the hall, shoving him between the shoulder blades every time he stopped to gawk. There was more than one staircase to choose from to make it upstairs but all came with the considerable risk of being seen. Still, the main staircase in the front of the house was the closest to my room and the quickest route.

With my mother's marble urn tucked under my arm, I directed him through the cavernous foyer, reminiscent of a medieval hall, and up the stairs to the left. We moved down the hall, along the gallery that overlooked the foyer, and finally darted into my room. To be on the safe side, I not only shut and locked the door, I added a ward to make it harder to open.

"Your house is..." Whatever he was about to say trailed off as he wandered around my room, staring alternatively at the elaborately painted night sky on the ceiling to the hand-carved mantel over the fireplace.

"Creepy. Yeah. Got it." I set my mother's urn on the floor and stomped over to the large armoire for more supplies.

"I was going to say cool."

"Mhmm."

"No, really. This place looks like it belongs in England or something."

"Well, it used to. Our family had it shipped over sometime in the 1800s," I replied distractedly, sorting through the various vials and jars in the cabinet.

"Why? I mean, why not build a new one?"

Dumping the things I'd need onto a silver platter, I grabbed a handful of candles and hip-checked the cabinet door closed. "Several reasons. One, this house has been imbued with magic for centuries. And two, after your family kept torching all of the other wood-frame homes, one of my ancestors got the bright idea to use stone instead."

"Oh." When I glanced up at him, his gaze darted away, actually looking ashamed for half a heartbeat.

"Sit over there," I said, gesturing to the antique chaise in front of the fireplace.

Thankfully Graeme didn't argue.

Once the lit candles and crystals were set up in a circle, I sat in the middle with the platter of herbs. Sprinkling the blend of dried greenery into the center of a square of paper, I rolled it tightly. I ran my tongue along the edge of the paper to seal it, just *waiting* for comments from the peanut gallery to begin.

Lighting the end, I inhaled and held it in while laying on my back, making sure the marble urn was right above my head. I closed my eyes, drawing more smoke into my lungs, and trying to relax my muscles methodically, from head to toe.

"Seriously? You're getting high right now?" Graeme sniffed.

And there it was...

Expelling the smoke sharply, I kept my eyes closed, trying my damndest to ignore his never-ending judgment. "If you think it's so easy to cross over, why don't you fucking do it? Oh, that's right. You can't."

He muttered something under his breath that sounded like "asshole" but he didn't say anything else loud enough for me to hear.

I took another drag, already feeling my body loosen. As much as I hated to admit it, the orgasm from earlier helped. But more important than my physical body relaxing was the fact my mind was finally slowing down. I didn't want to leave my body vulnerable for too long with a Hewitt around, so I was grateful Claudia had perfected this blend to help us transition quickly — in *and* out. It hit fast, but it wore off just as fast. I mean, Graeme had already fucked me, but he probably wasn't above smothering me while I was out of it.

Fabric shifted and there was a slight breeze as Graeme sat next to me, outside the circle.

"What am I supposed to do?" he asked quietly.

"Try shutting up?"

"Fuck off. I'm trying to help."

"You can help by shutting up."

"Oh my God. Could you be any more of a dick?"

Ignoring him, I inhaled another bout of smoke. My hand suddenly weighed a hundred pounds. It crashed to the floor, dropping the joint onto the silver platter. Heaviness spread across my whole body, meanwhile, my head spun until the colors behind my eyelids were nothing but a blur.

I knew the moment I'd crossed into the Land of the Dead by the smell alone. The sickly sweet scent hit me hard, a combination of frankincense, vanilla, and pomegranate. The next thing that washed over me was a cold, damp chill that seeped into the marrow of my bones. Despite my lineage, I hated this place, this land of "in-between" — between Heaven and Hell, where souls were left to wander and Necromancers came to commune.

Forcing my eyes open again, I blinked rapidly, trying to adjust to the dim, eerie light. It was a swirl of shadows and fog, lit here and there by the faint silvery glow of spirits as they drifted aimlessly.

Something bumped my elbow in the dark. I whirled away from the sensation and looked down. It was a man, except he was shuffling around on two bloody stumps instead of legs. His head was bent at an odd angle, his neck twisted and purple with broken bones. One bloody, mangled hand dragged a motorcycle helmet along the ground as he moved.

I backed away from it and continued through the fog, looking for my mother. Having her ashes nearby should have drawn her to me, but who knew how long it would take for her to find her way. Beads of sweat trickled down the back of my neck, but my hands felt like ice. Each second that passed made it harder to breathe between the smell of death and the oppressive fog.

"Cassius?"

"Mom?" My voice cracked as I spun in a circle, searching for her. Other than my dreams and photographs, I hadn't seen her in six years. Not since the night she died. And now, when I needed to keep my shit together, all of those lost, little-boy feelings rushed to the surface, blurring my eyes with years of unshed tears.

"Cassius, is that you?"

"Mom! It's me! I'm right here!"

She materialized beside me with a bright smile, her ghostly form still dressed for her fateful afternoon ride. Her long, black hair blew in a breeze that didn't exist and her pale arms embraced me. For the briefest moment, I would have sworn I felt their warmth instead of the whisper of cold wind. I wanted to bury my face into her, to smell her perfume again, but I knew that was impossible.

"What are you doing here, sweetheart?" She stroked my cheek with translucent fingers, her blue eyes wide with worry. "You know it's not safe."

"I need to ask you about that day," I said, swallowing down a flurry of nerves and wiping at my face.

She tilted her head to the side, brows furrowed. "My death day?"

I nodded, biting my lips together when the lower one wouldn't stop trembling.

"Oh, sweetheart. Leave the past alone. Look to your future, instead. It's brighter there. I promise you."

"I can't, Mom. I need to know what happened — from you."

She sighed and looked away, wringing her hands together. For a moment, I thought she was refusing, but finally, she spoke. "The crows told me there was a problem in the orchard. Lucius ran as fast as he could, but by the time we got there it was too late. Percy was screaming and crying and shaking Owen. When he saw me, he ran away. I tried to save Owen, sweetheart, but he was already gone."

"But *how?*"

"I don't know. There wasn't a mark on him. He just... died."

"So what happened when you went to the Hewitts?"

She shook her head, a small crease between her delicate brows. "Why are you asking all of this? Why now? What's happened?"

"We just want to know the truth, Mom. No one else will tell us."

"We?" She blinked, touching my cheek again. "Who is 'we'? Your father already knows all of this."

"Graeme and I."

The warmth vanished from her face. Her hand fell and her shoulders rolled back, lengthening her spine. "Graeme? Graeme *Hewitt*?"

"We just want the truth, Mom. Please. I know it's hard, but—"

"*We*?" Her gaze narrowed.

"Mom, please. You know we don't have a lot of ti—"

"The Hewitts are dangerous, Cassius. More than you know!"

"I think I have a pretty good idea," I shot back, biting my tongue a second too late. "I'm sorry. I'm just… frustrated."

Her eyes darkened. Literally. Inky blackness spread from the pupil until it consumed the entire eyeball. "Stay away from them, Cassius! Do you hear me? They will be the death of you! *He* will be the death of you!"

I made a face even as my stomach twisted into painful knots. "What are you talking about? Do you know something?"

She reached forward with both hands, her nails growing into long, black claws. They sank into my shoulders, crushing and puncturing at the same time. The copper smell was even more jarring than the feeling of blood running down my arms.

"How are you doing this?!" I stared at the thing that used to be my mother, immobilized in her clutches. "Mom, talk to me!"

A piercing screech sounded overhead. I looked up in time to see flashing yellow eyes and a sharp black beak diving straight for my face. One of the massive owl's talons scratched across my cheek, but it clearly missed its intended target.

"Ne te quaesiveris extra," my mother hissed. The owl screeched again and banked in a circle overhead. Her pale lips twisted with rage. With one, hard shove, she sent me flying backward, through smoke and flames, into the darkness.

Do not seek outside yourself.

Chapter Fifteen
Graeme

I didn't like this. Not one fucking bit.

Pacing back and forth in front of Cassius's drugged-out body, I alternated between chewing on my thumbnail and raking my hands through my hair. How long had he been under? I didn't even know. Five minutes? Twenty? Each second felt like a lifetime.

All I *did* know was the mild twitches and sighs had started to turn into full-body jerks and yelling. Not in English, of course, so I had no clue what he was even saying. I actually didn't know what language it was. Maybe Latin? Something old and not in my wheelhouse. Go figure.

What if he got stuck over there? What if all of the yelling was because he was fighting to come back to this plane? Realm? World? I don't know. This spirit-travel shit was another thing that was beyond me. My magic was nature-based, as Cassius so snidely pointed out every chance he could. I dealt with things I could see and touch. Natural processes from the natural world, not spirits and demons and shit.

Forcing myself to sit down, I got as close to the circle as I could, looking over his body and hoping for inspiration. He was right. I didn't know the first thing about crossing over, which meant I had no fucking clue how to help — or if I even could.

I hated this feeling. Sitting here and doing nothing when I was partially responsible for sending him over there. Ok, mostly responsible. I mean, *he's* the one who volunteered in the first place but it was because I couldn't leave him the fuck alone. I couldn't even explain why it mattered. Owen was dead. Knowing the reason why wouldn't change a damn thing about that. Except, *maybe*, to relieve me of some of my guilt.

Shouting, Cassius's eyes flew open. He jerked upright, crashing right into me.

"Breathe!" I caught him on instinct, holding onto him while he got his bearings. "You're ok. Just breathe, Cash."

A strange smell wafted off of him — like incense and fruits, tinged with smoke. He definitely didn't smell like that earlier when I was, ahem, next to him.

Cassius sucked in ragged gasps of air, like he'd surfaced from underwater, forcing me to focus on the here and now and not what happened an hour ago in the crypt.

He pulled back sharply, his brows furrowed. His eyes narrowed as they swept over me, like he didn't have a clue who I was or what I was doing here. Before I could even say anything else, he turned and fell forward on his hands, puking all over the floor. Thankfully from the looks of it, he hadn't eaten a very heavy lunch.

Trying not to make a face, I scooted back to give him some room. A red blotch on the sleeve of my olive henley caught my attention. I had two of them — one on each arm — and they definitely weren't there before.

"Are you bleeding?" I asked, although he wasn't exactly in a position to answer since he was still retching.

As soon as Cassius was done throwing up everything he'd ever eaten in his entire life, he wiped his mouth with his sleeve and flopped back onto the floor. He was always pale, but his skin was even paler now, with a grayish cast beneath the sheen of sweat.

Two blooms of crimson appeared on his shoulders the longer he lay there. As far as I could see, his sweater itself wasn't ripped but I was *not* imagining the blood on the light gray wool.

"You *are* bleeding! What happened?"

"Owl..."

"What?"

He closed his eyes, trembling from head to toe. "Do not seek outside yourself. Do not seek outside yourself. Do not seek outside yourself..."

"Do you need something?" I asked over his random mumbling. "Like, water or crackers?"

Shaking his head, he swallowed with a grimace. He rolled on his side and curled into a ball, his face lined with pain.

"Cash, tell me what to do," I said quietly, hoping he listened because I was about two seconds away from calling his ass an ambulance. Or his dad. Either way, the Corbins would probably kill me but I couldn't just sit there and do nothing if he really needed help. "Cash. Cash!"

Of course, he didn't answer. Stubborn bastard. Nor did he look at me. All he did in response to my growing panic was to wave me away with a groan. Before I knew it, his breathing evened out and deepened, indicating he'd fallen asleep.

Sighing, I rolled him from his right side to his left in the recovery pose, just in case he puked again. After that, I kept sitting there, watching the rise and fall of his shoulder. Every once in a while I checked the pulse in his neck to make sure he still had one.

"Fine time to finally stop talking," I grumbled, propping my chin on my hand.

I knew I should have left, for the simple fact that if his family caught me I'd be fucking dead. But it felt wrong to leave him like that, bleeding and unconscious. He might have been the biggest asshole I'd ever met, which was surprising considering I never thought anyone would beat Lennox in that regard, but he was still a person. And as much as he ragged on nature witches, I wasn't ashamed to be fucking compassionate.

Plus the selfish part of me still wanted answers.

Chapter Sixteen
Cassius

I felt like shit. I always felt like shit after crossing over, but this time was worse. *The* worst. My shoulders ached, my head was pounding, and every single muscle in my stomach was sore.

Rubbing my eye with the heel of my hand, I sat up and looked around. I was on the floor. What the fuck was I doing on the floor?

An image of Graeme flashed in my brain.

No, not an image. The real thing.

He was curled up on the floor next to me, sound asleep. And vulnerable again. Like the babies he accused my family of slaughtering. A pillow, a sheet — pretty much anything could asphyxiate him. Or I could crush his skull with my mother's urn. Wouldn't that have been poetic? Lydia Corbin strikes again, finishing off the last heir of the Hewitt line.

Shaking my head, I got to my feet and staggered toward the bathroom. I had bigger problems at the moment than Graeme Hewitt, that's for sure.

I stared at my face in the mirror for a minute, examining my cheek. I would have sworn there'd be a mark from that fucking owl, but there was nothing. At least, not there. There *was* blood all over the arms of my sweater, which was never a good sign.

Rinsing the vomit out of my mouth and brushing my teeth helped me feel somewhat human again, but I wasn't going to be completely restored until I took a shower.

As much as I didn't want to know what was going on under my shirt, I needed to see what the hell my mother did to me. Gritting my teeth, I peeled the garment off carefully, leaving behind a few fibers in the dried blood on my skin.

"What the hell, Mom?" I shifted one shoulder forward, closer to the mirror. In all the times I'd dealt with spirits, I'd never had one successfully touch me, let alone injure me in the real world. And I certainly wouldn't have expected my mother to be the first.

Ne te quaesiveris extra. Do not seek outside yourself.

What the fuck was that supposed to mean? Latin had been drilled into my brain as early as English had, but that phrase hadn't cropped up in my formal education.

He will be the death of you.

And who was the "he" she was talking about? Graeme? George? Were there any other male Hewitts left? George I knew to steer clear from, but Graeme? Even though I knew how dangerous Stormbringers could be, he didn't seem like he was too clued in about his powers. How could *he* possibly kill *me*? Unless it was by accident, like that time outside the library…

And what was with the goddamn owl trying to take my head off? Was Mom supposed to be an owl, too? No, she couldn't have been. Considering our family bird was a crow, it stood to reason that's what she was transforming into, from her black eyes to the way her fingers morphed into claws. Besides, crows were the natural enemies of owls. Maybe it was her way of protecting me? Protecting herself?

Then again... was that thing even my mother? It may have looked like her, but it could have very well been a demon just fucking with me. Either that, or she'd lost her maternal instinct sometime after her murder. The real Lydia Corbin would have never hurt her children unless it was for a very, *very* good reason. I suppose saving me from having my face ripped off by an owl demon might count, but damn. She could have just told me to duck.

Turning the shower on, I padded back to my bedroom to get some clothes from my dresser.

Graeme stirred on the floor. He gave me a sleepy smile and stretched, the hem of his shirt pulling up over his taut abs. Ugh. Someone shouldn't look that good first thing in the morning. "You're awake."

"Clearly." I slammed the dresser drawer shut, a bundle of clothes tucked under my arm.

Blinking, he sat up and considered my half-dressed form, his pouty lips turning down. "You have blood all over you."

"Hence the shower, genius." Rolling my eyes at his astounding brilliance, I retreated into the bathroom. I'd just shed the rest of my clothes right as the bathroom door swung open.

"What the fuck?!" I glared at Graeme as he marched right up to me. It was a little late for modesty, but I could still be offended by his brashness. "Get out!"

He looked at the puncture wounds in my shoulders and pointed, in case I had no clue what he was talking about. "What the fuck is that?"

"It's nothing."

"It's *not* nothing, idiot. You were attacked by something."

"I wasn't attacked," I huffed. I didn't know what it was, but it couldn't have been an attack... at least, I hoped it wasn't.

Graeme crossed his arms over his chest, lifting a dark brow. "Oh, ok. So coming back with giant holes in your body is totally normal?"

"Do you mind?" I stared at him, pointing at the door he

barged through. "I'd like to take a shower and I'd prefer to do it in peace."

Blockheaded as always, he didn't take a hint. "Why didn't you tell me it was dangerous over there?"

"Is this a joke?" I gave him a once over, wondering for a split second if I was still on the other side, or trapped in a dream. He thought waltzing around the spirit world was like a day at the beach? Granted, I'd never been injured before, but there was always the possibility when you were dealing with angry spirits or demons.

"Am I laughing?" he tossed back, his jaw shifting irritably.

"Say I did tell you how dangerous it was, what a risk I was taking," I said, crossing my arms to mimic his pose. "What would you have said?"

"Don't do it." He didn't even hesitate to answer, nor did he blink or crack a smile. He looked as serious as I'd ever seen him, not an ounce of bullshit to be found.

I smirked. "Yeah. Right."

"I'm serious." Still, no visible change in his expression or his breathing. He *was* serious and yet I didn't want to believe him. My brain told me *not* to believe him. But the way he looked at me, his mismatched eyes full of worry, made me think that maybe, just maybe, he was telling the truth.

Not knowing what to say to that, I simply turned and walked into the shower. I wasn't going to stand around all day, naked, waiting for him to take a hint.

I half expected him to follow me into the shower, because that's how much of an entitled dick he was, but he didn't. A moment later, I heard the bathroom door close and I exhaled a long breath, letting my shoulders relax.

See you later, asshole.

After I was showered and dressed, I returned to my bedroom with every intention of crawling back into bed for a few more hours. I had a history class in the afternoon, so I still had plenty of time for a proper nap in a proper bed, not passed out on the hard-ass floor.

But instead of settling into my nice, fluffy bed, *Graeme* was there. *On* my nice, fluffy bed. He sat up when I entered the room and raised his brows at me, like he was waiting for me to say something.

I certainly wasn't about to disappoint him. "Why are you still here?"

"Because I want to know what happened."

"None of your fucking business. How about that?"

"No, it *is* my business. We agreed we were going to get answers." I groaned and went to walk past him. He shot up and blocked my path, his arms crossed. "Why do you have those marks?"

"If I tell you that, you'll throw it back in my face that we're the freaks you always said we were. So thanks, but no thanks. I didn't find anything useful over there. I tried. I failed. End of story. Happy now?"

"So what now?" he asked with a shrug, apparently not buying one ounce of my casual dismissal. "We go back to hating each other?"

I scoffed. "I never stopped hating you."

To my surprise, he actually flinched. "Wow."

For a second I felt bad. Then I remembered what brilliant liars they all were and I absolved myself of guilt. Plus I couldn't shake my mother's warning, not when her fucking claw marks still stung my shoulders.

"Can you ever look at me and not see my father?" he asked quietly.

"Can you ever look at me and not see a monster?"

"I don't see a monster."

"Too bad I don't believe you." I pushed past him roughly, but instead of making my escape to the other side of the room, he grabbed my wrist and jerked me to a halt. Little surges of electricity ran down my arm from where he touched me, like he had a continuous current running through him.

"What's it going to take to change your mind?" he asked, with none of the hostility I expected considering he was on the verge of electrocuting me.

"I don't know why you'd want to." I yanked my arm free and rubbed my wrist.

"Because," he spat back, stopping just as quickly, his jaw clenching.

"That's not an answer."

He stalled, looking like he was in some sort of battle with himself before one side ultimately lost. "Because last night you apparently risked your life going over there to get answers for me. And while I watched you sleep, wondering if you were going to wake up again, I didn't see a fucking monster, Cash. I saw *you*."

"One and the same to you people." I slammed my shoulder into his, instantly regretting that decision as a burst of pain shot through my arm. Gritting my teeth and trying to ignore it, I stalked over to the balcony doors and yanked back the curtain, glaring out into the misty morning. The *one* good thing about this day so far — the fog would cover Graeme's imminent departure.

"Cassius?" Claudia called at the same time her knuckles rapped on the door.

"Fuck!" I threw up a wall of shadows and darted back to Graeme. He reached for me at the same time, grasping my arm with wide eyes.

The doorknob turned, catching the lock. "Why's the door locked?"

I hauled Graeme over to the balcony and shoved him out the door. "Get out!"

The lock clicked, but the ward held.

"Cassius! What's going on?" Claudia shouted.

"Wait!" Graeme whispered, right as I closed the door in his face and pulled the curtain back.

I sprinted across the room and launched myself into bed, yanking the covers up.

The bedroom door creaked open. "Cassius? What's going on? Why is it so dark in here?" Claudia whisked the shadows away as she stormed inside.

Mumbling pitifully from the bed, I focused my magic on my heart and slowed it down, along with my spastic breathing.

"Oh my God. Are you ok?" Claudia's steps hurried closer, but I didn't dare open my eyes. I felt her cool hands on either side of my face before one laid across my forehead. "Another migraine?"

Nodding weakly, I managed a pathetic, "Yeah." I knew the second she brought back the swirl of shadows, even with my eyes closed. "Thank you."

"I'll go get you some tea," she said softly, her footsteps already retreating to the door.

I waited until it closed again before springing off the bed and darting to the balcony. Slipping outside, I peered over the stone railing, hoping Graeme made it down without falling. Although there would have been some karmic justice in knowing he fell and smacked his head too. Not like he'd damage anything up there.

Suddenly, his face popped into view, inches from mine, and I nearly jumped out of my skin.

"That was close," he said with a mischievous grin, hanging onto the ivy like a damn squirrel.

Still clutching my thumping heart, I glared at him, half-tempted to shove him off the goddamn lattice. "What the fuck?! I told you to leave!"

"No, you told me to get out."

“Same fucking thing! You need to go before someone sees you.” I threw a cautious glance over my shoulder, in case Claudia crept back in.

“Meet me at the library tonight.” His mismatched eyes were practically glowing again, just like they had the night of Preston’s party.

“If it means you’ll leave, then fine. Now go.”

“One more thing.”

My molars ground together, suppressing the urge to throttle him. “What?”

He leaned up and grabbed me by the back of the head, yanking me close. As soon as I realized what he was doing, he pressed his lips to mine. A rush of warmth swept through me, along with a thousand more tingling sensations. By the time my brain managed to come up with a coherent thought, he was gone, climbing down the lattice as if he’d been doing it his whole life.

Landing on his feet softly, he looked up, giving me a wry grin, before darting off toward the gardens.

I closed my eyes and expelled a sharp breath.

He was so goddamn annoying! And yet, I couldn’t help the stupid little flutter in my stomach.

Chapter Seventeen

Graeme

Checking the time on my phone, I sighed, seeing only two minutes had passed since the last time I looked. I'd been waiting at the library for what seemed like forever. I even skipped my afternoon English lit class to make sure I didn't miss Cassius. Not that *that* was a great sacrifice on my part, but still. It was the thought that counted.

Maybe kissing Cassius right after he agreed to meet me wasn't the brightest move. I don't even know what came over me, except some madness in the moment. I blamed Shakespeare. Life imitating art and all that jazz.

Even as the sky grew darker, I didn't budge from my spot on one of the thick, stone railings that flanked the library steps. Something told me *if* he showed, it wouldn't be until after nightfall.

Finally — finally! — I spied him cutting across the commons, his hands tucked in his coat pockets and his collar popped against the autumn wind.

The damp, orange leaves I'd been swirling in a little cyclone exploded into the air when he reached the walkway that led directly to the library steps. They drifted down like autumn confetti. As soon as he took one step forward, the leaves behind him swirled around and settled on the ground again, laying out a pathway for him.

When he reached the stairs, he arched a dark brow, looking no more impressed with my leafy welcome than he did with anything else about me.

"Part of me didn't think you were coming," I admitted as he moved past me.

"I'm not failing this class because of you." He didn't even slow his steps. He just kept walking, right through the massive library doors.

Chuckling, I swung my leg off the railing and hopped down. I had to jog inside to catch up with him as he stepped onto the escalator. He was in black jeans again with a blue-collared shirt beneath his gray sweater. Despite his wool coat, I got a perfect view of his ass as we went up to the next level.

"Stop staring," he grumbled, stepping off the escalator.

"I wasn't."

He slid an annoyed look over his shoulder and dropped his messenger bag on a long, well-worn table, but didn't pull a chair out. "I'll be right back."

"Where are you going?"

"Getting books, genius. It's kind of an important part of research."

My initial happiness at seeing him was dwindling. Fast. I trailed after him as he disappeared into the endless stacks. "Can we ever have a civil conversation?"

"This *is* being civil." He stopped and turned toward the row of books, running his finger along the spines until he found whatever it was he was looking for. Pulling an old, faded book off the shelf, he flung it at me without even looking.

I caught it a second before it smashed into my face. The

second one he at least dropped in my arms instead of using it like a frisbee.

"Are we going to talk about the whole crossing over thing?" I asked.

"No."

"Why not?"

"Because I told you, it's none of your business." A third book thunked into my arms right before he disappeared around the corner of the massive bookcase.

"Do you still have those marks?"

"Would you lay off already?" he snapped, coming face-to-face with me as I rounded the corner to follow him.

"No," I shot back.

"Back off, Graeme." He gave me a withering glare before striding down the aisle. A moment later, a fourth book turned into another frisbee. I didn't have the hands to catch it, so it hit me square in the chest.

I let all four books fall to the floor and stepped over the pile, closing the distance between us. "Do you always have to be such a hard ass?"

"Do you always have to be such a pain in the ass?"

"Only if you want me to, baby." I slipped both hands around his hips and grabbed the ass in question, yanking his pelvis against mine. Personality aside, he was fucking perfect. The long, hard lines of his body melded with mine, like two puzzle pieces coming together.

He pushed against my chest, his fingers curling in the fabric of my maroon henley. "It's not happening, *baby*, so go bark up another tree."

"I like this tree." I backed him into the towering bookshelf and pinned him in place. I *really* liked this tree. For some stupid, inexplicable reason, Cassius was all I could think about these days. And whenever he was near me, all I wanted to do was touch him.

"The fuck you do," he scoffed. When I swept the dark strands off his forehead, he pulled his face away with a scowl. No matter what I did, he refused to look at me, but his body wasn't nearly as rigid as I'd expect. Well, except for one area. That was rigid as fuck, pressing against my thigh.

Sliding one hand up under his shirts, I reveled in the heat of his skin. For someone with such an icy exterior, he was fire underneath it all. I cupped the back of his neck with my other hand, brushing my lips against his cheekbone. "It doesn't have to be like this," I murmured.

His breathing came quicker and I swear the fingers that were twisted in my shirt pulled me closer instead of pushing me away. "Like what?"

"Our parents hate each other. It doesn't mean we have to."

"Speak for yourself."

Taking his face between both of my hands, I forced him to look at me. His stormy eyes met mine begrudgingly. Lightning might have been my power, but it felt like a bolt shot straight through me from that look alone. "Do you hate me, Cassius?"

"You know I do." His voice was hard, his face was hard, even his dick was hard. But the flicker of emotion behind that carefully cultivated facade, the way his grip tightened on my shirt... I didn't have to have divination powers to know he was fucking lying.

"That's a shame," I said, my lips brushing across his lightly. "Because I'm starting to kind of like you."

"I don't believe that for one second."

I caressed his face with both hands, dragging them down his throat to the silver chain around his neck. Lifting the crow skull out from beneath his sweater, I kept my eyes locked on his. Before I lost my nerve, I pressed down hard and fast, piercing the pad of my thumb with a wince.

Watching me with an unreadable expression, he simply

stood there, as still as a statue. It didn't even look like he was breathing.

Letting go of the skull, I lifted my hand, revealing the drop of crimson on my thumb.

He still didn't move, but I could finally see him breathing. His chest rose and fell faster until it stopped altogether when I dragged my thumb over the center of his bottom lip. The blood mixed with the wetness of his mouth and slipped off my skin, coating the inside of his lip.

His tongue peeked out, swiping the blood away.

His brain probably didn't even have time to register the coppery taste before I slanted my mouth over his, caressing his bloody tongue with mine. He inhaled sharply and, shockingly, pulled me closer, one hand on the back of my head and the other grabbing at my waist.

I kissed him back, as desperate for him as he apparently was for me. Both of our cocks were beyond hard, grinding against one another as our mouths ravaged the other's. Each of our hands clawed and grasped for whatever we could, trying to eliminate any possible space.

Oxygen was the only reason I pulled away, and even then Cassius continued kissing me, my throat, my clavicle, anywhere he could, throwing in a few bites along the way. "Fuck, Cash. I need you."

"Too bad," he mumbled, pulling my mouth to his again and replying between kisses. "We have to study."

"How am I supposed to study when you have me hard as a fucking rock?"

He spun us quickly and pushed me against the shelving. Unbuckling my belt, he tore open the front of my jeans and shoved them low on my hips. He freed my hard-on next, tucking the elastic band of my underwear underneath my balls, out of his way. "I'm not going to let you tank my GPA."

"How can you think about your GPA right now?"

Rather than answer, he kissed me again, stroking my cock right there where anyone could turn the corner. I suppose I should have cared, but I didn't. I was already too lost in the feeling of his hands and his mouth all over me, burning me from the inside out and making me want stuff I know I shouldn't.

Dropping to his knees, Cassius pressed his lips to the crown of my dick and then licked the slit gingerly. He made sure to make eye contact when he did it, equal parts amusement and desire in his blue eyes.

Tipping my head back, I closed my eyes and exhaled, trying to savor every moment. It turned to a gasp when the heat of his mouth enveloped all of my cock, his velvet tongue tracing abstract designs along the shaft as he moved up and down.

"Oh, God. Just like that..." I bit my lower lip to shut myself up, hanging onto the shelf overhead with both hands in case I passed out from sheer bliss. Thank God these bookcases weighed a thousand pounds and could support my weight, otherwise, we might have an embarrassing domino situation on our hands.

Cassius humored me a little longer, teasing me just so, before sucking hard, sliding back toward the head. Before I could warn him off of that particular move and that it would be game over in about two seconds, he swallowed the length of my cock to the hilt, only to do it again, hollowing his cheeks as he pulled his head back toward the tip.

"Fuck, fuck, fuck... Cash!" My fingers tightened on the shelf as my balls drew up. He massaged them gently while continuing to do magnificent things to my dick with his mouth. Despite the fact I wanted this feeling to last forever, I also knew every second we stayed was another chance at getting caught. Pretty sure the library would frown on BJs in the stacks, regardless of who we were descended from.

As soon as the first wave of my orgasm hit the back of his throat, he slipped his finger behind my balls and pressed against my taint. If my orgasm was comparable to a bottle rocket before, that little move put it in the mortar category. I doubled over, grabbing onto Cash's shoulder with one hand and the shelf behind me with the other before I crashed into him completely.

It was still several seconds after the last tremor wracked through me that I stayed in that position, trying to remember what planet I was on, and that my lungs actually needed oxygen. It was Cassius's self-satisfied chuckling that finally forced me to look up as he got to his feet again.

"Pick up the books," he said, grabbing my chin and pressing a chaste kiss to my lips. "And meet me at the table."

And there I stood — dick out, pants undone, chest heaving, watching the boy of my dreams step over the pile of books and turn the corner like he didn't just come in and wreck my fucking world.

Chapter Eighteen
Cassius

"Arsenic, lead, and belladonna," Graeme rattled off the ingredients, looking up at me with raised brows. "Where are we going to get any of that without getting on some government watchlist?"

I shot him an annoyed look over the top of my book. "My basement."

"You keep the ingredients for a seventeenth-century poison in your basement?"

"Well, not the belladonna," I said, flipping the page and scanning the text. "That's in the kitchen."

"Oh, yeah. Totally. Who doesn't keep belladonna in the kitchen?" He rolled his eyes and went back to scribbling in his notebook.

"It's a sedative," I pointed out with only a mild growl. Once again, the disparities in our magical upbringings were like night and day.

"It kills people!"

A guy and a girl walking by stopped suddenly, eyeing our table. They exchanged a look before moving on quicker than they were before, heads down and huddled together.

Leaning forward, I stole a quick glance around us before hissing my retort. "Say it a little louder next time! I don't think they heard you in New Hampshire!"

He expelled a short breath and grabbed another book, flipping through it as loudly as possible. Until that moment, I didn't even realize you *could* read a book loudly.

"What? What is it *now*?" I huffed right back at him, slamming my book flat on the table, lifting an irritated brow. "You've been fidgeting for an hour. It's driving me insane."

Throwing a glance over each shoulder, he leaned closer, lowering his voice. "You're honestly telling me your family doesn't have poisonous apple trees?"

"No, we don't." I held his stare, trying to make sense of the expression on his face. It was some mix of concern and confusion, not disbelief. "The only poison is the cyanide that is in *all* apples. Do I need to go eat one in front of you to prove it?"

"No." He glowered at the book in front of him.

"Ok, then what's with the face?" Not that I wanted to know the innermost thoughts of Graeme Hewitt, but if we were ever going to make headway on this stupid project, he needed to get it together. I thought a blowjob would help him focus on the task at hand. Apparently not.

"If it wasn't an apple that killed him, then what was it?" he asked, chewing on the end of his pen.

"I don't know."

"Your mom didn't say?"

Turning my gaze back to the book, I held my forehead in one hand in an effort to stave off a headache and avoid looking at him. "No."

"I mean, did you ask?"

"No, it totally slipped my mind," I replied, deadpan, trying to read the same paragraph on early modern alchemy for the third time.

"Why did you wake up talking about owls?"

"I don't know."

Out of nowhere, his hand landed in the center of my book and ripped it out from beneath my nose. "Bullshit."

Sighing, I tossed my pen on the desk and leaned back in my chair, folding my arms over my chest. He was never going to let it go until I threw him a bone, so I might as well get it over with. "I saw an owl. Ok? A big fucking owl that tried to tear my face off."

"What does that mean?"

"I don't know!" I closed my eyes and forced myself to inhale a breath and exhale it even slower. When I opened my eyes again, Graeme was watching me, his head cocked and his brows drawn with worry. "This may surprise you, but in our current situation, I know just as much as you do. I don't have the answers. Ok?"

He was quiet for a moment, chewing on his lower lip before speaking again. "Can I ask you something without you getting mad?"

I made a face for a split second before I bit my lips and schooled my features into something less hostile. "By all means."

"Do you think your mom did it?"

Swallowing thickly, I refused to let myself look away even though I was two seconds from flying out of this chair and strangling him if he so much as insinuated my mother was guilty. "Never. She would *never* hurt a child, no matter who his parents were."

He nodded, his gaze dropping to the book between us. "I didn't think so... She was distraught when she showed up at our house. I know I was young, but even then I didn't think you could fake that level of sadness."

"When I asked her about it, she said he was already gone by the time she got there. Did you ever look at the medical reports for a non-magical reason?"

Graeme's gaze flicked up to mine. "Yeah. My dad did.

They ruled the cause of death as natural causes. Something to do with weak heart valves or something. But my parents didn't believe them. They said it was your mom's magic that did it."

"She didn't have that kind of magic..." I looked away, blinking away the burning in my eyes.

"What kind did she have?" Normally I would have told him to fuck off, that it was none of his business, especially since she was dead. But for some reason, he sounded genuinely curious. And for the first time in six years it didn't hurt so much to actually talk about her.

"Birds," I said with a small laugh. "She could call the crows, like I can. And speak to the dead. Shadow work. But nothing that could harm, not like your parents accused her of."

Graeme gave me an unimpressed look. "Excuse you! Those crows almost pecked my eyes out. I wouldn't say that's harmless."

"In all fairness, you started it," I tossed back teasingly.

"If you would have just stopped walking, I wouldn't have had to trap your ass in a tornado."

"Oh, so it's *my* fault?"

"Well it's definitely not mine," he replied with a smile.

Lifting my chin, I gave him a slow perusal. This was the side of him I liked — the side I saw at Preston's before he turned into a total jackass. When he smiled and had that impish sparkle in his mismatched eyes and wasn't, you know, trying to fucking kill me.

The intercom overhead chimed softly, indicating we had ten minutes to clear out of the library. In the screaming silence that followed, I was struck by how much I was betraying my family. Revealing our magic to an outsider? No, not just an outsider. A sworn enemy. What the fuck was wrong with me?! Just because he batted his long lashes at me and had a nice smile. Jesus. I didn't even want to think about what we'd just done in the stacks.

We both stayed where we were, exchanging glances across the table, like we were each waiting for the other one to move first.

When it was clear he wouldn't, I closed my book and stacked it on top of the others. I reached for my bag, but my fingers clawed nothing but air. Looking up, it was dangling right next to me, suspended by Graeme's hand.

"Thank you," I murmured, slipping it over my shoulder.

"What are you doing right now?"

"Leaving...?" I blinked at him.

He rolled his beautiful eyes, the corner of his mouth tilted up in a half-smirk. "I mean *after* you leave the library. We could go get something to eat, if you want."

"Uh, no. I have class in the morning."

"So do I."

"Do you want congratulations?" Ducking my head, I made a beeline for the escalator, not sure where the hell he was going with this conversation. Studying and then food? That sounded like a date and *that* was *not* happening. Not in this town. And not with him. Ever.

"I still don't have your number," he said, hurrying after me.

"No, you don't."

"Don't you think I should?"

"Why? So you can hit me up for a booty call tonight? No thanks."

"No! Of course not! How about tomorrow night?" he asked with a laugh.

I stopped and spun so quickly he nearly ran into me. "No. Not tonight, not tomorrow, or any night from here until the end of time. Once, Graeme. That's all it was ever going to be."

He shook his head slightly as I spoke, like he couldn't believe a word I was saying. "But we—"

"No. We're lab partners. That's it."

"But you—"

"Don't make it personal," I snapped, walking toward the escalator again. I thought I left him behind when I started descending, but his voice was right behind me.

"Aw, baby. It's a little late for that. Don't you think?"

I stared straight ahead, doing my best to ignore him even though every single one of my senses was tuned into him whenever he was within a five-foot radius of me. I hated it. Hated him. How could I forget?

"What happened?" he asked as we stepped off the escalator.

"Could you be any more vague?" I gave him a scathing look as I strode toward the front door and shoved through it. I had to get away from him as fast as possible. Distance was the only thing that helped clear my head these days. Distance and the shock of cold night air in my lungs.

"I don't fucking get it, Cash. One minute we're talking. I mean, actually having a *real* conversation, and then the next you clam up. What gives?"

I turned the collar up on my coat, hoping it would block him as much as the wind. "You're imagining things."

"Just like I imagined you sucking my dick?"

His words brought me back to him like a boomerang. Grabbing him by the front of his jacket, I hauled him behind one of the large, sculpted columns in front of the library and shoved him into the shadows. "Would you shut the fuck up already?!"

"Why? Don't want to admit the truth, you fucking coward?"

"Don't want to get caught, you fucking moron! I don't know about your parents, but I know my family has plenty of people who will run to them in a heartbeat if they see us together."

"But we're lab partners," he threw back with a smile that bordered on a sneer. "Isn't that what you said? Why should it matter if anyone sees us together?"

"Because *some* people will use any excuse they can to murder a Necromancer." His jaw shifted, but I kept going. "I don't know what you want from me, but you better get used to the knowledge that you're not going to get it."

Like the prick he was, he smirked and bit his lip suggestively. "What if I already got it?"

"Then kudos to you. I can't wait to hear what shit the rumor mill is going to throw at my family next." Shoving away from him, I spun on the ball of my foot and strode away.

The entire way across campus, I cursed myself for being such a fucking idiot, for thinking Graeme Hewitt was anything but a manipulative piece of shit. When the rain started to fall, chilling me to the bone, I hated him all the more. Him *and* his fucking magic.

Chapter Nineteen

Graeme

Watching Cassius walk away from the library and not running after him took a surprising amount of self-restraint. For the minuscule amount of progress we made, he decided to throw us right back to square one. I had no idea what the hell happened or why a fairly decent conversation went south so quickly. Nor did I know why it bothered me quite so much.

Maybe it was because three hours ago we were ready to devour one another in the middle of the stacks. If he let me, I would have taken it further or at least reciprocated, but he insisted on actually doing homework. Then when it was time to leave? He looked at me like he'd rather cut his own dick off than spend one more minute in my presence.

And that dig about people talking? I mean, he wasn't wrong... Much like our Puritan ancestors, nothing stirred up the Winslow witch community like some good old-fashioned gossip. Except, I sure as shit wasn't going to tell anyone about us. Like there was even an "us" to begin with.

Cassius was right about one thing though — if people saw us, word would *definitely* get back to our parents. I didn't know what that meant for him, but judging how Dad reacted when he learned I was in class with a Corbin... it wouldn't be good. I was already on a short leash. Something as scandalous as this would land my ass under house arrest until I graduated.

Zipping my jacket up against the sudden chill, I stuffed my hands in my pockets and headed for my car in the parking garage, trying to think about anything except a moody, blue-eyed boy.

I was still mulling over the whole night and my strange interactions with Cassius the next morning when Preston dropped into the auditorium seat next to me for our meteorology class.

"You look like shit," he said, pulling out his pen and notebook.

"Thanks," I mumbled, burrowing deeper into my hoodie and trying to tune him out.

"India and I tried calling you last night. Where were you? I thought we were going to that fundraiser thing for her parents?"

"Shit, I'm sorry. I was at the library and completely spaced it."

He nodded, flipping to a fresh page. "It's ok. You didn't miss anything except a bunch of politics and petty squabbling."

"Isn't it always a bunch of politics and petty squabbling?"

He answered with a laugh. "In this town? Definitely."

Cam and Noah, two guys from our non-witch circle of friends, stopped in the aisle, tipping their chins up at us in greeting.

"You guys coming to the party Saturday night?" Cam asked, his thumb hooked around his backpack strap.

Preston and I shared a quick glance before we plastered on apologetic faces.

"I've got a family thing," I hemmed.

"Can't man," Preston said, sucking a breath between his teeth. "India and I have plans."

"Come on!" Cam pouted. "The rest of the swim team is going to be there! Like old times."

"I wish I could," I said with a grimace. "But you know my dad."

"Yeah, yeah. If you guys change your mind, hit me up. I'll text you the details." Cam nudged Noah and tossed his head further down the auditorium.

As soon as they were out of earshot, Preston turned to me with raised brows. "*We're* still on for Saturday though, right?"

"The equinox?"

"Yeah."

I shrugged, hoping he didn't realize I completely spaced that too. Using my dad as an excuse for bowing out of social obligations had become second nature over the years, I didn't even realize I actually *had* a family thing for once. "Yeah. Of course."

"Cool." He nodded and pulled his phone out, texting someone with a dopey smile on his face. Probably India. God, they made me sick.

Before I lost my nerve, I blurted out the words circling my brain. "Hey, can I ask you something?"

"Shoot."

"What's the deal with that Corbin guy?"

Preston lowered his phone, making a face before quirking a sandy brow. "You mean Cassius?"

"Yeah." I shrugged one shoulder, trying to look only vaguely interested in whatever the answer was, despite asking the question.

Preston shrugged as well. "I don't know. I mean, you know pretty much all there is to know."

"You guys are, like, friends, right?"

"Sure. I mean, as much as we can be. I haven't seen him for a while. And now that I'm with India, I don't have a lot of free time between her and the shit I have to do for my dad and the Congregation."

"Where's he been this whole time?"

"After his mom… you know… His dad flipped. Claudia was already away at college, so he didn't have to worry about her. But Cassius? His dad literally packed him up in the middle of the night and sent him to England to some boarding school. He didn't even get to go to his mom's funeral." Preston shook his head, genuine sadness in his hazel eyes.

"Why? That's so… extreme." Although, had the roles been reversed, I could totally see my dad doing the same thing. I might not have been sent to boarding school like Cassius, but any sense of freedom I had practically vanished that night.

Preston made a face. "Come on, man. His wife was just mur—died. He was trying to protect his kid."

"Yeah, I guess… so you didn't talk to him while he was gone?"

He shook his head. "Not really. A couple emails in the beginning, but they tapered off. I asked about him through Lennox and Arden, but… It was just hard, man." He shrugged. "Why are you asking about him?"

"Ainsworth made us lab partners." I blew out a breath and shook my head, tapping my pen idly on my book. "I'm just, I don't know… Trying to make the best of it, I guess. It seems like every other word out of my mouth pisses him off, and it's not like he'll tell me any of this shit."

"I mean, if my family was in a blood feud with my lab partner's family, I wouldn't be too chatty, either."

"*I* didn't fucking kill anyone," I mumbled. "But sometimes, the way he looks at me, it's like he'd murder me on the spot if he could. How can you hate someone so much for something they didn't even do?"

Preston's head swiveled in my direction. "Really? You're pissed because he doesn't like you without knowing you? Until I was friends with Lennox, Peyton had me *convinced* Necromancers baked babies in pies and ate them. That's what the old stories said. Hell, that's what our *parents* said. He even had a book about Necromancers and everything that he used to show me. We're all prone to pre-judging people."

"You have a book on Necromancers?"

He shook his head. "Not anymore. Percy stole it from Peyton and then his dumb ass lost it. It's a shame. It was a pretty cool book."

"Yeah, that sucks." I slunk down in my chair, staring ahead glumly while our teacher started rambling about pressure systems.

As usual, the only thing I could think about lately was Cassius. Instead of paying attention in class, joining in the stilted conversation with Dad at dinner, or even partying during the equinox gathering the following Saturday, I dwelled on a blue-eyed boy who looked at me like *I* was the fucking monster. No matter how many times I revisited that night at the library, I couldn't figure out what I'd done wrong or why he was so fucking pissed when he left.

India plopped down on the fallen log next to me, handing me a bottle of beer. "Why are you moping? It's the equinox. You should be celebrating."

"I'm tired," I lied, taking a swig. It didn't matter that we were underage and our parents were a mere twenty feet away, sipping their own homemade wines and meads. Congregation celebrations meant everyone, thirteen and up, was allowed to drink if they so chose and I *definitely* took advantage of that perk. It was one thing my dad hadn't taken away from me yet.

The firelight made India's copper hair especially vibrant when she cocked her head, silently announcing her disbelief.

"Just have a lot on my mind," I added. "That's all."

"Corbin?"

I turned my attention to the beer bottle, picking idly at the label.

Unfortunately for me, she knew me too well and wasn't about to let it go. "Why didn't you tell anyone Corbin attacked you that night before the Meeting?"

"I'm not so sure it was him," I replied offhandedly, rolling the cold, brown bottle between my palms to stop from picking.

"What? That night you said—"

"I know what I said." I cleared my throat, minding my tone when I continued. "But I don't think he'd do something like that. He's not afraid of a fight. He wouldn't attack me in the dark. He'd come at me head-on." Like he had... on so many occasions.

"Are you crazy?" India gaped at me, lowering her voice for the next part when she realized how fucking loud she was. "Of course he'd do something like that! They all would! They're not good people, Graeme."

I took another swig of beer to avoid having to answer her. At least right away.

She shook her head, either annoyed by my silence or my naïveté. "I'm going to go see if my parents are ready to get started. I want to be out of here before those freaks show up for their half of the ritual."

Before I could say anything, she got to her feet and ventured back to the main bonfire, leaves and twigs snapping under her shoes.

As soon as I was in the clear, I chugged half the bottle of

beer. I wanted to be out of here before Cassius showed up, too. I didn't want to inadvertently make him mad again, nor did I want to stand around and watch him do whatever ritual the Necromancers did in the dark half of the night. I'm sure I wouldn't be welcome, anyway. That's why the nature witches tended to clear out before midnight.

Forcing myself to my feet, I was one step away from my log when something crackled to the side. Pausing, I looked left, toward the bonfire. People from the Congregation were either milling about or standing in clusters, chatting about who knew what, their laughter bouncing off the trees.

Another dry snap echoed to my right, deep in the woods where I couldn't see beyond the light cast by the bonfire. Dad always said the North Woods were haunted. He drilled it into my head that I shouldn't venture near the old Winslow village unless it was with the rest of the Congregation for occasions such as these. I always thought he was full of shit. I'd never seen a ghost in my entire life, let alone a vengeful one. But maybe he was right.

The shadows in front of me shifted, moving between the trees.

Squinting in a vain attempt to see any sort of shape or detail, I took a step forward.

Something big and blacker than the night moved with me. Loud cracks sounded, scattering the underbrush hidden beneath a carpet of red and orange leaves.

A deep, guttural growl made the hair on the back of my neck stand up. People continued to laugh and talk behind me, unaware that something was circling us in the dark. Whatever it was, it was something decidedly *not* human and I was willing to venture not a fan of nature witches.

Backing away slowly, my gaze darted from side to side, looking for any sign of what it was. Just when I thought I'd zero in on it, the darkness would move again with dizzying speed.

As soon as I took a step, the crashing got louder. Twigs and branches snapped underfoot, from me and from whatever *it* was. The shadows shifted again. It was too fast, too loud, too big. Too… everything. And it was charging right toward the Congregation.

A female's scream shattered the night air.

I stopped abruptly and whirled toward the bonfire. There were two, all of a sudden, burning with an unnatural brightness. The main one and a smaller one moving in erratic circles. No, that wasn't another bonfire. It was a fucking person!

Sprinting back to the clearing, I tried to summon rain on the move, but it was hard to concentrate on magic and not trip at the same time.

People were screaming and shouting, so loud it sounded like the noise was pressing in from all sides.

Thunder rumbled along the ground as I ran. It took my brain a minute to register what it was, but it was a sound I recognized. Now I knew what I'd seen in the woods. It was Cassius on his fucking horse, lurking in the dark like always.

The female screamed again, refocusing my attention on what mattered more than some Necromancer with a chip on his shoulder.

Someone grabbed a blanket and threw it on the person, knocking them to the ground and patting at them wildly while one of the water witches conjured a deluge.

I slid to a halt, nearly crashing into Preston when he stood up from the blanketed lump, horror twisting his face.

"What the fuck?! What happened?" I asked.

"It's India," he said, breathing hard. His face was streaked with smoke, tear marks leaving trails through the soot.

"What?! What happened?" I turned toward her as Dr.

Dane waved away the group of people, making room for himself.

"Out of my way!" he barked.

Treadwell was also there, keeping the Tenneys away from the smoldering pile that used to be my best friend. Mrs. Tenney screamed and clawed at the air for her daughter, while Mr. Tenney looked like he was either a step away from throwing up or murdering someone.

"She's alive!" Dr. Dane shouted.

Peregrine rushed forward, dropping next to him. "Help me lift her. Carefully!"

A couple of the other experienced witches came forward, either to help physically lift her or use whatever magic they could to assist.

"What the fuck happened?" I asked, shaking Preston's shoulder to get him to look at me.

"I don't know." He blinked, releasing more tears down his face. "She was arguing with Lennox about the bonfire bull-shit. I was on my way over but she walked away. She wasn't even near the fire. But then she just… erupted."

"Lennox?! Where the fuck is he now?!" I was going to kill him. I was going to rip him limb from fucking limb before the Selectmen got their hands on him and tucked him away for safekeeping and a fair trial. He didn't deserve a fair trial. He deserved to burn in his own hellfire.

"I don't know," Preston mumbled. "I can't believe he would—" The thought died off in a strangled sob.

I scanned the area, searching the crowd for any of the dark families. There wasn't a Corbin, an Ambrose, or a Simms to be found. The only one with a murky allegiance was Dr. Colburn, who'd sidled up to Dr. Ainsworth for a huddle, making herself untouchable. Even the Olivers were gone.

"I gotta go." Preston hurried off after his father and the sound of car doors slamming in the night.

I spun in the opposite direction and stormed through the woods as fast as I could for my Jeep. Instead of tearing down the main path we used to get in to the North Woods, I turned east and drove straight for Norwood Bridge — an alternate entrance into the North Woods and the fastest route to the Corbin estate.

Chapter Twenty
Cassius

"What in God's name happened?" Dad asked as the three of us dismounted in the middle of the stable.

"I don't know," I replied, looking at Claudia and hoping she had the answer.

She was equally wide-eyed. "Lennox was there and India got on his case about the fire. I don't know what she said, but he yelled back and then he walked away. I saw him with his parents right before..."

"And where were you?" Dad asked, whirling on me. "Why were you late?"

"Me?" I blinked. "I just got there! I thought Lucius picked up a rock at the edge of the woods. I didn't see anything except you two riding toward me, yelling at me to go home."

Dad's face remained hardened. "No one leaves the house until I say so."

I gaped at him. "Dad, I have—"

"No, Cassius! Your professors will understand. I don't want either of you out of my sight until we know more about what happened. First the murder on campus and now an attack during the fall equinox?" He shook his head, stopping himself from saying what he was really thinking.

"Who said it was an attack?" I asked, but Claudia's question drown me out.

"What about work?" she asked. "I'm on call this weekend."

"No one leaves this house," Dad repeated. "That includes me. Nathaniel will understand or he'll deal with me."

Claudia and I exchanged a sullen look while Dad walked away, leading his horse down the aisle to its stall. And that was the end of *that* conversation.

Sighing, I turned Lucius's head and walked away, shoulders rounded.

After he'd been untacked, groomed, and given his customary peppermint, I headed up to my room to begin the lockdown my father insisted on.

As soon as I opened my bedroom door, I knew I wasn't alone. The cold gust of wind blowing in from the open balcony door was the first clue. The second was the figure that lunged at me, slamming the bedroom door shut and pushing me against the wall in the same breath.

"Was it him?!" Graeme's voice growled in the darkness.

"What are you talking about?"

"Your fucking cousin! Did he attack India?"

"No! He didn't!" I shot back, shoving Graeme away from me and stalking to the center of the room.

He didn't turn on the lights, but little blue sparks danced on his fingertips before they sailed through the air, lighting the candles in the wall sconces. Since I could see just fine in the dark, it was strictly for his own benefit. "If it wasn't him, who was it?"

"Who's to say it wasn't you?" I drew myself up as he came closer, matching his accusatory glare with one of my own. "You might not control fire, but electricity is close enough." In case he missed the point, I threw my arms wide, gesturing to the flickering candles.

"Everyone knows the Ambroses control fire. He's the only

one who—" Graeme's face twisted, a mix of horror and revulsion. He stumbled back a step, expelling a hard breath of air. "Your mother was a fucking *Ambrose*!"

"You think it was me?!" My eyes widened at the accusation. I wiped the surprise from my face and replaced it with anger. Taking a step forward, my jaw and fists clenched in tandem. "Why would *I* do something like that to her? To anyone, for that matter?"

"Still pissed about her outdoing you at the meetinghouse? I don't know. Do you people even need a reason to kill?"

I shoved him in the chest, black mist swirling between my fingers and adding force to the blow. "Fuck you, Graeme!"

Spinning away from him before I did something even more stupid, I stopped abruptly and cast a baleful glare over my shoulder. "And for your information, my power as it relates to fire is almost nonexistent! I can extinguish it because of my shadow magic. I can't fucking conjure it from nothing!"

"Fine. If it wasn't you, and you claim it wasn't Lennox, then who was it?"

"I don't know! Why the fuck do you keep coming to me for all of the answers?!" It was all I could do to keep from screaming down the walls out of sheer frustration.

"Well, she's not a fucking phoenix, Cassius! She didn't just spontaneously combust!"

"Maybe she did?" I spread my arms wide in a helpless gesture. "Stranger things have happened. You know magic finds a way to keep the balance."

He shook his head, crossing his arms over his chest. "I don't why I'm even asking you. It's not like I can trust a word that comes out of your mouth."

Incensed by what felt like a challenge, I stormed past him and rooted around in the top drawer of the cabinet. Shoving bones, crystals, and half-burnt candles out of the way, I found the small jewelry box in the back corner.

Yanking it out, I slammed the drawer shut and crushed the box against his chest. "There. Since you're so fucking convinced I have some dastardly agenda, take this and fuck off! I'll see you in class."

"What is it?" he asked, cracking open the antique box carefully. His brow furrowed as he lifted the amulet up for a closer inspection, his thumb running across the engraving on the black stone.

"What the fuck does it look like?" I snapped back. "It's an amulet. It pretty much negates my power against you. So feel free to *stop* accusing me of fucking murder every time you turn around!"

His eyes remained suspicious, but the rest of his face relaxed the tiniest bit. "Why do you even have something like this?"

"For this very reason. Because in order for us to be close to anyone outside our family, we have to bend over backwards proving that we're not evil incarnate. And you self-righteous assholes *still* blame us for everything."

Rather than ask if he wanted a demonstration, I simply did it. Summoning a ball of black energy, I hurled it at him while he was studying the necklace. It crashed against an invisible wall, scattering black mist like wisps of smoke.

He ducked anyway, covering his face with his arms. "What the fuck?!"

"See?" I held his bewildered gaze for a moment before I moved past him once more, out to the balcony. Turning my face up to the night sky, I closed my eyes and exhaled a slow breath, willing my anger to dissipate with it. Giving him an artifact like that was beyond stupid but necessary if we were going to finish this goddamn project for Ainsworth. Although, at this point, I wasn't sure it was simply my pride driving me to one-up him all the time. It's not that I wanted to impress him… but maybe I did. Maybe *if* I did, Necromancers wouldn't be as shunned as we were.

Graeme joined me on the balcony, resting his hand on the stone railing right next to mine. When he spoke, he was much calmer than before. He almost sounded sad. "Do you think this is happening because of us?"

"What are you talking about?" I opened my eyes and turned, startled to find him staring at me intently.

"You had a point about magic finding a balance. Nature does the same thing. So, did we disrupt something by being... together?"

I scoffed, turning my attention back to the starry sky. "Don't be ridiculous."

"How is that being ridiculous? Every marriage between a Hewitt and a Corbin has ended in bloodshed. Is that a coincidence?"

"No, that's centuries of hate and bigotry at work. Marriage is a convenient way to get close enough to murder one another." I bit off my answer before I added, *just like being fuck buddies*. I shot him a look anyway to see if he had a similar thought. Not surprisingly, he was still watching me, but his face was unreadable.

"Do you think it's all true?" he asked, his gaze flicking to the side, shyly, before coming back to mine. "The stories about our families?"

"No. I don't know. Maybe parts of it. My mom used to say there are three sides to every story. Ours, theirs, and the truth was somewhere in the middle. Regardless of what's true or why, a lot of fucking people have died. It's a miracle any of us are left."

"Then on behalf of the Hewitts, I'm sorry," Graeme said, so quietly I almost thought I made it up.

I furrowed my brow and looked at him. When he didn't elaborate, I asked the obvious. "For what?"

"For accusing you. And your cousin. And for what my dad did..." He swallowed hard, his gaze dropping, like the weight of his father's crime was hanging on his own shoulders.

"I'm sorry about your friend," I offered, clearing my throat softly, suddenly unable to look at him. "And your brother..."

His pinky stroked mine slowly. It was barely even a touch, the most minuscule amount of contact ever, and yet heat flared from that spot and spread through the rest of my body like wildfire.

My breath caught when he shifted closer. His whole hand covered mine and curled around it, holding it like it was the most natural thing in the world and not a profound act of... I didn't even know. Rebellion? Betrayal? Insanity? Insanity explained a lot of the past few weeks.

We stayed like that for a moment, each staring out at the darkness, the heat radiating between us. Those little tingles were back, racing up and down my arm and I wondered if he could feel them too.

After a while, he turned to face me and tugged me forward. With one hand still holding mine, he slid the other around my waist and pulled me against his chest, his eyes glimmering from starlight and the flicker of candles.

"What are you doing?" I knew I'd asked the question, but I hardly recognized my own voice anymore.

"What does it feel like I'm doing?" he murmured in return, brushing his lips along my cheek, down my face. Using his nose to nudge my head back, he pressed kisses to the underside of my jaw and the column of my throat.

"You have to go," I said, trying to remain firm and not melt into a puddle at his feet. "They're going to be looking for you. I'm sure Peregrine is calling for a Meeting as we speak."

"I don't care. I want to stay here. With you."

"Two seconds ago you accused me of setting your friend on fire."

"I didn't mean it."

"You mean your dick didn't mean it. Your brain certainly did."

"My brain is confused. All I know is that *you* are all I can think about these days. You're driving me crazy, Cash. It's like nothing in the world makes sense until you come around, then everything feels… right."

I shook my head, trying to tune him and all of his nonsense out. "Even more reason for you to leave. This is getting out of hand."

"Why are you fighting this?" He pushed me back against the railing gently, pressing his hips into mine. The fact both of us were hard wasn't even shocking at this point. It seemed to be a theme of our encounters. Scream at each other, try to hurt each other with words or magic, and then end up in a compromising position. I would agree with him on one thing and one thing only — it *was* confusing.

Still, my pride was on the line. He couldn't just fucking insult me *and* my entire family and expect me to take it lying down. Literally. Or standing or however he wanted to do it.

"You're insane," I said, though the words lacked their usual venom.

"Or bewitched." He tipped my chin up with one finger, meeting my gaze with a sexy smirk. "Did you hex me, Necromancer?"

"Why would I do something as stupid as that? I don't want to be associated with you for any longer than necessary."

"You tell me. You're supposed to be the evil one, after all."

"So I've heard."

I should have been prepared for it, but when he leaned in and captured my mouth with his, I was anything but ready. The softness of his mouth, the plush lips and velvet tongue, was completely contradictory to the words that fell from it. *He* was a contradiction, just like his eyes. An asshole, for sure, but also caring when he wanted to be. And funny and—

No, Cassius!

Something inside me overwhelmed that little voice, silencing it as our bodies pressed together.

Even through our jeans, his dick commanded attention, rubbing against mine until we were both sighing and whining for more. Little sparks of warmth flickered across my skin wherever he touched me. I didn't know if it was his magic, or just *him,* drawing feelings out of me that he shouldn't have been able to reach.

"Fuck, Cash. I have to have you."

I shook my head despite the fact I palmed his cock, stroking him through the denim. "No."

"Baby, please." He did me one better and unzipped my pants, sliding his hand inside to jerk me at the same pace I was teasing him.

"This is my father's house. He'll kill you if he finds you."

"We'll be quiet." His other hand caressed the curve of my ass, suddenly slipping between my cheeks and pressing into my hole enough to make me gasp. "See? You can be quiet when you need to."

My retaliatory glare didn't last long before his lips were on mine, his tongue invading my mouth. He lifted the hem of my shirt and pulled it off slowly, discarding it to the side. It was open season on my skin; his hands and mouth touched and kissed practically every inch of it while he worked down to my abdomen.

A shiver rippled through me, goosebumps spreading

across my body from him and the cold autumn night combined. Before he dropped to his knees, I took his hand and pulled him back inside where neither of us would freeze to death for the sake of our stupid hormones.

I helped him shed his clothing before kicking off my jeans. Walking backward to the bed, I bit my lower lip, taking in the sight of him completely naked. I didn't really have the opportunity to before, which was a shame because he was fucking incredible. Long, lean muscles and smooth skin still hanging on to what must have been a glorious summer tan.

Easing onto the bed on my stomach, I crooked a finger at him.

He closed the distance eagerly, stooping to kiss me, both hands in my hair.

As soon as he pulled away, straightening again, I licked the length of his cock. One small gesture that acted like an anchor, holding him in place without any physical effort. Graeme closed his eyes and exhaled, his fingers returning to my hair.

I sucked him into my mouth, swirling my tongue against him while caressing his balls.

"Your mouth is fucking amazing," he groaned, hips thrusting now and again. He really hadn't seen anything yet. The library was good, but it wasn't my best.

Popping off the end of his dick, I turned over onto my back and hung my head off the edge, pulling him back toward me by his hips. Instinctively, his cock slotted back into my mouth, sliding in all the way to the hilt with zero effort, thanks to the angle.

"Oh, fuck! Baby!" His eyes rolled up into his head, but not for long. He was too interested in watching his dick disappear down my throat again and again. I stroked his shaft when I wasn't deep-throating him, varying the speed and pressure and adding a twist on occasion.

Squeezing his ass, I pulled him in as far as I possibly could. He doubled over, bracing his hands against the mattress on either side of me. "Oh my fucking God," he rasped as I slid out from beneath his perch, wiping the saliva from my chin with the back of my hand. As soon as his gaze met mine, he grabbed my face in both hands and crushed his lips against mine. We collapsed backward onto the mattress, his tongue ravaging my mouth.

"I wasn't finished," I said in short bursts whenever I could wrest my lips from his.

"I don't want to come yet." Although his flushed and rigid cock would suggest otherwise.

His kisses made me dizzy, each one like another shot of the best alcohol in the world. Thankfully, he gave me a reprieve. Shifting onto his knees, he pulled me up with him before shoving me back down on all fours. I didn't have to guess what was going to happen next, especially when he grabbed a cheek in each hand and squeezed, spreading me wider. He dove in with a groan that sent tremors throughout my body.

"Oh, fuck…" I squeezed my eyes shut, reprimanding myself for talking when the goal was supposed to be silence.

As soon as his tongue circled the rim, a moan slipped out. I bit my lips together and fisted the comforter, willing myself to be quiet. He pulled back and spit at the area he was working on, lashing at my hole with his tongue like some sort of punishment.

"Fuck me," I sighed, wave after wave of pleasure rippling through every single nerve in my body.

A familiar burn spread through my entrance, accompanied by one of his long fingers. I pressed my forehead against the mattress, trying to keep my groaning to a minimum.

"Aw, baby. You're so goddamn tight," he murmured as his

finger slid in and out slowly. "I'm not going to last more than two minutes. You've got me so fucking hard."

He was hard? If the wind blew just right, I was going to come all over the place. And since wind was part of his bag of tricks, I wouldn't put it past him.

Forcing myself to swallow, I pushed myself up on my hands and glanced behind me. "Go to the cabinet."

He followed my gaze to the large armoire, his brow furrowing. Actually doing as I said without argument, he slipped off the bed and opened the doors cautiously, like something was lying in wait.

"See the blue bottle? Next to the quartz? Grab it. No, the *other* quartz."

After pawing through the collection of crystals, he found the one I was talking about. He uncapped it as he climbed back onto the bed, sniffing the rim. His nose wrinkled slightly, accompanying his curious grin. "What is this?"

"Altar oil."

"Well halle-fucking-lujah." He poured some onto his hand and immediately picked up where he left off, sliding his finger back in with ease. On the second pass, he added another. "Fuck, Cash... This stuff smells amazing. And who knew it would work like *magic*."

"Oh my God. Stop making puns and fuck me already," I breathed, trying to enjoy everything he was doing without having a fucking orgasm on the spot.

"Are you ready, baby?"

"More than ready."

He slid his fingers out carefully and snagged the bottle again, pouring more of the oil into his hand and coating his cock with it. Instead of going for it, though, he flipped me onto my back and wedged himself between my thighs.

I was surprised he'd want such an intimate position, but I wasn't about to complain. He could have fucked me upside down and I would have been happy, just as long as he was inside me.

Teasing my entrance with the tip of his hard-on, he raked his teeth over his lower lip, like he was hesitating. A look I didn't quite know how to interpret crossed his face.

"What's wrong?" My stomach twisted while I waited for the answer. That look generated a hundred different thoughts in my brain, none of them good. They all centered on one common conclusion — he finally realized *this* was wrong. *We* were wrong. On so many levels.

"Nothing," he replied with a small smile. "Just enjoying the view." Bracing one hand above my shoulder, he leaned down, kissing me with none of the reservation I saw a minute ago.

Despite the fact he'd started pushing inside, his lips never left mine. I'd be lying if I said I didn't notice him sliding deeper and deeper, but I was more concerned with his mouth and the way he took over mine completely. Somehow over these past few weeks he'd captured all of me and I didn't even realize it had happened until it was too late.

Unlike before, his thrusts were slower but deeper as a result. He caressed the side of my face, gazing down at me with those oddly beautiful eyes. "Is this what you wanted?"

"I know it's what *you* wanted." With a flick of his hips, he thrust in quicker, stealing my breath.

"Tell me you wanted it."

I shook my head, knowing full well what the repercussions would be for denying him. He didn't disappoint.

Pushing himself up onto his knees again, Graeme grabbed my thighs and yanked me up into his lap while slamming inside. He kept up the punishing pace, torturing himself as much as me if the look on his face was anything to go by. Cheeks flushed and eyes half-closed, his gaze stayed locked on mine, reiterating his silent demand.

"I want it," I panted, giving in to him at the same time I wrapped my hand around my shaft. "Fuck, Graeme. I want it. I want you."

"Tell me how much."

"So fucking much." Squeezing my eyes shut, I stroked myself harder, faster, trying to keep time with him.

"Mmm… I think you've had enough for now," he said with a dark laugh.

And then he was gone, leaving me beyond confused and frustratingly unsatisfied.

My eyes flew open, watching him pour more of the oil into his hand. Except this time, he rubbed it all over *my* dick. I must have made a face because he chuckled. "Don't tell me you haven't thought about it."

"I take it you have."

"Since the first night I saw you."

Once I thoroughly coated, he crawled up onto the bed and laid on his stomach, sending a smirk over his shoulder.

While I wanted to appreciate his ass — and I did — I was also somewhat distracted by the slashes on his back. They were still healing, three pink lines instead of the bloody cuts from the last time I saw them.

Rolling over, I straddled him from behind and massaged his ass cheeks. Even those were perfect, round and firm and everything a swimmer's body should be. How could he be so annoying and so sexy at the same time? It made my brain hurt.

He propped himself up on an elbow, gazing back at me with a furrowed brow. "Everything ok?"

Jesus, Cassius. Focus.

I gave myself a mental slap and nodded. "Yep. Just admiring your stupidly blessed genetics."

Of course he didn't buy it. He squinted for a second before reaching back and tapping my thigh. As soon as I moved off of him, he rolled over onto his knees, facing me directly. "Have you topped before?"

Well, shit. I'm pretty sure he knew the answer the second my gaze darted to the other side of the room. "Not with a guy," I mumbled, for clarification's sake. I didn't want him to think I was *completely* inept, just mildly inexperienced in this particular aspect.

I expected mockery of some sort or another insult. Needless to say, I was surprised when his fingers threaded through my hair, gently turning my head back toward him.

"You don't have to," he said quietly. "I should have asked first. I'm sorry."

"No, I want to." The words came out in a rush.

"But… you want to save it for someone you *actually* like. I get it."

"See? This is your problem. You just *assume* everything." For whatever reason, him being so goddamn nice was motivation to keep going. He was beyond annoying now and I wanted to prove him wrong. It's not that I didn't want to top him. Not at all. I just didn't want it to suck. He was clearly more experienced than I was based on our previous hookups, and I didn't want to lose face. But that concern went right out the window with the need to prove myself.

Before he could issue some other platitude, I seized his face and kissed him hard. Apparently the nice-guy act was just for show since he didn't waste any time stroking both of our cocks together in his hand, moaning into my mouth.

Breaking away, I turned him by the shoulders and shoved him back down to the mattress on his stomach. I resumed my earlier position and this time, I didn't hesitate. Slipping my fingers down his crease, I rubbed what was left of the oil on my hand onto him before sliding the first finger inside.

"Oh, yes," Graeme sighed into the mattress as my finger moved in and out. "Just like that, baby."

"Yeah?"

"Yeah."

"You want more?"

"Uh huh." To emphasize his point, his hips flicked backward, pushing against my hand.

Pressing a second finger inside, I stroked myself with my other hand, enjoying every muffled whimper and gasp he made.

I didn't let him enjoy it too long since I didn't want him coming on my hand. I wanted to be buried inside of him, to experience every bit of his orgasm from the inside out.

Shifting up behind him, I straddled his thighs and grabbed the bottle of oil again, reapplying to both of us. I lined my cock up with his hole and exhaled, pushing inside the tight entrance.

He clawed the mattress and bit his lip but it barely stifled the groan. Or maybe the groan came from me. I wasn't sure because all of my senses were fully engaged in my dick and what it was doing. Who it was doing it to and where we were only added to the thrill.

"Oh God," I whispered, sliding deeper and deeper until I came flush with his perfect ass. "Oh, fuck, Graeme..."

"Is it everything you imagined?" he asked, his breathing heavy and his fingers twisted in the sheets.

"More." Rocking my hips back and forth gently, I held onto his ass cheeks, partly for balance and partly because I wanted to watch my dick as it went in and out. Bottoming was great, but *this* was something else altogether. Now that I'd experienced it, I couldn't imagine sticking to one role ever again.

On the next thrust, he threw his hips back to meet mine. We both groaned.

"Baby... you feel amazing," he panted, meeting each thrust with unrestrained lust.

I stretched out over the top of his back and kissed him over his shoulder. Thanks to our similar height, it was easy to keep fucking into him while claiming his mouth as mine, too. And that's exactly what I was doing — claiming him. Every fucking part. No matter what happened after this, in this moment Graeme Hewitt was *mine.*

The need for air forced my mouth from his and I pulled away with a gasp. We were both breathing hard and sweating, our bodies moving together like they were meant to do this.

I paused, only so I could roll us both onto our sides. He draped his top leg over mine and leaned back into me, biting his lower lip when I resumed thrusting. The intention had been for me to jerk him off at the same time, but he whispered, "Harder," and shot that plan down.

One arm tightened over his shoulder and across his chest, while I gripped his waist with my other hand, holding him in place as best I could and driving myself into him, over and over.

"Fuck!"

I don't even know who yelled it. A shock of electricity rippled down my thighs and right through the very center of my body. Not the metaphorical kind. Actual goddamn electricity.

I couldn't help but cry out, both from the surprise and my own orgasm breaking over me like a wave. We fell away from one another, him forward onto his stomach, while I landed on my back, panting through the aftershocks and the strange prickly feeling running through me.

After catching his breath, Graeme rolled over with a satiated smile. "Wow," he breathed, his eyebrows lifting in a pleased sort of way. "That was—"

"What the fuck was that?" I pulled away from him,

studying his reaction for the real answer his lying mouth probably wouldn't give.

He blinked. "What?"

"What do you mean 'what'?" I scooted as far away as I could until my back hit the headboard. "Did you not *feel* that?"

His dark brows came together and he sat up, his mouth curving downward. "Feel what?"

"Oh my God. I know you're a weather witch, but get your shit together! You could have killed me just now."

Realization finally dawned on him. His eyes widened before he looked away, jaw slack. "Oh my God… that was magic? I thought it was… I don't know. Super intense."

"Electrifying," I deadpanned. Shaking my head, I crawled off the other side of the bed and headed for the bathroom.

So it wasn't just his hands that conducted the electricity. It was his whole body. That was… wow. Unheard of. No wonder people assumed he'd be the next Deacon. He had enough power to destroy an entire city if he wanted to and he probably wouldn't even break a sweat, if he could just get that shit under control.

I was waiting for the shower to heat up when Graeme appeared, slipping his arms around my waist from behind and resting his chin on my shoulder.

"I'm sorry," he murmured. "I didn't know that would happen. It never has before."

"Why did it?"

"I don't know."

"You don't know?" I turned and arched an eyebrow at him. "How can you not know what triggers your powers? That's witchery 101."

"I know what triggers them. It's just been getting stronger lately." He bit his lip and looked away sheepishly. "I go to do one thing, but something else happens. Or I don't mean to do it at all, and it still comes out. Like tonight."

"What did your parents say?"

He shrugged, still not looking at me. "Haven't told them."

"Why the fuck not? That shit is dangerous, Graeme! Active powers like that need to be discharged — regularly. Otherwise you could end up frying the next person you sleep with."

For some reason that last sentence is what provoked a reaction. His gaze darted back to mine, narrowed slightly. "The next person? You think I'm out there sleeping around with whoever?"

"I don't know and I don't care," I huffed at his indignation, hoping it covered the lie. "Fuck the whole campus if you want. It's none of my business."

"What about this?" he asked, reaching for me, his eyes soft, like a puppy I'd just dropkicked.

"This," I said, swatting his hand away, "was *never* a thing. This is lab partners. This is two people who belong to the same Congregation and whose families fucking hate each other. That's it." I stopped short of saying it was a mistake — which it was. A huge fucking mistake we'd now repeated, in every sense of the word, twice. There wouldn't be a third time. There couldn't be.

A flicker of anger darted across his face, the muscles in his throat tightening. "I refuse to accept that. Maybe you could have gotten away with saying that shit before, but not now."

"Refuse all you want. That's the way it is." I walked into the shower, but the door stopped before it caught the latch and swung open again.

Graeme stepped inside, closing the glass door behind him. "You mind?"

I shook my head. It would have been rude to refuse him a

shower. After all, he smelled like sandalwood and lavender and sex. He couldn't exactly go home like that. This fucked up thing between us might not be any sort of real relationship, but I wasn't *that* much of an asshole, either.

When I turned to hand him the body wash, I stopped abruptly, staring at the three lines on his back again. He accused *me* of doing that to him before the Meeting and of course he hadn't let me use his blood to see what the fuck he'd been talking about. But if it *wasn't* me, then what caused it?

Taking a step closer, I reached around him and held the bottle out to him. "Here."

"Thanks." He took it without question, but I didn't back away.

Since I was closer, I allowed my fingertips to trace the lines. He froze in place, the muscles in his shoulders bunching up. The scars appeared deeper on one end, tapering off to a finer line into nothing. Like a claw. Or a talon. The scars on my shoulders burned as soon as the thought settled and an involuntary shudder rolled down my spine.

"What are you doing?" he asked quietly.

"Tell me about this."

"I already did."

"No, I mean, walk me through what happened. Exactly. Step by step."

He turned slowly, his brows furrowed. With the confusion written on his face and how long it was taking him to answer, I figured he was going to refuse or start up with the insults.

Finally, he spoke, sounding no less confused. "I was going to the parking garage and the lights went out. Not all at once, like a power outage. It was one by one. Then I was surrounded by the same shadow thing you use. Someone or some*thing* hit me and cut me open."

"You never saw them?"

He shook his head.

"Did you smell anything?"

He glanced away, making a face as he tried to recall. "I don't know. Smoke. Leaves. Typical fall smells."

"How did it end?"

"I don't really know. I created a fog around myself and then the lights came back on. I don't know if it was because of that or because people were suddenly there. I have no idea."

"I really wish you would have let me use your blood that night." I could still try, but I doubted I'd be able to get anything useful from it. The visions were always clearer when the blood was fresh.

"How do you use it, anyway? I mean, I've seen you… lick it. I assume it's more than just a blood fetish."

I bit my lips together and looked away. I shouldn't be telling him any of this. I should tell him to fuck off, get out, and never talk to me again unless it was a Tuesday or a Thursday and only related to our stupid project.

Instead, I cleared my throat and actually answered him. "It's one of the easiest methods of divination for me. I use water too, but blood is more specific to the person. Obviously."

"So what do you see?"

"Everything? And nothing. It depends on what I'm looking for, what question I'm trying to answer."

"What did you see the first time you tasted mine?"

I *really* shouldn't have fucking said anything. This was opening a whole new line of questioning I didn't know if I was ready for. But my mouth kept on going before I could rein it in. "You were scared, like I said. Of me, my magic, my family."

"That's it?"

There was no way I was going to tell him I saw his feelings for me — the conflict brewing in his mind. He wanted to believe what he'd been taught to hate his entire life. He hated the idea of me, of me being a Corbin, but hatred wasn't the only emotion. He also wanted me, *Cash*, the guy he met at Preston's. Buried beneath the lust and confusion and contempt, I saw sadness. Loneliness. And more than a touch of guilt.

"You were pretty pissed about the crows," I replied quickly. It wasn't a complete lie. He *was* pissed.

"And what about in the library?" He couldn't help but give me an impish grin.

"All of the filthy things you want to do to me." I cracked a smile and shook my head. Also, not a lie. Underneath that perfect Hewitt exterior, he was a dirty bird with a wild side that had been beaten into submission over the years. For some reason, being around me made him tap into it, almost like it was primal. Maybe it was because he saw me as "evil" and thus he felt justified in giving in to his baser emotions. Or, I'd been paying too much attention in Psych 101.

Pinkness crept up into his cheeks. "Yeah, well. Can you blame me?" He gestured up and down my body.

I rolled my eyes and turned around, ducking under the sprayer on my side. "You're so annoying." Still, it didn't stop me from smiling like an idiot the second my back was turned.

Chapter Twenty-One

Graeme

Watching someone dry off after a shower shouldn't be sexy. It was a mundane task everyone did. But watching Cassius do it? Damn... If I didn't knock it off, I was going to give myself another hard-on. Considering what just happened I seriously doubted he'd be down for Round Two.

Like a cat stalking its prey, I moved closer. As much as I wanted to grab his hips and yank him into me, I didn't. It didn't mean I couldn't be near him, though. I couldn't help it. Ever since the first time I laid eyes on him, there was this pull. Like magnets. It made absolutely no sense. I should have wanted to be as far away from him as possible, and yet being near him was the only thing that felt right recently.

He was either oblivious to my closeness or choosing to ignore it. Either way, when he turned to leave the bathroom, he practically ran right into me.

"What?" he asked, eyebrows raised expectantly.

"What did you mean earlier when you said my powers had to be discharged?"

He stared at me for a beat, like he was waiting for me to crack some sort of a joke. When I didn't, a little crease formed between his brows. "There's no hidden meaning there. You have an active power. You have to let it out every once in a while, like a steam valve. How do you not know this?"

I shrugged, turning away from him to lean against the bathroom sink. "Magic wasn't really a priority after Owen died." I hated bringing up my brother — *period* — but I especially hated bringing him up to the guy whose mother died that same night. No, didn't die — was *murdered*. I saw the distinction now. And my father, no matter how distraught he was over Owen, was the cause of taking Cassius's mother away. I didn't know which was the worse crime — or if Owen's death had been a crime at all.

Cassius, on the other hand, didn't seem bothered by the remark. "Yeah, but you still should have had all of this explained to you during your conversion."

"I never had one," I admitted quietly. In the aftermath of Owen dying, the whole coming-of-age ritual was kind of passed over. Since I had no interest in being the next Deacon, I didn't care. I guess maybe I should have.

"What?!" His blue eyes nearly popped out of his skull. "Jesus. Graeme! No wonder your magic is a mess." He didn't say it insultingly, more like sympathetically, like it all finally clicked in his brain why I was such a fucking shit show.

"How do *you* know so much about weather magic? No one else in the Congregation seems to." I eyed him — less suspicious of his actual knowledge and more wary of the fact my family apparently didn't feel the need to explain jack shit. Maybe they assumed I would just *know*, innately, what I was supposed to do? But if that was the case, why was there a rite of conversion at all? There had to be a reason it was still hanging around after centuries. And if people were expecting me to be Deacon one day, then shouldn't I *know* this shit? Inside and out? Then again, maybe *they* didn't know and that's why they never said anything.

"Stormbringers and Necromancers used to be on the

same side, so to speak. We spoke to the dead that you all killed with your floods, droughts, and frosts." The surprise I felt must have registered on my face because the corner of his mouth ticked up into an amused smirk. "Yeah, that's right. Your kind used to be as hated as we were. *Are*. The only difference is that your ancestors tried to breed it out of existence, marrying into families with gentler, nature-based magic. We, on the other hand, embraced our power."

"Wow." A sudden twinge in my stomach had me walking away from him, back to the bedroom for my clothes. None of this was ever discussed in my family. Cassius could have been lying, but I had a feeling he wasn't. It was too... detailed to be something he made up on the fly. And he said it like I was a fucking moron for not knowing it. I mean, I guess I was. He knew more about my magic than I did which meant we were never on an equal playing field, no matter how much I thought we may have been.

"If you don't believe me, go ask Robert Winslow," Cassius said behind me. When I turned around, he was fully dressed in a t-shirt and pajama pants, which made me wonder how long I'd been standing there, holding my jeans and staring at the floor. "As the archivist, he can let you read the Book of Transactions. They also keep a record of each family. Yours should be there too."

I sank on the edge of his bed, still wearing nothing but a towel as my jeans hung limply next to me. "Who oversees the conversions?"

Cassius crossed his arms and shrugged. "Usually the Selectman from the family, but any Congregation member can do it."

"So you could do it?"

"Me?!" His eyes widened again. "You want *me* to do it?"

"Why not? You said anyone can. If I'm going to get a handle on this, then don't I have to do it at some point?"

"Yeah, but *I* don't know what you're supposed to do for your magic."

Shrugging, I gestured toward him with one hand. "I'll do whatever you did for yours."

He barked out a laugh. "You're joking."

I shook my head, dead serious. Magic was magic, right? Whatever he could do, I could probably do too if he showed me how.

"Let me tell you about my conversion," he said, sitting next to me on the bed. His thigh pressed against mine when he braced his heels on the side rail, his forearms resting against the top of his legs. "They take you down into the crypt and lay you inside a sarcophagus. Then they close the lid." He held my gaze as he spoke, his voice smooth and even. "It's up to you to get out in time."

I swallowed the lump in my throat. "In time?"

"There's only so much air," he said softly. "Until you accept death, truly make your peace with it, you're stuck in there. If it claims you in the process... well, the family has another ancestral spirit to add to the roster."

"They'd really let a thirteen-year-old die?" Ok, so maybe I *couldn't* do his type of conversion. Maybe it did have to be specific to your type of magic because there was no fucking way I was sealing myself in a sarcophagus with no way out. I pulled my magic from the atmosphere. If I was trapped in a stone coffin, there wouldn't be enough energy around me to get out again.

"Pulvis et umbra sumus," he replied with a tight smile. "'We are dust and shadow.' From dust we came, and to dust we shall return. You see it as a barbaric custom. We see it as a natural part of life. Everything dies. Some of us just die first."

Thunder rolled outside, rattling the glass in the window frames. Flashes of lightning brightened the night sky. Cassius turned toward the balcony door and considered it for a moment before looking up at me from his hunched position. "I take it you parked at the end of the orchard?"

"Mhmm." Rain pelted the glass, a soft staccato that calmed my racing thoughts. It always did. I loved rain, probably more than any other weather phenomenon.

"It's a long walk," he observed quietly, sitting up straight, running his palms over his thighs.

"Yeah."

"It's raining pretty hard."

"Yep."

"Did you do that on purpose?" His gaze slid toward me, curious but not reproachful.

"What if I said yes?" Contrary to what he must have thought, I didn't control *all* of the weather. The storm system had been heading in this direction for the past week, at least according to the real meteorologists.

"I'd tell you get dressed and enjoy your walk."

"And if I said no?"

Emotion flickered in his eyes — an indescribable one. All I knew was that it wasn't hatred anymore and whatever it was, I wanted to see more of it. "I'd say some higher power is telling us you were meant to stay."

I held my jeans up and tossed them away from me, never breaking eye contact with him. My dick was already starting to swell by the time I slipped off the bed. Standing in front of him, I tugged open the front of my towel and let it drop.

"Just because I'm not turning you out into the rain like a stray doesn't mean it's an open invitation for anything else," Cassius said, his gaze raking over me anyway.

"I'm showing my host gratitude." I stepped between his spread knees and pushed them open further, my fingertips caressing along the underside of his jaw.

"By electrocuting me?" His head tipped back regardless, letting me trace lazy designs over his throat, down his chest, all the way to the hem of his t-shirt. I hooked my fingers into it and dragged it upwards just as slowly, tossing it over my shoulder.

"You said you've already accepted death," I said quietly, sliding my fingers into his dark hair and angling his face up toward my mouth. "So what are you afraid of?"

His gaze burned into mine, so much that I swore *he* was using lightning against *me*. Tiny sparks danced over my skin as he ran his hands up my abs, around my ribs, and up my back. "You."

A slow smile spread over my lips as he pulled me closer. "Good."

"Why do you say that?"

"Because you terrify me."

We rushed toward one another, our mouths crashing against the other's. Even as the air dissipated from my lungs, I didn't pull away. In this new, confusing world, I didn't need oxygen anymore as long as I had Cassius. I took him, greedily, and I'd keep taking him as long as he let me.

Chapter Twenty-Two

Graeme

Morning light filtered in through the balcony door, slanting across my face and growing hotter by the minute. I rolled away from it and straight into Cassius's shoulder. He was facing away from me with one arm tucked under his head. From the steady rise and fall of his back, it was safe to say he was still asleep.

Pressing kisses along his shoulder blade, I slid closer and moved up the back of his neck. His scent was everywhere, but I buried my nose into his dark hair, inhaling the smell of his shampoo. Usually it was styled so perfectly with the longer part combed back. Knowing I was the reason it was such a mess made me smile. I liked seeing him like this — *not* perfect. Because not perfect meant not intimidating. Or at least as non-intimidating as Cassius Corbin could be.

He flicked a hand backward with a groan. A moment later, shadows swirled around the room, blotting out the sunlight.

"That's handy," I murmured as he rolled onto his back, blinking himself awake at last.

"You're still here."

I couldn't tell if he was disappointed or not. The scowl on his face could have been irritation at my presence or the fact he was clearly not a morning person. Then again, we didn't get a whole lot of sleep last night, so it's not like I blamed him for being moody.

"Is that ok?" I ventured quietly.

"I thought you would have left after the storm passed."

"That was never an option," I said, nuzzling the crook of his neck.

"It's reckless," he sighed, running a hand absentmindedly through my hair.

"Yeah, I know. Your family will kill me."

"Not just my family. Aren't you worried about your own?"

"Not really." That was a lie. I should have been worried, especially after not coming home last night and whatever the hell happened at the bonfire.

Fuck. India!

Like an asshole, I'd gotten so wrapped up in Cassius that I didn't even check in with her fucking parents. Rolling away from him, I snagged my cell phone and tried to wake it up, but it was dead.

"Shit. Do you have a charger?" I asked, holding up the phone.

"Should be one on that side of the bed," he said, gesturing vaguely toward his nightstand before scrubbing his hands over his face.

"Thanks." I found it and plugged my phone in, waiting impatiently for it to come back to life.

"Mhmm."

As soon as there was enough power, my phone started dinging and buzzing with all of the notifications. I knew I was in deep shit before I unlocked the home screen.

I groaned and started scrolling through the messages. There was a shit ton from my dad, big surprise. They started out demanding to know where I was and threatening all sorts of punishments if I didn't respond within a certain timeframe. Thankfully there were also a few from Preston, updating me on India's status.

According to all of the messages, they got her to the hospital in time. She was alive, barely, and had severe burns over most of her body. No one knew if she'd ever wake up again.

"India's alive," I said, ignoring the texts from my dad. I'd have to come up with a plausible excuse before I went home, but the ass chewing to end all ass chewings wasn't my primary concern at the moment.

"She is?"

I peered over my shoulder, frowning at his surprised expression.

He raised his hands like some sort of apology. "I know how serious burns are. I might not have fire magic, but rest assured I've gotten lectures on fire safety since I could walk. I had to practically sign a waiver any time I wanted to play with Lennox as a child."

"I should get going, though. My parents are going to be pissed." Pissed? Try furious, or livid, or irate. Hell, Dad was probably going to reach a level of mad they didn't even have a word for yet.

"Told you," Cassius said in a sing-song voice.

"Shut up."

While I gathered up my clothing, he grabbed his own phone and started scrolling.

"There's a Meeting tomorrow at seven," he said, all teasing gone from his tone. "Surprise, surprise."

I zipped up my jeans and turned to look at him. He appeared equally concerned, holding my gaze without blinking. "About India?"

"Didn't say. Probably." He sighed and tossed his phone back on the nightstand. "Guess it doesn't matter anyway. I'm on house arrest for the foreseeable future."

"What? Why?"

"My dad," he grumbled. "He's not letting any of us leave until we know what happened last night. God knows we'll be blamed for it. I mean, look at you."

I ignored that jab, regardless of how true it was. "Can't you sneak out?"

"No." A look of horror washed over him. If it was possible, whatever color was in his face drained from it and his pale eyes grew as big as saucers. "No, no, no…"

"What's wrong?"

He didn't answer me. Instead, he yanked on a pair of boxers and darted to the balcony, dragging me along in his wake until he whipped me toward the stone railing. "Climb over."

"What? I don't even have my shirt or my—"

"Graeme! Climb over!"

"Ok, ok. Calm down." I swung my leg over the railing. Well, I tried. It hit an invisible barrier just beyond the stone. Instead of using my leg, I leaned my torso over and pushed with both hands. Whatever the fuck it was, it didn't budge, like someone had erected a glass wall overnight. "What the fuck is that, Cassius?!"

"It's a protection spell. He must have done it right after we got home. Fuck!" Cassius stormed away from me. Chewing on his thumbnail, he paced back and forth. I couldn't tell if he was pissed because he was literally stuck with me or if he was trying to come up with some sort of solution. He always looked like he was scheming, so it was hard to tell.

"He who? Your dad?" I asked, just to clarify.

"Yes."

"Can't you ask him to break it, or whatever? Take it down?"

"Yeah. Sure. 'Hey, Dad, can you lower the ward so the son

of our arch-enemy can leave? What's he doing here in the first place? Oh, you know... we just spent the whole night taking turns fucking each other. No big deal, right?'"

Crossing my arms, I rolled my eyes. Fucking smart ass. "Well, when you put it like that, I can see where it's a problem."

"You think?!" Spinning on his heel, he stormed over to his dresser and yanked out fresh clothes. Instead of putting them on, he marched back to me and shoved them into my arms. "Put those on."

"I can't wear my own?"

"No." I must not have been moving fast enough for his liking because he stopped and stared at me, gesturing impatiently at the clothes. "It's easier to hide in shadows when you're wearing black, genius."

Made sense... I guess. I slipped into the joggers, relieved we had a similar body type, and tugged the hoodie on over my head. "So... what now?"

"I think I can get you out through the basement," he replied, yanking on his own clothes — his pajama pants and another hoodie. Stopping in front of me, his hands flew toward my face so quickly I flinched.

He frowned, fastening the amulet around my neck. Guilt hit me like a ton of bricks for thinking he was going to hurt me, even if it was only a split second.

"Doesn't the spell cover the basement?" I asked quietly.

"I don't know. I hope not."

I stuffed my phone and my wallet into the front pocket of my hoodie and was headed toward his bedroom door when a booming chime sounded through the house. It was as loud as church bells and Cassius immediately froze.

"What is that?" I whispered.

"The door."

"Why is that a problem?"

"Because the front gate is always locked, which means someone had enough magic to open it."

He crept to his bedroom door and cracked it open. The hallway looked deserted, but it was hard to know for certain with the dark wooden panels and expensive antiques on display. Someone could have easily been in the shadows of a doorway and I'd never see them.

Raised voices reverberated up through the belly of the house, turning my stomach into knots. I could only make out one of them definitively — my father's.

"Tell me what you've done to him!" Dad shouted.

Cassius and I exchanged a glance that summed up both of our feelings on the matter. We were scared shitless that one or both of our fathers was seconds away from dying at the hands of the other.

"You've truly lost your mind this time!" another male shouted, one I could only presume was Caius Corbin. In the few glimpses of him I remembered from my childhood, I couldn't recall a time when I'd ever heard him speak but it made sense that it was him. "But rest assured, this affront will *not* go unpunished!"

"I will call Treadwell myself unless you produce my son in the next thirty seconds!"

"Your son isn't here!" Caius snapped back.

"Then why is his phone tracking here?!"

Cassius and I both swore. He clenched his hand into a fist while I grimaced, kicking myself for not realizing how psycho my dad would actually be when I didn't come home.

"Give me your phone," Cassius whispered.

"What? No."

"Just trust me," he huffed, helping himself to my phone by rooting around in the hoodie pocket. "You'll only have a minute or two before the ward goes back up so don't fuck around."

"Ok..." I didn't like this one bit but I had to trust him. Mainly because I didn't have any other choice, but also because… just because. I was too jittery to come up with another reason other than my intuition.

His lips parted and he drew in a breath. My body hummed, waiting to see what he would say — what he would do. The last time we parted ways, at the library, had not been pleasant. And prior to that, I'd stupidly kissed him after he all but threw me out of the house. Needless to say, I hoped for a better goodbye this time.

Hope plummeted like a meteor when he swallowed and turned away from me, my phone in his hand. I took another step into the hall, watching him pad away silently.

As he rounded the corner, his gaze darted back to mine. I swear, he looked as shitty as I felt, which I suppose was something of a comfort. At least a sense of solidarity.

I didn't have time to dwell on it though. As much as I wanted to stick around and hear how the shouting match played out downstairs, I knew I needed to be ready to make a break for it. If I didn't reappear outside this house soon, my father would tear it apart, brick by brick, like the Big Bad Wolf.

Chapter Twenty-Three

Cassius

"Take this down! Immediately!" George thundered, beating his fists against the invisible wall between him and my father. "You fucking coward!"

"You don't want me to do that, George. At this point this barrier is the only thing keeping *you* alive," my father replied in a clipped voice, barely this side of civil.

"What's going on?" I asked, creeping into the foyer.

Claudia was there too, standing off to the side with her arms crossed and murder in her eyes.

"You!" George's attention snapped to me. "I knew it! You did something to him! Where is he?!"

Dad's jaw set and even though he was answering *my* question, his gaze never left his enemy's. "He seems to think we have his son. He claims his cell phone tracked to our house."

"Yeah. It's right here," I said, stepping forward and holding the phone up. "I mean, I didn't know it was his. I found it last night and picked it up. It was dead, so I charged it to see if I could return it."

Dad's eyes narrowed, but he didn't say anything.

"Graeme! Are you in there? Answer me!" George shouted, his wild eyes searching beyond us into the depth of the house.

"He's not here," I countered, taking a step forward. "I haven't seen him since class the other day."

"You stay away from him! Do you hear me?" George shouted. He actually tried to take a step into the house, only to run into the ward again. "If I see you near my son again, I'll—"

"That's enough!" Dad shouted, snatching the phone out of my hand and planting himself firmly between George and I. "If you think you can come to *my* home, threaten *my* son, and get away with it? You've got another thing coming. Take the phone and go." With a wave of his hand, the doorway shimmered. He thrust the phone into George's chest. His other hand, I noticed, was engulfed in the same swirling black mist as mine.

George clutched the phone so hard I thought he was going to break it. He held my father's glare for a moment before it sliced over to me. "If I find out you had anything to do with Graeme's disappearance, your little ward won't be enough to stop me or the rest of the Congregation."

"If you don't turn around and leave my property, he's not going to be the only one who disappears," Dad said with a terrifying calmness.

On that note, George spun on his heel and stormed back to his Volvo.

Dad stepped back into the house and slammed the door shut, leaning against it with a weary sigh. I turned to go, but his voice halted me in my tracks. "Cassius?"

"Yes?" I turned slowly, trying not to cringe.

"Where is the Hewitt boy?"

"I..." I shrugged and made a vague gesture, hoping I looked positively clueless and not guilty as hell. "I don't know."

"You didn't find his phone last night because we never made it to the equinox festival. So where did you find it?"

"Oh, um." I rubbed the back of my head, trying to think fast. "I guess it wasn't last night. It was the night before. On campus. I brought it with me last night to give it back to him."

Dad straightened and faced me directly, one eyebrow lifting slowly. "You said you didn't know it was his."

Fuck!

Claudia took a step forward, stopping at our father's elbow. The heat of their combined gazes burned hotter than the damn sun, boring a hole right through my lying heart.

I closed my eyes and expelled a short breath, preparing to plunge headfirst into a world of misery. "Ainsworth made us lab partners in my botany class. At first, I was pissed but I don't care anymore. It is what it is and I can't change it. I didn't tell you because I didn't want you to be mad."

"Mad?" The quirk in Dad's voice made me open my eyes. "Why on earth would I be mad?"

"I don't know," I mumbled. "Because he's a Hewitt?"

"He is not his father. I'm sure Samuel had his reasons, whatever they may be, for pairing the two of you. More importantly, you needn't hide things from me." Dad squeezed my shoulder gently. "Although it explains why you've been so distracted lately. Has it been hard? Working with him?"

I bit my lip and looked away, inadvertently catching Claudia's gaze. Dad may have been understanding, but Claudia looked like she was seconds away from biting the heads off of nails. "No," I blurted out, returning my focus back to Dad. "I mean, yes. I don't know. I'm just trying to focus on the work and move on."

"As you should." Dad shifted his hand from my shoulder to my cheek, giving it a light pat. "There's a Meeting tomorrow night, by the way. I don't know if you feel like going. Claudia's already said she's staying home."

"Are you going?" I asked.

He nodded solemnly. "I imagine it's an update on the events from last night. No doubt someone is going to blame us for it, or your aunt and uncle. I need to be there for them."

"I think I want to go," I said.

"Alright then." He gave my cheek one more pat and walked away.

Claudia stepped in to fill the empty spot, her dark eyes nearly pitch black with suspicion. "So what *aren't* you telling Dad?"

"Nothing," I huffed, walking away from her quickly. I didn't even know where I was going, I was just trying to get away from the interrogation. It didn't matter because she was on me like a shadow.

"Don't 'nothing' me, Cassius. You're hiding something. Something *else*. You might think you've fooled Dad, but it's plain as day on your face."

"What do you want me to say?" I shot back, using the time to rack my brain for a better answer. "After everything that's happened, I thought it would be better to keep him close, make sure he isn't running off to tell the Selectmen what a horrible, baby-eating monster I am."

"Because of the fight outside of the library?"

"And the crow thing."

She yanked me to a stop again, her eyes narrowed even more. "*What* crow thing?"

Shit! It was too late to lie now…

"The girl who was murdered? She saw me attack Graeme with crows..." Every new admission made me wince and I was sure she was going to smack me at any given moment. "On campus..."

Claudia made a face. "So what? She's dead."

I leaned closer, in case Dad happened to walk around the corner. "She wasn't the only one who saw."

Claudia's eyes tripled in size and her mouth popped open. "What?!"

"There was another girl with her."

"Cassius!"

I looked away, cringing under the weight of her stare. "I don't think Graeme saw her, but in case he did, I'm trying to appease him so he doesn't do something stupid, like try to blame *us* for that girl's murder."

"Who is it? Who else saw you?"

"I don't know. Sophia something. Ask Lennox. I mean, she left right away. So if she was going to say something, wouldn't she have already spoken up?"

She wilted with my confession, rubbing the space between her perfectly groomed brows. "Oh, Cash..."

"I know... Ok? I know. I just have to get through this semester and then I don't have to deal with him anymore."

She looked up at me, her lips pressed into a thin line. Disappointment oozed out of every pore. For the first time since coming home, I actually wished I was back in England, away from all of this.

"Please don't look at me like that," I sighed.

"You don't have to solve *all* of your problems yourself, you know. Otherwise, what's the point of having a family?"

"I'm used to relying on myself," I replied flatly. I didn't mean it in a spiteful way, but she flinched nonetheless. Wincing, my gaze fell to my feet. "I'm sorry. That's not what I meant."

"No, I know. I get it. You've basically been on your own for the past six years." She reached up and ruffled my hair, earning her a scowl. "Just remember, I will always be here for you, and if Graeme Hewitt so much as looks at you sideways, Lennox and I are more than happy to kick his ass."

"I know." I gave her a small smile and slipped away.

The moment I stepped into my room, I slumped against the door and closed my eyes.

I hated lying to them. Dad seemed sympathetic, but he was under the impression it was strictly in relation to the forced assignment. He would understand the reason we weren't ripping each other to shreds at Tennebrose. But inviting Graeme here — on *multiple* occasions, no less — to our inner sanctum? Even a man as patient as Caius Corbin couldn't be blamed for losing his shit.

And Claudia? She meant what she said. She *would* kick Graeme's ass without thinking twice and Lennox would be right there with her to help. I wished I could tell her everything, but I couldn't risk it. Maybe after the semester was over.

Pushing away from the door, I moved further into my room, glancing around for any sign of Graeme. His t-shirt was still there, but the zip-up he'd been wearing and his jeans were gone. Frowning at the forgotten shirt, I made my way to the balcony and opened the door, half expecting him to still be there like last time.

It was empty.

A ripple of disappointment washed over me as I peered over the railing. All that was there were crushed vines and ripped ivy leaves. For once, he listened. He really was gone.

Stepping back inside, I closed the door and pulled the curtains shut. My bed called to me, at least for a few more hours since Graeme sure as shit didn't feel the need to sleep.

I crawled under the blanket and buried my face in the pillow. It smelled like Graeme, mixed with my body wash. For some stupid reason that made me smile. Then scowl. And yet, I didn't swap it for another pillow as my eyes drifted shut.

Chapter Twenty-Four

Graeme

To say I was preparing for the ass chewing of the century was a bit of an understatement. By the time I hiked back to my Jeep and changed out of Cassius's muddy, dew-covered joggers and back into my jeans, I'd formulated a pretty convincing story. Here's hoping Dad bought it.

Rather than try to sneak in and pretend like nothing was wrong, I opted for a bolder move. I bought a cup of coffee and a bag of bagels and strolled in the front door as if all was right in the world. My eighth-grade acting teacher would be so proud.

Dad was on me like white on rice, flying out of the living room and into the front hall.

"Where the hell have you been?!"

I stopped, blinked, and held up the bag of bagels while trying to look as confused as possible. "Getting some breakfast?"

"Don't lie to me! I checked your room. You weren't there! So *where* were you?!"

Making sure I looked annoyed at yet another overreaction, I continued into the kitchen with an exaggerated sigh. "I'm not lying, Dad. I couldn't sleep, so I went to the hospital to see India. They aren't letting visitors in until later, so then

I went to the bagel shop. I got your favorite. See?" Setting the coffee and the bag on the counter, I opened it and withdrew one of the asiago cheese ones, holding it out to him.

Ignoring my peace offering, he pulled my cell phone out and slammed it on the counter so hard I jumped. It's not like I could say anything about taking it easy since he's the one who technically bought it. If he broke it, that was on him, even though I'm sure I'd be blamed regardless. "Then explain *this!*"

"Oh, you found my phone! Great! Thanks!" I feigned elation and made a move to retrieve it.

He slid it out of my reach, fixing me with a hard stare. "Why in God's name did a *Corbin* have your phone, Graeme?" The low timbre of his voice actually sent a wave of goosebumps down my skin.

Swallowing the lump in my throat, I tried not to look as guilty as I felt. As over the top as my dad could be, I didn't exactly enjoy lying to him, but I could never be honest either. Especially about the Corbins, which would forever be a touchy subject. "I lost it the other day. He must have found it. I don't know."

He leaned closer, his glare boring into mine, like my very soul was being judged. After an eternity, he straightened. "Don't let it happen again. God only knows what they did to it in the meantime. You should probably cleanse it before you even think about using it. I mean, with bleach *and* crystals."

Nodding, I forced a fleeting smile to my face. "I will. Thanks." I cleared my throat and glanced at the bag. "Do you think Mom's hungry? I could take one up there?"

Offering me a grim smile, he shook his head. "No. No, I don't think so. Not right now. She had another bad night."

"Was it the crying or the screaming kind of night?" I asked, even though my gaze sank to the floor, not really wanting to know the answer. It wouldn't have made a difference if I did. There wasn't anything I could do for either scenario. There wasn't anything *anyone* could do.

Even Dad knew there was no point in actually answering. He finally took his own bagel before disappearing, muttering a "Thank you" on his way out.

I exhaled a shaky breath the moment he left the room and sucked it back in, trying not to hyperventilate at the kitchen sink. That was close. Too fucking close. Which made me wonder how Cassius fared with his family.

After *another* shower to remove all traces of Cassius and mud from me, I changed and headed to the hospital for real. It was the least I could do since I hadn't bothered to check in at all overnight, like a complete asshole.

Surprisingly, Preston was the only one there when I walked into India's room.

"How's it going?" I asked quietly, glancing at the gauze-covered body in the bed. India looked like a mummy. If it wasn't for the fact her bright copper hair spilled all over the pillow, I would have never even recognized my friend.

Preston shook his head, standing up to give me a one-armed hug. "No change since last night. You just missed her parents. They ran home real quick to shower and change but they should be back soon."

"I brought these," I said, hoisting up the bag of bagels. Just like my mother, I didn't have much of an appetite at the moment. "I didn't know what else to get."

"Thanks, man." Taking the bag, he dropped back into his

seat but he didn't bother opening it. His attention immediately returned to India, his knee bouncing like crazy.

I eased into the chair next to him, half tempted to plant my hand on his knee to get him to stop. "Do they know what happened yet?"

He shook his head. "No... She was near the bonfire and the Selectmen think that maybe an ember caught her clothing. Or something. I don't know."

It was entirely possible but highly unlikely. Usually the only time your power turned against you was when you were attempting to do magic beyond your capabilities. Or if you were cursed. "Isn't it kind of unusual for a witch to be attacked by their own element?" To be on the safe side, I kept the curse idea to myself. He had enough to worry about without devolving into conspiracy theories.

Preston shrugged and shook his head sadly. "I don't know... Dad said it's possible, but I don't know if I really believe that. I mean, she did her conversion *in* fire. Like, walked into a bonfire just like the one last night and came out without a mark on her. I think someone did this to her. The question is, who?"

"Or what," I muttered.

His head snapped in my direction. "What are you talking about?"

Shit! I scratched the back of my neck and shrugged, making a noncommittal noise. "I don't know. Like, a demon or something. Aren't the North Woods supposed to be haunted?"

"I don't think Black Mary is responsible for this. It's not her style."

"Yeah, probably not. Do you have any ideas who could have done it, then?"

"You mean other than the Ambroses?" The muscle in his

jaw tightened and he ground one fist into the opposite palm. "No. No idea."

"Have you talked to Lennox?"

Preston snorted. "Yeah. He called me earlier, asked how she was..." He ran his hands through his sandy hair and held his head, propping his elbows on his knees. "I just don't know, Graeme. He was cool with India. I mean, mostly. They had something of a rivalry because of their magic but not like *that*. And he sounded upset. I don't want to think it's him, but you know those witches... their blood is as black as the Corbins'. I just don't know, man."

I laid a hand on his shoulder lightly. "It probably *was* an accident." God, I couldn't believe I was saying that when less than twenty-four hours ago I was convinced it was Lennox too. "A really, really shitty accident."

He looked up, his mouth pressed into a disbelieving line. His brows furrowed suddenly and he zeroed in my chest. "What the fuck is that?"

Blinking, I glanced down, completely forgetting the amulet from Cassius. I tucked it away sheepishly, the black stone cold against my skin. "An amulet. Can't be too careful with Necromancers around."

Preston nodded. "Good thinking. I should bring it up to Dad. He can make an announcement or something at the Meeting tomorrow night. Everyone should probably start wearing shit like that. Like back in the old days."

There wasn't much to talk about after that. I nudged his elbow and tipped my chin toward the bag of bagels, more so for his benefit than mine. He wouldn't be any good to anyone if he crashed from low blood sugar or something.

"Oh, yeah, sorry," Preston mumbled, pulling out a bagel for himself before passing the bag back to me.

I helped myself to a blueberry bagel and chewed in

silence, thinking about all of the shit that had been going on in Winslow lately. Melanie's murder. India's attack. Demons.

Mostly, I thought about all the stuff Cassius told me about my magic. How the hell was I supposed to discharge my power? I assumed he meant to use it somehow. But weather magic wasn't something you could bust out at any given moment. Depending on what sort of weather I was after, it took fucking *effort*. Wind was the easiest to manipulate unless Cassius was around. Then it seemed like lightning wanted to be front and center.

Maybe the whole conversion thing would help. It was a commitment ceremony, after all. Maybe finally pledging myself to the Congregation would help with whatever the hell my problem was. It didn't mean I wanted to be Deacon. At all. But I needed to do something to get a grip on my powers if I ever wanted to be with Cassius again.

Fuck! Why did everything always circle back to Cash lately? Everything! School, Cassius. Witchy shit, Cassius. What goddamn shirt to wear, Cassius! No matter what the first thought was, he was like an automatic follow-up, wondering how the first thought would impact him.

Sadly, I had as much insight into *that* as I did about my own magic.

If Cassius and the other Necromancers had to face death to fully embrace their powers, what the hell was I supposed to do? How do you *fully* embrace weather? Sit in a blizzard? Hang on to something during a hurricane? I had no idea.

I'd have to ask him more about it. Or Old Man Winslow. *He'd* probably know. But all of that would have to wait until after the Meeting and whatever bad news was about to fall.

As always, the Meeting started promptly at seven and according to my phone, it was seven minutes past as I slid in the eastern door and stole a quick glance around. Rather than interrupt the Deacon and his opening speech by trying to dart over to my family's box pew, I hurried up the stairs in the back to the gallery.

To my surprise, Cassius was there. He was the *only* one there since most everyone preferred the cushioned pews downstairs as opposed to the old, narrow benches in the gallery.

He sat up straighter, his gaze fixed on the people down below, as I edged onto the bench next to him. Mindful to stay far enough away to not be *that* obvious, I still stretched my arm out and laid my hand on the bench between us.

A second later, his warm fingers covered mine.

"I didn't think you'd be here tonight," I whispered, watching Peregrine gesture dramatically while he droned on about community safety and times of yore.

"My father knows how important this is."

"So why are you up *here*?"

He shot me a look out of the corner of his eye and shushed me irritably.

I rolled my eyes and leaned forward slightly. The rickety wood was already digging into my ass so I hoped this was going to be a quick Meeting.

Peregrine gave everyone an update on India and how to best help the family in their time of need, be it food, help around the house, or whatever skill one might possess. He said Mrs. Green was organizing some sort of rotating dinner list, so the casseroles and lasagnas could be delivered on a daily basis rather than bombarding the poor Tenneys all at once.

As Preston suggested, his dad told the Congregation to

bust out those old family heirlooms, blessing oils, and crystals. Everyone was supposed to charge them ASAP and practice our sigil skills while we were at it. I used to think it was all kind of bullshit, but then Cassius gave me his amulet and proved me wrong.

In a surprise twist, Peregrine wrapped it up and gave the pulpit over to Treadwell.

The chief stepped up the narrow stairs of the small, dark box and laid his hands on either side of the old podium. "I'm sure you're all wondering what I'm doing up here. Well, I am afraid I have more bad news. I had hoped the murder on campus was a one-time thing. Sadly, last night, we found another body. Decapitated, with the eyes removed. Now, Bob was able to keep it out of the newspapers" — he gestured to Old Man Winslow — "to keep the larger community from panicking. But I would strongly caution all of you to be on the highest alert and to please report anything suspicious to myself or the Tithing Man."

Ainsworth stepped forward, beneath the pulpit, and inclined his head, picking up where Treadwell left off. "Professor Colburn and I are staggering our classes so that one of us will always be on campus. Along with Mrs. Green." He gestured to the haughty blonde in the Colburn box for those who weren't familiar with one of Tennebrose's most feared professors. Instead of botany, she ruled over the history department with an iron fist. Regular people thought she was hot — witches dreaded having to pass her independent reading class, e.g. the history of witchcraft with a special emphasis on Winslow and another requirement specifically for witches. If we could, I'm sure we'd all take our required class with Dr. Hadder. He may have been a mere mortal with a reputation on campus for being crazy, but the "Mad Hadder" was still preferable to anything Temperance Colburn threw at you.

And then of course, Mrs. Green, stepped up and smiled cheerfully at everyone, dispelling the unease of Dr. Colburn's glare.

"Dr. Ainsworth?" Arden stood and waited until he was acknowledged before proceeding. "Is it true? Was it Sophia?"

Ainsworth and Treadwell exchanged a glance. When Treadwell gave a slight nod, Ainsworth faced Arden with a grim expression. "Yes, I'm afraid so. She was found at the observatory last night by the astronomy class."

Arden swallowed hard enough that I could see it all the way up in the nosebleeds. Barely even nodding, he murmured his thanks before resuming his seat.

And of course, Lennox was right there to comfort him, squeezing his shoulder and talking into his ear. Arden nodded to whatever Lennox said, but his head was still hung low and his shoulders rounded. If it was anyone else, I might have felt sorry for them. But it was Arden Simms, the snobby sidekick to Lennox Ambrose, number two and three on my list of enemies.

I caught Enemy Number One looking at me and faced him directly. "What?" Just because he and I had some sort of weird, hot-as-hell truce, didn't mean Lennox and Arden got a pass for being assholes.

"Sophia," Cassius said, his voice cracking, like the name should mean something to me.

"So? Who is that? And don't say another dead girl."

"She was with Melanie. You know? The girl who saw us fighting?"

My eyes widened and he nodded once I caught on. "Did she see us too?"

"I'm pretty sure she did, but she ran off so fast… I really don't know."

"Why didn't you say anything?" I hissed, snatching my

hand back. I don't know why, but it felt like we were back on opposite sides of the line again.

"Say anything about what?" he hissed back. "That not one but *two* people saw you getting your ass handed to you by a family of crows outside Dane Hall?"

"Fuck off. I wasn't getting my ass handed to me," I grumbled.

"*That* is your big issue? That you got beat up by birds?"

Ignoring the other jab, I huffed my next question. "So *now* what?"

"We need to tell Ainsworth," he said simply.

I shook my head, vehemently against that idea the second it fell from his lips. "The fuck we don't."

"Would you prefer to tell Treadwell? Or the Deacon?"

"No! We don't have to tell *anyone*. My dad will lose his shit. You have no idea! You think him showing up to your house was bad? What do you think he'll do if he finds out we *actually* got into it?"

"You don't think it's the tiniest bit odd that two out of the three people who saw us that day are dead?" Cassius squinted at me.

"You're right..." A sudden thought struck me. I turned and looked at Ainsworth. "What if he's next?"

"What if he *did* it?" Cassius countered, his voice barely audible.

My gaze shot back to him. "You think Ainsworth is behind it all?"

"Only one way to find out."

I shook my head, even harder than before. "No. No, do *not* say we're going to—"

"The morgue," Cassius said with a nod.

Chapter Twenty-Five
Cassius

In a moment of déjà vu, I was back at the hospital just before midnight, except this time I was actually waiting for Graeme in the parking lot instead of secretly hoping he'd bail on me. I rounded the front of my car as he was closing his door, looking less than thrilled to be here.

"You don't have to do this," I said. "I can go alone."

"No, I want to. I mean, I don't want to. But, I feel like I have to. It's my fault too." He shoved his hands in his pockets, rocking awkwardly on his heels.

Nodding, I turned and set off for the hospital. He fell into step beside me. For once he didn't seem hellbent on talking my ear off. I wanted to ask why, but at the same time, I had to focus on the task ahead.

We made our way into the basement quietly. Graeme's steps didn't falter until we reached the morgue doors.

I pushed the door open and gestured for him to go first.

He rolled his eyes and walked through, flipping on the lights as quickly as he could.

"Still creeped out by dead bodies?" I asked, heading toward the giant cooler.

"Yeah," he admitted bluntly, with none of his usual arrogance. "I don't think I'll ever *not* be creeped out by dead things." I mean, to be fair, most people were. At least he'd dropped the act and was actually being a little more humble these days.

"You want to know a trick?"

"What?" He eyed me warily, conveniently finding himself on the opposite side of the room, as far away from the cooler as possible.

"If you see the beauty in death, you won't be so creeped out by it. Not to get all Lion King on you, but it really is about the circle of life. The dead have a lot to teach the living, the living just don't want anything to do with it."

He didn't look convinced in the slightest. "Yeah, right. Thanks for the tip, Mufasa."

It was my turn to roll my eyes. Instead of arguing, I opened the large, stainless steel door and stopped at the threshold, eyes wide. "Shit!"

"What?"

It was empty. There wasn't a *single* body inside. Not entirely unusual for a small-town hospital, but the fact the murder victim wasn't here either? *That* was problematic.

I didn't answer him as I walked into the cooler and whirled in a circle, as if a body would suddenly appear if I willed it into existence hard enough.

Graeme opened the door wider and peered inside. "Where is she?"

"I don't know…"

"Well now what?"

"I don't know!" I swore under my breath and strode out of the cooler again, trying to think.

Treadwell said they kept it out of the papers to avoid panic. Maybe they kept Sophia out of the hospital for the same reason, which meant they had to take the body somewhere else. There was only one other suitable place for a dead body, pre-burial.

I grabbed Graeme's sleeve. "The funeral home."

"What?"

"I bet they took her to Kellermann's." The Kellermann family weren't witches, per se, but they'd been around long enough to have gotten the clue the supernatural existed. If the chief of police came to them in the middle of the night with a decapitated coed and told them to keep quiet, they probably didn't even blink an eye. It was, after all, just another day in Winslow, Massachusetts, where strange deaths and urban legends ran rampant.

"Ok… So, what? We break in there and do the little seance thing?" Graeme asked, brows lifted in anticipation of my answer.

I made a face at him and headed for the door. "No, we can't break in there. Are you crazy?"

"Oh, gee, I don't know," he snapped, trailing after me. "You have no problem coming to the morgue in the middle of the night, so why not crawl through the window of a funeral home?"

"Uh, because one of those is illegal?"

"Pretty sure poking around a dead body in a hospital is illegal too, unless you have M.E. attached to your name."

"Well, one day I will. I can always say it's for practice."

"You're going to be a medical examiner?" He snorted. "Go figure."

"And what are you going to be? A fucking weatherman?"

All he could do was scowl, so I knew I was right. That's not to say he wouldn't be perfect for the job. I mean, who wouldn't want to wake up to that beautiful face every day to hear the daily weather report?

"*Actually*," he said as we made our way back upstairs, headed toward the parking lot. "I was more interested in forecasting and technology to help the agricultural industries. Better predictions would help yield better harvests and save farmers time and energy."

"Look at you being a humanitarian. I didn't know you had it in you. So nice that you can remember the little folk from up on that pedestal of yours."

"God, you're pissy when things don't go according to plan."

"At least I *have* a plan," I snapped, lengthening my strides in the hope of reaching my car that much faster. Except, I didn't have a plan at all. I was winging it just as much as he was.

"Now where are you going?" he called after me.

"Home."

"Home? What about the ghost?"

"Spirit."

"Whatever!" He darted in front of me, blocking my retreat across the parking lot. "Don't you want to know if Ainsworth is in danger — or if *we're* in danger?"

"Of course I do. It's just not that simple. The easiest way to communicate with them is with a body or something personal from the deceased. We don't have either."

He crossed his arms over his chest. "Ok, so what's the hard way?"

I shook my head and sidestepped him. "No. I'm not doing it."

"Cash!"

"No, Graeme!"

"Why not?" He zipped in front of me again right as I reached for my car handle.

Biting my lower lip, I directed my glare past his shoulder. I understood his curiosity, even his concern for us and for Ainsworth, but he had *no* idea what he was asking.

"Cash, come on." He swayed closer, his voice lowering. Relenting, I let my gaze drift back to him. "I have to know why they died and… if it was because of me."

The guilt in his eyes ate at me. I wanted to smooth out the

lines on his face, reassure him in some way that neither of us were to blame, but my hands remained firmly at my sides. "I can try summoning her without the body. But I can't do it alone," I said quietly. "It's not like crossing over. It's a lot more work and her spirit is not the only thing that can come through."

He nodded, his face grim. "I'll help you. Whatever you need. Just tell me."

"It's dangerous, Graeme. All bullshit aside. You need to have your full strength. I can't hang on to a spirit, keep the veil closed, *and* possibly fend off a demon by myself."

"Meaning?"

"You'll have to go through your conversion first."

"But you said you didn't know how to do it."

"I don't. I'll go to the archive tomorrow and see if I can figure something out. If anything, I'll ask Temperance for help."

His eyes widened. "Dr. Colburn? You'd really ask for her help?"

"Yeah. I would. There hasn't been a Stormbringer in..."

"Over a century," he said, deflating.

"Exactly. I doubt anyone living knows how the conversion is supposed to go for that kind of power. Maybe she's got some resources that can help. Other than the archivist, no one knows more about Winslow than her."

He nodded, folding his arms across his chest and rubbing his bicep like he had a sudden chill.

I touched his elbow lightly before remembering we were in a very public space, even though it was after midnight. Glancing around, I shoved my hand into my coat pocket and cleared my throat. "Why do you always look like that whenever I mention your magic?"

"Haven't you heard?"

"Heard what?"

"I'm supposed to be the next Deacon."

"Yeah, I heard… You don't want it?"

He shook his head solemnly. "No. It's all I've heard about for as long as I can remember and look at me. I shock you every time I turn around and I don't even know I'm doing it."

"It doesn't always happen," I said quietly, holding up one hand like I was a mime, touching a pane of glass.

He glanced at my hand and swallowed. Slowly, he lifted his own and mirrored it, bringing it closer and closer. When his palm was still an inch away, blue flashes sparked across his hand. I braced for the zap a second before the lightning arced from his palm to mine, rippling through my hand and dispersing.

I tried to stifle a wince, but he saw it regardless.

"See?" His fingers curled into his palm and he dropped his hand immediately. "I don't know why it keeps happening. It's never happened with anyone else. But whatever it is, it's getting stronger."

"It's probably the feud." I shrugged, like that was the go-to answer for everything shitty in this town. At least, it was for our families. "Even our magic hates each other."

"Has yours been acting weird?"

He looked so hopeful, I felt like a dick for shaking my head.

"What if you do the blood thing?" He held his hand out, palm up. "Maybe you can see what's wrong with it?"

I glanced around again. Aside from a couple of cars, the parking lot was empty. Still, it was a risk. "I don't think that's a good idea…"

"Why not?"

"Someone could see us."

He snagged my sleeve and led me around the side of his Jeep. It was darker there and his vehicle blocked us from anyone who might be looking out the hospital windows.

Again, he held up his hand, in a silent, demanding way.

Seeing no way around his annoying persistence, I fished the crow skull out from beneath my sweater and grasped it carefully. As soon as I took possession of his hand in mine, another rush of electricity thrummed through my palm. I bit my lips and focused on piercing his finger as quickly as possible.

As soon as a bead of blood rose out of the cut on his skin, I lifted it toward my mouth.

I heard his sharp intake of breath as my tongue caressed the small injury. More electricity shot through me, traveling through my blood along with a whirl of images flashing through my brain.

It was a blur of faces and old buildings, even older books and rugged landscapes. I didn't recognize any of it or any of the people. Complicating matters was the fact they were all dressed like they were from the seventeenth century.

Once I realized I was looking at the past, I focused on the buildings and on the flashes of text I saw on the documents. Graeme's family name appeared at the bottom of a death warrant. John Hewitt, Sheriff of Winslow, ordered the execution of someone… but I couldn't see the name at the top. The writing was too spindly and it rushed by too quickly.

There were a few places I did recognize — Middlewich barn. The old gaol in the North Woods. The hanging tree, a single noose swaying in the breeze.

In the next instant, I saw a woman. Middle-aged with dark, wild hair hanging about her face. Her hands were bloody and streaked with dirt, much like the sores and mud caked on her bare feet. She was hanging from the noose, limp and motionless. Her eyes stared lifelessly while her tongue started to swell and turn black.

Slowly, her head swiveled toward me and lolled back.

Those dead eyes bored into mine, refusing to let me look away.

"Mors omnibus," she croaked right before sucking in a gasp of air, like a death rattle.

Something loud shrieked in my ear. A large, white owl swooped in, its talons leading the way. The sharp points scratched across my face like they had in the Land of the Dead except this time my mother wasn't there to fend it off.

I jerked back on instinct, landing hard on my ass in the twenty-first century.

"Cash!" Graeme was on his knees next to me, his mismatched eyes wide and his hands holding me while he searched for injuries or something.

I touched my face and pulled my hand back, expecting blood. There was nothing. No matter how real it felt, the owl hadn't been anything more than a vision — just like last time.

"What happened?" Graeme asked.

"I don't know..." I let him pull me to my feet, even though my legs felt less than stable. "I saw... a lot." An understatement, if I ever made one, but I couldn't exactly put my thoughts into words when I was too busy trying not to vomit from the motion sickness.

"Is that a good thing?"

"What were you thinking about right before?" I asked quickly, before I forgot everything I saw.

He furrowed his brow at me. "I don't know... Um, my magic? Why it's all fucked up? Should I have been thinking about something else?"

"Do owls mean something to you?"

He made a face. "Not that I know of... Why?"

"I saw another owl. First when I went to see my mother. And again, just now. They attacked me both times."

"Could it be your subconscious or something? Some sort of symbolism?"

"I don't know. I... I need to go home." I headed for my car, running a hand through my hair and holding the side of my head as my brain thumped. "I have to research some stuff. Some people. I have to go see Winslow in the morning. I need to find the fucking foli—"

"You're going to see Winslow in the morning?"

I stopped short and stared at him, my train of thought completely derailing. "What?"

"Winslow. You said you're going to see Old Man Winslow in the morning. What time?"

"I don't know. Whenever."

"Give me your phone."

I made a face but handed it over.

He typed something in quickly and handed it back. A second later, a text message popped up from him. "Text me when you go. I'll meet you there."

"Yeah. Sure." Slipping my phone back into my pocket, I hurried to my car and ducked inside before he could distract me any more than he already had.

Chapter Twenty-Six

Graeme

He wasn't going to text me.

From the confused look on his face to the way he peeled out of the hospital parking lot, I knew Cassius wasn't going to keep me in the loop on whatever fucked him up so badly. I mean, didn't I have a right to know? It was *my* blood, *my* magic, that apparently sent him into a tailspin. But maybe that's exactly why he wasn't going to clue me in — he saw something that completely and utterly freaked him out, something I didn't think was possible for a Necromancer.

So imagine my surprise when my phone chirped shortly after eight a.m. It was a message from Cassius, telling me he was on his way to the meetinghouse. I kicked the covers off and hopped out of bed.

Less than an hour later, I was hurrying up the hill to the meetinghouse — not the *Gazette* office, as I'd been expecting the night before. Cassius's Lexus was the only one parked outside. Since it was visible from the road, I pulled my Jeep around back and parked out of view, just in case.

I ducked in the eastern door and looked around the main floor. It was eerily quiet and empty.

"Cash?"

There was no answer.

I headed toward the front, turning around to look up into the gallery. It, too, was empty.

"Cassius!"

"Down here!" came his muffled reply.

I looked down at the worn floorboards, brows furrowed. "How do I get down there?" In all my years of being dragged to this damn building, I never once went into the cellar. I never had a reason to. Besides, there weren't any doors on the outside of the building or anywhere in the interior that indicated access to the basement.

Of course, he was a pain in the ass and didn't answer.

Right about the time my annoyance surged, his head popped up from the floor off to the side of the pulpit. "Do you need a written invitation?"

"Funny." I rolled my eyes and cut across the floor to the open staircase. "How was I supposed to know there's a trap door?"

"I thought everybody knew? How else do you expect to get into the archives?"

"I didn't realize Winslow kept them *here*."

"Where else would he keep them?"

"I don't know. Somewhere with central heating, maybe?"

"Quit whining already," Cassius sighed, leading the way back down the narrow stairs. "It's going to be a long day as it is without you pouting."

I was expecting the cellar to be dark and dingy. For being over three hundred years old, it wasn't too bad. Large flagstones made up the floor and the walls had been whitewashed probably a hundred times. The ceiling was low, but there were plenty of lightbulbs stationed along the wall to brighten everything up. It was noticeably colder than upstairs, but Cassius had started a fire in the massive fireplace set into the wall.

There were rows upon rows of old wooden racks, jam-packed with books and papers. It looked like each of the founding families had their own rack, along with communal ones toward the center. Other than that, the only other thing down here was an old, scarred table ringed by four chairs. Apparently Cassius hadn't wasted any time. He already had a pile of books on the table.

"What are you looking for?" I asked.

"I don't know, exactly," he replied, dropping into a chair and dragging a book closer. "Owls, I guess. Weather. Anything with our families in it. John Hewitt in particular."

"Who's John Hewitt?"

"He was the sheriff at one point or another."

"Ok. Why does he matter?"

"I saw his name last night in a vision."

Since it looked like he had a system already in place, I didn't want to come in and wreck it like a bull in a china shop. "Where do you want me to start?"

He looked up, blinking, like he was surprised I was actually going to help. "Um… these. I guess." He slid a stack of loose papers over. They were wrangled into a pile by the cracked leather cover they were shoved into, but not bound in any way. "Look for your last name. Or mine."

"Ok." I turned the cover and got to work sifting through the documents.

We sat like that for I don't know how long — him paging through the stack of books and scribbling things down in a notebook, while I thumbed through the loose pages, coming up cross-eyed and empty-handed.

The fire crackled to the side of us, illuminating only half of Cassius's face. At first glance, he looked evil as fuck. The shadows leapt across his angular features and made his pale eyes practically disappear. His dark hair, perfectly combed as usual, and choice of outfit — a gray plaid shirt underneath a navy sweater — made him look like he belonged at some prestigious university, like Oxford, not in the basement of a small-town meetinghouse, blowing cobwebs off of crumbling books.

But then he'd chew on his lip, or fiddle with his pen, and the sinister air around him disappeared. He wasn't evil. From the sounds of it, his family wasn't evil either. His dad could have killed mine the other day without anyone ever knowing, but he didn't. Caius could have taken revenge at *any* point over the past six years, but he didn't. If Necromancers were as evil and vindictive as my dad had led me to believe… then why was he still alive? Why was *I* still alive? Cassius could have just as easily killed me at any point in our history together… but. He. Didn't.

"Why are you staring at me?" Cassius asked.

I blinked, snapping out of the reverie I'd apparently fallen into. "I'm not."

"Uh huh." He went back to his book, rubbing his eye and looking more than a little tired, or maybe just downtrodden. "Find anything yet?"

"No. This is all wills and probate inventories from three hundred years ago. No one is going to give a shit that Black Mary had one bed, a set of silver candlesticks, and miscellaneous quires. What the fuck is a quire anyway?"

Cassius practically flew out of his chair and rounded the table, staring at the document. His lips moved as he scanned the list of items and then he bolted to the racks of books.

"Care to share with the class?" I asked, following after him.

"Which part?" By the time I caught up to him, he was actually scaling the racks to reach the top shelf. He groped along the top, nearly hitting his head on the ceiling.

"All of it. What are you looking for up there?"

"The first book."

"What book? You have a whole table full of books."

"The first Book of Transactions."

"Why?"

"Because that will indicated everything went to a Joy-in-Sorrow Oliver, presumably Mary's daughter. Maybe a sister-in-law."

"So?" It was really hard to pay attention to a history lesson with his ass in perfect view. I mean, it was directly in my line of sight thanks to him perching on the racks. Every time he rose up on the tips of his toes to reach further, the muscles contracted beautifully. The dark jeans weren't as nice as the riding pants, but it was pretty damn close.

"Stop looking at my ass and catch." Busted.

I looked up in time to see another massive book falling from the top of the rack. Thankfully I caught it with my hands instead of my face. "Would you stop throwing books at me?"

"I will when you start paying attention." He climbed back down and jumped to the floor in front of me, reclaiming the book and marching back to the table. "Mary Oliver is the lynchpin in this whole feud."

"Ok… what does that have to do with us? I mean, I thought we're supposed to be looking for something to help make my conversion so we can resurrect the dead girl's ghost or whatever."

He set the book on the table, on top of everything else, and flicked through the pages quickly. "Because… Mary… was… a…" With a brilliant smile, he stabbed a finger at a date in the ledger. "Stormbringer."

"Does that mean she was a Hewitt?" I looked at the page where someone had marked the date of her conversion and the powers she'd manifested. Rain, lightning, thunder, snow, fog — everything I could also do.

"No," Cassius replied, still smiling. "She was a Corbin before she married Josiah Oliver. And the quires in her will?

The ones passed on to Joy-in-Sorrow? It's a way medieval manuscripts were folded into pages, like folios. They might have what we need to figure out how to do *your* conversion."

"So now we need to find whoever the hell Joy-in-Sorrow is?" I asked, diving back into the wills with renewed interest.

"Exactly. Except, I don't remember hearing about anyone with that weird of a name in any of my family stories. Did your family ever say anything?"

I shook my head. "No. But as you can tell, my family let tradition go by the wayside. We're more like Easter/Christmas Catholics than the weekly, Sunday-mass kind."

"Funny you should mention Catholicism in the basement our Puritan ancestors built. They're probably rolling in their graves. Well, yours are, anyway."

The fire sputtered as a cold rush of air shot out of the hearth and swept through the room.

Cassius rolled his eyes. "Oh come on, it was a *joke*."

"That wasn't me," I said, more than a little miffed that he thought it was. I didn't blame him for every freaky thing that happened, so why was it *my* fault the basement of an old-ass building was drafty?

Another gust of wind raced down the chimney and blew the stack of papers off the table.

"Graeme..." Cassius sighed, stooping to retrieve the documents.

"It's not me," I said again, rising from the chair slowly and looking around for the source. Goosebumps fanned out across my skin, sensing something my eyes couldn't pick up on.

The firelight dimmed. The logs flickered and hissed as the flames faded. Shadows in the room stretched, longer and longer, like claws reaching through the air toward me.

I backed away from the encroaching darkness, but it followed. It surrounded me on both sides, like an ink spill, bringing with it a putrid smell unlike anything I'd encountered before. "Cash?"

"Graeme!" I heard him but I couldn't see beyond the shadows, they were so dark. "Don't move!" Like I fucking could. I *knew* I was in the cellar of the meetinghouse but it looked like I'd been swallowed into some sort of void.

The black tendrils reached for my face but stopped short. I felt like I should answer him. I *wanted* to answer him, but I was transfixed by those curling, finger-like wisps.

The moment I blinked, they rushed toward me again, turning into spindly claws. Before they could reach my skin, they smashed against something invisible and exploded like a puff of smoke. The blackness overhead plunged downward, crashing in on me like a wave, hard and fast.

Dropping to my knees, I threw my arms over my head, waiting to feel another knife rake across my back like the parking garage. Except, nothing happened. When I peeked out, the blackness continued to swirl around me but never actually made contact. I was tempted to see if *I* could touch *it,* but something in my little weather-witch brain told me that was *not* a good idea.

Cassius's voice reached me in my black bubble, but once again, I couldn't understand anything he was saying. It had to have been Latin. The only word I *could* make out made my skin crawl. *Daemonium.* I didn't have to be a Catholic or a Necromancer to know he said the word "demon" in a dead language.

A low, unearthly growl rumbled through the room. The longer Cassius spoke, the louder the growling got. By the end, a deafening roar ripped through the air, while Cassius shouted the words to whatever spell he was doing.

"Exilium!"

The darkness disappeared as soon as the word left his tongue. It receded up the chimney, like floodwaters seeping back into a river. A high-pitched whine wailed through the room. As the last of the shadow disappeared, a log in the fireplace cracked and snapped in two, sending a flurry of sparks upward.

Cassius rushed forward and grabbed my arms, pulling me to my feet. "Are you ok? Let me see." He spun me in a circle quickly. As soon as I faced him again, he grabbed the front of my hoodie and yanked it down, exhaling and closing his eyes.

"What?" I asked, suddenly more concerned about the relief on his face than whatever the fuck it was that just happened.

"You're still wearing the amulet."

"Is that why it couldn't touch me? What the fuck was that thing, anyway? Was that a *demon*? I heard you say demon."

"Yeah. That was a demon. Come on, we have to get out of here." He grabbed his jacket off the back of the chair and pushed me toward the stairs, a thousand percent serious about abandoning our project. When we were halfway up the staircase, he snapped his fingers. All of the light in the basement extinguished.

"Why are we leaving? You said we have to find that Joy chick. Or someone that knows something about weather magic."

"Because where there's one demon, there's always more. And I might not be able to control the next one," he replied, closing the trap door beside the podium and waving his hand over it. It pretty much looked seamless before, but whatever little ward he put on it made it completely undetectable.

"Wait." I stopped short and turned around, looking at him with a mixture of curiosity and awe. "You really can control them? Demons, I mean. For real?"

"Yes and no. It's complicated. Now can we go? We have to

get someplace sacred for a while, make sure there aren't any others out there."

"I know a spot." He looked dubious, but I didn't give him time to argue. Seizing him by the elbow, I led the way outside to the back of the building where my Jeep was. "Get in."

"Where are we going?"

"Just get in."

He huffed but thankfully climbed into the passenger seat without further commentary.

As soon as he closed the door, I sped away from the meetinghouse. Instead of driving toward the main road, back to town, I took off for a lesser-known road that led into the woods. If it could even be called that. It wasn't paved or even well-worn. In fact, if you didn't know it was there, you'd drive right by it, disguised by the trees and the bramble. It was also one of the only ways to access the old Middlewich barn. Thanks to the Deacon's many, *many* lectures through the years, I knew the barn was one of the most consecrated areas in and around Winslow. If we needed to hide out from demons for a while, that was the perfect place to go.

Chapter Twenty-Seven
Cassius

Riding in Graeme's Jeep was… odd. For one thing, it was off-road, which was uncomfortable given the uneven terrain. But also, we were *so* close together. I never realized how narrow of a vehicle it was until each bump sent our shoulders knocking into each other.

"Where are we going?" I asked again as we rolled over a large tree branch in the middle of the path.

"Middlewich."

My brows lifted, but rather than say anything, I turned my attention to the window. The woods around us were thick. Branches scraped the Jeep from every angle, along the windows, across the roof. It sounded like the forest was trying to claw its way into the vehicle.

"What?" Graeme asked.

"What?" I repeated, blinking at him.

"You made a face."

"No, I didn't."

"Yes, you did. Your face made a face. What's wrong with the barn?"

"Nothing's *wrong* with it." I sighed and ran a hand through my hair, carefully finger combing it back into place. "It was one of the things I saw last night. At the hospital."

"Oh." I could see him chewing on his lower lip out of my

periphery. A moment later, he asked, "Should we not go, then?"

"No, it should be fine. I mean. I didn't see anything happening there. It was just one of the places I recognized. Probably something to do with the trial."

"Trial? Black Mary's trial?"

"That's where it all took place. The meetinghouse wouldn't be built for another couple of decades. So, the court was established there." I snorted, shaking my head. "If you could call it a court. It was a mockery of justice."

"They said she was a scourge," Graeme said, cutting a quick glance in my direction, like he was afraid he'd said the wrong thing. "That she was going to kill the whole village. She had to be stopped."

"According to Amos Northrup, who lodged the first complaint against Mary," I countered, keeping my voice even.

"So if a Northrup started it, why do *our* families hate each other?"

"The story I've been told is that a girl in the Hewitts' household produced evidence that sealed Mary's fate. The Corbins, Mary's birth family, believed the Hewitts orchestrated the whole thing in an attempt to steal a very powerful artifact."

"What sort of artifact?"

"A book. Well, part of a book."

"So we've been killing each other for centuries because of a book?"

"No, we've been killing each other for centuries because your family manipulated the law to murder my family and steal from us."

He shifted uncomfortably in his seat. "What's so special about this book?"

"It doesn't matter now," I huffed, turning my glare back to

the window. "It's been lost for centuries." Stolen. It's been *stolen* for centuries, but I wasn't about to keep harping on that point when Graeme was clueless about it.

Neither of us spoke after that trip down memory lane. In a way, we didn't need to. Words were weapons, whether they were lies or spells or secrets.

That being said, sometimes words were a necessity.

I was about to ask him if he was sure he knew where he was going when the trees thinned out into a clearing. A large, gabled barn sat in the middle. It had once been painted red but the paint had faded through the decades. Now, it was mostly a worn, weathered gray with so many cracks in the planks that I knew I was going to freeze my ass off. I could keep Graeme warm with a little blood magic, but I was S-O-L.

He parked the Jeep alongside the barn and we climbed out, closing the doors as quietly as possible. I glanced around for any sign of a demon, grateful not to see anything except a flock of crows high in the trees.

Graeme slid one of the barn doors open, even though it protested on rusted hinges. Inside, the barn was even colder and draftier than I'd imagined. And unlike the basement of the meetinghouse, there was no fireplace here to light.

Folding my arms across my chest, I rubbed the opposite bicep, walking in a slow, tentative circle. "I haven't been here in years..."

"I'm sure not much has changed," Graeme said. "About the only time people come out here is the winter solstice."

"I can tell," I murmured, nudging a dead sparrow out of the way as I continued walking around the perimeter. Scanning the interior, I hoped something here would jog my memory from my childhood or give me some insight as to what the hell I actually saw in Graeme's blood.

"I'm glad you texted," Graeme volunteered, clearing his throat softly. "I didn't think you were going to."

"I told you I would. Still don't trust me?" I might have been going for teasing, but it came out sounding a little on the hurt side.

"I don't know." He scuffed his heel on the worn floorboards. "You seemed really freaked last night."

"Sorry. My head's kind of been all over the place lately." Like, ever since I came back to this fucking town and ran into you time and time again. Not to mention all the other… *stuff* between us.

He stepped in front of me, halting my wandering. His dark brows slanted downward, along with the corner of his perfect mouth. "Let's talk about it."

Laughing, I rolled my eyes. "Yeah. Sure."

Giving me an irritated look, he grabbed my sleeve and dragged me over to one of the benches that ringed the center of the barn. As soon as we sat, he raised his brows, waiting. Expecting.

I sighed, seeing no point in arguing with him anymore. "It's like lately, one thing leads to another. I came back for Tennebrose, but there was more to it. I wanted to find those folios that were stolen from my family. And then you came along and derailed all of that. And now we have demons to deal with on top of everything."

He smirked, like he was pleased he'd thwarted my plans — or that he'd become the sole focus of them. "Once again. What is so special about those folio things?"

"The missing folios are from something we call the Book of Lazarus. It's our grimoire, so to speak, but since it's incomplete, we haven't really been able to use it."

"Since when?"

"1667."

He straightened, the corners of his eyes tightening.

"Yeah. The year it all started. My family's magic has been limited all this time because of it." I ran my hands over my thighs, trying to ignore the slightly scared look in his eyes. I'm sure he was imagining all sorts of evil, awful things we'd be capable of if we were at full strength — and he wasn't necessarily wrong. "So, anyway. I gave up on the Book, at least for now. We have that stupid project for Ainsworth, who may or may not be a murderer or possibly the next victim, *and* your conversion — which I should have *no* part of. You should really tell the Deacon."

"I'd rather not. Once I realized they forgot about it, I thought I was in the clear. If I didn't do it, then I couldn't be the Deacon. Right? Plus I thought skipping it meant my powers would go away. But they seem to be getting stronger. I don't understand it and right now, you're the only person I can talk to about what's going on."

"We'll figure it out," I said, reaching for his hand. At the last second, I diverted to his knee and patted it.

"Is that why Stormbringers died out?" he asked quietly, staring at my hand as white and blue sparks flashed over his. "Because of this? Because we hurt people?"

I shook my head. "They didn't die out, Graeme. You're proof of that."

"Might as well have. It's not like I'll be able to be with anyone when I'm like this." A genuine sadness permeated his whole being and suddenly I wanted nothing more than to cheer him up again, even if that meant he'd go back to annoying the crap out of me.

Against my better judgment, I took his hand and laced my fingers through his. After the initial static shock, there was just a light buzzing in my palm that wasn't unbearable.

He tried to pull his hand away, but I held onto it. "The right person will make the effort," I said.

His gaze swept up to meet mine, his jeweled eyes searching. For what, I didn't know. An answer? Permission?

On some unspoken cue, we lunged at each other, our mouths crashing together. His hands slipped around my waist, pulling me closer, while mine held either side of his face. His lips were so goddamn perfect. And when they parted for me, giving me access to his tongue, I loved them all the more.

I let one of my hands fall, palming his dick through his jeans. It wasn't long before it got so fucking hard it made me want to drop to my knees right there and bring him some sort of relief. My own hard-on was teetering on the line between pain and pleasure, constrained by the unforgiving denim.

He moaned into my mouth and rocked his hips upward, grinding against my hand. I pushed back against him, rubbing my palm up and down along his length.

Tearing his mouth from mine, he closed his eyes and tipped his head back with a pained expression. "Fuck, baby. You kill me when you do that."

I kissed his throat, his jaw, anywhere I could reach while maintaining the speed and pressure on his dick.

He captured my mouth with his again, his hand fisted in the front of my sweater to keep me close. When his other hand landed on my cock, it was my turn to groan.

Pulling away, he looked at me with half-hooded eyes, desire written plainly in his gaze. "I want you so fucking bad."

"Which part?" I asked, nipping his lush lower lip.

He sucked in a breath and gave me a smirk. "Whatever I can get."

"In a dirty, old barn?" I wrinkled my nose for effect.

"Beggars can't be choosers. And I'm fucking begging you, Cash." He slid onto my lap, straddling me on the bench. His fingers slipped through my hair while his tongue invaded my mouth, taking what he was so desperate for.

He was right, though. I'd run the risk of being electrocuted and fuck him anywhere — or let him fuck me — if it meant some of that blissful relief only he seemed to provide.

"We shouldn't be doing this," I murmured, shaking my head with my feeble attempt at protesting. He responded by swiveling his hips, grinding against me so that we both groaned.

"I know," he whispered before sucking my bottom lip gently.

I grabbed his hips, thrusting up against him with a growl. "Then stop."

"*You* stop." He twisted his fingers in my hair and kissed me hard, pulling a strangled moan out of me.

Before we could get much further, the sound of beating wings erupted overhead. The family of crows from earlier swooped in through the open window up in the gable, twirling in the air and diving together in a frenzied rush.

Graeme ducked and slid off of me, eyeing the birds with outright fear. If he thought it was my doing again, he was wrong. I had nothing to do with summoning them.

As soon as he was clear of my lap, I jumped to my feet, staring up at the black whirlwind. Their voices screamed inside my head, a cacophony accompanied by their earthly cawing.

Flee!

Intruders!

Danger!

One crow landed in front of me, tilting its head and blinking rapidly, checking to see if I got the message.

"Thank you," I said to the bird. Nodding once, I pulled Graeme to his feet, ignoring the painful zapping in my hand.

The crow took off again, following the rest of its family back out the window.

"What the fuck was that?" Graeme asked as I hauled him toward the door.

"Someone's coming."

"Was that a sign or something?"

"No, they told me."

"They *told* you?"

I was about to answer when the barn doors were thrown open with more force than mere wind. We both jerked to a halt, staring at the man storming through the opening.

"Lennox!" I tried to recover from the shock, but then Claudia appeared behind him. "Claudia! What are you doing here?"

"Looking for you!" She didn't break her stride until she collided with me, her arms around my neck. "Let's go." With a glare in Graeme's direction, she wrapped her arm around my shoulders and hauled me toward the door.

"What the fuck?!" I tried to yank away from her, but Lennox's magic shoved me in the back with the gentleness of a hunting spear, forcing me outside with a yelp. "My God! What is the matter with you two?!"

"Stay away from him!" Lennox shouted behind us. "Do you hear me, Hewitt? I'm not going to warn you again."

"Get the fuck away from me, Ambrose," Graeme snarled in return.

I turned in time to see Lennox in Graeme's face, nearly chest-to-chest with him.

Graeme's eyes flashed and his jaw hardened, electricity rippling across his skin. Lightning arced from one fist to another with tiny crackles.

"Lennox!" Claudia snapped.

Lennox lingered for another second, his own hands

covered in flames. He took a step backward, slowly, his gaze locked on Graeme until the last second.

I couldn't do much other than snap, ridding both of them of their magic. Even if the amulet would keep Graeme safe from Lennox, this whole stupid thing didn't need to devolve into a literal firefight. Especially not over whatever this latest misunderstanding was.

Lennox shot me a glare, but Graeme's attention was focused solely on my cousin.

As soon as Lennox crossed the threshold, he flicked a hand behind him, slamming the barn doors shut so hard the old wood splintered.

"Someone want to tell me what's going on?" I asked, only to be jabbed in the back a second time. "Ow! Goddamn it! Stop!"

"Get in the car," Lennox growled.

"I'm going, already!" I yanked open the rear door to Lennox's Land Rover and climbed in, slamming it shut again.

"Are you alright?" Claudia asked once we were barreling out of the woods, as far away from Middlewich as possible.

"I'm fine! Jesus. What the fuck was that all about?"

"You disappeared, Cassius," Claudia replied with a glare. "Arden saw your car at the meetinghouse but you weren't there. You know what was? A demon! Excuse us for worrying."

"You thought a demon took me? To the barn?" I shook my head, not believing that half-cocked idea. "That makes zero sense."

"No, we thought maybe a demon *chased* you to the barn. It's the closest consecrated space," she shot back.

"Yeah, so imagine our surprise to see you there with a fucking Hewitt!" Lennox sliced a contemptuous look over his shoulder. "*Again.*"

"Again? What's he talking about?" Claudia asked.

"We're lab partners," I replied to Lennox, with as much indignation as I could muster. It wasn't that hard. I was fucking fuming. "And yes, there was a demon at the meeting-house. But it went after Graeme, not me. It must have come back after we left."

"Even more reason to stay the hell away from him!" Lennox cried.

"What were you doing at the meetinghouse in the first place?" Claudia asked.

"Research! Remember? Ainsworth made us pair up for our stupid project."

"What kind of botany research could you possibly be doing in the archives?" Claudia asked.

My head thunked back against the headrest and I covered my face with my hands. "Oh my God..."

"You were there looking for the folios, weren't you?" Lennox asked, shooting a suspicious glance over his shoulder as he narrowly avoided a tree.

"Folios?" Claudia whipped around in her seat, her eyes wide. "*The* folios?"

I lowered my hands, glaring at both of them, even if Lennox couldn't exactly see me while he was driving. "I *have* a father, you know. I don't need — or want — either of you trying to fill the role."

"I told you, I'm not losing any more family members," Claudia snipped.

"Neither am I," Lennox added.

"He's not like his father," I said on Graeme's behalf, like it would do one bit of good.

"I don't care!" Claudia yelled. "His family has been killing ours for centuries! And if you keep putting yourself in situations like that back there, they're not going to have any problem killing you too!"

I bit back a retort and glared out the window. Years

abroad had apparently done different things for my sister and I. I gained independence and learned to rely on myself, sometimes to a fault. She, on the other hand, became even more smothering and neurotic than when I left at twelve.

As soon as Lennox's SUV rolled to a stop, I threw the door open and marched up the front steps of the house.

"Where are you going?" Claudia asked, hot on my heels.

"To my room. That's what you want, isn't it?" I replied, stomping up each stair for dramatic effect. "To keep me under lock and key like a fucking princess in a tower."

"Does that mean I get to be the fire-breathing dragon?" Lennox asked, jogging after Claudia.

"Shut up!" Claudia and I both snapped at him. He raised his hands in surrender and turned away from us.

Scoffing, I rolled my eyes and continued up the stairs and down the hall. Claudia floated after me, like a waif. I slammed the door in her face and threw a ward over it.

"We're not done talking about this!" she shouted through the closed door.

"Yes, we are!"

"Just wait until Dad gets home!"

"That threat doesn't work anymore!"

She made a frustrated growling sound right before her footsteps stomped back down the hallway.

As soon as my phone connected to the WiFi in the house, a steady stream of texts dinged in my pocket.

I pulled it out and flicked through them, easing onto the edge of my mattress.

Graeme: WTF???

Graeme: Are you ok?

Graeme: What was that about?

Graeme: Why aren't you answering?

Graeme: Send something so I know you're not dead

Graeme: FFS Cash!

I typed a response quickly so he didn't do something stupid, like drive over here.

Me: I'm fine.

The little dots appeared and disappeared. Appeared again and disappeared. Finally, his reply came through.

Graeme: What happened?

That was what he spent nearly two minutes typing? *That* is what he came up with? How much deleting did he do before he sent two measly words?

Me: They ran into the same demon at the meeting-house and assumed I'd gone to Middlewich. It's fine. I'll see you Tuesday.

Graeme: What about Joy? And our project?

I bit my lip, analyzing all of my problems and trying to put them into some sort of logical order.

Me: I think your conversion is more important. Once that is out of the way, we can focus on the project.

Graeme: What about Ainsworth?

Me: Conversion, Ainsworth, project.

Graeme: What about your family's book?

Fuck. I shouldn't have told him about that... then again, maybe he could do some recon on his end and see if anything turned up on the folios or whoever Joy-in-Sorrow was.

Me: Conversion, Ainsworth, project, book. It's been missing for 350 years, it can wait a few more weeks.

Graeme: You sure you're ok?

Me: Yeah

Graeme: Ok. See you Tuesday

I tossed my phone behind me and flopped onto my back with a groan, dreading my Dad's imminent return.

Chapter Twenty-Eight

Graeme

I wasn't exactly a morning person, but for once I was awake before my alarm went off. Tuesday morning, I sprang out of bed and darted out the front door before Dad even came down the stairs. He shouted at me anyway, like it would slow me down.

"Graeme! Where are you going?"

"Class. Bye!"

Stopping by the bakery, I grabbed a couple of cinnamon bagels and two cups of coffee before heading to campus. Cassius and I had texted over the weekend, but it wasn't the same. I wanted to *see* him, to know he was really ok after getting caught by his family. *Again*.

I got to Dane Hall well before our class was even slated to start, so I had the maximum amount of time with him. Taking a seat on the stone steps, I started in on breakfast, scanning the crowd as people passed for any sign of the moody, blue-eyed boy.

Cassius appeared around the bend of one of the buildings, talking animatedly even though he was walking by himself. It took me a minute to realize there was a crow on his shoulder.

As soon as they were within earshot of me, the crow cawed and flew off, disappearing into a tree to roost.

"Good morning," I said, standing to greet him with a smile. "Who's your friend?"

"Just a friend," he answered coyly, taking the paper cup from me, the corner of his mouth tipped up. "Starting the experimentation part of the assignment early? Did you go with arsenic or belladonna first? I know it's not lead. Takes far too long."

"Nah, I'm not going to poison you, Corbin. I need to keep you around a while longer so I get a passing grade, since I'm so dumb and all."

He smirked at me and I hung back on the stairs, letting him go first. Instead of walking, he bit his lower lip, giving me a long, knowing look. Without making a comment, which I'm sure took great effort on his part, he finally made his way up the stairs. The black jeans were a hair too loose to be considered "skinny," but regardless, they hugged his ass perfectly. It took everything I had not to make an appreciative noise.

"What are you doing after class?" I asked as we neared the top of the stairs on the second floor.

He turned on the top step, his eyes narrowed. "No."

"What?" I blinked.

"No," he repeated, raising both eyebrows to drive the point home.

"I was going to ask if you wanted to go for a hike or something."

His brows dropped sharply and he gave me a disbelieving look. "A hike?"

"Mhmm. The North Woods."

Cassius canted his head to the side, his expression softening. "That actually works out better than I'd hoped."

Now it was my turn to make a skeptical face. "What does?"

"Tonight is the Harvest Moon."

"Ok..." I didn't like the way he said that. It was another one of those obviously witchy things that I should know but clearly didn't.

"It's the perfect sort of energy for your conversion, Stormbringer," he explained with none of his usual snootiness.

I opened my mouth to answer, but he shot me a rather evil sort of grin and turned, sauntering off toward our classroom.

Instead of taking my seat at the table across the aisle, I slid into the chair right next to him.

He looked at me like I stabbed him. "What are you doing?"

"Sitting down?"

"You can't sit here."

"Why not?"

He stole a glance around the room before leaning in. "Because!"

I leaned in a fraction closer. "Ainsworth is the one who wanted us to work together. Remember?"

"It doesn't mean we need to look so… so…"

"Friendly?"

"Yeah!"

Raking my teeth over my lower lip, I ran my hand over his thigh. "Like this?"

"Jesus, Graeme." His fingers curled around mine, stopping me from reaching my intended destination. He didn't let go, though.

I gripped the inside of his thigh and pulled myself closer, leaning toward his ear. "You don't want to be friends anymore?"

There was a soft exhalation before he murmured, "No."

"What *do* you want?"

Before he could answer me, Ainsworth swept into the

room. Our professor took one look at us, squinted suspiciously, and set his briefcase down.

"I hope you're all prepared to discuss atropa belladonna at length," Ainsworth announced. "Including its scientific and folkloric history. This *will* be on the final."

Message received, professor. I slowly pulled my hand from Cassius's lap and picked up my pen, clicking it loudly for our teacher's benefit.

He cleared his throat and began.

As much as I tried to focus on the lecture, I kept sneaking glances at Cassius. He was either completely engrossed in what Ainsworth had to say about nightshade plants or he was trying *very* hard to ignore me.

I sent a whisper of air toward him, curling it around the shell of his ear as gently as if I was caressing him.

He lifted one shoulder and grazed his ear, like he could block the sensation.

Sending another, stronger current his way, it was enough to ruffle his hair where it wasn't pomaded into place.

Cassius's stormy eyes shot toward me. A second later, his foot reached out beneath the table and nudged mine.

I nudged him back with an impish grin.

"Hewitt!" Ainsworth called out.

I jumped and looked up sharply. "Sir?"

"What is the scientific name for the nightshade family?"

"Solanaceae, professor."

Ainsworth smirked, considering me for a moment. "Very good." He resumed his lecture, clicking through slides as he went.

"We need elderberries," Cassius said under his breath.

"What?" I tipped my head in his direction, keeping my eyes glued to Ainsworth.

"Elderberries," Cassius repeated. "For tonight. And verbena if we can find some."

"If you're going to kill me, can it be with something *other* than poison?" He scoffed. When I stole another glance at him, he scowled at me. "Kidding," I whispered. "I know a spot."

"Just like the barn?"

"That spot was fine until your family came charging in like the cavalry."

"Maybe next time pick a spot that's more discreet."

"It's a three-hundred-year-old barn in the middle of the woods. How discreet does it need to be, for Christ's sake?"

Something hard slapped against the back of my head. I hissed and rubbed the growing welt, glaring over my shoulder.

Cassius also yelped and turned around.

A vine slithered back to its pot right as Ainsworth cleared his throat.

Cassius tucked his chin and busied himself copying notes from the whiteboard.

I slid down in my chair and scooted away from him. Or rather, away from the *temptation* of him.

As soon as class was over, Cassius and I both bolted for the door. Ainsworth yelled our names and told us to stop. We ignored him. It was a calculated risk, but I didn't feel like having my ribs crushed or getting smacked in the head again by a giant plant. Cash must have felt the same way.

"So what's the game plan for tonight?" I asked as we jogged down the front steps of Dane Hall.

"Do you know where Norwood Bridge is? Near the old

village?"

"Yeah."

"Good. Meet me there in an hour. Bring a change of clothes. And a towel."

"A towel?"

He gave me a wry grin and let his gaze drift over my body, like he was slowly removing each piece of clothing and picturing what was beneath. Raising his brows suggestively, he pivoted and strolled off in the opposite direction. A group of crows flew by overhead, keeping pace with him, like some sort of avian entourage.

I shook my head, half exasperated with him and half in awe.

Since I had an hour to kill, I ran home and snuck in the house for the supplies. I grabbed everything Cash told me to and stuffed it all into one of my packs as quickly as I could. I was on my way back out when that fucking crystal bell rang out, shattering the silence in the house.

"Graeme? Is that you?" my mother called.

Swearing under my breath, I debated whether or not I really wanted to answer her. The guilty part of my brain told me I was an absolute piece of shit if I didn't. She was sick and she clearly needed something. Besides, what kind of asshole pretends to ignore his sick mom?

So instead of leaving like I wanted, I crept toward her room, pushing open the door just a crack. "Yeah, Mom?"

"I need my pills." She shook an orange bottle at me. A few pills rattled in the bottom, but not many.

I crossed the room to her bed and took the bottle, squinting at the refill date in the light from the hallway. "Mom... you just got these last week." I mean, I remembered, since *I* forgot to pick them up at the pharmacy and got reamed by my dad for it.

"I have *headaches*, Graeme," she said, her voice brittle. I'm sure if I could see in the dark room, her eyes would be bloodshot and glassy, weighed down with heavy lids. She was always on the verge of a hysterical breakdown. Still. After six years.

At first I understood, but as the years dragged by, I couldn't help but be a little… bitter. Yeah. That was the right word. I was bitter that my mom was still upset about losing her child. I *was* an absolute piece of shit after all.

"Yeah, I know, Mom." Gritting my teeth, I twisted off the cap and shook out two of the pills.

She practically snatched them out of my hand, downing them with a glass of tepid water.

"Do you think you're going to make it downstairs today?" I asked, already knowing the answer.

"No."

"Do you want me to open the curtains? Let some fresh air in here?"

"You can go now," she sighed, flicking her hand toward the door and dismissing me now that my task was complete. It's the only use she had for me anymore. Errand boy. Servant. Daily reminder I hadn't protected the most precious thing in her world.

I didn't even bother saying goodbye. I stomped out of her room and down the stairs and drove straight to the hospital to check in on India. There hadn't been any updates in a while and I couldn't tell if that was a good thing or not.

Mrs. Tenney and Preston were at India's side when I walked in. Neither looked like they were in good spirits, which had my stomach knotting with every step I took.

"Graeme, sweetie. How are you?" Mrs. Tenney asked, standing to hug me. A real hug, not one of those one-armed social requirements.

I hugged her back, maybe a little too much, a little too long, but she didn't pull away until I did. Giving her a sheepish smile, I shoved my hands in my pockets and rocked back on my heels. "Shouldn't I be asking you that?"

She touched my cheek before gazing down at her mummified daughter. "Her lungs aren't healing the way they'd hoped. Too much inhalation damage, they said."

"But can't you…" I gestured toward India, hoping she caught my meaning. Beyond being a nurse, Mrs. Tenney was the go-to healer for the Congregation. She's the one who erased all of the claw marks from my fight with Cassius in under five minutes, so why couldn't she help her own daughter?

"If this was a regular burn, yes." When she turned back to face me, her blue eyes were filled with tears. "It's not. It's something… else."

"Like a hex," Preston added glumly.

"So her magic didn't backfire…" I said, looking at India. Only part of her face was visible. A red, angry mottling peeked through at the edge of the bandages. I could only imagine what the rest of her looked like.

"We reached out to Marcus and Jane, but they don't know anything that could help us," Mrs. Tenney said, wrapping her arms around herself.

"The Ambroses?" My eyes widened, glancing between her and Preston.

Preston bit his lip and shook his head, visibly holding something back, while Mrs. Tenney nodded at me. "Who better to ask than the other fire witches? We thought, perhaps, they might be able to sense something we were missing."

"Diane?" Dr. Dane appeared, knocking on the open door. "Can you come here for a moment?"

She forced a smile to her face and hurried over to join him in the hall.

My gaze snapped to Preston. "Spill it."

He sat up straighter, his jaw shifting irritably. "I've been thinking. About Lennox."

"I thought you said he didn't do it?"

Preston shook his head again. "I don't know. Something about that night has been bugging me. I went back the next day, after we talked, and walked the whole area. I found this." He pulled his phone out of his pocket and flicked through it before turning it around to show me a picture.

It was a bunch of lines scraped into the dirt. Lines and circles and triangles. And it looked an awful lot like—

"A demon sigil," I whispered.

"Yeah. And you know who knows all about demons?" The sickening feeling returned to my stomach, churning with nausea. "*Necromancers*," Preston continued, anger flashing in his eyes as he growled the word like a curse. Like I used to.

"But Cassius just got here… he didn't even know India," I said weakly.

"I'm not talking about Cassius, Graeme," Preston replied with a bit of a huff. "The Ambroses aren't just fire witches. They're Necromancers too. Lennox has all sorts of books like the ones Peyton had. Some dark shit. Like demons and blood magic."

"Why would he do something like that? You said he and India were cool."

"I don't know. But the next time I see him, he's either going to confess or he's going to get me some fucking answers on who really summoned the demon out there."

My throat felt like it was stuffed with cotton and no amount of swallowing would get rid of it, so I merely nodded. Lennox Ambrose was one of, if not, *the* biggest assholes I'd ever met. No doubt about it. But seeing how close he and Cassius were? If Preston went after Lennox, Cassius would go after Preston and where the hell would that leave me? Leave *us*?

Chapter Twenty-Nine
Cassius

As soon as I had everything I thought I could possibly need for this endeavor, I swung myself up onto Lucius's back and we were off.

I hoped Graeme really knew where the elderberries were, otherwise I'd have to make do with some other protective herb. Not that I knew which one would work, anyway. This whole thing was one giant risk and I, as a rule, didn't like taking risks. The only positive I could see in having *me* oversee Graeme's conversion rite was that I could lasso his spirit and shove it back into his body if things went really, *really* wrong. But if he took me out in the process? Well, then I guess we were both fucked.

Speaking of fucked... This thing with him was *so* confusing. When he wasn't around, I could think clearly. I could focus on research and translating the umpteenth medieval grimoire, looking for the demon that belonged to that sigil. It didn't help when there were so many different demons and so many different *levels* of demons — princes, dukes, marquises, and knights, each of which commanded their own legions. Last time I checked, a legion was six *thousand* beings. So despite Lennox's chastising, it was fucking impossible to have *all* of their sigils memorized.

But whenever Graeme walked into a room, he sucked all

the oxygen right out of it. I felt dizzy, like if I wasn't keeping my gaze fixed on him then I was going to fall over. Despite our verbal spats, he made me feel… That was it — he made me *feel*. Something. Other than anger, I hadn't felt anything else in such a long time. How the fuck did he do that? Granted, I still felt plenty annoyed when he was around. Angry. Resentful. But also, connected? Understood?

I made it to Norwood Bridge with time to spare and zero epiphanies on what I was supposed to do about Graeme once his conversion was over. I mean, as much of a pain in the ass as he was, I'd gotten used to having him around. But would he still want to *be* around after the demon-hunting and the semester was over? Would he actually help me look for lost folios? Or would everything go back to the way it was, where we tried to kill each other every chance we could?

Shaking my head, I dismounted Lucius. I needed to focus on the here and now and not worry about anything beyond tonight. Worrying about what had yet to come was as useful as lamenting over what had already passed. I, above all people, knew how limited our time in this world really was.

With the crows serving as lookouts in the trees, I started setting up the ritual space next to the river. I had no idea if it was even necessary, but I decided to err on the side of caution. Besides, Necromancy was nothing if not ritualistic in every sense of the word. We poured intention into each step of the process and followed the spells to a T, unlike the nature witches with their stupid feelings and hodgepodge spell casting.

Graeme's Jeep rolled up shortly after I finished, crunching branches and scattering rocks along the way. When he climbed out, I immediately knew something was off. He didn't smile at me like he normally did and he shoved his hands in his pockets, taking his time walking over instead of rushing to me like he had that morning.

"What happened?" I asked as soon as he was within earshot.

"Nothing."

"You *are* a shitty liar, you know that?"

"I just came from the hospital," he said, looking down at his feet as he traversed the leaf-covered ground, no less quieter than his Jeep had been.

Not quite sure what to say to that, I watched him approach warily. Turned out I didn't have to wait for long to find out what his problem was.

"Is Lennox a Necromancer?" Graeme asked, looking up sharply.

Furrowing my brows, I cocked my head, trying to figure out what his angle was. I thought he'd dropped the whole attitude toward my kind, but I guess not. "Why?"

"Answer the question."

"Not until you tell me *why*."

"Because Preston said Lennox has books on Necromancy shit. So is he? An actual Necromancer?"

"We *all* are," I ground out, not liking where this line of questioning was going. "All of the blood-born children from the so-called 'dark' families are. Not everyone can master it. Not everyone *wants* to because of that fucking look right there." I couldn't help but point at him and the murderous scowl on his face.

"Did he do it?"

"You've got to be fucking kidding me." I gritted my teeth and forced my gaze away, staring at nothing rather than look at him for one second longer. So much for moving past this. So much for him *not* being like the rest of them.

"Preston thinks he did. He found a demon sigil by the equinox bonfire," Graeme said, like he was intentionally provoking me. And like the idiot I was, I let him.

My gaze darted back to him. "Well Preston is dumber

than the fucking rocks he controls! Lennox wouldn't do that! *None* of us would!"

"Why should anyone believe that?"

"Because we have nothing to gain from it!" I snarled. "One of the basic tenets of Necromancy — power. Dominion over death. Killing a fire witch gains us nothing when we already *have* those powers. You know what we *would* want? The type of power we used to *kill* for back in the day?" I closed the distance on him, stopping just short enough that he didn't fucking electrocute me. "A Stormbringer. My ancestors would have chained you up and cut the still-beating heart out of your chest and drained every ounce of power they could from your body before they cast your spirit into the darkest level of Hell. But you know why we won't do that now? Because someone *stole* part of our grimoire, which means we *can't*!" My voice rose with each sentence until I was shouting so loud he flinched.

"I'm sorry," he said as I spun and stalked away from him for a bit of breathing room.

"Fuck your apology!" I snapped over my shoulder.

"Someone out there keeps summoning a demon, Cassius! If it's not you and it's not Lennox, then who is it?"

"How about you make your fucking conversion and then we can find out? Because I'm not crossing over on a demon hunt or bringing Sophia's spirit back by myself."

"Don't we have to go find elderberries or something?"

"Fuck the elderberries. The sooner we get this over with, the better for everyone. Come stand in the middle," I said, pointing at the circle and flicking open my pocket knife.

Graeme did as he was told, although his foot hesitated for a second before he stepped over the line of salt and crystals.

As soon as he was inside, I moved closer but stayed outside of the line. Murmuring a prayer in Latin, I sliced into my skin with the knife and turned my forearm over, letting the blood drip out and into his space.

A bolt of lightning arced through the air and struck the ground where the red droplets landed.

Graeme and I both jumped.

"What the fuck was that?" I stared at him, a little curl of smoke drifting up from where a leaf caught on fire.

"It just..." He gaped at his hand, clenching it into a fist. "I don't know!"

Something stirred in the back of my brain, but it was foggy and only half-formed. Working on instinct, I turned my arm over again and squeezed, pushing out more blood.

Another streak of crackling white energy hurtled toward me, colliding midair with the blood before it even had a chance to hit the ground. I jumped away from it, as horrified as I was confused.

"It's you," Graeme said, his mismatched eyes wide. "My magic has gone fucking haywire because of *you*."

I opened my mouth to reply. Finding I was at a loss for actual words, I closed it again and searched the trees, like they held the answer. In all my years of studying and training, I'd never heard about anything like this happening. Then again, maybe I needed to dive deeper into the histories or talk to someone with real experience — like Mary Oliver.

"You *did* hex me." Graeme's face hardened. "Didn't you?"

My gaze dropped to his, narrowing. "Are you serious right now?"

"Explain that!" He pointed at the scorched earth, his brows drawn into a sharp, angry V.

"I can't!" I yelled back at him. "I already fucking told you I don't have all the answers!"

"I'm not sure if I believe that anymore. You always seem to know *just* enough for some things and then conveniently you know nothing when it actually matters."

"What?" His words hit me as hard as a slap. I'd been nothing but honest with him, even when it was a fucking detriment to my family — like *right* now. He knew things about us that no one outside of our family knew and now he was throwing it all back in my face?

"What if this has all been some illusion, some fucked up mind game to pass the time? You get into the heads of birds. Who's to say you can't do the same to humans? Or haunt their dreams like a fucking hag back in the old days?"

Hag. The word was even more of an insult than implying I'd hexed him. A pain shot through my chest, so sharp it stole my breath.

"*You're* the one who wouldn't keep their fucking distance!" I said through my teeth, taking a step closer to him. "*You're* the one who keeps pushing for this to be something that it will *never* be!"

"Thank God for that." He gave me a once-over, his lip curled. "Now that your little secret is out, don't even think about coming near me again."

"There is no secret, you fucking asshole, because I. Didn't. Hex. You!"

"Like I would believe that after what I just saw."

Fury surged through my veins. I marched into the circle, making sure to step right on the salt and disrupt the line. Swiping my thumb in my blood, I drew a hasty cross on his forehead and clamped a hand over the top of his skull. It was a risk to close my eyes, but I did, my fingers digging into his scalp while I ground out a prayer in Latin. I couldn't curse him with the amulet on, so I did the only thing I *could* — I blessed him with the strength to follow his convictions and stay the fuck away from me.

As soon as I was done, he wrenched himself free, his mismatched eyes as wide as saucers. "What the fuck did you just do?"

I didn't bother answering. He wouldn't believe me anyway. He said so himself. Shoving past him, I stalked to the other side of the circle, kicking more salt out of the way and throwing my shit in the bag as fast as I could.

"Answer me!" he yelled.

That was the *last* thing I was going to fucking do. I'd been honest with him about everything — about more than I should have. And honesty got me nowhere. So fuck him. He could have silence instead.

Slinging the bag over my shoulder, I strode over to Lucius and pulled myself up into the saddle.

"Cassius!" Graeme was right behind me.

Clicking my tongue, I gave Lucius a swift kick to his sides. He whinnied and lurched forward, shouldering Graeme out of the way. I don't know if they actually collided or not, but Graeme stumbled backward before catching himself against a tree.

Lucius set off at the fastest pace he could manage through the tangled woods. I refused to look back. Even when the crows gliding along overhead offered an update on what he was doing, I declined. I didn't want to know what he was doing. I didn't fucking care anymore.

Chapter Thirty
Graeme

As soon as I got in the Jeep, I looked at myself in the mirror. I knew he'd smeared his blood on me like a fucking psycho, but I didn't realize he'd done it in the shape of a cross. What the fuck was *that* all about? And what the fuck had he said while he was doing it? I didn't hear anything about a demon this time, only the traditional closing of a Catholic prayer. Like the rest of Necromantic magic, it had to be some fucked up perversion of Christian liturgy. It just *had* to, because there's no way Cassius Corbin *blessed* me when he looked like he'd rather drown me in the river.

Hastily scrubbing it off, I, in turn, cursed his name under my breath. I threw the Jeep into drive and sped out of the woods as fast as I could. Only someone with something to hide would be that pissed. Right? And he's the one who mysteriously knew all about weather magic, yet he claimed he had no idea why my power literally went berserk when he started bleeding. Yeah, right. I called bullshit.

In addition to reminding me what a fucking liar Cassius was, this failed experiment proved he was more than likely hiding something. Whether it was about him or about his dickwad cousin, something wasn't right in that bloodline.

It was also a stark reminder I had to stay the fuck away

from him if I ever wanted to get a grip on my magic. I didn't know how he was messing with it, but clearly he was since it had never done this shit before. As much as I didn't want to talk to the Deacon about my magic, maybe that *was* the best option. Better than a fucking Necromancer, at any rate.

I'd no more than walked in the door when my dad rounded the corner, a grim look on his face.

"My phone died," I snapped, heading off his lecture. "Ok? It's not even fucking sunset yet. I'll take a battery pack with me next time so you can save your breath."

He frowned but didn't say anything, which was... odd.

I stopped and looked at him, a sudden rush of worry crashing over me. "What's wrong? Is it Mom? I only gave her two pills. I swear, she was—"

He held up a hand, his frown deepening. "Your mother is fine."

"Then what is it?"

He swallowed. "India."

The earth must have shifted on its axis. It was the only way to explain why everything went topsy turvy. One minute I was standing, the next I was shaking my head and stumbling across the kitchen, grasping the counter.

"I'm so sorry, Graeme." One of his large hands reached out and squeezed my shoulder, keeping me upright. I registered the sensation, but none of the comfort.

"I just saw her. I was, I was *just* there..." I said pathetically, like it mattered. I saw my brother the day he died, too, hours before, and look how that turned out.

"I know... Diane called. It doesn't make sense."

No. Nothing made sense. Nothing had made sense in weeks. Since... the night I met Cassius.

No matter what he said, I knew somehow this was all connected. To him, to us. We'd pissed off the powers that be and *this* was the punishment. People were dying and it was my fault. Again.

Tears welled in my eyes, bursting out before I could blink them back.

"Shhh. Come here." Dad folded me into a hug, like he used to when I was a little kid, and I let him.

Thunder rumbled overhead and rain plinked against the windows. All the while, Dad kept holding me. I sobbed and fucking sobbed. I tried to stop, but I couldn't. So many lives had been lost or ruined because of me, my magic, my stupidity. I didn't think I'd ever stop mourning my friend and cursing Cassius and hating myself for being the cause of so much fucking suffering.

A week later, I came face-to-face with the monster again in the worst place possible.

The sky was so gray, it didn't feel like daytime at all. The clouds overhead threatened rain, but I'd already cried all of my tears. No one in the greater Winslow area needed to worry about rain for a while. The wells had run fucking dry.

As soon as I saw them walking through the cemetery — the *Necromancers* — I straightened and took a step forward to stop them. Cassius's stupid amulet was burning a hole in my pocket. Not literally, but it might as well have been. I had every intention of throwing it in his smug face and telling him to fuck off as soon as he was close enough.

"Boys!" the Deacon snapped. It was only then that I realized Preston had been a step behind me, the hatred written plainly on his face for his former "friends."

Cassius's stormy gaze met mine across the distance. I felt nothing when I looked at him except rage. He must have felt the same thing, now that I was on to him, since he'd gone back to looking like the villain from a fairytale. How someone could manage to look so fucking evil just standing there was a mystery, but it was obviously a talent he'd mastered. Him and the rest of his twisted fucking family.

He stood between Claudia and Lennox, all three of them dressed in head-to-toe black. With their dark hair, pale skin, and the perpetual "Fuck off" carved into their foreheads, there was no denying how vile they were. I thought he was better than that. I thought he was actually nice underneath that hard exterior. How had I been so fucking stupid to let my guard down around him? It's a miracle I wasn't rotting in a pine box, too.

Dad laid a hand on my shoulder and pulled me back to his side. It was just us, of course, because Mom couldn't handle funerals. She couldn't handle anyone even mentioning death. So when she asked where we were going, Dad lied and said it was a work thing. I couldn't fucking handle funerals either, *Mom,* but I was still here trying to offer whatever pitiful condolences I could to India's family and to Preston. Except, I could never apologize enough for bringing death into their lives, all thanks to my disgusting fling with Cassius.

As they lowered India's casket into the ground, I couldn't help but wonder if she'd be safe. With a family of Necromancers standing fifteen feet away from her, would they leave her body alone? Should I come back tonight and set up some sort of vigil to make sure the fuckers didn't do something, like harvest her organs or resurrect her? They were so adamant about cremating their own to prevent that sort of thing, so what was stopping them from doing it to one of us?

Apparently I didn't have to worry. The Deacon ended the

service by blessing the grave and sealing it with an incantation so India's soul would find peace.

I stole a glance at Cassius at the conclusion of the spell.

His gaze flicked up to mine, the corners of his eyes tightening in silent challenge.

A gust of wind whipped through the crowd, cold and biting. All of the Necromancers immediately glared at me. I didn't care. Even if I was pushing against the good witches and breaking the stems in the delicate floral arrangements, I didn't call off the blustery attack.

Caius glanced between his son and I before leaning over to his daughter and saying something. Claudia nodded and hooked her arm through Cassius's, pulling him away. Lennox glanced at his uncle and Caius nodded, prompting Lennox to turn on his heel and follow his cousins. Caius stopped near Lennox's parents and said something to them, patting his brother-in-law's shoulder before he walked away.

The Selectmen from the Ambroses, the Simms, the Colburns, and the Olivers had their own little confab before they made their silent escape, one by one.

Good. At least now they knew they weren't wanted. Well, they probably knew it beforehand, but at least India's parents wouldn't have to be subjected to interacting with them.

My happiness at their disappearance was short-lived.

I thought the cemetery would be the last I would have to see any of the Necromancers. But oh no. The entitled assholes crashed the reception at the meetinghouse too.

Caius and Lennox's parents apparently had no issue marching up to India's parents, shaking their hands and murmuring condolences. Claudia even brought apple turnovers for the potluck. Like anyone in their right mind would eat something that came from a family with their own fucking poison garden. The verdict on whether or not they grew poisoned apples was still up in the air, given that Cassius was a giant fucking liar.

Once again, simply thinking about the asshole made him materialize. He was standing with Lennox and Arden off to one side, like a trio of alley cats, glaring down anyone who so much as looked in their direction. I couldn't help but wonder… three deaths. Three demons summoned. And three twisted-as-fuck Necromancers. Coincidence?

"I need air," I said to Preston, stomping toward the closest door. I shouldered it open and burst into the frigid wind still gusting around.

Closing my eyes, I tipped my head back and tried to inhale a calming breath.

The door behind me creaked open. The second my body started thrumming, I knew it was that fucking prick.

"You better not even—" My words faltered as I turned, opening my eyes to see Lennox and Arden, *not* Cassius. "What the fuck do you want?"

"Us? Nothing. We're just on our way to a barbecue," Lennox said with a shit-eating grin.

"Wanna come?" Arden asked.

"Might have a bonfire later, too," Lennox added.

Rage clouded my vision. A rush of freezing wind tore through air between us, dropping the temperature so fast my breath actually crystalized in front of me when I spoke. "If I find out you had anything to do with India's death, I swear to God I'll—"

"What?" Lennox challenged, darting forward so we were nose-to-nose. "You'll *what*, Hewitt?"

"I'll fucking destroy you."

He sniffed, giving me a disdainful once-over. "I'm not my cousin."

"What the fuck does mean?" For a split second I didn't

know if I should be offended on Cassius's behalf or just my own.

"It means I don't care how pretty you are or that the Congregation thinks sunshine comes out of your ass. I'll be more than happy to melt your fucking flesh from your bones and give them to Claudia as a Christmas present." Well that was a horrifying image… but I couldn't let it distract me.

"If I'm Deacon one day, things are going to get very bad for you, Ambrose."

"Who says you'll live that long?" Lennox smirked. "Especially now that there's a demon after you and you don't have your little fuck buddy around to protect you anymore."

I wanted to say he was lying, but I'd been attacked twice now by something I couldn't see. Still, despite the evidence in front of me, I didn't want to believe a word out of his fucking mouth. Especially the part about his own cousin. "The only demons I know of are you and your fucking family of freaks."

"Aw, what happened, weather boy? Cassius stop sucking your dick? Couldn't help but notice how *chilly* things were at the graveside."

I shoved him away from me as hard as I could before I fucking decked him. "Fuck you, Lennox!"

Sadly, Arden caught him before he stumbled too far.

Lennox laughed. "Maybe Preston will take over for him, especially now that India's out of the picture. You guys can console each other," he said with a mocking smile as he pantomimed jerking off.

I should have ignored him.

I should have walked away.

I should not have lunged across the distance I just created and tackled his smug ass to the ground, but that's exactly what I did.

We'd barely landed on the hard earth when I dealt punch

after punch to his fucking face, blood flying between it and my knuckles.

Something yanked me backward and slammed me into the ground, well away from Lennox. I assumed it was Arden, but when I pushed myself into a sitting position, Arden was kneeling next to Lennox, checking out the blood trickling from his lip.

Scrambling to my feet, I whirled around to see Cassius of all goddamn people.

"Get the fuck away from me," I seethed.

He circled around in front of me, conveniently putting himself between me and his dick cousin. "Then stay away from my family." Maybe if he'd just heard what his so-called family was saying about him, he wouldn't be so quick to defend him. But fuck if *I* was going to be the one to point that out.

"How about you tell your family not to start shit?" I straightened my suit jacket and pivoted on the ball of my foot. I was only two steps away when Cassius and Arden both yelled.

"No!"

"Don't!"

I threw a glance over my shoulder in time to see a giant ball of fire racing toward me.

Chapter Thirty-One
Cassius

It unfolded before my very eyes and yet it felt like I was frozen in time, unable to do a goddamn thing except stand and scream.

Arden snapped at Lennox, telling him to stop, to leave it alone and walk away. In return, Lennox told him to fuck off.

I felt the heat well before I saw orange bloom in my periphery. My head barely turned as a flaming mass sailed through the air, right past my face.

Panic exploded inside of me.

Arden and I both shouted in unison.

Graeme turned with the commotion. His eyes widened a split second before he threw an arm up, over his face. The flames stopped an inch away from him with a loud crack. They disappeared with a sizzle of smoke, like someone had thrown an invisible bucket of water on them.

Still, the smell of burning flesh filled the air.

The horrified look on Graeme's face unleashed a sudden sickness in the pit of my stomach. It wasn't panic anymore. My heart slammed against the inside of my ribcage and dread sent an icy chill down my spine as I followed Graeme's gaze behind me.

Lennox was sprawled on the ground again, a ring of black scorching the earth around him.

Arden was on his knees next to him, screaming.

A giant hole burned right through the center of my cousin's chest. The edges of his flesh were charred and red lines radiated outward on his skin. A *lightning* burn.

People began filing out of the meetinghouse, shouting questions and commands at us and each other.

"Lennox!" I bolted to his side and dropped to my knees. Lennox's black eyes were open, but unseeing. There was no breath. No blood. No movement of any kind, an absolute stillness only achieved in death.

"No, no, no!" I grabbed either side of his face and searched in vain for any sign of life, however minuscule. My vision blurred, my eyes stinging. Touching the hole in the center of his chest with a shaking hand, I willed myself to tap into whatever bone magic I had buried in my DNA. If I could put him back together, if I could fix his body quickly enough, I could call his soul back to it before it was too late, *before* he crossed over.

The crowd parted and Dad appeared, dropping to his knees next to me. He shooed me to the side and ran his hands over Lennox's chest.

Peregrine and Dr. Dane pushed through the crowd next, mimicking Dad's position, their hands hovering over Lennox.

Claudia edged around the gawking onlookers, her hands over her mouth. When she saw me, she sank to the ground and flung her arms around my neck. After a moment, she shoved me out to arm's length again, checking me over from head to toe. "Are you ok? Are you hurt?"

More tears spilled out of my eyes when I squeezed them shut, shaking my head.

She pulled me against her, pressing her cheek to the top of my head. I knew she was trying to be the brave one, but I felt her tears as they dripped down onto me. But then the drops came faster and faster, hitting parts of my body I knew she couldn't reach. They weren't tears at all. It was rain. A cold, drenching rain that cut through my clothes and froze me from the inside out.

Dad stood slowly and walked over to my aunt and uncle. I knew from Aunt Jane's high-pitched shriek that Lennox was well and truly dead. Beyond death, actually. His body was too broken to be repaired, which meant even if his spirit could be recalled, it didn't have a home.

As Dr. Dane shrugged out of his suit jacket and draped it over Lennox's lifeless body, Peregrine stormed over to Arden. "What in God's name happened?!"

Arden sniffed and swiped the tears off his face roughly with the back of his hand. It didn't matter with all of the rain falling, his cheeks were wet again within seconds. "It was Graeme Hewitt. He hit him with lightning."

"Out of nowhere?" George Hewitt snapped. "Yes, I'm sure that Ambrose played *no* part in instigating anything!"

"I didn't say that!" Arden shouted. "The Deacon asked what happened and that's what fucking happened! They fought. Graeme tackled him and started hitting him. Cassius broke it up."

All eyes were suddenly on me.

I lowered my gaze to the soggy ground, wishing I could seep into the earth like the water and disappear forever.

"And then what happened?" Peregrine asked.

Arden drew in a ragged breath.

Dr. Dane stood, clearing his throat. "Lennox used magic first. Arden and Cassius both saw it."

When I looked up sharply, Dr. Dane tapped his temple. Normally I would have been offended that he snooped around my mind without asking but at the moment I was grateful no one was demanding answers out of me. I didn't think I'd have the strength to actually speak without sobbing.

"So it was self-defense!" George scoffed. "Typical. Just like a dark family to ruin the day."

Peregrine held up a hand, silencing him from making any further comments. "Where is Graeme? Did anyone see him?"

Everyone paused and looked around. I got to my feet and walked over to the spot he'd been standing mere moments ago. All that remained was the amulet I'd so stupidly given him, staring up at me from the wet grass. Mocking me.

The dark clouds churned overhead. Another bolt of lightning split the sky, followed by a boom of thunder so loud I was sure it was right over our heads. It wasn't supposed to rain today, which meant, wherever Graeme had snuck off to, it was clear he was miserable.

Good. I hope he fucking choked on his guilt.

Dad didn't try talking to me until much, much later, after we were safely at home and everyone had some time and space to process the tragedy.

I had enough time to shower and change into something more comfortable and rake myself over the proverbial coals for a while before there was a quiet tap on my door.

Without waiting for an answer, Dad stuck his head in. "Got a minute?"

I snorted, keeping my gaze on the fire crackling in the fireplace in front of me. What else was I going to do? Short of driving over to the Hewitts' and snapping Graeme's neck, I didn't see myself doing much of anything for the foreseeable future.

"There are still some questions about what happened," Dad said, sitting on the edge of the chaise next to me.

"Namely, how Graeme withstood a hit like that. You know Lennox's fire magic is—was... formidable."

Sickness swirled inside of me, to the point I thought I was actually going to throw up. Instead of securing Graeme's trust, all that amulet had done was give him the upper hand in a fight that ultimately killed my cousin. Graeme still saw me as a monster, even after everything. And now Lennox had paid the price for *my* stupidity. If any Necromancer was going to die, it should have been me, not him.

"It's my fault," I said, bowing my head as another wave of tears crashed over me.

"Why on earth would you say that?"

"Because." The words choked me from the inside, unsure which way to go. I was torn between wanting to spit them out and swallow them down, to free myself from the guilt I'd been harboring but also to spare my father any more pain. Finally, I forced it out in one broken chunk because my family at least deserved the truth. "The amulet."

"You mean your mother's? The one for protection?"

Nodding, I drove the heel of my hand into my eye and turned my face away when the tears refused to stop.

He let out a long, slow breath. "Oh, Cash..."

"I'm so sorry, Dad! I didn't know this would happen! I thought he was different! I thought we could—" My stupid hope for what *could* have been died in a strangled sob.

Dad wrapped his arm around my shoulders and squeezed tightly. "None of this is your fault, son. *None* of it. You're not to blame for believing someone is good at heart. And you're certainly not to blame for what Lennox did."

"If I hadn't given Graeme that amulet—"

"Then Graeme would be dead. Or in the hospital. Would you still blame yourself?"

"Yes."

"Why?"

Now that we'd gone down this path, it was too late to turn around. "I've been seeing him… outside of class." I hid my face in my hands, unable to face him after that admission.

Dad pulled back slightly but kept one hand on my shoulder. "You what? What do you mean?"

I took a shaky breath and unleashed my entire history with Graeme Hewitt, minus a few moments that no father should ever hear. I told him about Graeme's desperation for the truth about his brother's death, about the murders on campus, our fight in front of Dane Hall, and of course the demon attack at the meetinghouse. His face got grimmer the more I spoke, but it wasn't until I told him about the freakish thing with Graeme's lightning and my blood that he cut me off.

"What was that last part?" he asked.

"About his powers?"

"Yes."

I gave a helpless shrug. "He never made his conversion. I assumed it was related to that. He asked me to help him with it so we went to Norwood Bridge last week. When I cast a circle, I used my blood for extra protection because of the demon thing. And that's when the lightning actually arced from him to the blood on the ground. I thought it was a fluke but we were able to replicate it. He said he didn't know why, that it's never done that with anyone else."

"I'm sure it hasn't," Dad said, blowing out a breath that sounded less tired and more amazed.

I frowned at him, not understanding why he was being so chill instead of screaming at me for being stupid and irresponsible — for *lying* to him all these weeks. "Why do you say that?"

"Because you're a blood witch, Cassius. Everyone has *some* iron in their blood, but you have more because of your magic. The same with Stormbringers. Like attracts like. Remember the story of Mary Oliver?"

"She was a Stormbringer. And the feud started because of her. So what?"

"People said she was dangerous. Volatile. They feared her. After she was tried and executed in 1667, no one wanted to identify as a Stormbringer anymore. The Corbins were shunned as a whole since that was the family she was born into. The focus in Winslow turned away from true magic, the kind Necromancers use, to magic found in the natural world."

"Graeme's not feared, though. Everyone fucking loves him."

"Because he's a Hewitt. He's from a line of witches with elemental magic. These people think that means he's automatically benevolent." Dad shook his head, like he pitied the lot of them. "They've never understood that the so-called 'good' or 'evil' essence of magic is in the heart of the witch, not their abilities. It's been the same way for hundreds of years. Some Necromancers should have been saints. Meanwhile, some elemental witches are right up there with Satan himself."

"Yeah, that sounds about right," I said, hanging my head.

"All I'm saying is, of course you two found each other. Your magic is more alike than anyone would ever want to admit, on his side of things *or* ours."

"So is that why he wouldn't leave me the hell alone? Our magic?" I asked, even though I didn't let him answer. "No matter what I did, he kept coming back around. I thought he was… I don't know what the hell I thought. I guess it doesn't matter now."

It was Dad's turn to make an uncertain face as he squeezed my shoulder gently. "I'd venture to say his feelings for you run deeper than they ever have with anyone else before. Because of your shared magic? Possibly. Perhaps that explained the initial attraction but he kept coming back because of *you,* Cassius. You're more than your magic. So is he."

"Yeah. Now's he a murderer, just like his father." Another round of tears fell. This time they burned hot with anger and humiliation, for letting myself get blinded by him and side-tracked from what was important in life — the Book and my family. So long as I lived, I'd never fucking forgive him — or myself.

Chapter Thirty-Two

Graeme

The rain hadn't stopped for over two weeks.

The weatherman said he'd never seen anything like it. A cell popped up out of nowhere and hovered over Winslow, refusing to budge no matter what sort of wind ripped through the air.

Most of the time it was a steady rain, keeping the world gray and cold. Other times the wind screamed and rain lashed the windows and the never-ending lightning turned night into day. The river rose and started to spill over the banks, worrying farmers and townsfolk alike with the potential for flooding.

The day I killed Lennox, Dad came home shortly after I did. He took one look at my bleary eyes and he smiled, hugging me tightly and telling me how proud he was. According to him, I'd protected myself and our family's honor.

I didn't give a fuck about the Hewitts' honor. A guy was dead and it was because of me. Whether or not that guy was a fucking prick from a family of Necromancers didn't matter. There was another death on my conscience.

There wasn't an investigation into the duel. According to Dad, Dr. Dane explained things to the point it wasn't needed. Funny how it was Arden and Cassius's memories that ended up exonerating me — my sworn enemies turned out to be my saviors, attesting to the fact I hadn't actually lifted my hands to cast a spell. It just… happened. Like so much of my fucking erratic magic.

If he was given the option, would Cassius have lied? Would he have toed the dark line and maintained it was all my fault? I didn't know and I couldn't exactly ask him. The one time I caved to my guilt and called, he didn't pick up. Nor did he answer any of the texts I sent, apologizing for what happened. I didn't name specifics, mostly because I didn't even know what the hell I was apologizing for. Killing his asshole cousin? Accusing him of hexing me? Trying to be his fucking friend?

After a week of laying low at the house, *again,* on yet another fucking "bereavement leave" as far as Tennebrose knew, I finally dragged my ass back to campus.

I marched into botany class, shaking rain from my hair, fully expecting to come face-to-face with Cassius. This time, I wouldn't be caught off guard. I had a speech prepared and everything.

But he wasn't there.

He wasn't there on Thursday, either.

Another weekend came and went. My calls went directly to voicemail. Texts, likewise, remained unanswered.

On Tuesday morning, with a modified speech rolling through my head, I strode into botany expecting to *finally* see his furious face or get swirling black mist thrown at me. And once again, he wasn't there.

After class, I followed Ainsworth to his office.

"Where is he?" I demanded.

"Come on in, Graeme," Dr. Ainsworth said, plopping into his chair and lacing his hands together on the desk. "Where is who?"

I closed the door but I didn't sit. I was too keyed up to sit. So I stood, arms crossed. "Cassius. Where is he?"

He raised his eyebrows and took his glasses off, setting them on the desk with a sigh. "If this is about your project, rest assured it's no longer a partnered assignment."

"I don't give a fuck about the assignment," I said, unfolding my arms and slapping my hands on his desk. "Where *is* he?"

Ainsworth blinked serenely, completely ignoring the fact I was beyond insubordinate and he had every right to slam my ass into a wall with another plant. "Why are you concerned with where Cassius is?"

Because he could be out there, plotting revenge? Because he could be summoning a hundred demons to rip me to shreds now that I didn't have his stupid amulet? Because no matter how much I tried to fucking hate him, all I wanted to do was see him, to know he was ok, and that I didn't totally destroy him?

A vine slithered around each arm and jerked me backward, depositing me into the chair as gently as a magically-possessed plant could. I didn't bother fighting it.

Once I was seated, Ainsworth fixed me with a look I couldn't quite decipher. "He dropped my class," he said at last.

It felt like a sucker punch to the gut. "But you said we couldn't! You said we *had* to take it this semester!"

"That was before..."

"Before what?" Before I killed his cousin? Before I completely fucked up everything?

He cocked his head, his lips pursed like he couldn't decide how much to tell me. "Before he withdrew from the university."

"He what?!"

When Ainsworth didn't offer any more details, I slumped

back into the chair, staring at the dark window. The rain picked up, tapping harder than before. No, not rain. Hail. And if I didn't get my shit together soon, I was going to seriously damage things — or people. Which seemed to be my specialty as of late.

Ainsworth glanced at the window before directing his gaze back to me. "How have you been?"

Snorting, I flung a hand toward the capricious weather, letting the boom of thunder answer for me.

He nodded. "I assumed that was your doing."

"I can't help it," I mumbled, picking at my jeans. "Just like I couldn't help it when the lightning killed Lennox."

"So it *wasn't* a duel?"

"No... he attacked me and I..." I waved one hand vaguely. "It just happened. Cassius thought if I made my conversion that I'd get more control over it."

"You never made your conversion?!" Ainsworth's eyes nearly bugged out of his skull.

I shook my head. There was no point in keeping it a secret anymore. I mean, it was bound to get out sooner or later, like when Peregrine stepped down and the Congregation was looking for their new fucking Deacon. "When Owen died Mom wasn't... well. And I think Dad just kinda forgot because he was too wrapped up in taking care of Mom."

"Oh my God..." He leaned back in his chair, blowing out his cheeks like a chipmunk. "So no one knows you haven't made your conversion?"

I shrugged. "I think everyone assumed I did it. I don't think anyone ever bothered to check the Book of Transactions, except maybe Old Man Winslow, but I don't know if he ever talked to Dad about it."

Ainsworth lunged forward, snatching his phone off the desk and dialing quickly. I swore under my breath, sure as hell he was calling Peregrine right then and there to rat me out.

Needless to say, I was surprised when he blurted out, "Temperance! Are you still here? Good. Come to my office at once. Bring that grimoire you were looking at earlier."

Oh, shit… maybe it would have been better if he *had* called Peregrine. I propped one elbow on the arm of the chair and held my head in my hand.

"Dr. Colburn is on her way," Ainsworth said, looking more cheerful than anyone who had reason to deal with a Colburn should. Just like the Corbins, her family was renowned for darker magic. And given her less-than-sunny personality, I doubted she'd be as thrilled to help me as Ainsworth apparently was.

"Why?" I asked.

"Because you're making your conversion tonight, so we can put an end to all this," he said, waving a hand at the window. A flash of lightning illuminated beads of rain on the glass, like jewels. "And once your magic is under control, we can resume our focus on your project."

"No offense, professor, but don't you have more important things to worry about? Like catching a murderer?"

"That is only a matter of time. Chief Treadwell has been very aggressive in his patrolling and Dr. Colburn has been researching various demons—"

"Demons?" I blinked, sitting up straighter. "So it *is* a demon?"

"I believe so. Anyone can cut out someone's eyes, but the decapitations in one stroke? No witch could do that without assistance."

"Wait… so is it a demon doing it on their own or someone controlling it?"

He grimaced. "We're not sure. It could be either. Why?"

"Cassius and I were attacked by a demon at the meetinghouse. And right before Lennox died, he said there was a demon after me. I think one attacked me on campus too, after that Melanie girl was murdered."

"My God! Why didn't you say anything?"

"I don't know." I looked away, my cheeks hot. "The whole thing was... complicated."

"I'll say. What else were you and Cassius up to these past few weeks?"

"I—we... Nothing." Thunder rumbled overhead, like the sky itself was calling me out on my bullshit. I looked anywhere but his face, not wanting to see whatever expression was waiting for me.

"I might be old, Graeme, but I'm not an idiot," Ainsworth said gently. "There's a reason I made the two of you work together."

"Yeah, what's that?" Unable to stop my curiosity, I glanced up.

"Ne te quaesiveris extra," he replied with a smile.

I rolled my eyes. "I don't speak Latin. And before you get on my case, it's *not* one of our requirements, nor do I think it should be."

"You don't recognize your family motto?"

"Clearly not."

He chuckled. "Do not seek outside yourself."

An uncomfortable chill prickled across my skin as my memory sparked in recognition. When he came out of his trance, Cassius was muttering that same thing, over and over. "What does that mean? In plain English?"

"Look within. You have all of the answers, Graeme, you just have to put it together."

Yeah sure. I didn't have a fucking clue where to even start. I'm sure this was some sort of teachable moment on his part, but I was too tired to deal with goddamn riddles.

Dr. Colburn strode into the room a little while later, a

stack of old books in her arms. She took one look at me and her nose wrinkled before her focus shifted to Ainsworth. "What's he doing here?"

Even if I expected her reaction, I was still a little miffed.

Ainsworth, on the other hand, smiled like nothing was wrong. "He needs your help, Temperance."

"I'll say," she muttered, marching over to Ainsworth's desk and dropping the stack of books next to his elbow. "The grimoire, as you asked. Plus some of the demonologies I've been referencing."

"Wonderful. What do you know about weather magic?" He raised his brows, looking up at her, his fingers laced together on his desk.

She, on the other hand, crossed her arms and shot me a side-eye before answering. "Only what's been recorded, which isn't much. Stormbringers were even more secretive than the Necromancers. At least *they* wrote shit down. India's untimely passing is exactly why we should return to the old traditions."

"The old traditions?" I asked with a frown.

Dr. Colburn faced me again, her icy blue eyes skewering me to my chair. "Nature witches work on instinct, on feelings. It's great when it works, but it can backfire — like what happened to India. Rituals are tedious and time-consuming to learn, but they ensure the practitioner's safety. Plus, having a compilation of rituals makes it easier to pass the traditions down instead of winging it for generations like a bunch of hippies."

"We don't know India's magic backfired," Ainsworth interjected.

"Well it wasn't Lennox! And even if it was, he's dead now so what does it matter?" With the look she shot in my direction, she might as well have just called me a murderer to my face.

Rather than dwell on her anger and proof of my guilt assailing the windows with a wet, slushy vengeance, I tried to steer the conversation back to a common enemy. "Do you think the demon has something to do with the university?"

They both went rigid, exchanging a glance.

"I mean, India goes to Tennebrose too. Or, she did…" I swallowed, continuing carefully. "And Preston found a sigil near the bonfire. Those two girls were murdered here. I was attacked here. There has to be some sort of connection to the Tennebrose. Right?"

Dr. Colburn's sharp features softened just a hair so I think I was on the right track. "Mind telling me what I'm doing here, Samuel?" she asked, pivoting on her heel and staring at her colleague again.

"Well, Graeme has a problem. You see, he never made his conversion," Dr. Ainsworth replied. He held up a hand the second Temperance opened her mouth. "I know, I know. But remember what you told me?"

"What?" she huffed.

"Astra inclinant, sed non obligant. The stars *incline* us, they do not bind us," he said gently, throwing a pointed glance in my direction.

She uncrossed her arms and leaned forward, bracing one hand on the edge of his desk. "Are you telling me he and Claudia are in *love*?"

"Claudia?!" I'm sure I wasn't meant to be a part of the conversation that was clearly *about* me, but I couldn't help it. It's not like they were whispering and the fact they were, like, five feet away meant I heard every word. "I don't want anything to do with Claudia!"

Ainsworth chuckled, looking quite pleased with himself. "Not Claudia..."

She straightened and reconsidered me with a tilted head and furrowed brows. "Cassius?"

My face *had* to have been on fire. Literal fire. It was the only way to explain the sudden burning in my cheeks, or the sweat collecting under my collar. Love was the furthest thing from my mind when it came to Cassius, but since I somehow lost the ability to speak, I couldn't exactly defend myself.

"Think about it, Temperance!" Ainsworth said with an enthusiasm I neither felt nor understood. "Cassius isn't just a Necromancer, he's a blood witch. Graeme isn't just a weather witch, he's a Stormbringer." As if he needed to emphasize his point, he jumped out of his chair and hurried to the window right as a flash of lightning illuminated the rectangle of glass. "Together, they have the power to undo the damage of the last three hundred and fifty years!"

I wanted to point out that Ainsworth had obviously lost his mind, but Dr. Colburn actually smiled. At *me*. Then him. "Do you really think it's possible?"

Thunder boomed, shaking the windows in their frames. A big, fat "Fuck no!" from the universe if *I* ever heard one.

"I don't understand," I admitted, glancing between the two of them. "Why do you care if we get along or not? And what does our magic have to do with any of it?"

"The feud has cost more lives than just Corbins and Hewitts. It's affected *all* of us," Dr. Colburn said, taking on an extraordinarily patient tone compared to what she walked in with. "Every time there's a new conflict, it puts the entire Congregation in danger. Our ancestors founded this town as a safe haven for witches but it'll never be truly safe until this thing between your families is over. For good."

"Your magic is what makes the two of you so unique," Dr. Ainsworth said, stepping up next to Dr. Colburn for my own private lecture. "You're like... a battery to one another. You're attracted to his magic, which makes yours stronger." He chuckled and threw his thumb over his shoulder toward the window. "Case in point. He's like a conductor, allowing you to tap into your magic on a deeper level. And *your* magic generates the power for him to do... more. More divination, more power, control. This connection makes both of you so much stronger than if the other wasn't around."

Well, that explained a lot...

"And," Ainsworth continued, "if you're going to be the next Deacon, wouldn't it be better to have the support of the entire Congregation? To know the Corbins and those loyal to them are just as happy with your advancement as the people who have always supported your family?"

"He can't be the next Deacon if he didn't make his conversion," Dr. Colburn pointed out.

"Oh! Right!" Ainsworth spun and grabbed the book on the top of the pile. "What do you suppose we'll need?"

She blew out a breath, sputtering, and waved helplessly. "I don't know. A storm, probably. Beyond that, I have no idea."

"Cassius said something about elderberries," I murmured. "And verbena."

They both looked at me, blinking.

"You told Cassius?" Dr. Colburn asked.

I nodded, even though I suddenly felt like that was a *very* stupid thing to do. "He was going to, um, help? We were supposed to do it during the Harvest Moon."

"Makes sense," Temperance said, looking at Ainsworth. "The Blood Moon would be better, if he can wait that long." Her gaze flicked to me, considering me from head to toe.

"He's waited this long," Ainsworth replied with a shrug. "Do you think you can get Cassius to come?"

"To the conversion?" I furrowed my brow, shaking my head. "Doubt it." Didn't doubt it. Knew with a thousand percent certainty he'd tell me to fuck off if I asked — provided he didn't kill me first.

"Have you tried apologizing?" Temperance asked.

"You know, I did. But Hallmark was out of cards that said

'Sorry I killed your cousin' that day." Being a dick to a professor like Colburn after she agreed to help probably wasn't a good idea, but how stupid did she think I was? Of course I tried apologizing! It fell on deaf ears. Or stubborn ears. Whatever the case may be.

Ainsworth chuckled, derailing whatever ass chewing I was about to get from his colleague. "Well, you have some time. I'm sure you'll think of something."

Doubtful. Very doubtful.

"I'll go dig up whatever I can on weather magic," Dr. Colburn said to Ainsworth before shooting me a parting glare on her way to the door. So much for that truce. Good job, Graeme, you fucking moron.

Ainsworth smiled brightly at me after she'd gone and rubbed his hands together. "Now, let's talk about this demon you saw."

Chapter Thirty-Three
Cassius

Unlike India's funeral, Lennox's ceremony was entirely private. Only the dark families were there: us and the Ambroses, of course, along with the Simms, the Olivers, and the Colburns. Even the so-called neutral families, like the Ainsworths, were forbidden from attending. As far as the rest of the Congregation as a whole was concerned, they were lucky my uncle didn't burn the meetinghouse to the ground — with them *in* it.

The cold October wind whipped around us, pushing us forward and buffeting us back, as the solemn procession made its way from our house, through the gardens, to the crypt.

It hadn't stopped raining since the day Lennox was murdered, which made our grief ten times worse. Our usual custom of having a pyre in the North Woods was abandoned in the days prior, anticipating more fucking rain. Even when we woke up to miraculously clear skies, Lennox's parents continued with our alternate plan in case Graeme decided to throw another temper tantrum. I didn't know if anyone else in my family had put two and two together, but I knew the unrelenting rain was his doing. Too bad he didn't drown in it.

Dad, acting as the minister, led the way for the procession, followed by Arden and I, the black casket resting on our shoulders. After the rest of the pallbearers came Lennox's parents and Claudia. The Simms, Colburns, and Olivers completed the small entourage.

We descended into the crypt in near silence, except for our shoes scraping and tapping on the stone steps. Aunt Jane's soft sobs echoed around the granite. Or maybe it was the wind, howling up above and moaning through the cracks.

Lowering the casket into the stone sarcophagus where we'd all made our conversion, the pallbearers stepped back while the rest of the group formed a circle. Lit candles were passed down the line until everyone had one, except Dad, who was holding the Book of Lazarus — or what was left of it.

He intoned a prayer in Latin and crossed himself. The rest of the group did likewise, bowing our heads.

I stared at the flame in front of me, trying and failing not to remember the last time I was down here. It was simply to return my mother's ashes to their niche, but before *that,* I was with Graeme. When I thought it was a brilliant idea to let him defile not only *me* but my family's final resting place. If it was possible, I hated him now more than I ever had at any time that came before. The flame on my candle flared brighter, confirming my thoughts on the matter.

Claudia's hand stretched out toward me.

Shifting my candle to the other side, I took her proffered hand, trying to find some comfort when she squeezed it gently. She'd been trying to cheer me up since the day Lennox was killed. Trying, and failing. But only failing because I wouldn't let her.

I marinaded in my anger, using it to fuel never-ending thoughts of revenge. I'd stupidly allowed myself to become sidetracked by Graeme and *his* quest for answers. But now, as Dad held *half* of our cherished grimoire not but five feet away, I was reminded why I really came home — to find the missing folios. Once I had them and the Book was reunited, there wasn't a Hewitt alive who could stand against me. It would be too late to bring my mom or Lennox back, but at least I could make damn sure no one else suffered their fate.

Dad moved around the sarcophagus, murmuring prayers designed to send Lennox's spirit on its journey instead of getting stuck between realms. Uncle Marcus followed behind him with a large silver vase, pouring a thick, fragrant oil all over the top of the casket.

Once Dad and Uncle Marcus were at the head of the casket again, the entire chamber smelled like earthy pine, softened with a hint of vanilla.

"In nomine Patris et filii et Spiritus Sancti," Dad said, closing the Book with a soft sigh.

"Amen," the rest of us replied, tossing our candles into the sarcophagus.

Dozens of flames latched onto the oil. The glossy black casket went up in a wall of white and orange flames.

Aunt Jane turned her face away, sobbing. Uncle Marcus wrapped his arm around her shoulder and shared a look with Dad before guiding his wife away.

One by one, the rest of the mourners made their way out of the crypt, including Claudia, until only my father and I remained.

"Are you alright?" Dad asked quietly. Lennox's casket cracked and split beside us as the flames gnawed through the lacquered wood.

"No, I'm not," I replied, gritting my teeth.

Squeezing my shoulder, he offered a fleeting smile. "Let's head up to the house."

I let him steer me away from the sarcophagus and direct me back up the stairs. He sealed the crypt and we made the return trip through the gardens in absolute silence. Before we could make it into the house, I took a step toward the stable. "Do you mind if I go out?"

"Be back before dark."

I nodded, ducking into the stable. Once Lucius's hooves were picked, I threw on a bridle as quickly as I could. I climbed up onto his back without a saddle and took off before the rain could come back and fuck up my day even more.

The cold air burned my lungs and stung my face, but I urged Lucius on faster. He wanted to run and I wanted to disappear, putting as much distance between myself and my problems as possible. If I fell and broke my neck in the meantime, then so be it. We all had to die someday, right?

We raced out to the far end of the orchard and were making our way back through the sloping hills when a group of crows cawed overhead. I reined Lucius in and he slid to a halt, snorting and flicking his tail irritably.

Danger!

Witch!

Hewitt!

"Show me," I said, watching the birds dive and twirl in the air.

They spun and swooped, careening toward the northwest — toward the North Woods.

Nudging Lucius back into action, we gave chase. Leaving the orchard behind, we leapt the split-rail fence in the back and cut across the open field that stretched between our property and the edge of the woods.

Graeme's Jeep appeared on the other side of the field, blazing a path through the long grass. He drove toward me for a bit and stopped, killing the engine.

The second he got out of the car, I let the crows do what

they wanted. And what they wanted, apparently, was to dive at him, claws outstretched.

Without any fear of witnesses, Graeme blew them away with a flick of his hand.

The crows tumbled through the air, caught up in what looked like a microburst, swirling and crashing into one another on winds that wouldn't let them go.

Giving Lucius a swift kick, I charged at the asshole, throwing a crackling black ball at him. It was enough to distract him, releasing the poor birds from the miniature storm he'd trapped them in.

"Cash, I'm not here to—" Whatever else he was going to say disappeared in a yelp as he scrambled up onto the hood of his Jeep right as Lucius barreled by.

Turning the horse's head, I circled around and glared at him. "I warned you last time, Stormbringer. Trespass again and I would kill you." The swirl of mist materialized between my fingers, churning in anticipation.

"Please listen to me," he said, not budging an inch from the safety of his perch. "I'm sorry, Cassius. I'm so, *so* sorry."

I didn't want to hear it. Any of it.

Clicking my tongue for Lucius to move, I launched the mist at Graeme as soon as we were close enough.

He swatted it away with another burst of air. The asshole was getting stronger, which did nothing for my already-shitty mood.

"I didn't mean to hurt him!" Graeme shouted.

"You didn't hurt him!" I flung another black sphere at him as hard as I could. "You fucking murdered him!"

Once again, he deflected it, scattering the mist into nothing. "I didn't know that would happen!"

Hurling orb after orb at him, I watched with growing frustration as each one shattered against a wall of wind. "I didn't give you that amulet to use against my family!"

"I was going to give it back!" he said, covering his face with his arms and bracing against each impact.

"When? After you'd murdered us all?!" My arm was on fire. The muscles screamed at me to stop, but my anger demanded I get some sort of justice for my cousin. For my own wounded pride.

Growling, he stood up straighter and flung a hand at me. I expected more wind or rain. Hell, I even expected lightning. I did *not* expect it to be a giant ball of fucking ice. It caught me in the center of my chest, knocking me right off of Lucius's back and onto the ground.

Gasping for a breath, I held my head with one hand and my chest with the other, trying to decide which one hurt the worst. It was the most miserable tie ever.

Graeme was in my face a second later, his distinct eyes wide with what looked like worry. "I'm sorry!"

"Fuck you!" I slapped away his outstretched hand. I would have slammed another black cloud into him if I had the energy, but since I didn't, I resorted to smacking him every time he reached for me.

He grabbed my hands, simultaneously stopping me from hitting him and using it as a means to pull himself closer. "Cassius, stop. Stop!"

"Get off of me!" I tried wrenching my hands out of his, but it was useless. Besides the fact I'd tired myself out, his magic kept sending waves of electricity into my nerves, pretty much rendering them useless.

"I need to talk to you."

"Do I look like I fucking care what you need?"

"Cash, please."

"Don't fucking call me that!" His attempt at getting into my good graces with that stupid nickname just pissed me off even more. "Let go!"

"Not until you listen!"

I finally yanked a hand loose. Dredging up whatever energy I had, I threw it into the center of his chest. The second I felt his other hand loosen, I kicked away from him.

He toppled backward into the long grass, grimacing and swearing.

Instead of climbing back up onto Lucius, like I'd intended, I seized the opportunity presented to me.

Launching myself at Graeme, I grabbed a fistful of his t-shirt and hauled him off the ground, right as my other fist drove downward. It connected solidly with his jaw, earning me another string of curse words.

He dodged the next punch, throwing an arm up at the last second to deflect it. A bolt of lightning crashed into the ground a few feet away from us, flinging bits of mud and grass in every direction.

"You missed!" I shouted.

He caught my wrist on another downward swing and threw his hips up, rolling us quickly and pinning me beneath him. "I'm not trying to kill you!"

"You might as well! Lennox's pyre is still burning. Just throw my corpse on top and you'll have one less Necromancer around. It's what you people always wanted!"

"Cassius, please. Listen to me!"

I couldn't. I *wouldn't*. Rage boiled inside me, as deafening as his thunder had been for over two weeks. Seething beneath him, I tried to shove him off, but he retaliated with a stronger zap of electricity.

My arms trembled and collapsed. He crashed into my chest, his brow creased. "Stop… stop fighting me."

Breathing hard, I squeezed my eyes shut and shook my head. "Never."

"I'm sorry about Lennox," he said, letting go of my wrist so he could touch the side of my face. His voice sounded *so* close, but I refused to open my eyes to see just how close that was. "I'm sorry for everything I did. Everything I said. Everything except *this*."

"What?" I snapped, opening my eyes to glare at him.

"This," he repeated, like it was supposed to be any more clear. "I'm not sorry that we happened."

"There is no we!" I practically screamed each word, enunciating as clearly as possible. "There will *never*—"

He silenced me with a kiss, rough and demanding. I strained beneath him, pulling back while trying to push him off, but he held on. His fingers wrapped around the nape of my neck, keeping me trapped against him. His lips pressed against mine, over and over, the kisses softening but not losing any of their desperate insistence.

"Please," he whispered between kisses. "Please, Cash."

"No," I answered, turning my face away and licking my lips.

Despite my reply, he kept kissing me, his lips whispering over my jaw, my cheekbone, ear, brow, nose, anything he could reach. Each one, combined with the tiny surges of electricity, was like a battering ram against my defenses. I clung to my hate, focusing on the pain of Lennox's loss, of Graeme's betrayal.

But it wasn't a betrayal, because *I* gave him the amulet.

So in the end, I could only hate myself for what happened to my cousin. It was *my* betrayal that killed him — not Graeme's.

Graeme's perfect lips brushed against mine, hesitantly, before he sealed our mouths together again. When his lips parted, I acted first, plunging my tongue into his mouth to tangle with his.

He groaned and angled his face, granting me better access.

I threaded my fingers through his hair, twisting the dark strands and pulling him as close as I could until my lips felt bruised. It was my penance, my way of inflicting pain on myself for my stupidity. The guilt of being with the guy who murdered my cousin would eat at me for eternity, so I might as well embrace it. If there was one thing being a Necromancer taught me, it was that you couldn't run from your problems. They were best dealt with head-on, otherwise you were in for a lifetime of suffering.

Limbs and tongues tangled together, our bodies were as intertwined as our fucking magic. One of my hands slid up underneath his t-shirt, slipping over the smooth skin of his ribs and his lower back, while the other remained fisted in his hair.

Out of nowhere, a piercing shriek echoed in my head.

The crows shot out of the bare trees, cawing and crying out to each other as they scattered into the sky.

I shoved away from Graeme with a cry of my own, pushing against my skull with both hands.

"What's wrong?" Graeme asked. "What's happening?"

"Demon," I spit out, squeezing my eyes shut and trying to forge a link to one of the birds up above, hoping to catch a glimpse of it. The birds were in a panic, their hearts racing faster than their wings could flap, carrying them away to safety.

"Come on." Graeme latched onto one of my wrists and yanked me to my feet, catching me when I stumbled thanks to the long grass snarled around my boot.

"Lucius!" I searched the area for my horse, but he'd gone. Probably back home to his afternoon oats, the traitor.

"Forget the damn horse," Graeme said, pushing me ahead of him toward the Jeep. Suddenly, he slammed into the back of me, smashing me against the side of his car.

"Fuck!"

Before I could turn around to yell at him, he was gone. I spun in time to see him sliding through the field, his hands clawing at the earth, tearing furrows in the dirt and ripping out grass in an effort to try and stop himself. A mass of flames and shadows had latched onto his foot. Inside, a huge, monstrous shape was barely visible to the naked eye.

Fear spiked through me. The mist was back, swirling through my fingers as it grew. When it was big enough, I hurled it at the center of the demon's back.

It roared, an unearthly sound echoing through the surrounding woods. In the midst of it, it stopped dragging Graeme, long enough for a bolt of lightning to strike the ground. It didn't hit the demon, but the current of electricity fanned out, shocking it regardless.

As soon as Graeme was free, he scrambled to his feet and sprinted back to me.

The demon turned, darkness spreading out around it and surging toward us like a tidal wave.

I lifted one hand and held it up toward demon, closing my eyes and focusing on the banishment spell I'd used in the basement of the meetinghouse.

"It's not working," Graeme said next to me.

I couldn't answer him because I was too busy trying to remember a fucking page-worth of Latin and not jumble the words as I hurriedly spit them out.

The moment the demon's sphere settled over us, the stench of sulfur burned my nostrils.

"Exilium!"

It was like pushing against a brick wall. I felt the power of my words, but they met with an unseen resistance. My eyes flew open, watching as the demon kept coming, shrouding us in its smoky black bubble.

Graeme launched another lightning bolt at it. It struck the demon in the back but didn't keep it down for long. "What's wrong? Why didn't it work like last time?"

"It's a different demon."

"So?"

"I'm not strong enough," I whispered with a sickening realization.

"Battery," Graeme said with a blink before grabbing at the front of my shirt.

"What? What are you doing?"

"Battery! We're batteries!" Yanking my necklace into view, he sliced across his palm with a hiss.

"What are you doing, you idiot?! Demons are drawn to pain and blood!"

"It's a little late for that," he snapped back, holding up his bloody palm. "Use it! Do the thing!"

I didn't have time to question him. The demon was gaining ground again. It was so close I could feel its heat radiating across my face, nearly choking me with the smell.

Dragging my tongue over the cut, I swallowed the blood quickly, a tingling rush of energy coursing through my veins. It was so much stronger than the other times I'd tasted his blood. Probably because there was more of it and because we were both pumping out adrenaline like crazy.

Another crackle of lightning tore out of the sky, piercing through the dark cloud in front of us.

Manifesting my own black sphere, I flung it across the field at the same time.

The demon howled, pushed back by our joint energy.

I resumed chanting, starting the goddamn banishment all over again.

"Cash!"

Before I could open my eyes to see what he was yelling about this time, something seized the front of my suit jacket and yanked me into the sky. The closer I got to the swirling shadows and flames, the more clear the demon became. Its fanged mouth opened, unfurling a forked tongue. Black claws sank into my flesh, burning my skin as it squeezed me tighter.

I squeaked out the remainder of the spell, using the last of my breath to utter the final word. "Exilium."

The demon snarled and pitched me across the field as it retreated back into the woods, leaving a trail of scorched grass in its wake.

I landed hard, my arm bent behind me in a way arms weren't meant to go. A loud *snap* sounded in my ears and a wave of nausea hit me before I'd even stopped rolling.

The last thing I heard was Graeme yelling my name before my eyelids sank closed.

Chapter Thirty-Four

Graeme

"Fuck, fuck, fuck." I didn't even know where to start with how bad this fucking situation was. Slipping my arms beneath Cassius's, I dragged him back to the Jeep and wrestled him into the passenger seat. And in a sickening parallel of six years ago, I did what Lydia Corbin did — I returned a broken son to his family. The only difference between now and then was Cassius still had a pulse and I'd be damned if he lost it because he was trying to save me.

"Hold on," I said out loud, which was stupid because he was fucking unconscious, and floored it.

The Jeep tore through the open field and burst through the split-rail fence at the back of the orchard. We picked up more speed once we hit the manicured lawn. Racing along the perimeter of the house, I slid around the corner and gunned it toward the front steps.

Oh fuck!

The driveway was lined with cars. Some I recognized immediately — like Arden's. And Lennox's parents. Double fuck! Cassius hadn't been exaggerating when he said Lennox's pyre was burning. It was his fucking funeral of all days, if the black and purple bunting hanging over the front door was anything to go by.

I didn't let it slow me down. I couldn't. Unless they wanted to mourn two family members today.

Slamming the Jeep into park, I threw open the door and raced to the other side. I blew the front door of the house open with a gale on my way by and turned my focus to Cassius, pulling him back out of the car.

Arden was the first one outside. "What the fu—what did you do?!" He rushed down the steps and nearly bowled me over to get his hands on Cassius.

"It was a demon," I said as Arden slipped beneath Cassius's other arm, actually helping me drag him toward the door instead of trying to be a dick and fight me. "Watch his arm! It's broken."

A flash of pain seared through my chest, squeezing the air from my lungs. Agony and the inability to breathe dropped me like a rock in the middle of the driveway.

Arden kept his hold on Cassius and hurried away as the rest of the dark families filtered into the courtyard.

Claudia stood at the front, her hand outstretched toward me, her fingers gnarled like claws. As soon as I was separated from her brother, she twisted her hand and pantomimed crushing something. That something was apparently my ribcage squeezing all of my internal organs. I guess now I knew why they called her a bone witch.

I gritted my teeth, trying to keep from yelling, but the more she squeezed, the less I cared about saving face. A strangled cry ripped out of my throat, lacking much power since I couldn't inhale more than a gasp of air at a time.

"Claudia!" Caius, who'd stopped to check on Cassius first, rushed over to his daughter and knocked her hand down.

As soon as her hold disappeared, I gasped in as much oxygen as I could and pressed a hand to my chest, just in case my bones were seconds away from falling out.

"He doesn't deserve to live!" Claudia shouted.

"That is enough," Caius snapped. "Everyone back in the house. Including you," he added, pointing at me. "You're not going anywhere."

Claudia snarled something under her breath and marched inside with the crowd.

There was no fucking way I was going into that house with a group of pissed-off Necromancers. I looked at my Jeep, calculating the distance and how fast I'd have to be.

Caius must have either seen the reservation on my face or he was a mind reader, because the next thing I knew, an unseen force picked me up and stood me upright.

Temperance walked up next to me, shaking her head. "You've done it now, Hewitt."

"I didn't do anything," I said in my defense as she nudged me toward the house.

"Really? You brought Cassius home unconscious on the day we said goodbye to Lennox. You have the shittiest timing in the world."

"You told me to apologize!" I shot back.

"Not during a goddamn funeral!" Without waiting for a reply, she shoved me through the front door and slammed it shut behind us.

With zero choice in the matter, I followed her through the castle-like house, jumping at every sound and moving shadow. She deposited me in a large sitting room stuffed with antique furniture and all sorts of creepy shit on the walls. Skulls and other taxidermy animals and birds lined the bookcases and the ornate mantel over the fireplace. A variety of flowers and colorful butterflies hung on the walls, captured beneath glass for the rest of time.

Standing in the center of the room, I took in all of the carefully curated objects, remembering what Cassius said. Ok, fine. Death could be beautiful, under the right circumstances. I doubted mine would be at the hands of my enemy, but that was neither here nor there.

I had no idea where the rest of the mourners were. Probably in the living room, plotting my demise. At least I had Dr. Colburn to keep me company, even if she was more of a begrudging ally.

"Do you think Cassius is going to be ok?" I asked, shoving my hands in my pockets.

"What kind of demon was it?"

Ok, *that* wasn't the comfort I was looking for. "Um, I don't know. It was a big black blob that smelled like sulfur. Every once in a while I thought I could see its eyes or claws or something, but they'd disappear back into the shadow."

"Did it have a bull's head? A crow's head? A lion?"

"Um…" I sifted through my memories, trying to catch a glimpse of horns on the replay. "Maybe? No. It all happened so fast. I think it was a bird."

She opened her mouth to say something but closed it as footsteps approached the room. We both turned expectantly toward the door, which was another stupid thing of me to do. Cassius was unconscious. There was no way he was going to come strolling in like nothing happened.

Needless to say, I wasn't surprised to see it was Cassius's dad.

He and Dr. Colburn exchanged a long, heavy look. She nodded, without saying a word, and walked out, sliding the pocket doors shut behind her.

"How is he?" I asked, watching Caius warily as he approached with measured steps.

"Alive." He gestured to the pair of chairs in front of the roaring fireplace, taking the one closest to him.

Sinking into the other, I more or less perched on the edge in case I had to make a break for it. Hopefully that ward thing wasn't in place.

He withdrew a small knife from his pocket and held it out to me. "I'm sure you're familiar with blood magic by now. Would you mind? It'll save us a lot of time and miscommunication."

I glanced between him and the knife and back again before finally taking it, slowly retracting my hand like it was some sort of test. When he didn't attack me, I looked at the knife. I only knew what Cassius told me about blood magic, about the things he saw, and I *definitely* didn't want Caius seeing any of that. But the last time Cassius used my blood, he asked what I'd been thinking about. So, maybe there was a way to leave out the sordid part of my relationship with his son by thinking about something else.

Once I got my thoughts under some semblance of control, I clenched my teeth and sliced the tip of the knife across the pad of my thumb.

"Just squeeze some on the blade," Caius said.

I did as he instructed before handing the knife back, relieved he wasn't going to tap into the source like a fucking vampire. It was kind of hot when Cassius did it, but his dad? Ugh. No thanks.

Holding the knife carefully, keeping it flat, Caius stood and walked to the fireplace. He flung his hand at the flames and for a moment I thought he threw the whole knife into the hearth, but apparently it was just to get the blood into the fire.

Biting my lips, I watched in silence as he searched the flames for whatever answer he needed. India had done the same thing — used fire to try and divine her future. Guess she didn't see the part where it was cut off before she even turned twenty-one.

After a *very* uncomfortable couple of minutes, Caius pushed away from the mantel and resumed his seat. The knife was nowhere to be found and he looked exhausted.

"Sir?" I glanced around, wondering if there was something I was supposed to be doing.

"I saw my wife again," he said quietly, staring at the flames with a sad, half-smile. "Thank you for that. And thank you for returning my son to me."

"I'm sorry, sir. For all of it. I didn't mean for Cassius to get hurt and I didn't mean for things to happen with Lennox. I know you have no reason to believe me, but I swear I didn't—"

He held up a hand, silencing me. "I know, Graeme. I know."

"I'll just be on my way then. I promise I won't bother any of you anymore," I said, rising to my feet, running my palms down the side of my thighs.

"Don't you want to see Cassius when he wakes?"

I couldn't help but wince. "I don't think Cassius wants to see me. Ever."

"I know he doesn't have much reason to show it, but my son has a big heart. Trust me. He'll want to see you."

"Did you use his blood too?"

The corner of Caius's mouth lifted in another smile, this one a little brighter than before. "I didn't have to. I'm his father. I've known about you since he blundered through a story about why he had your phone after the equinox."

"Oh." I felt a flush creep across my cheeks and looked away.

"Not to mention the trampled vines on the lattice outside his window," Caius added, arching a dark brow.

Shit…

He rose to his feet and gestured to the door. "I'll take you to him."

"Can I ask you a question?" The words flew out of my mouth before I could stop myself.

"Of course."

"Why… how are you ok with any of this? With me? I mean, I'm grateful you didn't let Claudia kill me. But… why not?"

Caius exhaled a long, weary sigh, like he'd been expecting this question. "Son, when you're older, you'll come to realize there are more important things in life than carrying the grudge of people who have been dead for almost four hundred years. This ongoing hatred cost me the love of my life. I wouldn't wish that pain on anyone, least of all my son. I raised him to be better than me. What kind of example would I be setting if I judged you for the sins of your father, instead of your own?"

A puff of air could have probably knocked me over. I'd gotten it wrong my entire life. Maybe Caius had changed drastically in six years, but I doubted it. People didn't change *that* much. The "villains" of my childhood weren't really villains at all. They were good people — *better* people — than the Congregation as a whole gave them credit for.

Like he could read my thoughts, Caius gave me a nod and clapped me on the shoulder, steering me out the door and up the massive staircase. He stopped at the end of a hallway I recognized from the last time I was in the house.

"He's just through there. Use the bell pull if you need anything."

"Thank you, sir."

I waited until he headed back the way we came before I faced Cassius's closed door. Expelling a short breath, I turned the handle and slipped inside quietly.

All of the drapes were closed, but someone had lit a fire in the fireplace. It took a moment for my eyes to adjust before I made my way to Cassius's bed quietly. I kicked off my shoes before climbing into it.

"Cash?" I slipped my hand beneath the sheets, looking for his. It was warm when my fingers curled around it. He squeezed mine in return, instinctively it seemed, since he didn't open his eyes.

I nestled down in the pillow next to him, watching him sleep. "I'm sorry," I whispered. "I don't care if you spend the rest of your life hating me. I'll never stop apologizing for everything I've done."

Chapter Thirty-Five
Cassius

Every part of my body was sore, from my head down to my toes. I'd never used so much magic in my life. I felt completely and utterly drained, like I could sleep for a week. With how stiff I was, I wouldn't have been surprised to hear my family knocked my ass out to do just that.

Rubbing my eyes, I pushed myself into a sitting position and glanced down at my arm, trying to take stock of what was left of my injuries. Of course Claudia had gone to work, repairing whatever bones I'd broken. Either she or Dad sutured the giant claw marks closed. The perk of living with two doctors, I supposed.

But how the fuck had I gotten from the field to my bed?

The answer, as it turned out, was laying beside me, passed out.

Reaching out slowly, I poked Graeme's arm, expecting to see his image disappear like a soap bubble popping. Instead, he inhaled and blinked himself awake. When his mismatched eyes finally focused they opened wide and he sat upright, throwing himself at me.

"You're awake!"

"What are you doing here?" I asked, peeling his arms off of my neck and pushing them back toward him.

I didn't miss the flicker of hurt on his face before he answered. "Making sure you're ok."

"You need to leave." Throwing back the covers, I eased out of bed carefully in case there were any lingering internal injuries. "If my family finds you, they'll fucking kill you."

"They know I'm here."

His words froze me in my tracks, halfway between the bed and the balcony door. I was concussed. And the crows must have done a number on my hearing with all of their shrieking. Or it was all a dream. "They what?"

"They know I'm here," he repeated, slipping off the bed and padding over to me. Maybe he was a ghost. Maybe I'd imagined he felt solid a few minutes ago. Or maybe he was somehow able to channel so much energy that he still felt solid. And warm.

Ghost or not, he took my face between his hands and leaned in.

His lips barely brushed mine when I reared back. "No."

"No?" He frowned, his dark brows furrowing.

"Thank you for bringing me home. But it's time for you to leave. And since they apparently know you're here, feel free to use the front door this time." I sidestepped him and headed for said door to open it and throw his ass out.

"I'm not going anywhere."

"You're sure as hell not staying."

"Cash…" He reached for my arm, but I jerked it away from him.

"Don't."

"Please, just talk to me."

"Talk to you? Talk to you about what, Graeme?! About how you murdered my fucking cousin but it's ok because you didn't 'mean' to? Or how you're the one who pushed for this… whatever the fuck it is… and then turned and threw it all in my face the second I didn't have a good enough answer for you?"

"I'm sorry. I'm sorry for freaking out on you. Please, Cassius, tell me what to do. Tell me what I can do to make it better."

"It'll never *be* better! Don't you see that? I hate you! I hate everything about you and what you represent! What you've said and done. But I hate myself even more and looking at you is a reminder of that."

"Our lives have been filled with hate. I'm fucking sick of it. Aren't you?" With his shoulders rounded and his eyes soft, he looked as tired as I felt. Like he was genuinely upset by the state of things.

Nevertheless, I steeled my spine. "Some of us don't have the luxury of pretending all is right in the world. But as soon as I find those missing folios and reunite the Book, I'll let you know if I've miraculously had a change of heart."

"Will you kill me then? When you have your precious book? Why wait?" He spread his arms and took a step closer. "Go ahead. I won't stop you this time. Or maybe I should go back outside and wait for that demon to come back, the one your cousin said was after me."

I stiffened. "Lennox said a demon was after you?"

"Yeah. Explains a lot. Don't you think?"

My mind whirled with the possibilities, piecing together the events of the past several weeks. "There's got to be a Necromancer involved, but it's not me," I said after a moment.

"Then who is it?"

"I don't know. We need to tell my dad." I opened the door again, but Graeme stopped me in the hallway.

"Wait. Are we…? What are we? Are we ok?" A small crease formed between his brows, his eyes dark and guarded, yet I saw a glimmer of hope.

"I don't know," I said truthfully. "We have more important things to worry about."

"Do you forgive me?"

"No." The hope in his eyes flickered out. "Maybe with time. But I understand, which is a start."

He smiled, brittle as it was. "I'll take what I can get."

I slipped my hand into his and held onto it, tugging him down the hallway. Keeping my eyes peeled for the telltale marks of a demon or a sign of any of the other dark families, I navigated through the house to my dad's lab.

Claudia intercepted us right outside of it. She took one look at our joined hands and her dark eyes flashed like hot coals. "You've got to be fucking kidding me, Cassius!"

"Not now, Claudia," I sighed, tightening my hold on Graeme's hand. Hopefully she wouldn't actually try to kill him if I was standing so close.

"What happened to 'lab partners'?" she yelled. "What happened to just getting through the semester? Now you're fuck buddies with him?! He murdered our cousin! Our mother is dead because of his goddamn family! What is wrong with you?!"

Each word out of her mouth was like a slap in the face. I was too stunned by the magnitude of her anger to formulate a response. Thankfully, I didn't have to. Dad's lab door swung open and he stepped out, frowning at the three of us.

"Enough, Claudia," he said. "Your brother is free to make his own choices."

"Are you serious?!" She whirled on Dad, her jaw about hitting the floor.

Graeme's other hand encircled my wrist, squeezing gently in some sense of comfort or solidarity.

Dad didn't say anything in the face of her outrage. He simply maintained his composure, fixing her with a patient stare, like he was waiting for her to come to the same conclusion he had.

"What do you think is going to happen when his family finds out?" she asked, pointing at Graeme even though she took a step closer to Dad. "If you thought things were bad before, this will end whatever peace the Congregation thought it had."

"Wars have been fought for less," Dad replied. "If love is the cause of this one, then come what may."

"Love?!" A look of pure horror washed over Claudia's face as she turned from Dad to us, apparently seeing us in a new, disgusting light.

I was just as shocked by Dad's statement. Looking down at our hands, my gaze traveled up Graeme's arm to his face. From the faint pink in his cheeks and the way he glanced down before looking up again, I knew it was true. He loved me. He fucking *loved* me. I didn't know how. Frankly, I didn't know why. But he did.

The inevitable question was — did I love him? Underneath all of the hate and anger and stupid lust, was there something else? Was it love that made my blood come alive? Love that made the knot in my chest loosen whenever he was around? I had no fucking clue. I'd never loved anyone before. Not like that.

"Unbelievable," Claudia whispered, shaking her head. She put her hands up in defeat and disappeared down the hallway as fast as her legs could carry her.

"Claudia!" Dad called after her, his frown deepening.

"It's fine, Dad," I said weakly, still in a state of shock myself at the revelation.

He shook his head and faced us again, his brows lifting. "Was there something you needed?"

I nodded. "We need to talk."

"About what?"
"About everything."

Chapter Thirty-Six

Graeme

Cassius and I talked to his dad for what seemed like forever. We retraced our relationship from the very first night we met at Preston's, all the way to the events that led to me sitting in the Corbins' kitchen drinking tea like an old friend instead of their sworn enemy.

We told him about our fight in front of Dane Hall, how it was the two murdered girls saw us. Our trip to the morgue (both times) and my battle with an unseen entity by the parking garage. Cassius crossing over to try and get information from Lydia. The disaster at the meetinghouse (again, both times) and my inability to control my damn powers.

Cassius added some additional facts even I was unaware of — that their family's ritual knife had apparently been used in the first murder. It had gone missing and mysteriously returned with no explanation. Other than tying the family to the murder, if the knife had fallen into the wrong hands, it could have been *very* bad for the Congregation. The knife, according to Caius, had the ability to kill any demon — or witch — and in doing so, it absorbed their powers, giving the wielder access to more magic than they had on their own.

As scary as *that* thought was, Cassius's ultimate concern was that someone was after the Book of Lazarus.

"What would happen if they get the book?" I asked,

glancing between them as they shared a long, weighted look.

"It wouldn't be good," Caius said, his thumb stroking the handle on his mug. "The book was written *by* Necromancers *for* Necromancers. It's not that a regular witch, or God forbid a mortal, *couldn't* read it, it's that they don't understand the magnitude of what they're dealing with. In the Middle Ages, Necromancers documented the rituals necessary to summon demons. Summon *and* control them. It's simple enough to summon one. They're always lurking about, ready to corrupt the willing. But controlling them? That's where non-Necromancers get into trouble. It's one of the reasons we forged the crow knife to begin with, to safeguard ourselves against demons."

"What if someone summoned a demon but couldn't control it?"

"Then we'd all be fair game," Cassius replied, staring into his tea. "No quicker way for a demon to enhance their power than to kill a witch and claim theirs."

"Lennox seemed to think there was one after me," I said quietly, not wanting to push my luck with Caius — or Cassius. "How would he know that?"

"Lucky guess?" Caius said, spreading his hands. "Your magic is unique. A demon would be drawn to it, naturally. But when you're with Cassius? It's even stronger. I can feel it right now."

Cassius and I looked at each other. Now that his dad pointed it out, the buzzing in my blood was there, humming along in the background. It wasn't just *my* magic or *his* magic — it was *our* magic that I'd been feeling all along.

"Or," Caius continued, interrupting the moment of warm fuzzies. "He knows because whoever summoned it told him about it."

"What if he's the one who summoned it?" Cassius asked, his words clipped.

Caius cocked his head, his frown deepening. "Do you honestly think he would?"

"I don't know... he was here when the knife was missing. He obviously knew about the Book. He hated Graeme," Cassius said, stealing a glance at me. "But this one was strong, Dad. This wasn't the same one from the meeting-house. The banishment spell almost didn't work."

Caius sat up straighter. "What do you mean 'almost didn't work'? That spell is designed to dismiss any demon."

"I'm telling you, it didn't work the first time I did it. It only worked when Graeme gave me some of his blood."

"Wait here," Caius said, standing abruptly and disappearing through the door to another room.

"That can't be good," I murmured, turning to face Cassius.

"No... it's not."

"If your dad said that spell should have worked the first time, why did it only work after you used my blood?"

"A demon that strong has the powers of a witch — either through killing them or because they've entered into a covenant."

"Ok... I get why that's a problem, but why did your dad look extra worried?"

"Because despite what our enemies would have you believe, forging a covenant with a demon isn't *that* easy, especially if you're actually trying to control it and not get yourself killed. If you're using it for some sort of stupid gain, like wealth or a lover, then sure, they'll cooperate because you'll be dead before you can enjoy whatever it is they've given you. But to send it out as your own personal assassin? That sort of magic is hardly ever recorded. You'd need a very old, very powerful grimoire like the Book—"

"Of Lazarus," I concluded.

"Exactly. And there aren't that many in existence, let alone here in the States."

"How many Necromancers are out there?"

"I don't know," he replied with a frown. "It's not like we have a club. Although, I *am* surprised no one has started a support group by now."

"Let me rephrase, smart ass. How many people would know about your family's book?"

He chewed on his lower lip, mulling it over for a minute. "I don't know... I imagine anyone in the Congregation *could* know about it. But even if they did, I don't think they'd know how to get to it."

Caius breezed back through the door with a rather unremarkable book in his hand. "Got it."

"What's that?" I asked.

Cassius supplied the answer, like it was obvious. "The Book."

"*That* is the Book? *The* Book?" I stared at it as Caius set it on the kitchen table, leafing through it gingerly. As far as sacred books went, this one was... nondescript. A thick, black leather cover was scratched and stained and the silver clasps were tarnished. It looked old, for sure, and smelled old from the must, but I was expecting jewels and gold and for it to be *big*, or at least thick, like one of those monster bibles you see in medieval monasteries. This thing was no bigger than any regular book you'd find in a bookstore today. "It looks like it could be anything, not some weapon of mass magical destruction."

Caius chuckled. "That's the point. Once upon a time having a book like this was a guaranteed trip to the gallows — or worse. That's why the Book was separated to begin with and some of the folios removed, to keep both the Book and the practitioner safe. You're right — at a glance, this looks like nothing. And should one section be found or, say, confiscated by the authorities, it would be practically worthless without the other."

"Which is exactly what happened when someone *stole* the folios, hobbling our family's magic for centuries," Cassius said with a bit of a growl, throwing a look his dad's way.

"Yes, but this is the part I was most concerned with," Caius said, spinning the book around and showing Cassius a page with all sorts of weird symbols on it. It looked like instructions on how to cast a circle, but the writing was entirely in Latin. The only thing that stood out, once again, was *daemonium*. "It tells a witch how to summon a demon and forge a covenant, but the part for controlling it once it's unleashed is in the missing section. So is the part about how to dissolve a covenant."

"So now what?" Cassius asked, looking up at his dad.

"There are three options. Find the witch, find the demon, or find the missing folios."

Cassius slumped back in his chair with a defeated sigh.

"Is that going to be, like, impossible?" I asked, glancing between the two.

"It won't be easy," Caius said.

"What if we divide and conquer?"

He cocked his head in a way very reminiscent of his son. "What are you proposing?"

"We were already in the archives," I said, glancing at Cassius. "I can go back and look for any mention of the folios. And Necromancers are clearly your thing, so you two can look for the witch."

"And the demon?" Cassius asked, his brows raising.

"The Congregation," I replied. "Ainsworth and Colburn are already looking for one. Treadwell is too, even if he doesn't know it yet. I would bet anything the one who killed those girls is the same one who attacked us in the field. Maybe even the same one who attacked India at the equinox."

Again, Cassius and his dad had some silent exchange until

Caius let out a weary breath. "It's not the worst idea I've ever heard. There's just one problem..."

"What?" Cassius and I asked at the same time.

He smiled, glancing between the two of us. "Since there is a demon like this out there with some sort of agenda against Graeme, I think he should stay with us for a while. At least until he makes his conversion."

"What?!" We both exploded again.

"Dad!"

"Sir, that's still a week away. There's no way in hell my dad is going to let me be gone from the house that long. And he if finds out I'm *here*? He really will bring the whole Congregation to try and tear the house apart."

A familiar high-pitched whine howled outside, like the wind, but creepier. There was a *tap, tapping* along the window, followed by a screech of something sharp against the glass.

We collectively froze, glancing around.

"Is that—"

Before I could even finish my question, something hard slammed against the window, cracking it.

The three of us jumped, staring at the splintered glass.

The smell of smoke and sulfur seeped through the cracks, but nothing else came through.

After a few minutes, we let out shaky breaths.

"I think Lennox was right," Cassius said, his voice barely above a whisper. "I think a demon is hunting him. They've never attacked the house before."

"You're not going anywhere tonight," Caius said, looking at me with the utmost seriousness.

No argument there. But what the hell was I going to tell my dad?

Chapter Thirty-Seven
Cassius

Never in a million years did I think Graeme Hewitt would be in my house — in my bed — *with* my father's approval. Not only approval, his decree. Maybe the whole sharing a bed thing wasn't part of the decree, but he refused to let Graeme leave and I refused to let Claudia murder him in the middle of the night, therefore it seemed like the logical choice as far as sleeping arrangements went.

"So... are we going to talk about it?" Graeme asked, staring at the painted ceiling overhead. The constellations glimmered with flashes of gold in the firelight.

"Talk about what?" My heart rate accelerated. He was going to ask me the question I'd been asking myself ever since Dad basically outed him. Maybe a part of me had known all along, but that look downstairs confirmed it.

"Really?" He shot me an incredulous look.

"We need sleep. We both need sleep. It's been a... long day."

"Did you lock the door?" he asked after a minute of awkward silence.

"Yes. Why?"

"Just wondering if I should sleep with one eye open in case your sister comes." When I glanced at him, I could see he was toying with the amulet around his neck — something Dad insisted I give him again until this whole mess was sorted out.

"That's why you're in here and not a guest room."

"Oh." He sounded pouty in the near-dark.

"What?" I sighed.

"I thought maybe you just wanted me here..."

"I..." What the hell was I supposed to say to that? I did. I wanted to keep him safe from Claudia, from demons, from whatever else might be trying to kill him on any given day. But I wanted to beat the hell out of him. He took my already complicated life and made it a thousand times worse. Just like a Hewitt to take and take and take and never give anything back. He'd taken my time, my energy, my focus, and what was I left with? Pain. Death. Confusion. A veritable mess of emotions.

I was surprised and relieved my dad didn't kill me because of all the lying I'd been doing, especially about Graeme, but now Claudia hated me. Sure, my sister and I weren't as close as we were before Mom died, but she was still my sister. I didn't ever want to intentionally hurt her. Seeing the look on her face when she saw Graeme and I together — not once, but twice now — made my stomach clench.

And there was no way Graeme's family would be ok with this. He'd said as much. Needless to say, his phone call to his dad had not gone over well. He claimed he was staying at some guy named Noah's house, which his father vehemently objected to. It ended in a screaming match and Graeme damn near throwing his phone.

"I don't know what you want me to say," I said weakly, knowing *full well* what he wanted me to say. But what he wanted and what I was capable of were two different things.

"Do you hate me, Cassius?" It seemed like just yesterday

he'd asked me that question on the balcony. A lifetime had passed since then, for both of us.

"You know I don't."

The sheets rustled a moment before he pressed himself against me, propping his chin on my shoulder. "That's better than what you said last time."

I turned slightly, resting my cheek against his forehead. "How do you know it's real? Not just our magic?"

He toyed with my fingers in the dark, each featherlight touch completely innocent, but sending little ripples of energy straight to my dick. "I *don't* know. But if magic is part of who we are, then why would it be any less real?"

"You realize the last time Necromancers and Stormbringers were on the same side half of my family was wiped out, right?"

"I don't think that's going to happen this time."

"If your dad had his way, it would."

"I'm not going to let anyone do anything to you or your family."

"Is that Graeme Hewitt, the future Deacon, I hear?"

He poked my ribcage. I laughed and swatted his hand, squirming away.

"Keep it up and I'll nominate *you* to be Deacon when the time comes," Graeme grumbled, snagging my waist and hauling me against him, my back pressed to his chest. Burying his face in the side of my neck, his lips brushed against my pulse point. "Wouldn't that be revolutionary?"

"A Necromancer as Deacon?" I closed my eyes, melting into him. "Hell would have to freeze over first."

"I could help with that," he murmured against my skin, sliding one hand up my stomach, his fingers splaying over my bare chest.

"I know something else you could help with…" I turned my face toward his, enveloped immediately by his kiss. His hand drifted south, rubbing along my length over the top of my underwear. His own dick pressed against me, hardening by the second. Gripping the base of my shaft and stroking slowly, he kissed me harder, rolling his hips against me for his own relief.

Pulling his mouth from mine, he licked my lips teasingly and shifted on top of me. Leaving a trail of kisses down my throat, he made his way across my chest and along my abdomen before settling between my legs. Mouthing my hard-on on top of the fabric, he chuckled like a sadist when I whined.

"What do you want?" he asked, nosing along my cock and teasing me with his breath, running his hands along the inside of my thighs. Hooking his fingers around the waistband, he pulled my boxer briefs down a millimeter at a time, drawing out the torture.

"You." I threaded my fingers through his dark hair, trying to redirect him to where I wanted him.

"Me, huh?"

"Stop being a—" The rest of that insult ended in a groan as his mouth descended on my dick. "Fuck…"

Humming his amusement, he swallowed the length of me. The vibration, the heat, the wetness. It was a miracle I didn't come on the spot.

He paused, only to work my boxer briefs off completely and toss them to the side. Before he could resume, I caught his jaw in my hand and dragged him forward, kissing him roughly.

"On your side," I murmured. "And lose the underwear."

"Yes, sir." In the blink of an eye, he was naked, laying on his side as instructed, with his head toward the foot of the bed.

Scooting down so we were better aligned, I wasted no time sucking the head of his cock into my mouth. He swore under his breath, his hips thrusting once before he went back to my dick, licking and sucking along every inch of it.

A cold breeze wafted through the room. For a moment, I thought the balcony door may have blown open. Then the distinct smell of sandalwood and lavender filled the air.

I popped off the end of his dick and looked at him with an arched brow. "Did you just levitate that?"

He bit his lower lip, sliding his slick fingers along my crease. "You looked like you were enjoying yourself. I didn't want to interrupt."

With a flick of my wrist, the bottle zipped in my direction. I poured a bit onto my hand and ran it between his cheeks as well. "Magic in the bedroom was dangerous the last time."

"After today? I don't think I have enough energy to turn on a lightbulb."

"That's unfortunate for me," I murmured, slipping a finger inside of him. He gasped and clenched around the intrusion, glaring at me.

"My stamina has nothing to do with magic," he said, teasing my rim while I moved my finger in and out of him slowly, adding more of the oil when necessary.

"Good." Still working my finger inside of him, I leaned down and sucked on his cock again, desperate to get him ready before I had my own orgasm from the things he was doing to me.

"I can't take it anymore," he said, pulling away from me. Before I could ask anything, he pounced, straddling my lap and kissing me feverishly. My cock rubbed along his crease, both of us slippery from oil and pre-cum. To be on the safe side, I poured more into his hand. Instead of coating himself with it, though, he reached behind him and stroked my dick with it before spreading the leftover around his hole.

"What are you doing?" I asked.

"What does it look like?" Holding my cock steady, he eased himself down onto it with a series of gasps and groans.

"Oh, fuck. Graeme." I bit my lip, gripping his waist. It was just as amazing as before. Maybe more so with the help of gravity, ensuring he sank all the way down. "I thought you didn't ride?"

"Horses, you idiot." He swiveled his hips once before rocking them in a smooth, steady pace.

My grip on his waist tightened. I hauled him downward at the same time I thrust up, reminding him I wasn't a fucking pony ride. He cried out, bracing one hand against my chest for balance.

"Fuck, Cash."

I kept doing it, enjoying the way he squeaked now and again, trying to keep his outbursts to a minimum like last time. His cheeks flushed and eyes half-closed, he stroked himself in time with me until it looked like he was right on the edge. Then he stopped suddenly and leaned down, kissing me softly before sliding off of my dick.

"Your turn," he whispered, grabbing the bottle of oil and applying a fresh coating.

He nudged my legs apart and settled between them, teasing me, only this time it was with his cock. I was about to make a comment about what the fuck was taking him so long when he finally sank inside. We both let out the breaths we'd been holding as our bodies melded together.

My eyes fluttered closed as the feeling of being full and stretched overtook my other senses. "You feel amazing," I said, tilting my hips up to meet his tentative thrusts.

"It's like you were made for me," he panted, driving into me in a slow, steady rhythm that hit all the right spots.

"Maybe I was." I ran my fingers through his hair and grasped the back of his head, pulling him down so I could kiss him as deeply as he was fucking me.

He pressed his forehead to mine, breathing hard and picking up the pace. I jerked myself in tandem with him. Release was there, I could feel it gathering in every single fucking cell. I just needed a little more…

"Don't stop. Oh my God, Graeme…"

"I'm going to fucking come, Cash."

"Not yet," I breathed. My balls were so tight I was sure they were going to explode on their own at any second.

"I don't know how much longer I can last. You feel too fucking good."

"Fuck me harder."

I didn't have to tell him twice. He gripped my hips and slammed into me, again and again. I stroked my cock furiously, the muscles in my thighs tightening around his waist.

"Get there, baby," he pleaded, squeezing his eyes shut.

"I'm close…"

"Oh fuck!" He gave a final thrust, burying himself inside of me, crying out with the release. His orgasm hit me hard, ricocheting throughout my nervous system like fireworks. It wasn't lightning this time but it was damn close. My whole body vibrated from the intensity, but thankfully it didn't hurt. It did, however, push me over the edge into my own orgasm.

I muffled my cries into his shoulder until the last surge of energy dissipated. His forehead fell to mine again, both of us covered with sweat and the sticky remnants of my release.

"You're ok, right?" he panted, swallowing hard.

"Yeah."

"No lightning?"

I rolled my head back and forth in the negative, too exhausted to say more.

"Oh thank God. I felt this… buzzing and I was afraid it was happening again but I couldn't stop."

“I felt it too. But it was different this time. Maybe because you expelled so much energy earlier.”

“Does this mean we have to fight off a demon every time we want to have sex?”

“God, I hope not. Guess we’ll find out after your conversion, though.”

“Right.” He looked away, a sudden solemnness on his face.

“What’s the matter?” Caressing his cheek, I guided him back to me.

When his gaze drifted up to mine, his eyes were glassy. “I’m scared. Between the conversion and a fucking demon after me… I just—”

I captured his face between my hands and pressed my lips against his, as much to comfort him as it was to shut him up. Talking about anything heavy was going to ruin our happy little moment and after everything lately, I didn’t think it would have been good for either one of us.

He let out a shaky breath, the corner of his mouth ticking up. “What was that for?”

“Because I think I love you too.” Just saying the words made my heart rate triple. At the same time, it spread that warm, thrumming energy around my body even faster.

He gave me the dopiest smile ever and dragged a knuckle under his eye to wipe away a non-existent tear. “Those are the nicest seven words you’ve ever said to me.”

“And I already regret them,” I replied with a biting smile.

A genuine smile curved his lips as he leaned down, kissing me with so much passion it was hard to believe it was the same guy who tried to kill me two months ago. Then again, it was hard to believe I’d ever feel anything for a Hewitt other than bottomless hatred. Yet here we were.

Chapter Thirty-Eight

Graeme

"How long are we supposed to do this whole buddy-system thing?" Cassius asked his dad over breakfast one morning. "Midterms are over now."

Not surprisingly, Claudia was absent. I hadn't seen hide nor hair of her since the other night when their dad gave us his blessing. For the most part, Cassius and I had been hiding in his room in the hope of avoiding her. The only time we came out was for food and only if Caius was there.

"Trouble in paradise already?" Caius chuckled, glancing between us.

At least Cassius looked as uncomfortable as I felt. While he chugged half of his cup of coffee, I ducked my head and concentrated on my omelet, pretending this wasn't the most awkward moment of my life. It was bad enough his *dad* was the one to point out I was in love with his son… now this? Jokes over breakfast?

Maybe it would have been easier if the demon killed me. At least then I wouldn't be in this weird in-between stage with Cassius. He knew I loved him. With the way Cassius looked at me after his dad said it, there's no way in hell he *didn't* know. I mean, *I* didn't say the words (thanks a lot Mr. Corbin — Dr. Corbin?), but I didn't deny it either.

So I guess I couldn't blame Cassius for not, exactly, saying the words either. *I think I love you*. It was still better than the alternative, which was him screaming how much he hated me all the time.

"In answer to your question," Caius continued, dabbing the corner of his mouth with a cloth napkin. "At least for a few more days. The Selectmen are meeting tomorrow night to discuss the demon when Peregrine gets back from his business trip. Temperance found something she believes will be useful. Do you have classes today?"

I assumed he was talking to Cassius until I remembered what Ainsworth said.

Glancing between the two of them, I cleared my throat. "Yeah. Meteorology, chemistry, and geography."

"Normally I wouldn't suggest skipping, but in this case, I'm sure your professors would understand. Otherwise, Cassius can go with you. It's not safe for you to be on your own, even if it is at Tennebrose."

My attention shifted to his son. "I've been meaning to ask. Did you *really* withdraw?"

"I'm going to get more coffee." Cassius stood abruptly and retreated into the kitchen. His mug, however, remained on the table.

"Excuse me," I mumbled to his dad before hurrying after him. "What the fuck?"

"I can't believe Ainsworth told you," Cassius said, shaking his head even though his back was to me, his palms braced against the granite counter.

"Well, considering we were lab partners, yeah. He kind of had to. Besides, I would have figured it out when you didn't come back to class. *Ever*. Can't you rescind it?"

"No." Jesus. He didn't even give me a second to finish speaking!

Stepping up behind him, I slipped my hands around his

waist and pressed my cheek against his shoulder. "Can't you at least try?"

His whole body stiffened against me. I knew the answer before he even whispered, "No."

"Seriously? What about—"

"I don't want to talk about this right now. We have more important things to worry about."

"I'd say this is pretty important."

He turned in my arms, pressing himself back against the countertop and making no attempt to touch me. "I'm going back to England."

I took a step away from him, head cocked. "You're what?"

"The University of Ashbourne has a place—"

"No!" I cut him off, shaking my head. Anger replaced confusion in the blink of an eye. "You don't get to leave me here after everything while you run off to Hogwarts and pretend like none of this ever happened!"

"I'm not running anywhere," he said, crossing his arms.

"Sure sounds like it. Is it because of what you said the other night? In bed?"

"No."

"Coincidence, then?"

"It's done, Graeme. All of this shit started when I came back, so it's time to leave before anyone else dies. My feelings on the matter are completely irrelevant."

I'm sure he didn't mean it, but I couldn't help but feel it was entirely my fault and entirely related to what happened with Lennox. He was just being nice for a change and not blaming me when he absolutely should have been.

"Anyway, don't worry about Ainsworth's class. I did my part." Cassius sidestepped me and disappeared down the hallway to his father's lab. And when I say lab, I mean *lab.* Full-blown, medical research laboratory with microscopes, a centrifuge, an autoclave, hot plates, and an incubator.

Anything and everything a doctor or scientist could ever want for their own research purposes.

He retrieved a small specimen container from the refrigerator and set it on the counter, gesturing for me to take a look. Inside was a handful of completely normal-looking apple seeds.

"And now I'm supposed to grow them?" I asked, picking up the plastic container and studying the seeds.

"You *are* a weather witch, aren't you?"

"So everyone keeps telling me." I set the container down again. "What did you do to them?"

He wandered to the other side of the lab and grabbed a beaker full of clear liquid. When he returned, he wafted it beneath my nose, raising his eyebrows. "Smell anything?"

I shook my head.

"I replicated Acqua Tofana, as I said, only I made it a concentrated dose. Once I was sure I could do it consistently, I infused the pips with it. Now it's your turn." He gestured to the glass dome cloche and the potting soil.

Nodding, I picked up one of the seeds with a pair of tweezers and buried it in the soil. Clearing my throat, I laid both hands over the pot and focused on creating a nice, gentle rain. As soon as I felt the cool mist on my palms, I lifted them, revealing little white puffs floating in the air. Tiny drops of rain descended on the soil.

The corner of Cassius's mouth lifted, growing bigger by the second. "That's really cool."

"Thanks." I tried to be flippant about the praise, but inside I was glowing. So much so that the raincloud evaporated and a miniature sun appeared in its place. Pretending it was all part of the process and not because I was blushing, I set the cloche over the top, turning the whole thing into a little terrarium. If I did it correctly, it would regulate itself in a fairly consistent weather pattern and hopefully soon we'd have an apple big enough to test.

"I'm heading out," Caius announced from the doorway. "Are you two going to be alright?"

We both nodded.

"I'll see you tonight." Caius disappeared, leaving us alone again, staring at one another with a weighted silence closing in.

"What are the chances we can go outside today?" I asked, pressing my hands together in a hopeful prayer.

"I don't know, weather boy, what's the forecast?"

I rolled my eyes. "I was more concerned about a demon than a little rain."

Cassius chewed the inside of his cheek, glancing at the old, wavy glass in the windows. "As long as we stay close to the house we should be ok."

"I don't even care if we just walk around it. I'm dying for fresh air."

"Nature witches," he muttered, shaking his head while moving toward the door. I let the dig go, especially since it lacked his usual snappiness.

We exited through the doors off the breakfast room onto a large, stone terrace. The sprawling steps led down to a gravel path I knew would take us to the gardens, and ultimately the Corbin crypt.

"So is everyone in your family a doctor?" I asked.

"Pretty much. Doctor, scientist, professor. Anything related to anatomy."

"Do you... want to be?" I snuck a glance at him.

"Want to be what? A doctor? Of course. Otherwise I wouldn't be doing it."

"So you're not doing it because it's what your family expects?"

"Is this about the Deacon thing again? Just tell them you don't want it. It's that simple."

"No, this is about you making up some bullshit reason to leave. You just said you do things because you want to, not because of obligation. So that means you *want* to go back to England."

"What if I asked you to come with me? Would that make you happy?"

"I don't know. Would you mean it?"

"Not right now I wouldn't."

"You know, you act all annoyed by me, but I think you like it."

"Trust me, it's not an act."

We turned down another path, the gravel crunching beneath our shoes. I honestly didn't know where to go from there, conversation-wise. Talking about the future was risky. Talking about the past was off-limits. And in the present, all I wanted to do was kiss him and beg him to stay with me.

So, I did the next best thing — tried to get under his skin and ruffle a few feathers.

"I don't think anyone has ever challenged you before," I said, stepping in front of him and blocking the way. "You accuse me of always getting my way, but look at you. You refuse to cooperate and act like it's the last thing you'll ever do, but you always end up submitting."

"Yeah," he replied with a smirk. "Because it's the easiest way to shut you up and move on with my day."

I leaned closer, like I was going to kiss him, and diverted at the last second to speak softly in his ear. "There are other ways to shut me up, you know."

"I don't think anyone has ever challenged *you* before, your majesty," he shot back. "They all bow before the Hewitt name and give you everything you want."

"Would you prefer they run away screaming, like people do when they hear yours?"

"Let them hate, so long as they fear," he quoted, tipping his chin up.

"Of course you'd quote someone as diabolical as Caligula."

"Accius," he corrected. "But I'm impressed you know Roman history at all."

"There's more to me than my good looks, you know. There *are* a few brain cells up there."

"A few? That's being generous."

I gaped at him, trying to decide how serious he was. He finally cracked a smile, glancing away.

"You can drop the asshole act any time," I said, only half-joking.

"I told you, it's not an act."

Cawing up above drew Cassius's gaze to the sky. He held a hand aloft as a crow swept downward, landing delicately on the offered perch. Aside from being mesmerized that wild birds continued to seek him out, I was even more struck by the dirty white cloth hanging from its beak.

"What is that?" I asked as Cassius lifted his other hand.

The crow dropped whatever it was into Cassius's palm before hopping up onto his shoulder and turning around to see what Cassius was doing with it.

It was a little cloth doll with brown yarn for hair. There wasn't a face or clothes. It was like one of those kitschy voodoo dolls but creepier. Except for the smear of dark reddish-brown across the center of the doll's chest, there was nothing to indicate what the hell it was. No colors, no markings. Nothing.

"It's a poppet," Cassius said, turning it over. "Ow! Shit!" He sucked his index finger into his mouth and glared at the doll.

The body had been pierced with pins at all sorts of different angles. They weren't stuck through the thing, like a voodoo doll, the pins were *inside* it, poking out through the cloth and stuffing.

The crow made a little grumble noise and ruffled its feathers, like it was irritated.

"Where did you get this?" Cassius asked the bird.

Blinking back, the crow tilted its head and made a couple of rattling and clicking sounds, ruffling its feathers again.

I obviously didn't have a fucking clue what was going on between the two of them, but Cassius's chiseled face turned to ice in the blink of an eye when he practically shouted, "What?!"

Leaping off his shoulder, the crow swooped downward and took off again, heading north. Cassius sprinted after it, clutching the doll.

I, in turn, followed him. "What's wrong?"

"The crypt," was all he said as we barreled down the path.

Oh, goodie. Just where I wanted to go.

Chapter Thirty-Nine
Cassius

Running as fast as I could, my lungs were burning by the time we reached the crypt. Instead of going in, however, I followed the crow to the back of the mausoleum and slid to a halt.

Graeme skidded to a stop next to me, grabbing onto my arm to steady himself.

"What the fuck?"

I don't know who said it, or if I'd merely thought it. Either way, I was fucking speechless.

There was a whole group of crows on the ground — dead. Not just dead, *slaughtered*. Heads and wings ripped off. Black feathers and broken little bodies were everywhere. Blood splatters streaked across the back of the crypt and left dark pools on the grass. It was recent, but not too recent. Thankfully decay hadn't set in on any of the birds.

The crow who'd led us to the massacre sat on the top of the crypt, cawing loudly, screaming out a warning to any other corvid in the area.

Graeme stooped and picked up one of the bodies, cradling it gently. Against all odds, it was intact, save for the fact its head was facing the wrong direction. "What happened? Who would do this?"

I clenched the cloth doll so hard the needles inside of it

pierced my hand and blood ran from between my fingers. "Something evil," I whispered, too struck by the horror to speak at full volume.

"Can you do something?" he asked, holding the dead bird out to me like it was merely a broken toy and not a creature that had been senselessly *murdered*. "Can you fix it?"

The living crow cawed again, agreeing with Graeme.

"It might be too late," I said, holding the poppet out to him, trading it for the crow. How this one managed to not have its body ripped to shreds was a miracle. It may have only been a dozen birds, give or take, but the carnage made it look like twice that. An entire family gone in one fell swoop.

Since my hand was already bleeding, I made another fist and squeezed more blood onto the center of the dead bird. Closing my eyes, I cupped it between my hands and whispered the necessary words. I couldn't save all of them. I knew that. Their bodies were too mutilated. But I could save this one. I just had to fucking concentrate.

The sound of my heartbeat thundered in my ears, drowning out the world around me. Once I was in control of my own pulse, I lowered it until I couldn't hear anything at all except the deafening silence.

Whispering the resurrection spell, I channeled my magic through my hands, searching for a ghostly crow flying through the aether.

Graeme shifted next to me.

The living crow cooed and edged closer on the rooftop, its black claws scratching the stone.

Wind rustled through the trees and the branches scraped together, tearing off another batch of brightly colored leaves.

A cold tendril caressed the side of my face and slithered around my neck, creeping down my body like a serpent until it latched onto my heart.

I hung on to that feeling as hard as I could until a tiny flutter sounded beneath the rest of the noise.

Finishing the prayer as quickly as possible, I whispered the final, "Amen" and held my breath.

"Did it work?" Graeme whispered.

I opened my eyes and looked at the limp bird in my hands. The crow glided down from the crypt and landed on my shoulder, cooing again.

"Cash?"

I couldn't answer him. I was still focusing on that chilly ribbon wrapped around my heart, holding on to it with all of my magical abilities, even as the wind tried to rip it free.

The fluttering turned to a thump.

"Come on," I whispered, stroking the dead crow's chest feathers with my thumb.

One clawed foot twitched.

"Was that...? Did it move?" Graeme's fingers tightened on my arm.

The crow on my shoulder hopped along my other arm. Its black beak flashed forward, poking and preening its mate.

"I feel you," I whispered to the crow in my hands. "She feels you too."

The chill in my heart unwound itself, slipping away like a piece of silk. I'd done what I could. I brought the soul back and gave them another chance. It was time to let go and trust he'd find his way.

So I did, releasing my tenuous grasp on the fragile spirit with a ragged exhale.

The thumping stuttered and grew quiet.

The living crow preened her mate again, alternating between coos and caws. Every time she nudged him, his body rocked back into position, unmoving, unflinching.

The hot, humiliating sense of failure crashed down on

me. Squeezing my eyes shut, tears spilled down my cheeks. "I'm sorry. I tried."

Cawing loudly, the crow on my arm jabbed her mate again with her beak.

"Holy shit," Graeme breathed, damn near breaking my arm by squeezing it so tight.

My eyes flew open. Blinking away the tears, I watched both of the male's feet stretch and curl, like he was waking up from a heavy slumber.

The thumping exploded inside my head, turning to a steady drumming and picking up speed.

I turned the bird over onto his feet, still cradling him. Light shone in his black eyes and his feathers ruffled, shaking off droplets of water. That's when I realized I was still crying like an idiot, dripping tears all over him.

The female darted forward, preening beneath his chin and along his throat. The male tipped his head back, cooing at her.

"You fucking did it," Graeme said.

I'd never been more proud of my magic than that very moment. People wanted to vilify us as Necromancers, hate us for centuries for our morbidity, but they never saw this. They never saw what we could really do because they didn't *want* to. It was easier to see us as evil instead of being capable of doing anything good.

"Are you ready to go home?" I asked the lovers.

They both cawed their agreement. The female took off first with a few powerful flaps of her wings.

"Go get her," I said with a laugh, tossing the male into the air gently. He climbed higher and higher while she pirouetted around him in a dance, dipping and swooping until they both disappeared into the trees.

Dashing the tears from my face, I turned toward Graeme with my eyes downcast. "Sorry for—"

He seized my face in both hands and kissed me.

I pulled away after a moment out of a genuine need for air. Thanks to the crying, my nose was stuffy and I'm sure I looked even more like a damn vampire with the red-ringed eyes now.

Graeme let me pull back, but he didn't let go of my face. "You are fucking incredible. That was… a miracle."

"Born out of tragedy," I replied grimly.

We both turned toward the rest of the carcasses.

"What does this have to do with all of that?" Graeme asked, holding up the poppet. "Is it a demon thing?"

"No," I replied, crouching down and running a hand over one of the headless birds. "This was a witch's doing. It's some sort of curse."

"I thought you said they're not worth the effort?"

"Generally they're not. Whoever did this seems to think it is."

"Who would want to curse your family?"

I stood slowly and met his gaze head-on. "The same person who would be after the Book of Lazarus? Or the people who hate us and wish we all ceased to exist? Pick one."

"I can't believe the Congregation would do this."

"Maybe. Maybe not." I slipped my phone out of my pocket and snapped a couple of quick pictures. "Dad can ask those assholes tomorrow night at the Meeting and see what kind of reaction we get — to that and to us."

"Us?" Graeme's brows shot up.

"Yes, 'us.' Isn't that what you keep bugging me about? Trying to get me to say shit like 'we' and 'us.'"

"Yeah, but like, I didn't mean we had to make an *announcement* in front of the whole Congregation."

"Ashamed of me already?"

"No. Absolutely not. That is *not* what this is about."

Folding my arms over my chest, I cocked my head, waiting for him to continue.

"Dude, you *know* my dad. Ok? Is that something you want to risk?"

"I'm not risking anything. I'm already one of the most hated people in Winslow, remember?"

Rather than continue the fight, I turned back to the massacre and sighed. Waving my hands back and forth in slow, circuitous patterns, I collected all of the pieces of the dead crows with my magic and assembled them in a pile, along with a mound of twigs and crispy leaves.

"Would you mind?" I asked, gesturing to the pile.

"Mind what?" He blinked.

"A little spark or two."

"Oh. Right." He cleared his throat and nodded. Blue lines rippled across his hands and flashed forward, igniting the leaves. They crackled and snapped as the fire spread, latching on to the little corpses.

Despite the warmth from the miniature pyre, I felt frozen to my core. I repeated the words for Requiem Æternam, making the sign of the cross for the avian souls. When the prayer concluded, I spun on my heel and marched toward the house.

"I'm not ashamed of you," Graeme repeated as he caught up to me. Lacing his fingers through mine, he matched each of my strides with his own. "How could I be? You're the most out-of-this-world, intense person I've ever met in my entire life. You're smart and passionate and have the most amazing ass I've ever seen."

"Wow. You know how to make a guy feel special."

"And that!" he said, pulling me to a stop again. "That snarky, deadpan delivery. You're a complete package. I couldn't ask for anything more."

"Except someone Mommy and Daddy approve of." I arched an eyebrow at him, daring him to refute it.

His shoulders rounded. "It doesn't mean I'm ashamed of you. I would shout it from every rooftop in Winslow if you wanted me to. I just… you're the first thing in my life they haven't controlled. You're mine," he sighed, shifting closer and resting his forehead against mine. "To hold hands with, to kiss, to… be myself around. I'm afraid once they know about you, about *us*, I won't have that anymore. We'll be under a fucking microscope and I don't want that for either of us."

"I'm still going to the Meeting," I said sternly, despite the fact my insides felt like goo. Once he explained his reason, it made sense. And to be honest, I felt the same. Obviously my family knew, as well as our extended circle thanks to him showing up the day of Lennox's funeral, but no one on the other end of the spectrum was aware of our… friendship. We couldn't hide forever, but we could at least delay the headache — and the scandal — a little bit longer.

Chapter Forty
Graeme

"I need to swing by my house before class so I can grab a few things," I said, swiping my keys and my cell phone off the table. "Are you coming with me?"

"I'm pretty sure that was the order."

"Don't sound so thrilled about it."

He shot me a look on our way to the door. "You were fine skipping three classes yesterday, but today you just *have* to go? For one?"

"It's Ainsworth's class! You think I want him on my case?"

"I think you're trying to get me to re-enroll."

"Would that be such a bad thing? You know Mrs. Green can wave a magic wand and make the whole dropping out thing go away. You're a Corbin, for fuck's sake! You can come and go from the university at will."

"Can we just go, please?" he sighed, rubbing his forehead like he had a headache.

"Fine." I wasn't anywhere near giving up on our fledgling relationship, but I wasn't going to keep harping on about it either.

We climbed into the Jeep and made our way down the long driveway in silence. Cassius only spoke when we reached the looming, iron gates at the end of the drive. Brick columns stood on either side, topped with two rearing horses. Instead of a metal fence surrounding the property, it was guarded by a tall, thick wall of hawthorn. I wondered how my dad had been able to get past such a defense system, physical and psychic, but didn't voice the question out loud. Guess he really was more powerful than he let on.

The drive back to Winslow was equally silent. It was almost a relief to reach our destination.

"Wait here," I said, parking on the street in case I had to make a quick getaway.

"I was planning on it," Cassius murmured.

Rolling my eyes, I got out of the Jeep and headed inside.

The house was quiet, which meant Dad had already gone to work. Lucky for me.

Heading upstairs, I ducked into my room and stuffed some clothing and other necessities into a bag. The row of crystals on my bookshelf winked in the sunlight, glittering with all of their different colors and facets, drawing me in like a magpie. Struck by a sudden thought, I stepped over to it and scanned the shelf. Zeroing in on the dark green stone in the back, I shoved it in my pocket without dwelling on it.

I grabbed my backpack too and was on my way back to the stairs when a shaft of light in the hallway stopped me in my tracks.

Normally, the door at the end of the hall was closed. It was Owen's room and from the moment of his death it had been turned into a shrine. No one went in there. No one opened the curtains. Which meant the door shouldn't be open and there shouldn't be a swath of sunlight pouring into the hall.

Lowering my bag to the top of the stairs, I edged down the hallway toward the room. On my way past my mother's closed bedroom door, I held my breath, hoping she didn't hear me.

The door to my brother's room was still covered with a

drawing he'd made and his name stamped onto a fake license plate. Shoving aside a flood of memories, I touched the knob, pushing it open the rest of the way.

It swung inward with a low creak. I blinked against the sudden light and the shock of what was in front of me.

In the middle of his room, Mom sat on the floor in her nightgown, rocking back and forth. The trunk at the end of Owen's bed was open, its contents scattered on the rug. A worn-out baseball glove, rocks he'd collected, toys, books — the typical treasures of a nine-year old.

The sunlight illuminated her like a halo. As soon as I was close enough, I heard her whispering. Like a prayer. Except... it was in Latin and we sure as fuck weren't Catholic.

Creeping around her slowly, I glanced between her face and the book clutched to her chest. It was small, unremarkable, and *old*. The only time I'd seen anything like that, with its yellowed, whisper-quiet vellum and tarnished clasp was in the Congregation's archives — and at the Corbins'.

"Mom...?"

She kept rocking, repeating the same verse over and over. The words made my skin prickle uncomfortably. I pulled my phone out slowly and dialed Cassius's number, hoping he picked up even though he was literally outside.

He answered after the first ring, concern lacing his simple, "Hello?"

"I'm going to put you on speaker phone," I said, barely above a whisper. "Just listen."

I hit the button and held the phone closer to my mom, hoping he could hear her frenzied whispers.

It sounded like she was only halfway through the verse when he shouted my name. I took him off speaker and pressed the phone to my ear. "What is she saying?"

"Get the fuck out of there!" he shouted, the sound of a car door dinging in the background.

"Why?"

"She's summoning a—"

The rest of his warning was lost. Something hard hit me across the back, sending me flying across the room and face-first into the wall. My phone clattered on the floor next to me.

I scrambled into an upright position, throwing an arm over my face as a blinding light filled the room.

Cassius thundered up the stairs, chanting his own prayer as he ran. Shadows raced ahead of him, twisting and turning and blotting out the strange light.

As soon as it dimmed, I lowered my arm, facing the creature trying to take shape in front of us. It mostly resembled a man. No, an angel. Huge white, feathered wings stretched out to each side, nearly filling the room. In one hand, it held a long, shimmering sword. The most disturbing part, however, was the giant owl head. Its sulfurous eyes narrowed on me a second before it let out an ear-piercing screech.

"In nomine et virtute domini nostri Jesu Christi. Exilium!" Cassius hurled a giant ball of black mist at the creature as he crossed into the room.

Without warning, a surge of electricity shot through me and ripped out of my hands. Two bolts of lightning chased the black mist through the air. They exploded together in the center of the creature's chest.

The thing screamed this time, a decidedly inhuman sound, as it winked out of sight, leaving nothing behind but singed, snowy feathers and the disgusting smell of rotten eggs.

Mom collapsed on the ground, the book flopping out of her hands.

Cassius darted forward and snatched it off the ground before running over to me. He reached for my face, but yanked his blood-covered hand back at the last second and wiped it on his pant leg instead.

"What did you do?" I asked, grabbing his wrist and pulling his hand forward to study the long slash across his palm.

"Improvised. Let's get out of here."

"My mom," I said pathetically as he hauled me to my feet. She was still on the ground, unconscious.

"She'll be fine."

"How do you know that? What if it comes back?"

"It won't without the book. Come on!" He tucked the book in question under his arm and yanked me toward the stairs again.

I had no choice but to follow him.

At the base of the stairs, he came to a halt, pointing at something on the wall. "What the fuck is that?!"

I peered around his shoulder and made a face at the picture frame. It was a red shield with a white chevron through the middle. Three white owls, two on top and one on the bottom, completed the heraldic device. Beneath it was the Latin quote Ainsworth gave me crap for not knowing. "The family crest. Why?"

"He will be the death of you," Cassius said.

"What?"

"That's what my mom told me right before she repeated that quote right there," he said, pointing at the motto. "She said 'He will be the death of you.' I thought she meant you, but what if she was talking about that demon?"

"*That* was a demon?"

"They're not all horns and cloven feet," he said, resuming his march out the front door and down the steps.

"Where are we going?"

"Home."

"Shouldn't we go tell Ainsworth? Or your dad?"

"You want to tell the Selectmen your mother was summoning a demon to do God knows what?"

I shifted my weight to my back foot, looking away. "Not... really..."

"Ok then. Now that I have folios, I can reunite the Book, get rid of that thing once and for all, and then we can all move on with our lives."

Planting my hand in the center of his chest, I pushed him into the side of the Jeep. "What does that mean for us?"

It was his turn to glance around awkwardly, like he could pluck an answer out of thin air. When that tactic apparently failed, he closed his eyes, his jaw clenching. "There isn't an 'us.'"

"Bullshit."

His eyes opened, narrowing. "There *can't* be an 'us.' We're destined to fucking hate each other, just like owls and crows. Three hundred and fifty years of hatred doesn't go away after a few fucks. And for good reason," he snapped, holding the book aloft. "I wonder how your mother got ahold of this! I mean, after all this time, what are the fucking odds? It shows up in a Hewitt household after all."

"You can't pin this one on my family. Not this time. We've never had anything like that in our lives. Not like the—the Northrups! Preston said his older brother used to scare the shit out of him with a Necromancy book but they didn't have it anymore because Percy lost it. I'll bet you anything Owen fucking took it. Or Percy gave it to him. Whatever. It doesn't matter because you have it back so your argument is null and void."

"You are so fucking stubborn." He shook his head, not looking the least bit convinced.

"You're one to talk."

"Give it up already, Graeme. This was—"

"Stop."

"—never going—"

"I love you!"

"—to work!"

Ignoring him and his never-ending negativity, I took his face between my hands and forced him to look at me. "I love you," I repeated, enunciating each word. "I don't know why. I don't know how. All I know is how I feel when I'm with you and the thought of you leaving? You might as well rip my heart out and take it with you, because you're it for me, Cassius. I know it, just like I know when the leaves will drop or when the first snowfall comes. I fucking *know* it. And I know you feel it too. On some level."

"You're crazy." He might have been shaking his head, but the lines of his face softened.

"Tell me I'm wrong." I held his gaze, refusing to blink or let him look away.

"You're not wrong." He hooked his fingers into my belt loop and yanked me forward so I was right up against him. His lips were there to greet mine, angrily at first until they turned gentle and content.

"Are we going to go kill a demon now?" I asked, pulling back so I could meet his gaze.

"If we're lucky."

"Good."

"Why is that good?"

"Because that means we can have sex again."

"Oh my God," he groaned, shoving me away from him and sliding into the passenger seat.

Chapter Forty-One
Cassius

"Do you want to, like, call your dad or something?" Graeme asked as we descended into the basement.

"He's in surgery all day," I replied. "You mind getting the lights? I mean, *I* can see, but you probably want something."

"I don't know. Maybe I shouldn't see what you're about to do." Nevertheless, little blue sparks flew across the room, lighting the multitude of candles scattered around.

"You mean read a book?" I spun suddenly, invading his personal space and bugging my eyes out at him. "It's terrifying."

"Smart ass." He shoved me forward with a roll of his eyes.

I set the folios on the main altar and retrieved the rest of the Book from its iron box. Seeing the two halves come together on the table, laying side by side, made my heart seize. The main portion of the Book had a dark cover, beaten to Hell and back, whereas the missing folios had a lighter cover, stained and battered through the centuries. I laid a hand on each half and exhaled, letting my eyes drift closed for a moment. I'd done it. Finally. After nearly four hundred years, the Book of Lazarus was reunited.

The two sections radiated energy beneath my palms, their

words whispering back and forth to one another like lovers who had found their way home again.

"I can't believe after all this time," I murmured, running my fingertips over the white folio, "they're back together."

"So... what does this mean for the Congregation?" Graeme asked, edging into my line of sight cautiously.

For a moment, I was tempted to tell him something dark and twisted — the truth. With this Book, I could do every horrible thing people accused Necromancers of. The knowledge that had been kept from us for centuries was all *right* here. We were no longer hobbled with only half of the information. Now, I could destroy this town and everyone in it. All I had to do was utter the right words, send the right demon, and Winslow would be no more.

But I didn't.

Because I *wouldn't* do those things.

Since meeting Graeme, all I'd done was defend myself and my family against insults and accusations. I tried to show him we weren't the monsters they made us out to be. And even though I had the Book and the means of taking revenge on behalf of my mother, of Lennox, of *all* the Corbins who had been slaughtered through the centuries by fear and bigotry, I wouldn't. Because then I'd be the thing they hated and my dad taught me to be better, to not let my anger consume me no matter how brightly the flame burned.

"Hey," Graeme's voice was in my ear at the same time his hand glided over my shoulder, rubbing gently. "Are you ok?"

"Yeah." My voice cracked and I cleared my throat. "Yeah, just... it's a lot. Everything, lately. I guess I'm feeling it more than usual today."

"Do you want to talk about it?" he asked, propping his chin on my shoulder.

"No. We have way more important things to worry about. Like demons. And your conversion."

"You *can* talk to me, though."

"Mhmm." I gave him a brief smile and reached for a platter of crystals, dragging it closer to me.

With the Book in the center, I assembled a crystal grid around it and lit more candles. It wasn't until I was finished that I realized Graeme had gone eerily quiet. Glancing up, I saw him fixated on something above my head. I pivoted slowly and tried to follow his line of sight. He could only have been looking at the skulls.

"Is that a..." He swallowed the rest of the question.

"A child's skull? Yes." Aside from the size, the double-row of teeth was a pretty big clue.

"Wh-why do you have a child's skull?" he asked, folding his arms over his chest and obviously trying very hard to keep his tone as light and non-judgmental as possible. "And, um, *whose* skull is it?"

"It belonged to a relative," I replied, amused with how uncomfortable he was. "I don't remember which one. And as to the why, sometimes kids are easier to connect with. They want to talk and they rarely lie convincingly. They'll tell you things adult spirits won't."

"That's fucked up."

I frowned at him.

He held his hands up. "Sorry. Those teeth are... Ok, I can't find the beauty in that. It's creepy as shit."

"Where, exactly, do you think your adult teeth come from? The fucking Tooth Fairy?"

"I didn't think about it until *now*, ok?" He shot back with a glare. "Love and light, remember? That's what we're all about. Not skulls with four rows of teeth like a fucking shark!"

I couldn't help but snort. "Love and light? Really? I didn't get the warm fuzzies from your mother today."

"Whatever. What are we doing down here anyway other

than me watching you play with your rocks?"

"Research. If you want to help, look for this symbol," I said, sketching it quickly on a sheet of paper and handing it to him.

He frowned at it. "This looks like the demon sigil from the bonfire."

"It's the sigil from the dead girl at the morgue," I corrected.

"No, this is what Preston showed me." He held his hand up, the cut from the other day still raw and angry. "Look in my head if you have to. I'm telling you, it's the same symbol."

"I don't need to look. I believe you." I grabbed the top book and started flipping. "These are the last of the demonologies I have to sort through. I'm hoping it's in here somewhere."

"And if it's not?"

"Then we're fucked."

"You suck at pep talks," he grumbled.

"I'm a realist."

"More like a pessimist."

I shrugged, taking the quasi-insult in stride. No one had ever accused Necromancers of being cheery folk.

We thumbed through the old books in silence. So many of the sigils looked similar, it was slow going, especially when Graeme kept bitching about cobwebs and trying to wipe them on me.

Shoving my last book at Graeme, I rubbed my eyes, trying to get the dryness to go away. "Does that look like what I drew? My eyes are crossing right now. I'm so sick of looking at demon shit."

"Yeah, I think so…"

Blinking rapidly, I took the book back and compared it to what I'd sketched. The lines, the circles, even the cross-like shapes all matched. I read the description of the demon quickly, swearing under my breath.

"What's wrong?" Graeme asked, craning his neck to try and read over my shoulder. "Who's Andr—"

My hands flew up, one clamping over Graeme's mouth and the other holding the back of his head in place so he couldn't squirm away and blurt it out. "Do not finish that name. He's a *very* big problem. We need to go back to your house and talk to your mom and find out what the fuck is going on."

He shook his head and I lowered the hand from his mouth, letting the other drift down the back of his neck and rest on his shoulder. "I don't think that's a good idea."

"She's been communicating with one of the Grand Marquises of Hell! I don't think *that's* a good idea."

Rolling his lips together, he cast about the room, probably trying to find some way to make this my fault or point out how wrong I was. He must have come up empty-handed since his mismatched gaze lifted slowly. "Do you really think my mom is the one who sent a demon after me? Or killed those girls...?"

"There's an easy way to find out," I said, picking up a knife from the altar and waving it at him.

"I was afraid you were going to say that."

Within the hour, we were back at Graeme's house. Once again, he parked in the street instead of the driveway.

"You're not going to hurt her, are you?" he asked as he let us in the front door.

"I haven't hurt you, have I?"

"She's different, ok? She hasn't been the same since Owen died. She's... fragile."

I slipped the knife out of my pocket and held it out to him. "Then you cut her."

His fingers curled around the hilt of the blade, over mine. "Ok."

With that sorted, we climbed the stairs, pausing now and again to listen to the sounds of the house around us. It was mostly quiet, except for the old stairs complaining under our combined weight.

The knife I used earlier to slice open my own hand was still laying at the top of the stairs, crimson droplets splattered on the wooden floorboards.

Graeme led the way down the hall at a snail's pace and tentatively pushed open the door to his brother's room. Except for the toys and things on the carpet I'd seen earlier, the room was empty.

"Where is she?" I asked, glancing around as the house ticked and creaked, the appliances downstairs adding a soft hum to the air.

"This way." He led the way down the hall to another room with a closed door. He turned the knob carefully and peered inside. From the looks of it, the room was nearly as dark as mine tended to be. "Mom?"

"Not now, Graeme," came a pitiful reply.

He stiffened in the doorway. I laid a hand on his shoulder, nudging him forward.

"I just need to check something really quick," he said, trying to sound casual except for the fact his voice wavered.

A deep sigh sounded somewhere in the dark. As soon as my eyes adjusted, I saw the lump laying on the bed, unmoving. "What's wrong with her?" I whispered as we crept closer.

"I don't know," he whispered back. "Depression, I guess.

But no matter what Dr. Dane gives her, it doesn't help. It's been worse lately. Like, a lot worse."

"Worse how?"

"She barely eats. She won't leave this room. She says she's in a lot of pain but she won't let anyone near her."

"Yeah, I don't think it's depression..." I reached for the light on the nightstand but Graeme seized my wrist.

"Don't! It makes her headaches worse."

I yanked my hand out of his grip and turned on the lamp anyway.

Mrs. Hewitt hissed and rolled away from the light, clamping her hands on her eyes. From what I could see, she was beyond sickly looking. Pale, gray skin. Sunken eyes. Dark wild hair. An army of pill bottles littered the bedside table. "Graeme! Get out! Get out of here!"

I half expected him to listen, but he stood firm, his hands clenched at his sides. "Mom, what were you doing with that book?"

"I said get out!" She flung her hand backward, knocking us both back with a gust of wind. We tumbled to the floor, colliding with one another.

"She's a weather witch, too?" I looked at Graeme accusingly.

He shook his head, his eyes wide. "Just air."

"That's not 'just air.' Can't you feel that? That power?"

He shook his head again, looking as bewildered as he had when the demon appeared in his brother's room.

Suppressing my irritation to a growl, I ripped the knife out of his hand and lunged at the bed.

"Cassius! Don't! You're going to hurt her!" He leapt on top of me, wrestling my arm down.

"Get off of me or I'll fucking hurt *you*!"

Mrs. Hewitt turned toward us again, her jade eyes practically glowing with rage, so much so she didn't even look human anymore. "Cassius?!"

Oh, shit...

One look was all I needed. One look and I knew she was going to kill me. The only thing I could do was to make peace with my life and embrace the end of it.

The veins in my head throbbed so hard and fast, it dropped me to my knees. The knife fell uselessly from my fingers. It was a pressure, a pain, unlike anything I'd ever experienced. It was so overwhelming I couldn't breathe. I couldn't manifest magic. I couldn't do anything except hold my skull in both hands and scream.

The scent of blood filled my nose. I expected it to be my own, but it wasn't. As soon as I smelled it, the pressure was gone, replaced by a high-pitched shriek of fury.

Graeme grabbed my arm and hauled me to my feet, shoving me toward the door. "Come on!"

"The blood!"

"I got it." He jabbed me in the back, pushing me down the stairs. A series of items smashed along the wall, narrowly missing his head as we ran. A glass of water, a vase full of flowers, and perfume bottles all shattered, showering us with glass as we raced downward.

"I thought she was fragile!" I shouted over my shoulder, sprinting for the front door.

"Today must be a good day."

"You're not funny."

"Wasn't trying to be."

We took the front steps two at a time, pulling up short in the front yard as a very familiar Volvo turned into the drive.

"Oh fuck," Graeme said. "Get in the Jeep."

He didn't have to tell me twice. I hauled ass to his car as his dad threw his own vehicle in park and bailed out.

"Graeme!" Mr. Hewitt thundered. "Stop right there!"

He did not. If anything, the very real possibility of both our deaths spurred Graeme to run faster. He dove into the driver's seat and jammed the START button before the door had even closed. As soon as the engine turned over, he peeled away from the curb. Something hard hit the back quarter panel, but Graeme didn't stop.

I twisted around to see what his dad did, but the back window was covered in ice. Guess that explained how Graeme ended up being a Stormbringer. Not only did his mother have weather magic that she'd apparently kept hidden from everyone, but his dad was a fucking water witch. Throw in a little fire magic somewhere up in the family tree and voila — a perfect recipe for a Stormbringer.

"You want to rethink this whole 'us' thing?" I asked, dropping back in my seat and letting out a shaky breath. "I'm pretty sure both of your parents just tried to kill me."

"Pretty sure they're going to kill both of us if they get the chance." He handed the bloody knife over and then gripped the steering wheel with both hands. "I hope this is enough."

I took it with a sigh, relieved that the shit show back there wasn't all for nothing. "Plenty."

Chapter Forty-Two

Graeme

Once we were back at the Corbins' house, we returned to the basement with the bloody knife.

It was like descending into a dungeon. For all Cassius's bitching that death wasn't creepy, I remained mostly unconvinced, especially when there was a variety of skulls staring down at me from the shelf — including the little goblin skull he claimed was a child's.

Thankfully, instead of trotting out more skulls to play with, he pulled out a large, shallow silver dish. He filled it with water and took the knife from me, swishing the blade around until it was clean and the water swirled with streaks of crimson.

Cassius leaned closer, squinting at the whorls with a preternatural concentration.

I'd never been good at divination. Ever. He teasingly (or not so teasingly) made fun of nature witches' reliance on intuition, but until now it hadn't been a problem. There was never a need to master divination, or even practice it with any sort of regularity. So imagine my surprise when images rolled across the surface of the water like a silent movie with next to no effort on my part. That must have been another perk of our magical link or whatever it was.

"What in the..." I took a step closer to the bowl.

He threaded his fingers through mine and squeezed. I got the hint and shut up.

The first few images didn't make sense to me. It was like trying to see through red-tinted fog. I could make out tall, dark trees, the trunks knotted and stretched, like screaming faces were trying to push through from the other side. It had to have been the North Woods.

Flashes of people I didn't know came next. The poppet from behind the crypt was lying in a shallow grave. A crow scratched at the dirt, unearthing it and cawing, its beak bloody.

More blood coated an ornate knife. Its hilt was fashioned in the shape of a crow, black gemstones glittering in place of eyes.

There was a glimpse of Melanie's hand, its vibrant pink nail polish a shock of color in the red water and against her corpse's gray skin.

Out of nowhere, my back burned, like the scratches were fresh all over again as Tennebrose's parking garage materialized. The bonfire flared to life before my eyes, India's scream filling my ears until it ended in a gurgle. India's face morphed into Sophia's, rolling away in the murky water, blood gushing from her neck.

The stench of rot and sulfur filled the air. Instinctively I backed away, but Cassius held on to my hand, keeping me rooted to his side. Miniature versions of ourselves darted across the water, facing off against that huge ball of fiery shadows.

Suddenly, the water rushed upward with the force of a geyser, knocking Cassius off his feet. He stumbled backward into the cabinet, taking me with him as he coughed out a mouthful of bloody water.

He dashed the water from his eyes. "Son of a bitch!"

"Are you ok?" One sleeve was soaked, so I used the other sleeve to help dry his face.

"Yeah. It's just… never done that," he said, pushing his wet hair off his forehead.

"So now what are we going to do?"

"We go to the Meeting and tell the Selectmen everything, like we did with Dad."

"But the Blood Moon is tonight," I hedged.

"Ok, so you do your conversion and I'll go to the Meeting," he replied with a shrug. When I didn't immediately agree, he frowned. "What?"

"Ainsworth and Colburn wanted you at the conversion."

He crossed his arms over his chest. "Why? In case you die?"

I blinked rapidly, opening and closing my mouth a few times like a guppy. Fuck me! I hadn't even considered that *that* was the reason. "I mean, I thought it had more to do with, like, moral support or because of your blood magic. But, yeah. Maybe. Fuck…"

He uncrossed his arms and grasped my shoulders. "Ok. Look. Meetings are always at seven. We'll go there, explain what we have to and then go do the conversion. You'd have to wait for Ainsworth anyway. There's no way he can skip out on a Meeting as important as this."

"Yeah, good point." I relaxed the tiniest bit. "So what are we going to do until seven?"

He hooked his fingers into the front of my jeans and yanked me forward, his expression serious. "I think you need to relax."

"If you say so. I mean, you *are* the expert," I murmured right before his lips slotted against mine.

And by relax, apparently Cassius really meant *relax*. He drew a bath, complete with a ring of candles alternating with crystals. Dried flowers floated on the surface of the water, along with some sort of scented oil. Shoving a cup of tea at me, he told me to "center" myself. Whatever the fuck that meant. I turned to take my shirt off and the door clicked shut behind me.

"Cash?" Glancing over my shoulder, I couldn't help but frown when I realized he left.

With a resigned sigh, I stripped off the rest of my clothes and climbed into the tub, easing myself down into the water. Once I was situated, I picked up the cup of tea and took a tentative sip. Whatever it was, he'd at least sweetened it with honey, which I appreciated.

"Ok..." I tipped my head back against the edge of the tub and exhaled. "Center myself... Centering... Piece of cake."

Ten minutes later, I was sweating my ass off from all the steam and the tea had mostly gone cold. Was this centering? Was this what he wanted me to do? I had no idea.

Do not seek outside yourself.

For some reason, those words popped into my head. First Cassius said them when he was coming out of that weird seance/trance state. Then Ainsworth said it again. Today, they all but jumped off the family crest and smacked me in the face. What the fuck did they mean?

Look within, Ainsworth said. *You have all of the answers, Graeme, you just have to put it together.*

Put *what* together? Did Ainsworth actually know something or was this one of those teacher tricks, trying to get me to realize my full potential or something?

Closing my eyes, I let my mind wander through the past few months, when everything started to get bad. Or at the very least confusing. It all centered around Cassius.

Cassius came home from England to go to Tennebrose. We met. We fought. Melanie saw us and died. I was attacked by a demon on campus… after several fights with Cassius. India was attacked by a demon… after she and Cassius got into it at the meetinghouse. That Sophia girl, who also saw us, died. All roads led back to Cassius.

Cassius, the Necromancer.

Cassius, the demon expert.

Cassius, the sworn enemy of my family.

Did he somehow know my mom had that half of the book? Had this all been some fucked-up plot to get access to it? When he realized I wouldn't go down without a fight, did he decide to change tactics and distract me with… other methods? He himself said he gave in just to shut me up. What if that was a lie? What if he gave in to make himself a Trojan horse?

No.

I refused to believe any of that was true about him. He *wasn't* evil. As much as we'd fought, I knew he was good beneath his dark and prickly demeanor. He could have killed me countless times. His father, his sister. They all could have killed me at any point over the past week. God knows his cousin actually tried…

Maybe *Cassius* was really the target? Someone who wasn't happy he came home? I mean, someone had killed all of those crows behind the Corbin crypt. Someone had created that fucked-up poppet for a reason. What, I had no idea, but it probably wasn't good.

Did that mean we were *both* targets? Killing both of us would definitely bring an end to the feud. Dr. Colburn said the Corbins and the Hewitts weren't the only ones affected by our fighting. She's the one who said the Congregation would never be truly safe until we laid down our figurative arms. The Colburns were historically aligned with the Corbins, which meant they had Necromantic powers if they wanted them… That's what Cassius said. *All* the dark, blood-born witches had the capability. What was Temperance's specialty again? Divination? Maybe she saw a future with both of us dead, resulting in peace for all the Winslow witches.

Cassius's little story about his conversion also crept into my mind. They were willing to sacrifice thirteen-year-olds for the sake of their magic. Why should an eighteen and a nineteen-year-old be any different? But if that was her plan all along, why drag it out? Why not kill us at any old time?

My stomach was thoroughly in knots by the time the bathwater went cold. If this was what Cassius meant by centering myself, I was pretty sure I failed miserably.

I exited the tub knowing three things. One, it was safe to assume someone wanted one or both of us dead. Two, I was scared shitless to actually make my conversion knowing it was entirely possible to die during the middle of it. And three, no matter how fucked up it was, I was one-hundred percent in love with the boy in the next room.

Wrapped in a towel, I walked back into Cassius's room fully prepared to be yelled at for not being any more relaxed than when I'd gone *into* the bath.

"What's wrong?" Cassius asked the moment he laid eyes on me from his bed. He was shirtless, the burgundy sheet pulled up to his waist. His dark brows slanted while he waited for the answer.

"Nothing." I don't know why I bothered lying to him anymore, but I dropped my towel anyway in the hope of deterring more questions.

He lifted the sheet for me, revealing he was, happily,

naked beneath it. I slid in next to him and pressed myself along the side of his body, resting my head on his chest.

He wrapped an arm around my shoulder and hugged me closer. "You're going to be fine."

"I kind of wish you didn't tell me people die during these things," I admitted. Cassius's fingers tightened on my bicep.

"It hasn't happened in a really long time," he said quietly.

"Just like there hasn't been a Stormbringer in a really long time..."

"Graeme." He lifted my chin gently. "You're going to be fine. I promise I won't let anything happen to you."

I ran my finger down the crow skull around his neck, mindful of the sharp beak. "Does your power let you see the future? Or only what's been?"

"Both. But sometimes I don't realize I'm looking at the future unless I ask a specific question."

"Can you look and see what's going to happen tonight?"

"It's not *that* specific," he said with a quiet chuckle. "If it was, we'd play the lottery and sweep Vegas whenever we felt like it."

"Too bad. I'd feel a lot better knowing how that *and* the Meeting are going to go."

"Whatever happens, I'm with you," he said, pressing his lips to my forehead.

"Does that mean you're not transferring to Ashbourne when this is all over?" I looked up again, stupidly hopeful.

"I don't know. I mean, it's not like I have a reason to stay at Tennebrose..." he said with a dramatic sigh, looking off into the distance with a wistful expression.

"I think your boyfriend would really like it if you stayed."

"Boyfriend?" His brows shot up as he returned his gaze to mine, all traces of joking gone from his face.

"Yeah." I smiled sheepishly, scooting up to sit next to him and pressing a quick kiss to his shoulder.

"When did I get one of those?"

"I told you, you're it for me. So you might want to figure out if we're going to hyphenate our last names the same, or if I'll be Hewitt-Corbin and you'll be Corbin-Hewitt."

"Oh my God." He shook his head, rolling his eyes skyward. "I haven't even said I'll date you and you're already planning a wedding?"

"Admit it, we've pretty much been dating since the semester started."

"Trying to kill one another doesn't equate to dating."

"It hasn't been all bad... there's been study dates, and sleepovers, and lot and lots of naughty time," I said, kissing his throat and shoulder every couple of words.

He tipped his head back, his fingers tracing idly over my bare thigh. "There hasn't been one proper meal and no, bringing me a bagel does not count."

"I tried to take you out to eat after the library. You said no. An aggressive no, if I recall, not a flirty 'try harder' no."

"Because you were being reckless!"

"Uh, *you're* the one who got me off in the stacks where *anyone* could have found us."

"*After* you got me off in Peregrine's office, of all places."

"Alright, fine. Let's do a 'proper' date with dinner. Do you want flowers, too?"

"Yes," he shot back with an arched brow and a challenging smirk. "And I'd like to have a lengthy, meaningful conversation over drinks and candlelight instead of you just trying to find a way into my pants."

"You're not wearing pants now," I pointed out, dragging my fingers down his chest, along the flat plane of his stomach, straight to where his dick was tenting the sheet.

"No, I'm not."

"Is this supposed to help me relax before tonight?"

"Well, it might if you'd stop talking."

"Does that mean you want to—"

"Oh my God!" He seized my face between his hands and kissed me.

Chapter Forty-Three
Cassius

Graeme drove his own Jeep to the Meeting, while I rode with Dad. Claudia said she'd meet us there since she was coming from the hospital. There were fewer cars than on a regular Meeting night, which meant Dad and Graeme were able to park next to each other.

"I don't see my dad's car yet," Graeme said as we walked up to the meetinghouse together.

"I'm sure he'll show. Dad said all the Selectmen were coming."

"What do you think we should do? Should we sit by each other? Oh my God. If he sees me in the Corbin box, he'll go berserk. Not to mention your sister."

I threaded our fingers together, squeezing his hand lightly. "We'll sit in those open pews at the front. Together. Your dad's not going to try anything with the rest of the Selectmen there."

"Yeah. You're right..."

At the very front of the meetinghouse, we paused again, staring at the door in front of us. Without even thinking about it, I'd walked to the western side of the building, to the door the dark families used. Other than tradition and symbolism, there was literally no difference between the doors but it was one of those things that just stuck thanks to our Puritan ancestors.

We both looked down at our joined hands and back up at the western door. To spare him the heart attack he looked like was two seconds away from having, I let go of his hand and opened the door, gesturing for him to walk in first.

"Breathe," I whispered as he walked by me. "It's just a door." Walking through it didn't make him "dark" or "evil" — it simply meant he was closer to my family's box pew than his own, which he seemed to realize once he crossed the threshold and exhaled the breath he was holding.

Inside, the Selectmen who were already there had gathered beneath the pulpit, talking animatedly. Ainsworth and Temperance were among them, along with Peregrine and Treadwell.

Dad, who'd followed us inside, gave me a brief nod and stepped around us to join his peers.

As discussed, we settled onto one of the open pews at the front. Thankfully these were wider than the ones in the gallery, so it was marginally more comfortable. Physically speaking. Having everyone stare at us was another matter entirely.

Peregrine stopped talking mid-sentence, his gaze fixed on the two of us, sitting mere inches from one another. Graeme's knee bounced like crazy. It took everything I had not to slap my hand over it to stop him.

"Caius?" The Deacon's gaze cut to Dad.

Dad raised his brows in return and checked his watch, pretending to be oblivious to the elephant in the room. "I believe Marcus is running a tad late. Have you heard from the others?"

Peregrine and Treadwell shared a look. Ainsworth, meanwhile, looked at the two of them curiously before shifting his focus to Temperance.

Bob Winslow hauled the giant Book of Transactions up from the cellar and heaved it onto a table. "Are we ready?"

"Nearly," Peregrine replied.

As the rest of the Selectmen filed in, assuming their seats in the chairs that ringed the center of the room, I stole a glance at Graeme. He was abnormally pale and he'd gone from bouncing his knee to cracking all of the knuckles in his hands, each and every joint possible.

I wanted to reclaim his hand, to let him know that it would be ok. Except, then his dad walked in the door and I wasn't so sure everything *would* be ok.

George Hewitt threw open the eastern door and stormed inside, looking like he was on the warpath. "Deacon," he all but shouted, marching right up to Peregrine. "I need to file a grievance with the Selectmen, as well as you, Chief," he added, looking at Treadwell.

"Can it wait? Samuel and Temperance have something urgent they need to discuss."

"No! It absolutely *cannot* wait!" George turned his fury on me, striding over so quickly I thought he was going to bowl me over. "Earlier today this… this *Necromancer* broke into my home and attacked my wife! We just got home from the hospital, where she had to have over a dozen stitches in her arm because that *lunatic* sliced her open!"

I sat there, stunned, but at least Graeme tried to offer a defense. "Dad, he—"

George seized a fistful of Graeme's jacket and yanked him to his feet. I stood as well, but it didn't stop him from dragging Graeme away from me and depositing him roughly on another pew, closer to the "good" witches. "He's corrupted my son, our future Deacon! He's trying to tear this Congregation apart! Everything that has gone wrong in Winslow started when that *Necromancer* came back. It's high time he returns to wherever his father banished him all those years ago!"

Every time he snarled the word *Necromancer* my skin crawled. Despite my rising anger, my attention was solely on Graeme. His wide, mismatched eyes darted between me, his dad, and my dad. A shimmer of blue and white ran back and forth on his hands, even as they gripped the pew like it was the only thing keeping him stationary.

Dad strode forward, planting himself between George and I. "One more word out of your mouth about my son and it will be your last, Hewitt."

As much as I was trying to pay attention to Dad and George, I kept watching Graeme out of my periphery. The lightning arcs were getting bigger, rushing up and down his arms. Graeme still seemed unaware of what was happening, even though there was a clap of thunder so loud it sounded like it broke right overhead.

"Enough!" Peregrine shouted, stepping between the two Selectmen and spreading his hands out like a referee. "Let us not descend into savagery while there is a common enemy amongst us."

"The only enemy I see is *them*," George snarled, his gaze locked on Dad's.

"Spoken like a Hewitt," Uncle Marcus shouted as he came in the western door. Another boom of thunder rolled through, shaking the walls of the meetinghouse so hard dust floated down from the rafters.

Diane Tenney entered the fray next, stepping up next to George. "Of course you'd rush to your brother-in-law's defense, even though it was *your* son who cursed my daughter!"

"You have no proof of that!" Uncle Marcus yelled. "And even if you did, Lennox is dead! You will not tarnish his name any more than you already have, hag!"

The Selectmen who weren't involved in the fight all gasped, murmuring amongst each other.

A streak of crackling energy ripped across the room, its destination unknown. But I knew the source. Snapping my fingers quickly, the room plunged into darkness. The lightning fizzled into nothingness before it could strike anyone.

I darted over to Graeme as his hands began to glow again. "Graeme, focus," I whispered, dropping to my knees in front of him. I covered his hands with mine despite the painful shocks slicing through my palms. "You can control it. I know you can."

One of the fire witches reignited the oil lamps and candles in the room and there was another round of gasping, followed by even louder chatter all around us.

I ignored them and whatever commotion was going on behind me. Squeezing Graeme's hands in mine, I kept my gaze on his and concentrated on lowering his racing heartbeats. Slowly, the zaps radiating through my palms started to diminish. Somewhat.

"I'm sorry," he whispered, resting his forehead against mine and shutting his eyes.

"Don't be sorry." I let go of one of his hands to thread my fingers through his hair. "We'll fix it all tonight. Ok? After this, we'll fix it."

Graeme nodded, keeping his forehead pressed to mine, his hands squeezing tighter.

"Do you see?" George shouted again. I didn't dare turn around but I knew without a shadow of a doubt he was referring to us. "He's poisoned my son's mind! He's corrupted his powers!"

"He's done nothing of the sort," Temperance countered. "Maybe if you pulled your head out of your ass, you'd see what was really happening!"

"And what is that, exactly?" Bob Winslow asked, a pen at

the ready to jot it all down in the Book of Transactions. I'm sure tonight's entry was already quite lengthy. One for the history books, as Bob would say.

"It's true love," Ainsworth said happily, like everyone wasn't on the verge of tearing each other limb from limb. "For the first time in over three centuries, the stars have aligned and brought these two together. It should be celebrated, George, not reviled."

"Oh, shut up Samuel!" George snapped back. "I know you're in on this whole thing, what with assigning them to the same class! What were you thinking?"

Ainsworth's cheeks reddened. "That maybe someone should give them a chance to actually get to know one another before they decide the other is a complete asshole? Maybe form their own opinions instead of regurgitating whatever shit they've been taught? And look! Look what happened when given that very opportunity!"

"I don't believe it," George said, his teeth on edge. "My son has clearly been hexed."

"Oh, for Christ's sake," Dad scoffed. "Are you *that* pigheaded, Hewitt?"

"Can we get back to why we're *really* here?" Treadwell interjected. "I have three murders to solve and a demon to kill. I don't give two shits about whose kids are shtupping whose, alright?"

"First we have to find who's summoning the demon. *Then* we can kill it," Temperance said.

"Yeah, about that…" I touched Graeme's cheek gently and rose to my feet. He clung to my hand, standing with me. "George is half-right. We did go to their house today, not to attack Graeme's mom, but to—"

"It's her," Graeme blurted out. "Mom's been summoning the demon. I saw it. Cassius saved me from it. And I'm the one who cut her, to get her blood so Cassius could use it for scrying. He didn't do anything wrong."

For once, George was stunned into silence. Peregrine, on the other hand, took a step forward, his jaw slack. "Your *mother*? Are you sure?"

"Positive, sir," Graeme mumbled. "She had the Book—" I squeezed his hand sharply and he cleared his throat. "She had a Necromancy book and she was reading a spell in Latin. Then a demon appeared."

"Where's the book now?" Peregrine asked.

"I don't know," Graeme replied, fairly convincingly considering he knew damn well where it was.

George finally found his voice and turned to the Deacon. "Perry, you don't honestly think Marian would do this, do you?"

"Whether she would or not is irrelevant," Treadwell said. "The fact of the matter is she *did* and three people are dead as a result. She needs to answer for those crimes."

"No!" George shouted.

I produced the poppet from my jacket pocket and handed it over to the chief carefully. "We found this yesterday in the center of a ritual space. A *dark* ritual space. And when I used Mrs. Hewitt's blood for scrying, I saw the same doll, along with the murder victims."

"More lies," George hissed.

"He's not lying," Graeme snapped. "I saw the same visions in the water. Dr. Dane can look in my head if he wants to. Or Dr. Colburn and Mrs. Green can do their own divination on the poppet. Cassius is telling the truth."

"Did you see which demon it was?" Temperance asked.

I nodded. "When it manifested in Owen's room. We confirmed it through its sigil."

"And?" Her blue eyes widened, waiting for me to go on.

"It's a Marquis."

She swore, along with the rest of the dark families. The nature witches all exchanged looks and shrugged.

Treadwell cleared his throat. "Can we kill it?"

I bit my lips and deferred to my dad.

Dad looked grim. "Not without difficulty. Best case scenario is to sever its link to this realm so it can't cross over again. But there is still the matter of the witch responsible for it all."

"Well, it's not Marian!" George shouted.

"How are we going to find out who that is, for certain?" Bob Winslow asked, throwing a pitying look at Graeme's dad.

Treadwell considered the poppet in his hand before holding it out for Mrs. Green to touch. "Can you get anything off of it?"

Mrs. Green took the poppet and turned it over, studying it. "Not much, I'm afraid. There is a dark magic over the whole of it. Very dark. I feel… hatred. Betrayal. Vengeance. This is a talented and dangerous witch, *whoever* it is." Another sympathetic smile for George.

"We have another option," Dad said. "To ask the spirits what they know."

Uncle Marcus shook his head. "You can't do that, Caius. The Marquis could be there, waiting for that very thing. It could use you as a vehicle to come through, unbidden."

Graeme yanked on my hand. When I turned to glare at him, he was already glaring at me. "Isn't that what you were going to do? To find Sophia's spirit?"

"Yeah. So?"

"You didn't tell me you could be possessed by a fucking demon!"

I stared at him for a moment. "I told you I'd need your help! Did you think I just wanted a cheerleader?"

"I don't know because I don't know anything about your creepy ass seances!"

"I could be possessed by a demon. Also, if I die over there, my body dies here. There. Now you're caught up on the dangers of crossing over and working with spirits," I said flatly.

"But you still did it? For me?" His gaze softened.

"I really did try to get you answers. Mom honestly didn't know how Owen died."

"It was aortic stenosis," Dad said with a frown, interrupting our conversation. "Owen had a severe case. He was born with it. It's all there in his medical history. His death, while tragic, was absolutely mundane. Nathaniel can attest to that."

Dr. Dane nodded. "It's true. Lydia had nothing to do with Owen's death. Something I've explained ad nauseam." I didn't miss the way his gaze flicked to George pointedly.

"Then how did *she* die?" I snapped, narrowing my eyes at George as well. "How was my mother killed?"

George tipped his chin up, seething in defiant silence.

"The official cause was an arterial air embolism," Dr. Dane replied on his behalf.

"From what? There wasn't a scratch on her! How did a fucking air bubble get in her artery?" The truth hit me so hard it felt like someone dumped ice water over me. "It wasn't you," I said, looking at George. "It was her. *She* controls the air."

George swallowed, shifting his weight to the other foot.

"Marian was the one who killed my mother! Wasn't she?!" I was going to be sick. Everything I thought I knew was flipped on its head. It wasn't a vengeful Hewitt continuing a blood feud. It was a grieving mother who lashed out. A Hewitt by marriage, sure, but I don't think it would have mattered *who* brought Owen back to her, Marian would have had the same reaction. "You've been lying this whole time! For six years, I thought it was you..."

Graeme's hand squeezed mine tighter. "Dad...?"

George looked at Graeme and closed his eyes. "I'd just lost Owen. I couldn't lose your mother too."

"So you lied to me?"

"It was for the best."

"You lied to all of us," Peregrine added, looking just as hurt as Graeme, if that was somehow possible.

"It was easier for you to think I was at fault," George said to Peregrine. "You know Marian has had a difficult go of things. She hasn't been the same since Owen... Some days she's more ghost than human."

"That's because she's been consorting with demons," Dad interjected. "And apparently you've been too stupid to see the signs! Make no mistake about it, Marian is guilty of *murder* and I'm going to insist the Selectmen reconsider *my* grievance from six years ago."

Graeme and I exchanged a glance, silently checking in with the other in light of the many revelations. He looked as unhappy as I did, but his grip tightened on mine.

Peregrine raised his hands to quiet the various mutterings. "George, you and Thomas will bring Marian back here, to the meetinghouse, so we may question her. Determining her guilt or innocence in this matter has to be our priority before we resurrect old grievances," he said, looking at each of the men in turn before his gaze fell to Dad.

"I will not hand my wife over like some prisoner," George said.

"Dad!" Graeme's brow furrowed in disbelief.

"No. I've heard enough nonsense for one night." George strode forward and grabbed ahold of Graeme, tearing him away from me. We grappled to hang on, but George's anger was stronger than both of us.

"Dad! Stop! I can't leave!" Graeme tried to wrest himself free from his father's large hand, turning every now and again to look at me, his eyes wide.

I teetered to the side, watching helplessly as Graeme's dad dragged him toward the exit.

George yanked the door open — or tried to, anyway. The door only opened an inch before it slammed shut by something unseen.

I looked at Dad, but his hands were balled at his sides.

It wasn't me.

It wasn't Graeme.

George growled and pulled on the handle again, and again it only opened an inch before something on the other side jerked it shut.

My gaze slid to Ainsworth, who was the only one present with his hand held aloft. It was twisted like he was opening a doorknob — or holding it shut.

Using his dad's stunned frustration, Graeme yanked himself free and sprinted back to me. We collided hard, his arms around my neck and mine around his waist.

George whipped around, eyes narrowed. "Graeme, come here."

He shook his head. "No. I'm staying."

"He's not leaving, George," Ainsworth said, his hand twisting in the opposite direction. The door swung open easily, a tree root slithering away into the darkness. "You can go, but Graeme stays."

"Absolutely not!" George took a step back in our direction. "Graeme, let's go! Now!"

"Give it up, George. He's not leaving," Temperance snapped. "And you're not going to come between him and Cassius. So unless you want to lose another son, you better get on board real fucking quick."

"Holy shit," I whispered, stealing a glance at Temperance. "How'd you get Dr. Colburn on your side?"

"Fuck if I know," he whispered back.

Treadwell moved forward in the aftermath of Temperance's blunt directive, raising his hands to George in a friendly, entreating way. "Let's do as the Deacon said, ok? Let's go get Marian and get to the bottom of everything. Graeme will be fine. You *know* he'll be fine. But Marian might not be."

George's glare shot from Treadwell straight to me. I saw my death in his gaze, just as I had earlier with his wife. I clung to Graeme even tighter. His lips brushed across my temple, so I was pretty sure he saw the promise behind that look, too.

Without another word, George pivoted on his heel and stalked out the open door. Treadwell turned and shot a look at Peregrine, or Ainsworth, it was hard to tell, and followed after, pulling the door shut behind him.

There was a collective exhale from the remaining people.

"Well that went over better than I'd hoped," Ainsworth said brightly. We both looked at him incredulously. "Well," he continued with a shrug, "the meetinghouse is still standing, so that's a start. And everyone has a pulse! Celebrate the little things, boys. It'll make your lives a lot happier."

He had a point, but we still shook our heads, trying not to smile. So much for *not* telling the Congregation about us...

Ainsworth clapped his hands together. "Alright then! Who's ready to make their conversion?"

Chapter Forty-Four

Graeme

"I thought it was just going to be us?" I whispered to Ainsworth as Cassius and Dr. Colburn set up a circle even more complicated than the last one Cassius did. Standing off to the side, Caius and Old Man Winslow were chatting in low voices. When they heard what we had in store for the Blood Moon, they both insisted on coming. Bob, I could kind of see. Committed as ever to his role as the Congregation's archivist, he lugged the Book of Transactions out to Norwood Bridge after that spectacularly disastrous Meeting, intent on capturing it all for posterity.

"Bob's here to record the event," Ainsworth replied. "He's quite the stickler for following timelines and unfortunately yours is about six years too late. Poor guy. Don't mention it. He's absolutely gutted he overlooked the whole thing."

"And Caius?" Even if he approved of whatever this thing was with his son, it didn't mean he wasn't intimidating as fuck, not only as a Necromancer but also as one of the top cardiothoracic surgeons in New England — something I only learned about when I accidentally found a drawer full of awards he'd won while Cassius and I were working on our apple tree project in his lab. Yet another difference between him and my father. Dr. Corbin hid his accomplishments and let his work speak for itself, versus Dad who would have had each and every single one of them framed and sitting on a mantel.

"I think he's trying to be supportive," Ainsworth replied with a chuckle.

"More than I can say about my own dad, I guess."

"Well, hopefully your dad will come around."

"Really?" I gave him a skeptical look and crossed my arms. "You think we're going to be able to have family barbecues in the summer and split the holidays between Cassius's house and mine? After tonight, I think it's safe to say I'm on my own. Hopefully Caius doesn't mind me crashing there for a bit longer."

"There's always on-campus housing." He said it so smoothly, I almost missed the all-knowing smirk on his face. "Room and board are available for all legacies."

I blinked, my jaw dropping. "What? Dad said—" I bit my lip, silencing the rest of my stupidity before it could fly out of my mouth. Dad said it wasn't an option because I lived in Winslow, therefore I didn't qualify for housing. Yet another lie. It seemed that's all he told me. How could I trust *anything* he said ever again?

"We're ready," Dr. Colburn announced, dusting her hands off.

Ainsworth nodded and patted my shoulder before joining her near the riverbank.

I turned and sought out Cassius. He was at the water's edge, his arms wrapped around himself against the brisk night. His breath clouded in front of him, meanwhile the rush of water over rocks provided a calming backdrop.

"Thank you for being here."

"Where else would I be?" The corner of his mouth lifted into a smile. "Someone has to keep your blood warm, otherwise you're going to freeze in that water."

"Yeah, about that... I saw this and it made me think of you." I fished the bloodstone out of my pocket, the same crystal I'd swiped from my house earlier, and offered it to Cassius on the palm of my hand. The flash of red was barely visible in the moonlight, but in sunlight it shone beautifully against the dark green stone. "If I make it through this thing alive, will you, Cassius Corbin, be my boyfriend?"

"What are you, a penguin?" Shaking his head, he nevertheless took the bloodstone with a small smile. I'd almost swear there was a blush too, but it was hard to tell in the silvery light.

"I'll take that as a yes." I smirked and pulled him in close for a kiss.

"Whenever you're ready," Ainsworth called behind us.

Cassius pressed his forehead to mine. The weight of everything I wanted to say — every apology, every "I love you," just *everything* — hung between us, suspended like the cloud of our mingled breath. I don't think either of us wanted to ruin the moment by saying the wrong thing, so we said nothing.

At last, I drew a deep breath and exhaled, forcing myself to walk away from him.

Dr. Colburn held an old, brittle book in her hands and Dr. Ainsworth had a bowl with some black, liquidy substance in it.

"Are you ready?" Ainsworth asked, raising his brows at me behind his glasses.

I swallowed and nodded. "As I'm going to be."

Disrobing in front of a group of adults was already weird enough. Add in my newly-declared boyfriend's dad? Fucking mortifying. I stripped out of my shirt and pants, leaving my boxer briefs firmly in place. Everything else could go, but those and Cassius's amulet were staying on throughout this whole process and I didn't give a shit what any of the Selectmen had to say.

The ground was cold and hard beneath my feet as I walked to the center of the circle, trying not to stab myself on sharp twigs or rocks. Couldn't we have postponed this until summer? I'd even take spring. Then at least I'd have a chance at warm weather versus the frosty October night I was now standing in the middle of.

As soon as I was situated, Ainsworth stepped forward with the little bowl. He dipped his fingers in and smeared the sticky liquid in the center of my chest, beneath the amulet. By the time he was done, I had what looked like a protective sigil on my skin.

He nodded and stepped back, glancing at Dr. Colburn.

"Summon a storm," she said, as if it was as easy as ordering a pizza.

"Yeah. Sure. Coming right up."

Cassius shot me a look and I got the meaning loud and clear. *Don't piss off Dr. Colburn right after she stuck up for you, dumb ass.*

I bit the side of my cheek and got to work. Bowing my head, I focused on the temperature changes, the varying pressure in the air, all of the elements required for a storm.

The wind picked up and the air got noticeably colder as it whipped across my bare skin. Clouds gathered overhead, obscuring the bright glow of the Blood Moon. Rain came in soft spritzes until the storm gained momentum, making it fall faster and heavier. Thunder rumbled, not that far away.

"Into the water," Temperance said over a boom of thunder.

Steeling myself for the fucking cold, I left the safety of the circle and crept down the riverbank. A few rocks jutted out into the water, worn smooth by the gentle insistence of the river.

The dark water had no more than swallowed my ankles when I gasped like an idiot. I hoped Cash didn't mind topping for the next week because I'm pretty sure that's how long it was going to take for my dick to come out of hiding.

By the time the water rushed over my bare thighs, a strange warmth had spread through me, radiating from the chest outward. That must have been Cassius's magic. Maybe it was cheating to have another witch help you during your conversion, but if no one was going to leave clearly written instructions then we couldn't be blamed for winging it.

The water was still fucking cold, but as I sank in up to my chest, the heat streaming through my body made it tolerable. Plus, the fact I was soaked from the top down thanks to the rain helped with the adjustment.

Thunder struck again and the rain fell in sheets. The people on the bank were almost impossible to see with the combined darkness and the driving rain. It wasn't until lightning illuminated the area that I could even tell which black shape was Cassius.

I tipped my head back and closed my eyes again, focusing on the storm overhead. This whole process was about a spiritual death, leading to a spiritual rebirth — according to Cassius. It was deeply personal and no two experiences were the same. So while that left some wiggle room for the actual ritual, it also meant I had no idea what the hell I was supposed to be doing, other than hanging out in the middle of a storm I'd created until something profound happened.

I don't know how long I floated there, doing a backstroke now and again to stay in the same general area before the current carried me away. The lightning kept flashing behind my closed eyelids, crackling as it got closer and closer, chasing the thunder.

It was peaceful, the chaos of the storm. It reminded me of autumn and why I loved it so much. As long as I had Cassius to keep my blood warm and circulating, I could stay in the water indefinitely. I didn't think *he'd* be too happy about it, though.

On second thought, Cassius was a lot like an autumn storm. Wild, unpredictable, but strangely comforting when you were prepared to withstand it. Maybe that's why I loved him, even more than I wanted to admit out loud. Loving someone that much, giving them that much power over you, was bound to fucking hurt, but I couldn't let him go. Not now.

The warm buzz of happiness surged through every muscle, growing hotter.

Too hot.

Unbearably hot.

Someone on the riverbank shouted.

I opened my eyes in time to see a bolt of lightning hurtling downward. It struck the river's surface right in front of me. Blue and white crackles radiated from the center, scattering in every direction. The electricity washed over me, contracting every muscle to the point of agony.

I couldn't move.

I couldn't breathe.

All I could feel was a violent surge of power. Pain prickled over every inch of my skin like a thousand needles driving into me at once. Each second was a lifetime. And then?

I was free.

The lightning dissipated and my muscles relaxed. My legs gave way and my body drifted upwards, floating again.

More lightning arced overhead in the clouds, flashes of bright white among the dark, roiling shades of gray and blue and purple. It was beautiful. Certainly a beautiful way to die. Cassius would be happy for me.

Faintly, over the howl of the wind and claps of thunder, I heard someone scream my name.

I drew in a breath to answer but water rushed into my mouth, down my throat, filling my lungs as the river swallowed me whole.

Chapter Forty-Five
Cassius

I was soaked to the bone from the wind and the rain, but that wasn't what made my blood run cold or my hands shake.

Graeme had been under the water for several minutes already. His heartbeat started out strong but faded as time went on. I was torn between listening to that dimming pulse and searching for any silvery wisps floating upward, any sign his soul was trying to depart.

"What else does it say?" Ainsworth said, turning to Temperance and holding a flashlight up to try and read the book over her shoulder.

"It doesn't!" she snapped, angling the book so he could see it clearly. Or as clearly as possible with rain pelting us from every direction. "It's not a grimoire, Samuel! It's a goddamn journal entry from two centuries ago. You're lucky it said anything at all."

"What does it say exactly?" Dad asked.

Temperance spun the book around to show him.

"Moon full this Day. A Chilly air. After Meeting tonight Cyrus Oliver went to the river. Revd mr Dane performed Convrsion. Some rain & haill came and ice ran in the river. Cyrus was Safely Delivrd through Divine protection, though a fatagueing

Event. He is very weiry. I came home but Could not compose to Sleep."

She bugged her eyes out in exasperation, emphasizing how *not* helpful that entry really was. "That's it! The next entry is a week later and talks about traveling to Boston."

"That's not very helpful," Ainsworth said flatly.

"Hence my point!"

I couldn't listen to the Selectmen bicker anymore. They'd distracted me long enough and I lost track of Graeme's heartbeat.

Cupping my hands around my mouth, I shouted his name into the wind. There was no response. No movement beneath the water. Worst of all, I couldn't hear his heart.

Another streak of lightning darted through the sky, slamming into a tree and splitting it down the middle. Half of the ancient oak peeled off and crashed into the river, near enough to where Graeme had gone under that I shed my coat and my boots and ran into the water.

"Cassius, don't!" Dad shouted.

I ignored him.

As soon as the water was deep enough, I dove beneath the surface and groped along the craggy bottom.

Squinting against the blurry darkness, I opened my eyes underwater and searched for any human-shaped forms. I swam slowly, feeling my way along in the cold dark until I ran face-first into the top of the downed tree, nearly poking my eye out on a branch.

Surfacing with a gasp, my teeth chattered as I hauled myself up on the limbs, looking around for any sign of Graeme from up high.

"Where is he?" Ainsworth shouted.

"He's not here!"

Samuel and Temperance looked at Dad, who shook his

head, also searching the area. That alone gave me hope. If Graeme was dead, Dad would have told me to come back. He couldn't sense his spirit either, which meant he must have been alive. Somewhere.

A flash of white further down the river caught my eye.

I leapt out of the tree branches and let myself drift downstream toward it, dodging rocks along the way. As soon as I could get my feet beneath me, I ran as fast as I could toward the riverbank.

Graeme clung to the muddy earth, his fingers dug into the ground like grappling hooks as he tried to haul the rest of his body out of the water.

"Graeme! Are you ok?" I slipped my arms around him and helped him scramble up the slope onto dry land. Well, as dry as it could be with the downpour.

"Are you hurt?" I swept my hands over him, checking for blood or broken bones.

"I'm cold," he whispered, trembling against me as I pulled him into my lap.

"Oh, shit." In the frantic search for him, I'd clearly forgotten I was supposed to be the one keeping him warm. I concentrated on his heart and the blood rushing through his veins, raising the temperature slowly so I didn't boil him alive from the inside out. "I'm sorry."

"'S'ok," he mumbled, turning his face into the side of my neck. The wind died almost immediately, while the rain tapered off into a light mist.

"You scared me," I said, rubbing the blue-tinged skin on his arm, hoping to speed his recovery. "I thought you were gone."

"Can't get rid of me that easily." He tried to laugh but ended up coughing.

"Yeah, you're like a wart. Or a hemorrhoid."

"Aw, babe. You say the sweetest things."

We both chuckled as the Selectmen rushed over to us.

"Are you alright?" Ainsworth asked, draping a large towel around Graeme's bare shoulders.

"Do you feel any different?" Temperance added. Bob loitered behind her with the Book of Transactions, one finger shoved between the pages to mark his place. He seemed to be having a hell of a time juggling his umbrella, his pen, and the Book but you had to admire his dedication.

"I don't know," Graeme replied.

I helped him to his feet, keeping both hands on him in case he collapsed. Even after he was standing, his arm stayed slung over my shoulder.

"Do something," Temperance said impatiently. "Something you've never done before. Or something that requires a lot more magic."

"Like what?" He frowned at her, stealing a glance upward as the last of the clouds drifted along, clearing the night sky and revealing the bright Blood Moon.

"Make it snow," I suggested. All of the elements were already in place, he just needed to drop the temperature. Drastically. "For me?"

He gave me a small smile before closing his eyes. My arm tightened around his waist, keeping him close.

In what seemed like no time at all, the temperature plummeted. A wall of pale, gray clouds rolled in from nowhere. Tiny particles drifted downward lazily, melting as soon as they landed. Then larger flakes fell, faster and thicker, until the area was covered in a light blanket of white. With no wind, the night was absolutely still, only the sound of the river filling the silence.

"Marvelous," Ainsworth said, clapping his hands.

"Not just a weather witch, but a *real* Stormbringer. After all these years." Dr. Colburn clutched the diary to her chest, actually looking like she might shed a tear.

"Can I get dressed now?" Graeme asked, his dark hair dusted with snow.

"Oh! Yes! Of course." Ainsworth blinked and handed Graeme a plastic bag. "Bob, did you get it all?"

The archivist snapped the heavy tome shut and patted the cover. "Officially logged."

Graeme ducked his head, trying to avoid the awed way the others were looking at him as he tugged his pants back on. He used the towel to wipe off the remnants of the protective sigil on his skin and yanked his shirt over his head.

A blast of cold air whipped along the river so hard it scattered the snow from our feet.

"You've made your point, your majesty," I said, stuffing the towel into the plastic bag. "You can kill the wind."

Graeme turned slowly, his gaze sliding over his shoulder to the dark woods on the opposite side of the river. "It's not me."

A sickening moment of déjà vu hit me. I reached for Graeme but my fingers swiped through nothing but air. Pressure seized the center of my chest and lifted me off my feet, hurling me backward.

Chaos broke out on the bank.

Graeme yelled my name.

Dad and Ainsworth ran toward the river.

Temperance and Bob were shouting at everyone.

I slammed into a tree so hard I saw stars. Crashing to the ground, I narrowly missed smashing my face against a rock half-hidden beneath the snow.

"Cash!" Graeme slid down the slight hill like he was sliding into home base, his eyes wide. "Are you ok? What happened?"

"I don't know."

A large, broken branch sailed through the air, headed straight for us.

"Get down!" I grabbed Graeme's shoulder and yanked him out of the way, leaving myself exposed in the process.

The branch stopped suddenly, an inch away from my face, another tree root gnarled around it. It hovered for a moment before the root turned and launched the branch back across the river like a missile.

"Ainsworth," we said at the same time, scrambling to our feet.

I pressed a hand to my sternum and tried to keep up as Graeme raced back to the riverbank. He wrapped a hand around my elbow and helped drag me forward.

The riverbank was cloaked in an unnatural darkness, but that didn't stop objects from flying back and forth across the river — rocks, more branches, gusts of wind so sharp they felt like knives slicing across your skin.

Graeme hesitated on the edge of the darkness, but I barreled through it to find my dad.

"Cassius! Take Graeme and go!" Temperance shouted. She and Bob were huddled together behind Dad's protective black shadows, each clutching their respective books like their lives depended on them.

"What's happening?"

"It's Marian," Dad shouted.

A hailstorm of river rocks rained down on us from overhead. Dad threw himself over the top of me, using his hands to protect my head and neck. In doing so, the wall of shadows dropped, exposing everyone.

"Fuck!" Ainsworth shouted, a smear of blood on his forehead.

"Professor!" Graeme ran over to him, pressing his sleeve to the gash.

Across the river stood Marian Hewitt, looking like a ghost. Her dark hair blew wildly around her shoulders and the pale, sleeveless nightgown she wore was dirty and torn.

The white gauze wrapped around her forearm was bleeding again, the dark stain spreading wider. She may have been human, but the ferocious look on her face was anything but. Hollow cheeks, sunken eyes, and a thin-lipped mouth twisted by pure rage.

As soon as the shadows cleared, she pointed directly at Dad. He opened his mouth but all that came out was a scream. Clamping a hand over his chest, he sank to his knees before eventually toppling over completely.

I threw a crackling ball of black energy at her, again and again, until she dropped her hand and my dad stopped screaming.

Ainsworth, recovered from the rock to the head, pushed his hands together like he was crushing a can. Across the river, two trees surged toward Marian, their branches outstretched like long, twisted fingers. She waited until the last second before leaping out of the way and fleeing into the night like a wraith.

"Dad!" I dropped to my knees next to him. His heart was pounding wildly, but so was my own. With all of the adrenaline in both of our systems, I couldn't slow either of us down.

He gasped, a deep guttural noise, mouth gaping like a fish sucking in a dying breath.

"No, no, no." I pushed him onto his back and scooted closer, interlacing my fingers and driving the heels of my hands into his chest, counting off the number of compressions.

"Caius!" Temperance appeared on his other side, one hand hovering over his temple. She looked at me, her blue eyes welling with tears. "He's—"

"No!" I didn't slow the compressions at all.

"It's in his heart!"

"What's in his heart?" Graeme asked, appearing next to me. "What did she do?"

"The same thing she did to Lydia. An air embolism," Temperance replied.

When compressions failed to restore the beating of his heart, I laid both hands over his chest. Using my magic, I pushed as much blood through his heart as I could, forcing it through his body and up to his brain. Those were the two most important things. The rest, we could deal with later.

"Nathaniel is on his way," Ainsworth said, pocketing his cell phone. "And Thomas alerted his officers. They're on the lookout for Marian."

"They won't hurt her, will they?" Graeme asked.

I didn't hear the answer.

I wanted to scream at them all to shut up, that I didn't give two fucks if they shot Marian Hewitt dead in the middle of downtown Winslow, but I couldn't waste a single ounce of energy. My own blood pounded in my veins, throbbing at the temples, squeezing painfully as I poured more and more magic into my father's dying body. The second I stopped, the death clock would start. I'd barely been able to retrieve a crow's tiny soul from the Land of the Dead. I wasn't naive enough to think I'd be able to keep my father's from going where it was destined.

"Cassius," Bob's voice said, thick and warbled.

His concern became apparent when something wet trickled down my lips and dripped from my chin. Blood splattered on my dad's gray, woolen coat. I wiped my nose hastily with the back of my hand, trying to ignore the smear of bright red on my skin. Dad's blood was more important. Keeping it going was more important than my own vein rupturing under the strain.

"Let me try something," Graeme said, laying a hand on my arm. "Please? Trust me."

I was too exhausted to even speak, so I rocked back on my heels, dropping my hands to my thighs.

He gave me a terse nod and leaned over my dad, holding one hand over his chest and the other along his side. Exactly where you'd place defibrillator pads.

A flash of white shot from one palm, arcing into the other from within Dad's body.

Dad's torso jerked and fell still.

I held my breath, waiting.

Temperance's hand hovered near Dad's temple again. I didn't miss the glance she shot in Graeme's direction.

He repositioned his hands, ready to try again, when he slowly froze into place.

A shimmery flash in my periphery drew my attention to the side. I knew it was a spirit before my head fully turned. The pale, silvery glow was the first clue, as was the cold tendril coiling around my torso, making a connection.

"Mom?"

Her translucent figure wavered in front of me, getting blurry. I dashed the tears from my eyes and rose slowly, happy to see her, happy that it wasn't Dad. But then again, there's only one reason she'd be here.

"Hi sweetheart." She tilted her head to the side, giving me a sad smile.

I shook my head, taking a cautious step closer. "Don't take him. Please."

"Oh, honey. You know it's not up to me."

"Tell him to stay! Tell him to fight! I can't lose him too! Not yet!" I tried to choke back a sob, but it came out regardless.

She rushed forward, wrapping her pale arms around me and pressing cool lips to my temple. Even if I couldn't feel it, I pretended I did, for both our sakes. "Shh… Cassius. It's ok. It'll be ok, sweetheart."

"Nothing has been ok, Mom. Nothing. Not since you died. And especially not since I came home."

"I know, honey… I'm so sorry. I wish I could be there for you."

"Why didn't you tell me Marian Hewitt was the one who killed you?"

She frowned, trying to brush the hair off my forehead. "How did you find out about that?"

"She tried to kill me too. And Dr. Dane said it was an arterial air embolism."

Closing her eyes, she bowed her head slightly. "I told you they were dangerous…"

"Would have been nice if you were a little more specific. Maybe then I could have stopped her from hurting Dad."

"There's nothing you could have done to stop her, sweetheart. She's hexed. Until she's released or the curse is broken, she's as strong as the Marquis she's been summoning."

"She's *hexed*?"

Mom nodded solemnly.

"Ok… How do we stop her?"

"Find the witch."

"Do you know who that is?"

"Ne te quaesiveris extra." *Do not seek outside yourself.*

"Stop with the riddles, Mom. Who is it?"

"You already know, Cassius. I can't give you the answers."

"Did the witch bind you? Are they keeping you from speaking?"

Her hand drifted to my face again, a whisper of cold caressing my skin. "I love you. It *will* be ok. I promise, sweetheart. But now it's time for you to leave."

"Are you taking Dad with you?" I asked, dreading her answer.

She smiled softly. "Not tonight."

In the next instant, the coldness wrapped around me was

gone. I was back on my knees next to Graeme, watching as he delivered another shock to Dad's heart.

Dad jolted again, a little more violently than before since Graeme apparently gave him a stronger round of lightning.

I searched the woods, looking for any abnormal light, any wrinkle in reality. Like an idiot, I called out for my mother, even though I knew she'd gone.

Graeme looked at me, his brow furrowed. Before he could say anything, Temperance cheered.

"Caius! You're ok! Hold on, ok? Nathaniel is coming."

Dad sucked in a regular breath, his head lolling to the side.

I grabbed his hand and squeezed it, needing to confirm for myself he was still warm. "Dad? Don't move, ok? We have to get you to the hospital."

"Simply marvelous. Another one for the history books," Bob said, cracking open the Book of Transactions, pen flying over the page. Ainsworth stood next to him, hands clasped and head tipped back.

Stealing a brief moment to express my own gratitude, I turned and grabbed Graeme by the shoulders and dragged him forward, kissing him quickly. "Thank you."

He nodded mutely. The relief on his face disintegrated into unease as his gaze cut across the river again to where his mother had been standing.

Chapter Forty-Six

Graeme

Three days passed since the night of my conversion. Three days since anyone had seen my mother. And three days since my father refused to speak to me.

After Nathaniel arrived and stabilized Caius, the remaining Selectmen carried him to a car and whisked him to the hospital. Cassius went with him while I insisted on helping Treadwell look for my mother.

My first stop was at home, except Dad made sure there was no way I'd get inside. Apparently Caius wasn't the only one who could put up a ward. I couldn't even step foot on the porch before I ran smack dab into an invisible barrier.

I shouted at the house until he appeared in the window. He took one look at me and closed the curtain.

Calls went unanswered.

Texts ignored.

He fucking hated me, of that much I was sure. Upholding the Hewitt name meant everything to him and I'd committed the worst sin of all — I sided with the Corbins. He believed in the righteousness of the feud so much, I doubted he'd ever forgive me.

With that realization weighing on me, I met up with Treadwell in the North Woods. He redirected me to one of his officers and we set off on a UTV to comb our section, looking for any trace of my mother. As far as the officer knew, she was only a missing person, not a cursed witch with an axe to grind.

"Is she familiar with these woods?" the officer asked, navigating the UTV over the rocky ground and between trees as carefully as he could.

"I didn't think so. I mean, it's been years since she's been out here. Or, so I thought..." Turned out I didn't know a lot of shit about my parents. A large part of that was them fucking *lying* to me for, oh, my entire life. But maybe the other part was that I didn't *want* to know. I didn't want to be a part of this magical community and that willful ignorance turned around and bit me in the ass, more than once.

We searched for her as long as we could, until the UTV was about to run out of gas and the officer called it quits. He marked our progress with his GPS and headed back to civilization.

Since going to *my* home was out of the question, I went to the hospital to be with Cassius. He was asleep in the chair, his coat scrunched under his head and propped against the wall.

Not wanting to bother him or Caius, I covered Cassius with one of the spare blankets from the little closet and crept out again.

Exhausted beyond belief, I slept in my car in the hospital parking lot, hoping Claudia didn't find me out there and murder me in my sleep. I suppose I could have gone to the Northrups' house, or even Ainsworth's, but I wanted to be close to Cassius in case he called.

Day Two was more of the same. After checking in with Cassius, I went back to the woods to start the search over in the daylight. Still, no sign of my mom.

On the third day, Treadwell brought out dogs. Shepherds and bloodhounds crisscrossed the North Woods with a small army of police marching behind, kicking over leaves and checking inside hollowed-out tree trunks.

When we got closer to the old Winslow village, the dogs stopped tracking. They whined and backed up, refusing all commands to go forward. Some even tried to pull their handlers in the opposite direction or bit at their leashes, trying to free themselves.

"Chief?" One of the K9 officers raised his brows. He didn't have to finish his question out loud. I knew what he was asking. All of the officers did. While some came from branches of the founding families, others were entirely disconnected from the Congregation. It didn't mean they were unaware of the fact that not everything was what it seemed. They were *fully* aware, more than most of the people who lived here, that Winslow was not like other towns and its denizens were not always entirely "normal."

Treadwell nodded. "Why don't you head east, toward Norwood Bridge? Maybe she crossed there."

The officers returned the nod, steering the dogs away from the old village and back to the relative safety of another part of the woods.

Dread prickled along my spine. Did the dogs sense the horror of the village, steeped in a history of violence and hatred? Or was it something else? Was there a demon lurking nearby? A vengeful spirit?

"Just… stay behind me," Treadwell said as he took the first purposeful step toward the village.

Stormbringer or not, I wasn't about to argue with him.

We made our way through the woods as quietly as we could. The only sound was our boots crunching on brittle branches and sweeping through thick piles of brightly-colored leaves. There were no birds. No insects. Not even the whistle of wind, high in the trees. It was completely and utterly silent, except for us.

"If we find her, how are you going to convince her to come with us?" I asked, keeping my voice low.

He chuckled. "Ask her nicely."

"Yeah, good luck with that."

"You doing ok, kid?"

It was my turn to chuckle, but it definitely wasn't out of amusement. "Not really, no. I just found out everything I thought I knew was a lie. My dad hates me. My mom is either straight-up psycho or hexed and tried to kill my boyfriend's dad, in addition to two of my classmates *and* my best friend. Oh, and I'm pretty sure I'm going to fail all of my classes this semester because I haven't been to class in weeks because of the demon hunting my ass."

Treadwell considered it for a moment and shrugged. "Could always be worse."

"Really?" I shot him a look.

"Just saying."

"I appreciate the sentiment, Chief, but I don't really want to challenge the universe right now."

We walked onward, creeping through the woods as quietly as we could, straining to listen for the sound of someone else. Some*thing* else.

The old village wasn't that far from where the dogs refused to move. In what seemed like no time, the trees thinned out and the clearing yawned before us.

Remnants of an archaeology dig from years ago were still in place, rows of string tied into squares and tarps draped over pits in the ground. Buckets of tools and sifting screens had been tipped over, spilling their contents everywhere.

The only building still in existence was the old gaol. A squat stone-and-timber-frame building sagged between two trees, its small, dark windows glaring at us as we moved past it. The front door was padlocked shut and there was no way anyone could fit through the windows, so it was safe to assume Mom wasn't in there.

"I can't believe they left everything out here," I said, edging around a discarded glove like it might suddenly grab my ankle.

"You talking about the original settlers or all of the archaeology students who were murdered a while back?"

"Both, I guess."

He shrugged again. "After the bodies were collected, no one wanted to come back out here. Not that I blame them. And as far as the village… well, same reason. Black Mary doesn't like people bothering her and no one wanted to give her a reason to come back."

"Do you think she's as evil as they say?"

He shot me a look out of the corner of his eye. "You don't?"

"I don't know… I used to come out here all the time as a kid and didn't think about it. If she was that evil, she could have killed me countless times. Same with the rest of her descendants."

"Yeah, you and Corbin. That was, uh, an interesting development."

I snorted. "Tell me about it."

"My advice? Take happiness where you can find it. Life's too fucking short for the rest of the bullshit."

"That's the problem, though. Our happiness comes at the expense of other people."

"Fuck 'em. It's your life. Don't forget that."

Nodding, we fell into an easy silence as he ventured further away from the old village. I don't think I'd ever spoken to the chief that much in my entire life, but I was suddenly grateful for his company and for his dedication to finding my mom. It hadn't escaped my attention that none of the other families were trying to look for her.

"How much further are we going to go?" I asked. We'd already been out here all day and the light was fading.

"Figured we'd go check the caves real quick and cut back over to Norwood Bridge before sunset."

"Do you think she'd really go that far north?"

Something rustled the leaves up ahead.

Treadwell stopped, throwing his arm in front of me to keep me behind him.

I held my breath, waiting to hear something else.

A little snarl accompanied the sound of more leaves rustling. Wings flapped.

Treadwell crested the small hill and immediately came to a halt. He reached for his radio and called for his lieutenant. When the other man's voice replied, Treadwell mumbled something too soft for me to hear.

I scurried up the hill after him to see what the problem was.

Before I could reach the top, he whirled around and put his hands up. "Don't."

"What?" I couldn't help but look behind him.

He found my mom after all.

Dead.

Hanging, to be exact.

A noose was cinched around her neck and her head hung at a funny angle. She was still in the tattered nightgown from the other night, covered in blood and dirt. Her lifeless eyes seemed to be looking right at me. Her swollen tongue peeked out of her mouth, a trickle of brown fluid dried on her mottled gray skin.

One rope was thrown over a branch and tied off to another tree, meanwhile a second rope dangled from underneath her nightgown.

Scratch that — the second thing wasn't rope. It was her fucking intestines, which were currently being feasted on by a possum. A couple of turkey vultures lurked nearby, apparently displeased at having to wait their turn.

I didn't realize Treadwell had physically turned me away from the sight until I broke free and collapsed against a fallen tree, expelling whatever was in my stomach.

"I'm so sorry, Graeme," Treadwell said as I stood, wiping my mouth with the back of my hand. "As soon as the others get here, I'll have someone take you home."

At a loss for words, I simply nodded. I mean, what was there to say? My mom had spent the past few months murdering my friends, attacking whoever she felt like, including me, and cursing my boyfriend and his family. Now she was dead. Whether she was crazy, hexed, or had been corrupted by a demon was a moot point.

In a way, I knew it would always end like this. Maybe not like *this*, but I knew things would never be the same. We might as well have buried her the day we buried Owen since that was the day my mother really died. That thing hanging there wasn't my mom. That was an imposter, someone who'd lived in our house for the past six years but hadn't been a part of our lives.

Maybe now she was reunited with Owen. Maybe now she'd finally find the peace that so obviously eluded her in this life. Maybe now I could stop feeling so fucking guilty.

Chapter Forty-Seven
Cassius

Necromancer or not, I was getting *so* sick of funerals. There had been too many in Winslow as of late. Graeme's mother was just the latest town tragedy. The story his father spun was that she'd been unwell and succumbed to illness at home. No one in the community questioned it, since Marian had been absent from the public eye for years. But the Congregation all knew the truth now.

There was no reception for Marian, no gathering at the meetinghouse. Frankly, I was surprised George even let anyone attend the funeral. He didn't talk to anyone or even look at them. As soon as Peregrine sealed Marian's grave, George left without acknowledging his son in any way.

After his dad learned about our relationship that night during the Meeting, Graeme pretty much moved in. It was temporary, until his university housing application was processed. Dad said he could stay as long as he wanted, but things with Claudia were still somewhat, um, icy. Besides, I think he wanted space for himself to process all of the shit we'd gone through.

Surprisingly, Claudia started to come around. Sort of. After we brought Dad home from the hospital, she and Graeme ran into one another in the hallway outside Dad's room. Graeme and I both expected a fight, but she inclined her head and mumbled her thanks to Graeme for saving Dad's life. After that, it seemed like the ice began to thaw.

Peregrine was the one who kept us apprised of the funeral arrangements since George refused to speak to his son. It broke my heart to watch his father shut him out, but there was nothing I could do. Leaving Winslow wasn't an option anymore, not unless Graeme came with. I'm sure Dad could have talked to his friends at Ashbourne to see if they'd take Graeme too, but it was far easier for us to stay at Tennebrose.

As Graeme predicted, Mrs. Green was able to reverse my withdrawal from the university. She logged it as a temporary leave due to a family emergency and reinstated me, no questions asked. My professors let me make up the midterms I'd missed and life carried on.

"Are you sure you're ready to go back to Tennebrose tomorrow?" I asked Graeme as we walked away from his mother's grave. We were the last two there. The rest of the Congregation had left over an hour ago.

"Yeah. We have to turn in that progress report for Ainsworth."

"I'm just saying, if you need more time..."

"I'm fine," he replied, stopping to face me. "Really. I'd been living with my mom's ghost for the past six years anyway. I'm just sorry so many other people got hurt, or killed, because of her."

"I know." I touched his cheek softly, wishing I could take his pain away. "At least we have this chance to start over."

"Yeah..."

I slipped my hands into his and gave them a light squeeze. "Are you sure you're ok?"

He nodded, pulling me closer before disentangling our hands so he could wrap his arms around my neck. I let

Graeme decide when he was ready to leave and until then, I stood with him, holding him.

Upon our return from the cemetery, we walked into a house brimming with all sorts of delicious smells. My mouth watered at the same time suspicion crept into the back of my mind. Despite the fact Dad was a notoriously awful cook, he was still on bed rest most of the time, which meant it was Claudia's doing. Unless someone sent a group of caterers to the house.

I was honestly more prepared for that than to see Claudia in the kitchen, cooking and baking up a storm from the looks of it. She stopped when she saw us come in and dusted her hands off on a towel.

"I didn't know what you like to eat," she said to Graeme. "So I made a little bit of everything. There's a roast chicken, shepherd's pie, lasagna. And of course dessert."

I reached for a wicker basket and dragged it closer. Peeling the cloth napkin aside, I started to help myself to an apple turnover when Claudia slapped my hand.

"Dinner first," she said, unfazed by my glare as she whisked the basket away to the other side of the kitchen.

"You didn't have to do all of this," Graeme said softly.

"I know." She gave him a fleeting smile. "Cassius, can you set the table while I finish up?"

"Sure." I grabbed the stack of dishes from the counter while Graeme scooped up the bundle of silverware and cloth napkins.

Dad managed to come down for dinner, lured by all of the smells, he said. I think it was to keep an eye on Graeme and Claudia.

It was strange, the four of us sitting around a table, but comforting in a way. After all of the shit that had gone on recently, a family dinner felt normal. We chatted amicably about work, school, and how Ainsworth helped Graeme secure a job on campus in addition to getting the ball rolling on his housing.

"He is full of surprises," Dad said, in reference to Ainsworth. "But good ones. I mean, look at the two of you."

"Fate has a way of working itself out," Claudia said, glancing between us.

I smiled and squeezed Graeme's hand. He squeezed my hand in return, but there wasn't even a hint of a smile.

Dad, however, actually managed to get a chuckle or two out of Graeme by cracking the *worst* jokes known to man.

"Dad, please," I groaned, holding my forehead and covering my face with my hand. "No more!"

"Ok, ok. Last one." He cleared his throat and looked at Graeme very seriously, waiting until all eyes were on him before continuing. "Does an apple a day keep the doctor away?"

I rolled my eyes and shook my head. He'd officially gone from being a "cool dad" to the most embarrassing kind in the blink of an eye.

Graeme stole a glance at me before shrugging one shoulder at Dad. "I don't know. Does it?"

"Only if your aim is good," Dad said, laughing way too hard at his own joke.

Graeme laughed, a genuine laugh. I couldn't tell if it was at my dad's lame joke or because of how hard *he* was laughing, but it made me smile in spite of my protesting.

"Oh my God," Claudia groaned with me and slapped her napkin onto the table. "I'm getting dessert."

She returned shortly thereafter with two dishes, a cheesecake and a Boston cream pie, because once again she didn't know what Graeme preferred. The answer, apparently, was both.

After we were thoroughly stuffed and the dishes were done, we disappeared up to my room.

"That was nice of your sister," Graeme said, undressing and slipping under the covers with a contented sigh.

"She has her moments." I crawled into bed next to him. When he opened his arms, indicating he wanted a hug, I settled down on top of him, burrowing my face into his neck.

"I'm sorry," he murmured, wrapping his arms around me. "I'm sorry that my mom—"

I picked my head up and scowled at him. "Stop. You have nothing to apologize for. We can't control our families."

"She almost killed your dad. Legit, one of the nicest people I've ever met. And she almost fucking killed him. For what? Because he's a Necromancer? Because he's Lydia's husband? I don't get it."

Well, there went the hope of having any fun time before bed. I mean, after everything we ate I knew anal was off the table, but I thought we could still get off some *other* way. So much for that. "I don't know…"

"Why did she kill Melanie? And Sophia? And fucking India, for Christ's sake. She's known India her whole life! Why would she send a demon after my best friend?"

"I don't know…" Yep. Definitely no sex. Couldn't even get hard if I wanted to.

"Why would she send it after *me*?"

I opened my mouth to answer, but he kept going. Burying my face into the side of his neck, I exhaled, waiting for him to get it all out of his system.

"What if it comes back? The demon, I mean. Do you think it's still hunting me? Am I strong enough for it now? Or do I need you to do what you do?"

"Don't worry about the demon," I said into the side of his neck. "It's not coming back."

"Yeah, but how do you know that?"

Lifting my head, I met his gaze once more. "Uncle Marcus took care of it. Dad gave him the Book of Lazarus and the rest of the Necromancers helped. They summoned the Marquis and killed it. Well, bound it and *then* killed it, so there's no chance of it reappearing, with or without a witch's help."

He didn't look relieved in the slightest. The crease between his brows remained, as did the downward curve of his mouth. "There's so much about what happened that doesn't make sense. Answers have only led to more questions."

"Do you want me to cross over? I can ask your mom. Or, if you really want, I can bring her here and you can talk to her. Your blood should be enough of a connection to summon her."

"No. Absolutely not. I appreciate the offer, but no. She was a liar in life, what makes you think she'd tell the truth now?" He scoffed, the muscle in his jaw tightening. "Let's just… try to move on." I might have believed him if he didn't look so upset, like he didn't intend to follow his own suggestion.

"Whatever you want." I gave him a soft smile before pressing my lips to his. His arms tightened around me and I was pretty sure he was never going to let go.

"Should we take the tree with us?" Graeme asked, shoving his laptop in his backpack. "Or do you think pictures are enough?"

"I'd hope pictures are enough," I replied, pawing through my messenger bag and making sure I had everything for botany. "He can't honestly expect us to haul a fucking tree in there every three weeks. Although, we should go see how it's doing anyway. I haven't checked on it in a couple days."

"You haven't checked on it?" Graeme gasped with exaggerated outrage. "Are you going to ignore our children too?"

"We don't *have* children, smart ass."

"Well, not with that attitude."

We walked into Dad's laboratory and smiled at our poisonous apple tree, stupidly proud of our creation. As I figured, it was fine. It wasn't like an orchid that you needed to baby with misters and the appropriate ratio of sun and shade.

Having long since outgrown its glass cloche lid, the tree was now in a giant planter, biding its time until we took it outside. I was actually hoping Ainsworth would come over and help with that endeavor since I didn't feel like wrestling the tree into a wheelbarrow and taking it out to the poison garden by myself.

"See?" I smirked at him, gesturing magnanimously. "The tree is growing proportionately and the apples—"

"Where the fuck are they?" Graeme asked, his jaw slack.

I stared at the tree, taking a step closer and gaping just like Graeme. "I just saw them, like, two days ago! There was enough for at least half a peck!"

"Did they fall off or shrivel up or something?" He stooped to check underneath the desk and the surrounding floor space.

Gently cradling one of the broken stems, I considered every possible scenario in which our little experiment had gone wrong. Except, it hadn't. The entire tree had been picked clean of all its fruit.

A memory from last night hit me hard.

Apple turnovers. My mother's specialty. *Claudia's* specialty.

I tried to take one and my sister stopped me, but then she never brought them out for dessert. With two other dishes, it didn't seem necessary and I didn't think anything of it. Until now...

Darting past Graeme, I sprinted down the hall to the kitchen, searching high and low for any sign of the wicker basket. I couldn't find it anywhere or proof the turnovers were ever there.

"What's wrong?" Graeme asked.

"Claudia," I said, swallowing hard. *Fate has a way of working itself out.* "Call Ainsworth." Snatching my keys off the counter, I spun and headed for the door.

"What's going on?" Graeme asked as he dialed.

"Just fucking call him!"

Graeme didn't argue or ask any more questions. I heard the phone ringing as we ran out to the garage. Ringing and ringing and not being answered.

"It keeps going to voicemail."

"Try his office."

"Ok."

I put the car in drive and floored it, trying to think of something else I could do in the meantime, like send him a crow or see if there was a friendly spirit hanging around. They were always bugging the shit out of us, asking for favors, maybe it was time they did us a solid and helped out in return.

Graeme shook his head, lowering his phone. "No answer there either."

"Shit!"

"You think Claudia is really going to hurt Ainsworth? For what?"

"Us. Think about it, think about everything you said last night. Every single person who was attacked or killed by the demon had some sort of interaction with me."

"Yeah, I thought that too, but how would Claudia know about any of that shit? Did you tell her?"

I shook my head, my grip tightening on the steering wheel. "Some of it, yeah. But I'm not the only one in my family who talks to crows. I told you, there are people all over this town spying on one another. That includes the wildlife."

"Ok, but if it was someone getting rid of potential witnesses to our magical standoff outside Dane Hall, then why didn't Sophia die right away, at the same time as Melanie?"

"Maybe the crows didn't see her. I don't know. But I told Claudia about Sophia after the equinox, when I had to tell my dad why I had your phone. And she was the next one to die."

Graeme kept trying to call Ainsworth as we drove, hanging onto the door handle every now and again as the Lexus whipped around curves in the road.

"Claudia's said time and again she wouldn't lose any more family members," I said, not slowing down in the slightest. "Lennox said the same thing. I'd bet anything the two of them teamed up after you threw me off that ledge by the library and it's been downhill since then."

"Dude, it was an *accident*! You know I didn't know what the fuck I was doing!"

"It doesn't matter! Lennox knew you were being hunted by a demon. At the time I thought it was a coincidence, because he knew what happened at the meetinghouse, but what if it wasn't? What if Lennox was helping Claudia?"

"But I thought you needed the second half of your grimoire to control demons like that? I thought that's why you wanted it so bad?"

"It is! I mean, it was. But somehow they found a way without that part of the Book. Maybe there's another grimoire, or they took what information was in our piece of the Book of Lazarus and filled in the blanks."

"But what about my mom? We *saw* her with that demon. And your family's grimoire. Not to mention the fact she tried to kill your dad right in front of both of us."

"The poppet," I said suddenly. "The poppet from the crypt. You know the crow is our family symbol. I thought it was part of a curse, and it was, in a way, but it wasn't *against* us. Claudia or Lennox or whoever the fuck used the crows as a sacrifice. Using their blood and the power of our ancestors twenty feet below them, whoever made the poppet would have had enough energy to control your mother. And given how old and ratty that doll looked, they'd probably been at it a while. The crows we found that day were just renewing the energy supply."

"Would that sort of control be enough to make her summon a demon?"

I nodded. "If a witch is strong enough, it's entirely possible. And I don't know if you know this, but Claudia is extremely powerful."

"I kind of got a clue when she almost crushed me to death in your driveway. But why would she go after Ainsworth? He didn't do anything."

"He brought us together. Everyone said so, even Dad."

"Then why wouldn't she just kill me and get it over with? I mean, she had the perfect opportunity last night or *any* night I've been at your house."

"I don't know. Maybe she changed her mind about you. Maybe she doesn't want to hurt me. We'll worry about that later. Right now, we have to get to Ainsworth before she does."

We sped through Winslow at double the speed limit, praying there were no cops out running radar near campus. I didn't even bother trying to find a parking space. I slammed on the brakes right in front of Dane Hall and threw it in park before sprinting up the stone steps. Graeme was right behind me as we raced up to the second floor and down the empty hall toward Ainsworth's office.

The light was on, peeking out beneath the closed door.

I turned the handle, but it was locked. Rapping quickly, I threw a glance over my shoulder at Graeme. "Professor? It's Cassius! I have to talk to you!"

Something glass crashed and shattered inside the room.

I turned the handle again, as if it would magically open this time.

"Move," Graeme said. As soon as I darted out of the way, he kicked the door open and burst through it.

Ainsworth was on the floor, white foam spewing from his mouth. Several glass jars had been knocked to the floor in what looked like an attempt to stand up. The vines he normally controlled with ease limped along the floor, shriveling before our very eyes.

"What poison did you use again?" Graeme asked, rolling Ainsworth onto his side so he didn't choke on the foam.

"Acqua Tofana," I replied, pawing through his collection of various specimens and herbs. "A combination of arsenic, lead, and belladonna."

"Is there a toadstone?"

"I'm looking!" I grabbed a couple of different jars and hurried over to them, careful not to drop any more glass on the ground. "Start giving these to him."

Graeme took the first jar and made a face. "A bezoar? How the fuck is a hairball going to help him?"

"It's been proven to negate arsenic," I said, mixing another concoction in a jar.

Gagging, like *he* was going to throw up a hairball, Graeme shook one out onto his palm and pushed it between Ainsworth's lips. "Professor, you have to swallow."

"Water!" I said impatiently, shoving a stainless steel bottle at him.

Graeme held Ainsworth's head up and tipped some of the liquid into his mouth.

Ainsworth sputtered, spewing water and foam all over the place. His wheezing didn't improve at all.

"Now this," I said, taking the water bottle back and shoving my concoction at Graeme. "For the belladonna."

"What about the lead?"

"There's no antidote. I can help him later with whatever's in his body."

He nodded, holding the tonic to Ainsworth's lips. Ainsworth grimaced and tried to pull away, but Graeme held on.

"I know it's disgusting," I said. "But it'll save your life."

As soon as he'd finished the contents of the glass, we pulled Ainsworth up into a sitting position and let him recline against the backside of his desk. He heaved a couple of breaths, looking abnormally pale.

Graeme stood and picked up the wicker basket of apple turnovers, holding it aloft. "Looks like you were right."

"Fuck…" I blew out a sharp breath and returned my attention to Ainsworth. "How are you feeling?"

"Like I survived a seventeenth-century poisoning," he said with a groan. "How did you know?"

"Cassius put the pieces together," Graeme said.

"You have to tell Treadwell. And Peregrine. Quickly."

"Why? Is she going there next?"

Ainsworth nodded, his reply getting lost in a severe coughing fit.

Graeme and I both pulled our phones out. "I've got Treadwell," he said.

Dialing Peregrine's number, I waited impatiently while it rang. He finally picked up on the fourth.

"Cassius, this is a surprise. Your sister was just here."

"Don't eat or drink anything she gave you!" I blurted out.

"What? Why?"

"The apple turnovers are poisoned. She nearly killed Ainsworth just now. We'll explain later, but you have to tell the rest of the Selectmen, in case they're next. Graeme is already calling the chief."

"Yes. Of course. Absolutely." He hung up and I exhaled, dropping my chin to my chest. Fuck, Claudia! Why?

Graeme hung up with Treadwell a moment later. "He's on the lookout for her. When she shows, he's going to have her arrested."

"See, boys?" Ainsworth rasped. "This is why it's so important for witches to study botany."

Graeme and I shared an exasperated look while Ainsworth chuckled, right before it devolved into another coughing fit.

Epilogue
Graeme

Big, fat snowflakes fell from the gray sky, catching along bare tree branches and sticking to the pavement. The day was quiet and the falling snow made it look like Tennebrose was stuck inside a snow globe. Despite everything that had happened, I felt at peace in that moment, inhaling the freezing December air.

Cassius and I had just finished our last final of the semester — Ainsworth's. We thought after that whole thing with the poisoned apples he might let us slide, but nope. Two grueling hours later, we finally escaped Dane Hall into the cold, wintery afternoon.

"How do you think you did?" Cassius asked, slipping his hand into mine as we descended the icy stairs.

"Probably bombed it. You know I suck at Latin. Why do we have to know the stupid genus names anyway? It's way more beneficial for us to know all of the folk names."

"Like bat wings? And eye of newt?"

"Yeah. Exactly!"

"Well, I wouldn't worry about it. Our apple tree project has more weight than the final. And guess what I have..." Cassius pulled his hand from mine and lifted the flap on his messenger bag, withdrawing the paper and holding it out with a smirk.

I turned it over and laughed at Ainsworth's scribbled comment on the back.

A+ Experiment was a success. No need to replicate.

Destroy all notes and documentation of this process immediately.

"I mean, he has a point," I said, handing the paper back with a chuckle.

"Yeah… wouldn't want anyone else getting a hold of that recipe," he said, looking out over the commons.

"Any word from Claudia?" I asked quietly.

Biting his lip, he shook his head, stuffing his hands in his coat pockets this time.

I wrapped my arms around him, pressing my forehead to his. I should have known better than to ask, but it also felt wrong avoiding her entirely. She was still his sister, after all, and like he'd told me once upon a time, we can't control our families.

As promised, Treadwell arrested Claudia as soon as she showed up at the police department bearing poisoned turnovers. She was taken immediately to the old gaol in the woods and locked inside while she awaited trial by the Selectmen.

Three witches acted as the investigators, one from each faction, as it were. Dr. Dane, Old Man Winslow, and Mrs. Oliver — a "light," neutral, and "dark" witch, respectively, to ensure there was no bias in the investigation.

They all concluded the same thing — Claudia was beyond guilty.

The curse against my mother was actually the original agenda. It all came about after Claudia learned Mom had the stolen Corbin folios in her possession.

One night after a shift at the hospital, Claudia stopped by the cemetery to collect some graveyard dirt for a spell. She stumbled across Mom at Owen's grave with the white Book of Lazarus, apparently in the middle of trying to resurrect Owen. For obvious reasons, Mom wasn't successful.

Originally, Claudia planned to steal the Book back herself and murder wasn't even in the cards. But in doing the necessary research on my family, trying to uncover all of our strengths and weaknesses, she learned the truth — that *Mom* was the one who really killed Lydia Corbin. Thanks to Bob Winslow and his excellent record-keeping skills, Claudia put two and two together. The record of Mom's air magic and the air embolism noted in Lydia's autopsy report was all Claudia needed for motive.

Then Cassius came home and nearly died outside the library, all thanks to me, and a new plan was born.

Using my mother as a spiritual vessel of sorts, Claudia and Lennox got Mom to summon the demon that ultimately wound up murdering my classmates. I, of course, was a target as well but Cassius inadvertently thwarted their attempts to kill me, first by giving my magic an unforeseen boost and then by being there to fend the demons off, time and again. The day in the field, Cassius was simply collateral damage. Apparently demons weren't too picky about who they killed, especially if it was a witch.

Claudia picked that particular demon because it had a penchant for sowing discord among humans, but also because it was known to transform into an owl. She wanted my family's emblem to be the cause of misery and death in the hope it would become as reviled as the Corbin crow was by the rest of the Congregation.

It was no surprise to anyone Lennox helped her before his own untimely death. And as we'd suspected, each of the murders was done to protect Cassius or as some sort of punishment on behalf of the Corbin family.

Then came the cherry on top.

In addition to cursing Mom and using her like a puppet

for months, making Mom do her dirty work and carry the magical and psychological burden of being linked to a demon, Claudia was the one who ultimately forced Mom to hang herself like a helpless marionette doll. Not only that, but it was the same tree from 1667 that the Congregation hanged Black Mary in. Mary Oliver's death sentence became the catalyst for this stupid, centuries-long feud, a feud that accomplished absolutely nothing other than destroying families each generation, and Claudia apparently thought it was fitting to hang a Hewitt in the same tree.

The final part of her mission was to take out the rest of the Selectmen for what she saw as a miscarriage of justice for her mother's death. The fact they'd been willing to overlook the evidence and not hold anyone accountable for Lydia's murder was too much for Claudia to stomach.

Her plan was nearly flawless. There's no doubt it would have worked — had her brother and I not intervened. Cassius (and his relationship with me) was the one wildcard Claudia could have *never* predicted.

Claudia hadn't spoken a word since her arrest. Not during her trial. Not during her sentencing. Not a peep. Everything we knew was discovered through divination or telepathy, not because Claudia herself offered any sort of explanation or defense.

Cassius tried to reach out to his sister, but she wouldn't even look at him let alone talk to him. She saw his love for me as the ultimate betrayal to their family, much like my own father. He tried to explain that his feelings for me in no way diminished his pride in his family or their heritage, but she refused to believe him. And since she wouldn't even acknowledge his presence, there was no hope in her giving him a reprieve from his guilt.

At the conclusion of her trial, Claudia was sentenced to life in prison in the witches' gaol, deep in a cavern in the

North Woods. It was a fate worse than death. Surrounded by stone and iron, the condemned were left in the dark, where time stopped. There was no magic. No modern amenities. Nothing. It was you and your thoughts and the never-ending darkness, until the Committee came to release you — which could be years, or decades, later.

Caius was the only one who ventured out to the gaol. Claudia didn't need food or blankets, or anything of the sort, but he tried to bring her comfort regardless. And each time he came back a little more crushed, a little more dejected. She refused to speak to him either, still angry and disappointed in him for allowing Cassius to "dishonor" their ancestors.

"I'm starving after that test," I said as a shiver rippled through Cassius's body, reminding me to focus on the present. Pulling away, I cupped his cheek and stroked my thumb along the sharp line of his cheekbone. His skin was cold beneath my palm, but it made me smile the way he leaned into it. "How about we go get something to eat?"

"And then what?"

"I don't know…" I bit my lip and slid as close as I possibly could, wriggling up against him in spite of our heavy jackets. "Maybe we go back to my place… watch some movies and just chill. What do you say?"

"Netflix and chill? Really?" He arched an eyebrow at me. "You expect me to believe that?"

"Ok, fine. It can be Prime if you want." I gave him a bright smile until he laughed and shook his head.

"Yeah. That sounds good." He smiled, threading his fingers through mine and resuming our walk to my Jeep. "But don't forget, we have to go order our boutonnières for the Foolstide Ball at some point."

"Yes. I know. Oh, and before *I* forget, I found this the

other day and thought of you," I said, digging in my pocket and holding my closed fist out to him.

He stopped walking, eyeing my hand with a raised brow again. "Are you giving me more pebbles for my nest? You know, I'm running out of room with all the rocks you keep 'finding.' I'm going to have to buy a bigger shelf. Or I'm going to start keeping them at your place so *you* can dust them."

"Last one, I promise," I said with as much seriousness as I could manage.

"That's what you said about the *last* crystal," he retorted with a smirk, slipping his palm beneath my fist anyway.

I dropped the offering into his hand and waited, biting my lower lip.

Cassius's gaze lingered on mine for a minute before he looked down at the rose quartz heart in his palm. The stone of pure, unconditional love. A smile pulled at the corners of his mouth as he ran his thumb across the smooth pink surface. "What am I supposed to say to this?"

Getting down on one knee, I presented him with a closed black velvet box. "Say you'll marry me. Tomorrow, after graduation, after med school. I don't care. All I know is that I'm never going to love anyone the way I love you. I know we're young, barely even adults most days, but I'm afraid if I don't ask you right now and stake my claim, some other penguin is going to find a better stone and take you away from me." I cracked open the box and swallowed down a rush of nerves when his eyes doubled in size. "Cassius Corbin, will you please marry me?"

He was taking *way* too long to fucking answer. I knew he could hear my heart pounding like crazy, even without his blood magic abilities.

Finally he shook his head, a half-smile on his face. "You're such an idiot. There will never be another penguin for me." He caught my face between his hands and pressed his lips to mine. Even as I stood up, he kept kissing me, which I guess was his way of saying yes.

Tearing myself away for the moment, I pulled the ring out of the box and slid it onto his finger. The emeralds flashed in the gray light, a dark green stripe set in black gold. Green might not have been the color most people associated with romance, but the boy loved his crystals and I knew he'd recognize the symbolism. After all, people said emeralds represented "successful love," since they were associated with love and truth, especially in marriages.

Cassius smiled at his hand and kissed me again. I knew, from the ardency of that second kiss, he recognized the deeper meaning and my heart soared. It might not have been the most romantic time or spot to propose, but damn did I nail the ring.

"Do you have any idea how happy you've made me?" I asked, resting my forehead against his.

"Oh, I'm sure we'll both regret it at some point."

I scoffed and made a face at him. "You're such an asshole."

"But for some reason, you love me." He grinned at me, suddenly the picture of innocence as he resumed walking toward the parking garage.

"Yeah. And don't you forget that." I squeezed his hand, the one with the engagement band on, to drive the point home.

"How can I? You're like a leech. I can't shake you no matter how hard I try." The corners of his mouth lifted slightly and I caught the tail end of a glance in my direction.

"A leech? I'll show you a fucking leech." I yanked him back to me and grabbed his face between my hands, kissing him hard. He twined his arms around my neck and melted against me, giving as good as he got. We kissed until we were both dizzy from the lack of oxygen, but even after we broke apart, we stayed tangled in each other's arms.

The falling snowflakes formed a ring on the ground

around us, like our own protective circle. It was just him and me. The rest of the world didn't matter. Blood feuds and witch politics meant nothing inside that circle. The only thing that mattered, the only thing that would *ever* matter, was that Cassius and I had each other. A Corbin and a Hewitt. United in true love at long last.

One for the history books, as Old Man Winslow would say.

The End

Acknowledgements

Malum Discordiae took me longer to write than most of my books. There are several reasons as to why (mostly my crazy writer brain), but none of them are relevant to the finished product. What is relevant are the people who stuck with me throughout the process.

Anna — Your initial curiosity about a random moodboard I posted turned into a back-and-forth exchange that spurred me on to finish this book. Every time you asked me questions about the characters or the university, I had to write *something* to give you an answer. And then somehow you took my bumbling words and turned them into the most beautiful (and creepy) edits, which in turn inspired my writing. I can't even begin to tell you how grateful I am. You waited patiently for this book and I can only hope it met your expectations.

Amy — You know you're like my ride or die at this point, right? I remember sending you the crypt scene *ages* ago and waiting nervously for your feedback. At that point, I still had no idea what I was doing or where I was even going with these two. But as always, you looked past the choppy rough draft and saw their potential. Same with the dueling magic in the field. That scene could have been so cringey, but you made sure that didn't happen. I appreciate you and our friendship so, *so* much!

Kendra — Your unwavering support is nothing short of amazing! I am so grateful to you for always sharing my work and being a sounding board when I need it. It goes without saying how much I value your opinion and your feedback! Thank you for being in my corner!

Savanna — Thank you for being my formatting guinea pig! I tried to add those little extras to make it special, so I hope you love them. And thank you for coming along with me on this wild journey. You've read all of my books from the very beginning and I appreciate it *so* much!

Julia, Stefka, Gloria, & Kelsey — I appreciate each and every one of you so much! I know I can count on you guys to read whatever craziness I throw at you and you won't even bat an eye. You have no idea how much that means to me. The fact that you take time to not only read my stuff but then turn around and shout about it from the rooftops is absolutely mind-blowing. I'm so grateful to have met each of you. Thank you for being at the heart of my tribe.

About the Author

International best-selling and award-winning dark romance author Ashlyn Drewek has always been a hopeless romantic. She's also fascinated by the dark, macabre things in life (you can blame a love of Halloween and Edgar Allan Poe for that one).

Most of her time is spent making up stories in her head or researching some obscure topic just because she's that much of a nerd. The degree on the wall says she's a historian, but the paycheck says she's a first responder.

Ashlyn lives in Northern Illinois with her patient husband, fearless daughter, and a house full of animals.

For information on news and upcoming releases, check out her website at www.ashlyndrewek.com to sign up for her newsletter or follow her at any of the social media options below.

facebook.com/ashlyndrewek
twitter.com/ashlyndrewek
instagram.com/ashlyndrewek
bookbub.com/profile/ashlyn-drewek
goodreads.com/ashlyndrewek
pinterest.com/ashlyndrewek

Also by
Ashlyn Drewek

The Leander Welles Series:

THE MYSTERY OF LEANDER WELLES — a dark, psychological romantic suspense about a criminal psychiatrist who falls in love with her patient. Finalist for Suspense in the 2021 Next Generation Indie Book Awards.

THE RATIONALE OF LEANDER WELLES — a dark, psychological romantic suspense about an alleged murder who falls in love with his psychiatrist… or does he?

THE DAMNATION OF LEANDER WELLES: OR, THE DEATH & LIFE OF BENNETT REEVE — a dark MM friends-to-lovers romance about a cutthroat lawyer and an enigmatic millionaire and what happens when two dark souls join forces. A prequel to Book I and II.

THE WRATH OF LEANDER WELLES — a dark, MM romantic suspense about love, revenge, and how far a psychopath is willing to go for both.

The Solnyshko Duet:

THE KIDNAPPING OF ROAN SINCLAIR — a dark MM romance about an American college guy who is kidnapped by a Russian criminal.

THE VENGEANCE OF ROAN SINCLAIR — a dark MM romance about love in the aftermath of trauma and finding your new normal.

MM Contemporary Standalone:

THE DELIVERANCE OF MAREK SOMMERS — TBD

Paranormal & Dark Fantasy:

OUT OF THE DARK — a slow-burn MF paranormal romance about vampires and Chicago cops and what it means to fall in love when you're not supposed to.

THE COVENTRY CAROL — a darker MM Christmas novella with hot Santa smut, anti-Christmas feels, and a cannibal hitman.

Printed in Great Britain
by Amazon

25807390R00256